MOTIVES for MURDER

WITHDRAWN

Edited by Martin Edwards

MOTIVES for MURDER

BY
MEMBERS
OF THE
DETECTION
CLUB

*A Celebration of Peter Lovesey
on his 80th Birthday*

sphere

SPHERE

First published in Great Britain in 2016 by Sphere

1 3 5 7 9 10 8 6 4 2

MIX
Paper from
responsible sources
FSC
www.fsc.org FSC® C104740

Sphere
An imprint of
Little, Brown Book Group
Carmelite House
50 Victoria Embankment
London EC4Y 0DZ

An Hachette UK Company
www.hachette.co.uk

www.littlebrown.co.uk

Contents

Introduction

Motives for Murder is the sixth collection of stories to be published by members of the Detection Club. The first, *Detection Medley*, appeared as long ago as 1939, nine years after the Club came into existence, and seven years after it adopted formal Rules and a Constitution. *Detection Medley*, like this book, benefited from having a foreword by a highly distinguished member – in that case, A.A. Milne, whose brief but successful career as a crime writer tends nowadays to be forgotten. Several of the stories in *Detection Medley* – there were also a few non-fiction articles – had been published during the preceding years. In contrast, all the contributions to *Motives for Murder* are freshly written.

So what is the Detection Club? John Rhode, who edited *Detection Medley*, gave an account of its foundation by Anthony Berkeley. After making the point (unnecessarily, it may be thought) that the Club was not a trade union, Rhode said that: 'The principal reason for its existence is that members should meet at intervals for the enjoyment of each other's company'. It was, to use a contemporary term, the first significant social network for crime writers. From the start, members financed the dinners at which they socialised, and the hire of premises where they could meet, by collaborating on literary projects. These included 'round robin' detective stories with each chapter written by a different author, such as the much-admired *The Floating Admiral* and *Ask a Policeman* (both of which have been very successfully republished in recent years). Among the contributors to these projects were such legendary figures in the world of crime fiction as G.K. Chesterton, Dorothy L. Sayers, and Agatha Christie, all of whom served lengthy terms as Presidents of the Club.

In 1979, a second short story collection, *Verdict of Thirteen*, was put together by Julian Symons, who had succeeded the Queen of Crime as President following her death in 1976. Symons' 80th birthday was honoured by a further collection, *The Man Who . . .*, edited by his successor as President, H.R.F. Keating. The Club's 75th anniversary was celebrated in 2005 by the publication of *The Detection Collection*, edited by Simon Brett, who had in turn taken over as President after Harry Keating stepped down. The following year, Harry's own 80th birthday was celebrated by another book of stories, called *The Verdict of Us All*, edited by Peter Lovesey. The support given by members to these projects illustrates the strength of the enduring friendships fostered by the collegiate nature of the Club.

The Club flourishes to this day, and in addition to holding three dinners in London, members continue to enjoy collaborating on literary projects. The June of 2016 saw the publication of *The Sinking Admiral*, masterminded by Simon Brett; it is another 'round robin' mystery novel, with chapters written by a diverse group of members, including Simon and Peter, and packed with playful references to *The Floating Admiral* and the distinguished authors who wrote it.

In November 2015, Club members elected me as their eighth President. I was aware that Peter Lovesey would be celebrating his own 80th birthday the following September (although looking at him, none of us can quite believe it; we would dearly love to know his secret). Discussions with his old friend, Professor Douglas Greene, whose Crippen & Landru imprint published *The Verdict of Us All* in the United States, led me to resolve that my first act as Club President would be to try to put together a new book of stories to be written by Club members in celebration of this milestone. Members proved highly enthusiastic about the proposal, as did Peter's publishers, Little, Brown.

The only snag with the project was that, if the book were to be written, edited, and presented to Peter in time for a celebratory dinner at the Dorchester, the timescale was exceptionally tight. But a large number of members rose heroically to the challenge, and so did everyone at Little, Brown and Crippen & Landru, who are respectively publishing the book in the UK and the US.

Peter is, unquestionably, a worthy recipient of this accolade from his friends and colleagues in the Detection Club. His distinguished career as a crime writer began in 1970, with the publication of *Wobble to Death*, a prize-winning

Victorian era novel which introduced Sergeant Cribb. More Cribb books followed; the series proved enormously successful, and was televised. Peter's stature as a crime writer was very quickly recognised, and he was elected to membership of the Detection Club as long ago as 1974. More than four decades later, he remains a loyal and enthusiastic member, a valued contributor to our writing projects, and a highly agreeable dinner companion. His personal memories of early encounters with Detection Club members of the Seventies form an appropriate afterword to this book.

His career of sustained literary excellence has garnered many awards, including the Crime Writers' Association's Diamond Dagger, and CWA Gold and Silver Daggers. His interests are wide-ranging, and several of his stories offer intriguing 'motives for murder'. Two splendid examples from his popular series about Bath cop Peter Diamond are *Bloodhounds* (the title comes from the name of a group of crime readers who play a central part in the story) and *The Secret Hangman. Keystone,* a non-series mystery, offers another unusual motive, as does one of his Sergeant Cribb books, *A Case of Spirits,* while *On the Edge,* as Peter puts it, 'takes as a motive the unusual, but real situation of women who were expected to go back to dull lives as housewives after having made a real, satisfying contribution during World War 2, as plotters. Their unlovable husbands went back to their previous jobs. Two women get together and plan to kill their spouses and break free.'

In addition to his award-winning novels, Peter has established himself as a prolific and highly accomplished exponent of the short story; a collection of stories therefore seems an especially suitable way to celebrate his achievements. I asked each contributor to write a short personal preamble to his or her story, and you will see how those stories refer, in one way or another, to Peter's life and work.

My thanks go to Len Deighton for his lively foreword, and all the contributors for coming up with splendidly original stories (and in one case, a sonnet – a Detection Club first!) at relatively short notice, despite the many other calls on their time. I'm grateful to Peter for giving his blessing to this project and contributing the afterword, to Doug Greene for inspiring me to crack on with it, and to Katherine Armstrong, the editor at Little, Brown primarily responsible for the book, as well as to Georgia Glover of David Higham, the Club's literary agent, and to David Shelley, Thalia Proctor and their other colleagues at Little, Brown, and everyone at Crippen & Landru for their support and hard work in bringing an ambitious project to fruition with speed, efficiency, and enthusiasm.

Martin Edwards

Foreword by Len Deighton

Why do we become writers, and how do we start? Peter Lovesey wrote his first book after responding to a writing competition, choosing a time and setting familiar to him. He won! Since that time Peter has delighted us with a whole library of high quality fiction books and we all know how many hours he must spend on each one, and how disciplined he must be. Fortunately he is still at work and we can look forward to many more stories. I hope this light-hearted foreword and this tribute amuses him and amuses our readers too.

'*What do you writers talk about when you get together at your Club?*' many people ask. Recalling this question, I asked myself about the Detection Club which welcomed me in so long ago. What do we all have in common? Why do we write? How do we write? Where and when do we write? Is the desire and ability to assemble 100,000 words or so into a coherent narrative a talent, a trick or an affliction?

Several Club members have told me that they knew

they would become writers even when they were children. For most of our members writing came naturally, sometimes with a background of the law, medicine or English Literature studies. Some members were self-effacing, and echoed the American writer Russell Baker, who said: '*The only thing I was fit for was to be a writer . . . I would never be fit for real work, and writing didn't require any.*' Ouch! Wait a minute, Russell.

Some writers find their vocation only in middle-age or later. The enviable gifts of music or drawing usually become apparent in childhood but the writer's abilities are apt to develop more slowly and improve with experience.

'*Of making books there is no end,*' the Bible tells us and perhaps that is a measure of our obsession. Even after our ideas are on paper, shaping them into a carefully researched whole, with convincing characters and satisfying plot, is long, hard work. Those of us who labour slowly need a partner who understands that 'work' sometimes entails staring out of the window for hours on end while rendered deaf to questions. Ideas? That's the easy part. What author has not been angered by the proposal: '*I have an idea for a book: you write it and we'll split fifty-fifty*'?

Dr Samuel Johnson said: '*No man but a blockhead ever wrote except for money.*' How much money Sam earned is yet to be discovered but anyone embarking on a writing career in the expectation of riches is likely to be disappointed. Perhaps George Orwell came nearer to present-day reality when he said that the only way for an author to get rich was by marrying a publisher's daughter.

Was it Hemingway, Maugham or Oscar Wilde who described literary shindigs at which all the publishers were at one end of the room talking about art, and all the writers at the other end talking about money? Perhaps all three said it. A writer's book is likely to represent the author's deep emotional feelings. For a publisher a book – good or bad – is no more than a product from which they can earn money.

Writers toil in a bizarre world. One needs no more than a ream of paper and a pen to enter it; ladies, gentlemen, sportsmen, comics, TV personalities, distinguished scholars and ignorant buffoons all have a chance of becoming a successful author. In the vast and prosperous business of publishing, everyone is paid a living wage except those who provide the vital product. Those who teach 'creative writing' earn good wages, those who do the 'creative writing' starve.

The failings of publishers are many and varied, and provide a consistent topic of conversation when writers get together. Even when we discussed his work as Hitler's Minister of Armaments, Albert Speer found time to tell me: '*My book,* Inside the Third Reich *never reached the top of the* New York Times *bestseller list. It was* Everything You Always Wanted to Know About Sex *that always remained at number one.*' He may have been joking; he had a sharp sense of humour.

Memoirs occupy a favoured place in the book world. Their authors can provide a rags to riches storyline and, unlike judgmental biographers, can incorporate explanations, excuses and a deservedly happy ending. Lately we have seen many authors select a sequence from their own life, dust it with glitter and Grand Guignol, and present it as fiction. Even more successful have been auto-biographies with misery and melancholy as the theme.

Hemingway said that '*good books are truer than if they really happened*' and my respect and admiration go to writers who create an intriguing world and describe it in realistic terms. Raymond Chandler's Bay City was a place where crooked politicians bribed vulnerable policemen and chased them down 'mean streets' that strangely resembled Santa Monica. But the imagination of Harry Keating (who preceded Simon Brett as President of the Detection Club) surpassed that. Harry's gripping stories about Inspector Ghote's Bombay were written long before Harry journeyed to the subcontinent and yet they convinced a vast number of his loyal readers that they had been there. Peter's first novel, *Wobble to Death*, which introduced the remarkable Sergeant Cribb, was a perfect example of totally original people in a convincing historical setting and became a milestone in detective story writing. The love Peter has for the Victorian period is evident on every page and intro-duces his readers to the mysterious world of the six-day cycle race in London's 1880s!

Enclosed societies of any sort attract writers. Some fine books about murder in monastic orders have been written; some set in medieval times and some in modern ones. Josephine Tey described a historical murder investigated from the hospital bed of a present-day detective. Some writers begin books and '*just follow to where the characters lead*'. I believe a planned structure provides a tighter and better result. Detective fiction demands a structure and that is what I like about it.

A. J. P. Taylor told me '*When I want to find out about something, I write a book about it.*' Although Taylor's books were mostly concerned with modern history, I found it described the motive and foundation of some of the most interesting fiction. Technical and historical research can bring an exciting extra dimension to a fiction book.

Those members of the Detection Club who are lawyers or doctors find writing fiction a natural development. Into their offices come men and women with dramatic human stories. Whether for the purposes of law or medicine, their professional training enables them to define it, arrange it and give it a cause-and-effect pattern. And this skill is a great advantage when they write fiction, a fact demonstrated by physicians such as Conan Doyle, John O'Hara, Sinclair Lewis, Somerset Maugham, Zane Grey, Michael Crichton, Robin Cook, A.J. Cronin and Anton Chekhov.

I am a very slow worker and so I have to work every day and am awake in the night to scribble notes. My books usually take me more than twelve months of continuous work to write. I envy writers who produce books at a lightning speed but I have found that the more time I spend, writing, checking, rewriting, dumping unsatisfactory chapters, and sometimes, as with *SS-GB*, scrapping the completed typescript and beginning again, the better the final result. For me, the word processor provided the perfect tool. Eric

Ambler reluctantly turned to a word processor, hated it and went back to his electric typewriter. Julian Symons wrote his books in exemplary handwriting with no changes or crossing-out to be seen.

It was an advertising copywriter who told his underlings to *'Slaughter your darlings'* but it has been said in many different forms. It is much easier said than done; it hurts. My own device is to consign the condemned print-out to a high-shelf and dump it when my love has languished.

Tony Godwin, a memorable top man at Penguin Books, told me that when he looked at a freshly submitted type-script he concentrated on the written dialogue. Tony said that all other aspects of fiction writing – plot, characters, and descriptions of the environment, and so on – can be learned and improved. But convincing dialogue is rare and vital. Even Tony admitted that very fine fiction books can be written with very little dialogue, just using the voice of the author. But dialogue is the most powerful weapon in an author's hands and provides an opportunity that should not be neglected.

Stage plays and screenplays are almost all dialogue, sometimes hurriedly-written, rewritten and obvious, but actors can bring dead words to life. Somerset Maugham, who is perhaps unique in successfully writing both plays and books, said; *'There are three rules for writing a novel. Unfortunately no one knows what they are'*. He might as well have been talking about dialogue for that was the basis of his reputation.

As far as the writer is concerned realistic dialogue is

certainly not good dialogue. Anyone who has read the transcript of a business meeting or court case knows just how tedious and repetitive it is. But contrived artificiality can be worse. Dialogue in fiction needs to be informative and entertaining; and convincing too. It must not only fit the character, it must increase the reader's knowledge of the characters, and the situation, while moving the plot along.

So you have found a publisher? Now your troubles start. There are wonderful editors and I owe a lot to them, but beware the editor who – red ink ready – wants to write your book without all the hard work. And beware the publisher who will slap on your book a crude and inappropriate cover that will make you cringe. What can you do? How about writing a story in which a serial killer runs riot through a publishing house? I'll buy it.

Len Deighton

The Reckoning Of Sins

Alison Joseph

When I was invited to contribute to this anthology, I thought long and hard about how to pay tribute to Peter Lovesey's unmatched talent in creating utterly believable characters in beautifully structured crime stories. I concluded that the solution was DI Peter Diamond actually making an appearance. But try as I might, I could not persuade DI Diamond to make the journey from Bath to London, and he certainly had no reason to have any kind of dealings with a nun. Defeated, I pressed on with the story. But, as I wrote, the influence of Peters both Lovesey and Diamond began to make itself felt. Even without appearing in the story, it is DI Diamond's view of the world that we glimpse, and his wisdom and compassion that lie at the heart of this story.

'What on earth is that?'

Father Julius looked up from his desk as Sister Agnes struggled into his office, her arms wrapped around a large square parcel.

'A painting,' she said. She thumped it down on the floor.

'And why, might I ask . . . ?'

'From my ex-husband.'

'Oh, good heavens. Not him.'

'It arrived today. I don't want it. The convent doesn't want it. So I thought you could look after it for me.'

Julius' office was a narrow space attached to his church. A small leaded window shed beams of spring sunlight onto the threadbare carpet. Outside, there was the hum of London traffic, the rumble of distant trains. He sighed. 'Why has that awful man come back into your life?'

'He hasn't. Some lawyer in France had the order's address. One of Hugo's great-aunts in Burgundy has died and they're clearing her house. There's a note from the lawyers about Hugo feeling I was owed something from the estate. Given that I shared my life with him in France for those years—'

'Deeply miserable, terrified years . . . ' Julius interrupted.

'There is that. Anyway, this arrived.' She lent the painting against a wall, and unwrapped the packaging.

It was a still life. It showed a glass sand timer, a parchment with a quill pen and an old-fashioned weighing scale, next to which sat two bright oranges. The parchment had two columns of numbers written in black ink, sharp against the creamy paper.

'It's anonymous. School of someone or other,' she said. 'Probably Spanish, seventeenth century, the note said. Which, if it's true, makes it enormously valuable.'

'Knowing Hugo, it'll be a fake and worth about three quid.'

She laughed.

Julius bent towards the painting. After a moment he said, 'He must be trying to buy your forgiveness.'

'You think?'

'It's the reckoning of sins. The columns of numbers – it's bookkeeping. Spiritual bookkeeping, invented in Italian monasteries. It's a balancing out, God's forgiveness versus our own sinfulness. We all have to settle up at some point, I suppose was the thinking. Hence the sand timer, and the fruit which is bound to perish.' He sat back in his chair. 'Reminds me, I'm supposed to be doing this year's tax return. Father Ignatius was nagging me.'

Agnes crossed the room, filled the kettle, switched it on.

Julius picked up a pencil on his desk and studied it. She wondered if he'd ever changed in all the time she'd known him. Still the same soft white hair, the clear blue eyes with their wire-rimmed spectacles, the soft Irish lilt in his voice even after all these years. She wondered if he saw her the same way, unchanged; tall in her jeans and shirt, hazel-eyed, though with her short brown hair now flecked with grey.

'What are you thinking?' He smiled up at her.

'Nothing.' She opened a tin of tea.

'How long we've known each other,' he said.

'That kind of thing.'

'How's work at the hostel?'

'Oh, same old. The chaos of abandonment. The tip of the iceberg. We've got our silent stowaway. We can't progress his case till he tells us his age, and he still won't speak. Saliya's still ... well, Saliya. Throwing her weight around. And Kayleigh's missing again. Kayleigh who was dating your window cleaner.'

'Bernard? I'm not sure you'd call it dating. And he's not really my window cleaner. I just give him jobs to do while he's living in my doorway. He should go back to Bath, he's got friends there. Even the police looked out for him there, he says.'

She bent to the fridge, found a carton of milk.

'He slept at the abbey,' Julius went on, 'the one with the angels climbing the pillars towards Heaven. He said one of the coppers used to say that if you stared at them hard enough you'd see them move.'

'Hmm. Guess the coppers in Bath have time on their hands.'

Julius studied the painting. 'Just like Hugo to try to get you to forgive him this way.'

'Forgive him?'

'Indulgences,' he said. 'The medieval Church used to sell them. You could buy your way out of purgatory. It's typical of Hugo to hope the whole thing might still work.' He looked up at her. 'I fear him reappearing, you know. I don't want to have to rescue you again.'

She poured the tea, handed him a cup. They sat in silence, listening to the bursts of spring birdsong through the traffic rumble.

'You could sell the painting,' Julius said. 'And send the money back to Hugo.'

'He just wouldn't get it. And I don't want to ever see him again—'

There was a sudden loud hammering on the door. A man stood there, tall, broad and smart, making the office, as he strode into the room, seem even smaller and shabbier.

'Is he here? My darned brother? Is he?' His voice filled the space around him.

'Who—' Julius was on his feet.

'Bernard, of course.' The man looked around him, at Julius, then at Agnes, waiting for an answer.

Julius eyed him. 'No,' he said. 'Bernard is not here.'

'He owes me.' The man had a well-cut grey coat, well-cut grey hair. 'Where is he?'

'I'm sorry, but who are you?' Julius faced him, tall and calm.

'I'm Mansell. Mansell Ledger. I'm his brother.'

He had the same blue eyes as Bernard, Agnes saw. But this man was clipped and kempt.

'Sleeping rough,' Mansell went on, with a sneer. 'It's laziness. He just can't be bothered. Well, tell him I'm looking for him. He'll know what it's about ... ' His eye fell on the painting. 'What the hell's that?'

'It's hers,' Julius said.

He bent to look at it. 'It's – it's fantastic.' He glanced up at Agnes. 'If you ever want to sell it ... ' He straightened up, smoothing his trousers. 'I'm an art dealer. Here.' He fished in a pocket, handed her his business card. She read the name, THE LEDGER GALLERY, an address in Central London.

'I'm going now,' he announced. 'But if you see that brother of mine, tell him I need to speak to him. Urgently.'

Julius showed him out. Agnes heard the firm closing of the door.

'An unpleasant man,' he said, coming back into the room. 'Bernard mentioned him the other day. They're twins, apparently.' Julius sat at his desk. 'In fact, I got the impression Bernard was scared of him.'

'Perhaps that's why Bernard's gone too.'

'Perhaps he's eloped. With your Kayleigh.'

'We're supposed to protect our inmates,' she said, 'not encourage them to run off with the first man who shows an interest.'

Julius sipped his tea. 'Yes. I can see that.'

Agnes sighed. 'There has been something a bit edgy about her recently. Secretive. I think I need to have a chat with her.' She put down her mug, got to her feet. 'I should go. I'm due on the night shift.' She reached into her bag, pulled out a mobile phone, looked up at him. 'What's so funny?'

'Just, your order using technology to keep an eye on you. Why else would they let you have one of those?'

She laughed. She pointed it at the painting and clicked. 'An image of the picture,' she said.

'For contemplating your sins,' he said.

The late afternoon sky threatened rain. She dodged the bikes and buses on Tooley Street, walked past the hoardings of building sites, with their gleaming new office blocks

rising up behind them. She thought about their foundations resting on the ancient clay, buried in layers of the
city's past. She thought about Bernard's angels, climbing
the pillars towards Heaven.

She reached the river, listened to the slap of the waves
below. She was aware of a background hum of anxiety
about Kayleigh. A thin, straggly white girl, raised in rural
Lincolnshire, with no father and a mother who, given the
choice, chose drink, she'd pitched up on the streets three
months ago and was brought to the hostel late one night
by a duty officer, swearing and shouting, claiming she was
fine as she was and why can't people leave her alone . . .

She was calmer now. She seemed happier too, away from
her former, shadowy life. Her eyes were brighter, her hair
shone with newly pink-dipped ends.

Sister Agnes left the river's edge, turning south towards
faded Victorian facades of quiet poverty, down-at-heel food
stores. As she reached the hostel, she was aware of cars,
activity, blue lights, the door of the hostel wide open.

She was greeted by Rachel, her co-worker, her eyes wide
with shock.

'They've found Kayleigh. She's dead.'

The hostel kitchen was full of people, some uniformed,
some not, all apparently holding mugs of tea. Agnes was
handed one, sat at the table, listened.

' . . . A body of a young woman, found earlier today by
workers on a building site, now identified as Kayleigh
Ashton, apparently pushed into the pit after a struggle . . . '

'... Post mortem being carried out ... gap in the hoardings, at the back of the site, one of those big new office blocks near London Bridge, CCTV is being checked ...'

'... If anyone knows anything, please talk to us. People she was seeing, places she might have been going, had her behaviour changed in any way ...'

Gradually the kitchen emptied. The police drifted away into the London night. There was silence around the table.

'Poor cow,' someone said.

'She was working, isn't it,' Saliya said. 'It'll be a client.'

'She'd stopped. Her boyfriend wouldn't let her no more.'

'Maybe it was him, then. Angry with her, innit.'

'Who?' Agnes looked at Saliya.

Saliya shrugged. 'You know what men are like. Want you to themselves. They'd rather kill you than let someone else have a go.' She yawned, theatrically. 'I'm off to bed, me.'

Agnes went to her room. She lay on the bed. Across the river, the City churches chimed. She thought about the hostel kids, safe under this roof. The ones out there, not so safe.

She took out her phone, pulled up the image of the painting. She looked at the timer, the balance, the careful lists. Forgive us our trespasses, she thought. She wished she'd had that conversation with Kayleigh. Before it was too late.

At nine the next morning, Detective Sergeant Rob Coombes arrived. He had a nervous correctness, short mousy hair and took three sugars in his tea.

He stirred the spoon round in his mug. 'We've spent the night combing the site. Struck lucky. The girl's phone was there. Best weapon in the fight against crime ever invented. Whoever killed her didn't think to take it off her, can't have been professional. We've gone through the numbers. There's an Irish one, turned out to be a half-sister in Galway. Poor woman's distraught. Said no one cared about her, not a jot. There's a lot of recent activity from one number. A voicemail. Mansell, it says. Warning her off his brother. Bernard.'

'Well, well,' Agnes said.

He looked up at her. 'You know him?'

'I know them both. Bernard's local, sleeps in the doorways of churches. Mansell runs some kind of art dealership. I met him yesterday. He was looking for his brother. Fuming. Said he owed him.'

Rob was making notes. 'This is all good.'

'Unpleasant man.' She fished in her pocket. 'Here's his business card. He runs a gallery in Mayfair.'

Rob wrote down the details. 'There's one other thing – the girl was pregnant.'

Pregnant. The word stuck in Agnes' mind, as she cleared the breakfast in the hostel kitchen. She took a cup of tea into the quiet of the office. She sat at the desk, staring at Mansell's business card.

Half an hour later she emerged from Bond Street tube station. She walked along Grosvenor Street in the morning

sunlight, wondering at the poised elegance of the buildings, the sheen of luxury.

She turned off the main street, checked the address,
found herself outside a glass-fronted exterior.

She pressed the bell.

A woman was sitting at a central table. She buzzed her in.

The gallery had dark blue walls. Overhead spotlights
glinted on gold-painted frames. The woman was about
forty, in a pencil skirt and a black polo neck sweater. She
had pale skin, well-cut dark hair and orange lipstick. She
looked up with a professional smile.

'Can I help you?' Her voice was low, cultured.

Agnes hesitated. 'I have a painting I want to sell,' she
said. 'Mr Ledger gave me his card.'

The woman was weighing her up, scanning her jeans, her
charity shop jacket. Agnes felt too thinly disguised and now
revealed as a fraud. She took a breath, held out her hand.
'My name's Sister Agnes. I'm a nun.'

Another flicker of disbelief. 'And how did you meet my
husband?'

'Well ... I work in a hostel for homeless kids. Near St
Simeon's Church, Bermondsey. Your husband turned up
at the church yesterday, looking for someone. And then
he saw the painting, which I'd just acquired. And in the
end ... I'm here.' She looked at the woman's expression. 'I
know it sounds unlikely,' she added.

The woman leaned back on her chair. 'It was his brother,
wasn't it? That he was looking for?' Her tone was level.

'Yes.'

'Oh, those two. Do sit down.' The woman indicated the seat opposite her. 'My name's Gina. Gina Ledger.' She sighed. 'They're twins, you see. They have a toxic relationship. They each think the other one owes him.'

'Owes him what?'

Gina tapped an orange-painted nail on the polished mahogany. 'Everything. Money. Status. Women.' She seemed cool, unperturbed. 'So, this painting.'

'My ex-husband has given it to me as a way of expiating his guilt. I don't want it. It's a Spanish still life, we think.'

The face softened. She gazed at Agnes with a new interest. 'Are nuns allowed husbands?'

Agnes shrugged. 'I was very young. I'm half French. I was married off, in France. My parents thought he was from a suitable family. They weren't to know that that meant knowing everything about money and nothing about love.'

Gina considered her. 'I see. And the painting?'

Agnes took out her phone, clicked on the image, handed it to her.

Gina stared at it. 'If it's authentic . . . it's worth a fortune. I hope you're keeping it safe.'

'It's safe as houses,' Agnes said.

As Gina studied the phone, Agnes surveyed the gallery. There were various portraits, with porcelain skin, lace collars, sharp dark eyes. There was a Virgin and Child, a benign, clay-white face, a tiny man-like baby, both haloed in gold leaf. Further along hung a huge work in angry red and black. It seemed to show the flames of hell, dancing devils, skeletal humans languishing in pits.

Gina handed her the phone. 'Did my husband find his brother?'

Agnes shook her head. 'He seems to have vanished too.'

Gina got to her feet, paced the gallery. 'It's never stopped, those two. Not since childhood. What one had, the other wanted.'

Behind her, the red and black of the painting. She turned to Agnes. 'So – so your husband didn't love you.'

Agnes blinked up at her. 'I think – I think he didn't know the meaning of the word.'

'Did he tell you he loved you?'

'Yes. Yes he did. Often.'

Gina touched the picture frame, then turned to Agnes. 'There's a woman,' she said.

'I see.' Agnes took a deep breath. 'Mrs Ledger,' she said. 'It's not just the painting that brought me here. In our hostel, there's a girl . . . '

Gina's face drained. She stumbled to her chair. 'Go on.' Her eyes were fixed on Agnes'.

'Kayleigh,' Agnes said.

'I knew it. What's happened?'

'She's dead.'

Gina slumped on her chair. She leaned her head on her hands. After a while she looked up. 'When? Where?'

'Last night. It's all with the police now.'

'Yes.' She straightened up. 'Of course.' She shook her head. 'They both . . . well . . . ' She patted her hair back into place. 'A toxic childhood,' she said. 'Never enough to go round.' She fixed her gaze on Agnes. 'Poverty, it leaves scars—'

She was stopped by a buzzing at the door. Her face tightened. 'You must go,' she whispered, as the door swung open. Agnes saw the coat, the grey hair, blue eyes which settled on her.

'You again?' He threw her a smile. 'Come to sell us the painting?'

Gina went to him. 'Mansell – this is Sister Agnes.' She took the coat he handed her. 'You've met, I gather ... '

'We've met, yes. I was after Bernard. Not that I've got anywhere.' He strode to the desk, flung himself into a chair. 'Vanished into thin air. And this time he's in more trouble than ever before ... '

Gina murmured a hush.

'Don't shush me,' he said. There was a flash of anger in the cold blue eyes.

Agnes felt a familiar tightening of fear.

He got to his feet. 'I need a drink,' he said. He crossed the gallery and went out to the back. They could hear slamming of cupboard doors, loud swearing. 'Gina!' The voice came from the back. 'Where the bloody hell is the bottle opener?'

Agnes was on her feet. 'I'll go,' she said.

At the door Gina grabbed her hand. 'Thank you for telling me. Thank you so much.' She relinquished her grip. 'I must – I must go ... ' She buzzed the door open, and Agnes found herself out in the expensive sunlight.

Agnes walked to the tube station, seeing in her mind the nervous pallor, the trembling, orange-painted fingers.

Did your husband love you, she'd asked.

How to explain? That the whispered words of love came afterwards, with the begging for forgiveness, the promises that it would never happen again, never . . . .

She'd seen the look of recognition in Gina's eyes.

There was a ringing from her jacket pocket.

'Hi, it's Rob. Detective Sergeant Rob Coombes. Quick update. We've got more of the CCTV. About 21.30, night before last. We can see a girl, I think it's Kayleigh. There are passers-by, a guy on a bike, a woman in a cab. And there are two men, arguing, shouting, nearly coming to blows. One's your Bernard, doorway-sleeper. The other man – looks similar. Same height but kind of neater. His brother?'

'Almost certainly,' she said.

'Where the girl was found, there's a gap in the hoarding. The wrists show grip marks, there are signs of a fight before she fell. The hoarding where she fell was damaged. The images are rubbish – no full coverage. Where she fell, there's a sheer drop, then darkness. I'll keep you posted.'

That evening, in her hostel room, Agnes sat at the window. The sky was slashed pink with the setting sun; the distant strip of river between the railway arches glowed red.

In her mind, a building site at night. One girl. The rage of two men. A sheer drop, then darkness.

One brother, living in church doorways. The other, with wealth, art and beauty. She thought of his elegant, nervous wife. She lit a candle and settled in prayer.

In her mind, her memories. Her fear. Her bruises. Always feeling the one to blame. *No wonder Julius had to rescue me.*

And even now, Hugo wants to control me.

She spent a restless night dreaming of the home she'd shared with Hugo in the Loire. The hallway looked similar, with its wide carpeted staircase, only it seemed to be painted blue and decked with paintings, all hung crookedly. She woke to an early dawn, urban birdsong, a clench of anxiety.

Rachel found her at breakfast. 'Agnes – someone here to see you.'

Gina stood on the doorstep. She was in a tailored navy raincoat, stylish heeled boots.

'I'm sorry . . .' she began.

'Come in.' Agnes led her into the office.

Gina sat down heavily into a chair. 'The police came. First thing. They've taken Mansell in for questioning. It's all as I feared. My husband's number on the girl's phone. For some weeks, it seems.'

Agnes took a seat next to her.

Gina shook her head. 'Anything Bernard has, Mansell wants.' Her eyes welled with tears. 'As boys, they had nothing. Grew up on a struggling farm, out near Bristol somewhere. Then the farm was sold, and for the first time they had money. Bernard spent his on whisky. Mansell put it into the business. Bernard's convinced he's owed something, even now.' Her hands lay in her lap, the fingers tightly entwined. She spoke again. 'I – I wasn't entirely honest with you.'

Agnes waited.

'I was there,' Gina said. 'The night that girl went missing. I'd followed Mansell. He'd taken the car. I followed in a cab. I'd had enough of his lies. I ran to the building site. They were shouting at each other, the two brothers ... I heard it all. Fighting over a girl, the two of them ... ' Her voice cracked. 'And she was there, laughing, taunting them about the baby. About how they'd never prove which one of them was the father. She was saying it was her baby. "Only mine," she was saying. Laughing at them.'

'Then what happened?'

Gina's expression was tight, shadowed. 'They turned on her. All that rage ... I was frightened for her. She ran, and they chased her. I went after them, tried to reach her – that's when Mansell saw me.' Her eyes darkened. 'He was furious. "Why have you come?" he was shouting. He – he grabbed me. Pushed me into the car ... ' She put her hands to her face.

'And Bernard ... ?'

She breathed, settled herself. 'He was still there.' Her fingers worked in her lap. She spoke again. 'My worry is ... there's a gap, in the time. Between the girl running away, on to the building site. And my husband seeing me.'

'You think ... '

'I think one of them pushed her. But I can't be certain which one.' A catch in her throat. She looked up. 'When your husband told you he loved you ... did you believe him?'

Agnes met her eyes. 'For years, yes.'

'What changed?'

Agnes breathed out. 'I was rescued.'

Gina stared at her hands in her lap. 'There's no one to rescue me.'

'You could—'

'Rescue myself?' Her smile was empty. She shook her head. 'I have too much to lose.' She got to her feet. 'Thank you for listening.'

They went out into the hallway. Agnes opened the door for her.

Gina stood at the top of the steps. 'In my mind,' she said, 'I just keep seeing it, over and over ... the rage of the men, the way they turned on the girl ... and then she runs away, and I can't see her, and then there's my husband, putting me into the car ... ' She looked up at Agnes. 'What can I do? Life must go on.'

Agnes watched her go, the polished heels against the worn stone steps.

She turned and went inside.

Her phone rang.

'Julius?'

'Bernard's back,' he said. 'He's here.'

Bernard was sitting by Julius' desk in an armchair. He had a large mug of coffee at his elbow, and was eating a bacon sandwich with hungry desperation. His hair was a chaotic shock of grey; he had the beginnings of a beard. He wore a stained and tattered jacket that had once been brown corduroy.

He waved the sandwich at Agnes, continued eating.

Julius poured a coffee, pulled up a third chair for her.

Bernard spoke. 'Oh, Father. Sister. I have sinned. I know that well enough.'

Agnes draped her coat over the back of her chair. 'You were there, that night, at the building site?'

He gave a nod. 'I was with Kayleigh. And that bastard brother of mine. Words were spoken. Harsh words. I regret every one of them now.'

He swallowed, hard. Took another bite of sandwich.

'Bernard—' she faced him. 'What happened?'

'She fell. Kayleigh. Into the hoardings there. Into darkness. I couldn't see her. Couldn't see where she'd gone.' He swallowed. 'I was running after her, I grabbed hold of her – then she'd gone. I looked and looked. All I could see was blackness.' Another bite of sandwich. He looked up at Agnes. 'And I'm to blame. She only knew my brother because of me. What I have, he wants. And he wanted her. And Kayleigh ... the thing with that girl is, she's never known love. She doesn't know what it looks like. So attention, of that kind – she turns towards it like a flower towards the sun.'

Agnes spoke. 'This baby,' she said. 'It could have been yours or his.'

Bernard shook his head. 'No,' he said. 'No, no. Not mine.'

Julius touched his arm. 'Bernard ...'

Bernard turned to him. 'No lies, Father. I promise you. I know it can't be mine. Kayleigh and I ... we didn't ... we weren't ... And my brother knew that too.'

Julius glanced at Agnes.

'Father – I am destined for hell.' He put down his sandwich, stared at it on its greasy wrapping. 'I knew it was his baby. We all knew it was his baby. But she was taunting him, saying he couldn't prove it. He got angry then. It was like she'd unleashed something ... and then I saw him grab her, and there's the pit, and ...' He shook his head. 'Then Mansell vanished. Don't know where he went. I could hear his car. And I stood there, alone, staring into the blackness, the darkness. I thought I could hear a cry ... a tiny sound ... And then silence.' He put his hand across his eyes. 'I could have saved her,' he said. 'But I was a coward.'

Outside a siren, the change of tone as it passed by.

He spoke again. 'And the irony is, he never wanted a child. He's made it perfectly clear for all these years, married a woman who felt the same – but the minute that poor girl makes him think it might be mine, then he wants it. I hear it even now,' he said. 'That cry for help from the depths.'

'Bernard,' Agnes touched his arm. 'Will you speak to the police?'

He gave a weary nod. 'Though the law can't help me now.'

Agnes reached for her phone.

'I keep thinking of them angels,' he said. 'The ones climbing the ladders to Heaven, on the abbey. I used to say to them, when you get there, put in a word for me.' He gave a thin smile. 'They'll have their work cut out now, I can tell you.'

*

Agnes sat in her room. She lit a candle, took out her prayer book. The light was fading, and the city sky was pink with the setting sun.

She opened the book.

'Render therefore to all their dues: tribute to whom tribute is due; custom to whom custom, fear to whom fear, honour to whom honour. Owe no man anything, but to love one another; for he that loveth another hath fulfilled the law.'

One young woman, pushed into a pit. Three witnesses – an angry man, a wife, a brother … And then something happens. A gap in the hoardings, a struggle, a push. Then blackness, and a small, final, haunting cry.

In her mind, the scene replayed itself. The two brothers, the girl taunting them both, the husband turns on the girl, grabs her as she tries to get away – and then, before his brother can catch up with him, he's bundled his wife into the car, leaving Bernard, standing there, alone.

Agnes closed her prayer book, blew out her candle. She thought about Gina's brittle resignation. She thought about the reckoning, the calculation of our guilt.

And without Julius – would I have had the strength to leave?

She picked up her phone. She stared at the image of the painting for a long moment.

I know what I have to do, she thought.

The Mayfair streets seemed to have lost their gloss under the grey drizzly morning. Through the glass doors of the gallery, Agnes could see Gina, standing motionless in the glint of the spotlights.

Agnes rang the bell.

She turned sharply, buzzed the door open. She spoke. 'They released Mansell for now. They're talking to Bernard. It depends whether he tells the truth.'

'And what is the truth?' Agnes said.

Gina met her eyes, then turned away. She was wearing a chunky orange necklace, a white linen shirt, navy trousers. She wandered to her desk.

Agnes spoke. 'I've come to say, you don't have to sell my painting after all. I shall donate it to our mother house in France.'

'Oh.' She faced her, a hint of disappointment in her voice. 'Well, it's up to you.'

'I'm not allowed to own anything.'

A brief smile. 'That's why I could never be a nun.'

There was a composure about her as she stood by her desk. Agnes thought how well she belonged there, so crisp and tailored. Even the Madonna seemed to smile her approval.

Agnes breathed. 'Well,' she said.

'Well.'

They looked at each other.

'Marriage,' Agnes said. 'I keep thinking of your husband, whisking you away from the building site the other night, pushing you into the car.'

Gina gave a shudder at the memory. 'Mansell wants to blame Bernard.'

'And Bernard wants to blame himself. But what price will you have to pay? That's what I keep thinking. Last night,

I was imagining, how would it have been if I'd stayed with Hugo. Constantly paying the price. I was looking at my painting, on my phone, and thinking of the reckoning. And you . . . ' she faced Gina. 'There'll be other girls, other Kayleighs. And you'll be silenced.'

Gina's composure drained away. She tried a smile. 'We all pay a price.'

Agnes sighed. 'I suppose we do.' She sat at the desk. 'The problem,' she said, 'is that Bernard doesn't know what happened that night. He didn't see it all. Whereas your husband saw everything.' She looked up at her. 'In my mind, I see Kayleigh, taunting your husband about his baby. And you, standing there, knowing that the one thing your husband had refused to give you, he'd given to her.'

Gina lowered herself on to the chair, her eyes fixed on Agnes.

'The men were still shouting at each other,' Agnes went on. 'Kayleigh ran away. And you followed. It must have taken a minute, to grab her wrists, a struggle, a push. And she was gone. And then, your husband, realizing what's happened, running, scooping you up, whisking you away, before his brother can see. Which leaves Bernard, alone, staring into the blackness of the pits, hearing that last faint cry.'

Gina got to her feet, stared at the walls. Behind her a flash of red, the flames of hell.

'Of course,' Agnes went on, 'it suits your husband too. To have Kayleigh out of the way. No wonder he's standing by you, blaming his brother . . . '

Gina spoke. Her voice was level. 'You have no proof.'

'No,' Agnes agreed.

Gina paced the gallery. She turned to Agnes. 'I – it's – it's all a blur.' She ran her finger along a picture frame. 'All I could see was that girl, her hand across her belly. All I could hear was her shouting, laughing, about having a baby, my husband's baby . . . ' Her finger went to the next painting. 'For years . . . for years we argued. Me and Mansell. It was the only thing I wanted. A baby. Months, years, of fighting. I was ill with it. At one point he said I should leave, find someone who wants a baby . . . '

'But you couldn't leave.'

Gina shook her head. 'I think . . . looking back . . . he had the power. He made it so I felt I couldn't leave.' She looked around her, glancing at the shining gold frames. 'I had too much to lose.'

She sat down heavily opposite Agnes. 'And now it's too late. There is nowhere to run.'

'They arrested her?' Julius handed Agnes a cup of tea.

She nodded. 'I called Rob Coombes on my phone. She walked out to the car. Calm as anything. I watched them handcuff her.'

'Well, well.' He leaned back in his chair. A flicker of sunlight illumined the room. 'And Bernard's gone back to Bath,' he said. 'He'll do better there.'

Agnes sipped her tea.

'Your painting's gone. Shipped to France. As instructed. I bet your mother house sells it for a fortune.'

'I thought you said it was a fake,' she said.

'I know those nuns – they won't let a small thing like that get in the way,' he said, and she laughed.

A few weeks later, a postcard arrived at Julius' office. He handed it to Agnes. 'It's from Bath,' he said. 'From Bernard.'

It was a picture of the West Door of Bath Abbey. Agnes turned it over. 'All settled here,' she read. 'I'm working at the abbey. Mostly window cleaning. Until I fall off a ladder. Hope you enjoy the picture. PS if you stare at the columns carefully, you can see the angels move.'

Alison Joseph is a London-based crime writer and award-winning radio dramatist. She is the author of the series of novels featuring Sister Agnes, a contemporary nun, based in an open order in London. Her other novels include Dying to Know, *a crime novel about particle physics featuring DI Berenice Killick, published 2015. Her new series features a fictional Agatha Christie as a detective, published by Endeavour Press. Alison is a member of Killer Women, and was Chair of the Crime Writers' Association from 2013- 2015.*

The False Inspector Lovesey

Andrew Taylor

The first time I met Peter was at an Awards Dinner of the Crime Writers' Association. Typically, he found the time to come up and introduce himself to a very new author. Equally typically, he had just won the 1982 Gold Dagger with The False Inspector Dew, *a brilliantly stylish crime novel about a man who pretends to be the detective who had arrested Dr Crippen and his lover, Ethel Le Neve. The book remains one of my all-time favourites in the genre. The story that follows is a humble homage to a wonderful writer and a very kind colleague.*

On my twenty-first birthday (more or less), the doorbell rang shortly before three o'clock in the afternoon. Auntie Ag was passing through the hall at the time, so she answered it.

The man on the doorstep raised his hat. 'My name, madam,' he said, 'is Lovesey.'

He had a droopy face like Mrs Conway-down-the-road's basset hound. He wore a long brown raincoat and carried a briefcase. Under his arm was a newspaper.

'Yes?' said Auntie Ag.

He pointed to the newspaper, the *Lydmouth Gazette*. 'I understand you have a room to let.'

'Yes,' said Auntie in a warmer voice.

Mr Lovesey placed his hat on his chest, covering his heart. His eyes slid past Auntie and found me in the shadows at the back of the hall.

'I'm looking for a bed-sitting room with half-board,' he said. 'For a week at first. Possibly longer.'

'The only vacancy at present is the first-floor front. That doesn't happen very often, I can tell you. It's a very popular room with professional gentlemen. My last lodger, Mr Forster, was a chiropodist. Lovely gentleman.'

Except he drank, I thought, and used to pinch my bum on the landing. Also, from Auntie's point of view at least, there had been the problem with the rent. Still, he had been better than Mr Taylor, over whom Auntie said it was best to draw a veil.

Mr Lovesey nodded. 'Perhaps I might see it?'

Auntie raised her voice but did not turn round. 'Margaret Rose? Go up and raise the blinds.'

I went upstairs. The blinds were already up because I had been in the middle of giving the room its usual sweep, dust and polish. I collected the cleaning materials and hid them in the bottom of the wardrobe.

Auntie Ag sailed through the doorway with Mr Lovesey in tow. 'South-facing,' she said in her most refined voice. 'And beautifully light. Remarkably quiet, too, despite the fact it's so convenient for the High Street, as well as handy for the park at the top of the road. A very nice class of neighbourhood.'

Mr Lovesey's eyes swept around the room, lingering for a moment on the tin of polish on the bedside table. Auntie saw it too, and I knew I would hear more about it later.

'Do try the mattress,' Auntie urged. 'I think you'll find it everything a mattress should be.'

Mr Lovesey sat down on the bed and bounced obediently.

'Plenty of room for your clothes. See?' Auntie opened the wardrobe door and found the rest of the cleaning materials. She closed the door. 'The gas fire's on a meter, not that you'll need to use it at present.' Her eyes swept around the room. 'Own basin, hot and cold water. Our bathroom's along the landing – it has a brand new Ascot water heater. That's on a meter too, of course.'

'What about meals?'

'I always say that a man needs a good cooked breakfast.' Auntie frowned, as if daring him to suggest otherwise. 'As for supper, two courses every evening, rain or shine. Eat with the family, naturally. Sunday lunch is available too, but that's extra.'

'Personal laundry?'

'By arrangement, Mr Lovesey. That's another extra, of course.'

'Of course.' He cleared his throat. 'And, er ...?'

'Four guineas a week, in advance.' The chiropodist had paid three. In theory.

'And the other lodgers?'

'There's only Mr Plantin at present. A very quiet

gentleman, a librarian. He has the room across the landing.'

'Excellent,' said Mr Lovesey. 'Well, I'll take the room for a week, if I may.'

'If you stay longer, I'll need to ask for references.' Auntie Ag gave him one of her closely rationed smiles. 'By the way, we're able to offer a discount of ten shillings for cash. There's such a saving on the bank charges and the paperwork.'

Some gentlemen smiled when she said this, guessing why she preferred cash. But Mr Lovesey merely nodded and took out his wallet.

'And what do you do, Mr Lovesey, if I may ask?'

'I'm a tax inspector, madam.'

There was a short silence. 'How nice,' Auntie Ag said.

'I'd like to move in this afternoon,' he said. 'Would that be possible?'

'Of course. Why don't we go downstairs and settle the details in the warm? Margaret Rose can air the room and make up the bed.'

The only thing I know for certain about me is that my name is Margaret Rose, like the Queen's sister.

I know that because when they found me in the porch of St John's Church I was wearing a luggage label attached to a piece of string around my neck, and the label said 'My name is Margaret Rose.' I was wearing nothing else apart from a nappy. I had been wrapped in several blankets, Miss Ingham told me later, and placed in a wooden box that had once held oranges. I was in good health and quite plump, so someone must have been looking after me properly.

Miss Ingham showed me the luggage label when I was about twelve. They had kept it in my file in the Home. The label said PADDINGTON-SWANSEA – ACCOMPANIED on it. The end bit had been torn off. Maybe the passenger's name had been there.

I had been taken to the Lady Ruispidge Church of England Girls' Home, which was hidden like a guilty secret in a cul de sac off the Narth Road about a mile outside town. Miss Ingham was the assistant matron. The Lady Ruispidge C of E Boys lived in a separate Home a mile outside Lydmouth in the opposite direction. I suppose they wanted to discourage us from breeding.

We went to school on the bus. I passed my 11-Plus but they said I couldn't go to the Lydmouth High School For Girls because of having to pay for the uniform and all the other extras that nice girls needed.

So I went to the Secondary Modern instead and dreamed of ways to escape. The only thing I wanted to keep was my name, Margaret Rose, which was mine. Even my birthday probably wasn't mine, though it might have been. Miss Ingham said that they made a guess from my height and weight when I arrived.

'Everyone should have a birthday,' she told me later.

Before the war, Miss Ingham said, a lot of her girls went into service when they left the Home, but most people couldn't afford servants now. So her girls usually became waitresses or worked in shops. Or, like me, they were sent

to be a live-in home help in a nice family which went to
church on Sundays. You called the lady 'Auntie' and helped
out however you could, and in return the lady fed you and
lodged you and taught you domestic skills, which would
come in handy if you were ever lucky enough to find a husband and have a home of your own.

I didn't particularly want a husband, but I liked the
idea of having a home of my own. But not in Lydmouth. I
wanted to live somewhere you can make dreams come true.

Anyway, in the meantime, that's how I came to be with
Auntie Ag in Victoria Road. I went to live with her when I
was sixteen. But I knew I wouldn't be there for ever.

You have to have dreams, don't you?

The more you look, the more you see. So I kept an eye on
the lodgers and their lives. You could say that was one of
the more useful things that Auntie Ag taught me. She preferred to take single professional gentlemen. She said that
on the whole they were less trouble than ladies.

Mr Lovesey moved in the same afternoon. He didn't have
much luggage – a briefcase, a metal box with a carrying
handle, and a small suitcase. Auntie Ag made a great fuss
of giving him a receipt for three pounds, fourteen shillings,
and entering the transaction in a notebook she normally
used for shopping lists.

The next morning, he went out with the briefcase after
breakfast, saying he probably wouldn't be back before the
evening. I went up to dust his room and make the bed after
breakfast. Apart from his toothbrush and shaving things

on the shelf over the basin, you'd hardly have known he had been there. The wardrobe in the first-floor front was a big one, with shelves on one side of it, as well as the hanging space. He must have put all his clothes in it.

No sign of the box or the suitcase. So they must be in the wardrobe along with everything else. The wardrobe door was locked and the key had gone.

I plucked a hair from my head, moistened it with my tongue and pasted it over the crack at the top of the wardrobe door.

Auntie Ag had a nose around upstairs after lunch. I heard her moving around in the first-floor front when I was clearing away. When she came down, she told me off for not making the tea sooner, but she did it without putting her heart into it. She had something else on her mind.

While she was having her nap, I went up to the first-floor front. My hair had gone from the door. Auntie Ag had a spare key for the wardrobe. But you didn't have to be Sexton Blake to deal with that lock – a hairpin was all you needed.

Mr Lovesey didn't have many clothes. The collar and cuffs of his one spare shirt were frayed. The box turned out to be a small typewriter in a metal case.

The suitcase was locked as well, but the hairpin soon dealt with that. Inside I found three odd socks and a bundle of something wrapped in an old and very grubby shirt.

The something turned out to be several types of Inland Revenue forms and about three dozen postage paid brown envelopes with OHMS printed on them. Finally, there was a paper folder containing printed letterhead.

The address on the letterhead was a Tax Office in Birmingham. The letterhead belonged to Mr P.H. Lovesey, HM Inspector of Taxes.

'Put the kettle on, Margaret Rose,' Auntie Ag said after her nap. 'I've got to pop out to the phone but I won't be a moment.' She went into the hall to put her hat on. A moment later, she poked her head into the kitchen. 'We'll have the Rich Tea biscuits. And mind you put the lid on the tin properly afterwards.'

I filled the kettle and put it on the ring. I turned the gas down low. The front door banged. We didn't have our own telephone, which annoyed Auntie Ag because several of her neighbours in Victoria Road were connected to the Exchange.

I slipped out the back door without bothering with a hat or coat. I went down the side of the house to the front gate. I waited, watching Auntie Ag waddling towards the telephone on the corner. Once she was inside, I walked quickly after her. The door of the box was on the far side of it. I stood out of sight at the back and listened to the rattle of coins. She couldn't see me as long as I kept away from the front and sides where the windows were.

The only danger was that one of the neighbours might notice me and tell Auntie Ag. I pushed that possibility out of my mind. If you want your dreams to come true, sometimes you have to take chances.

A moment later, I heard her saying, 'Could I speak to Mr Lovesey, please?' She was one of those people who think you have to shout if you want to be heard at the other end of the telephone. 'Yes, Lovesey. L-O-V-E-S-E-Y. He's an Inspector ... What? He's where? Dead? Are you sure? Oh ... Well, I'm so sorry to hear that. How sad. No, there's no one else I want to speak to, thank you. It was just him.'

Auntie Ag was very quiet for the rest of the day. Mr Lovesey came home at about five o'clock. He joined Auntie, Mr Plantin and me for supper an hour later.

I was always allowed to eat with the rest of them in the dining room. Auntie would have preferred me to have my meals by myself in the kitchen. But Miss Ingham had been firm about this, saying I needed to learn table manners and so on.

Mr Lovesey was complimentary about the baked beans and tinned peaches, though his long face and droning voice made everything he said sound rather sad.

'Will you be in Lydmouth long?' Auntie asked as she passed him the jug of evaporated milk.

'I don't know exactly,' he said, looking gloomier than ever.

'So you're not going to be based here? Or does the Inland Revenue say "posted" as they do in the Services?'

'Oh no. I shan't be here permanently.' He poured a thin white stream over the peaches, frowning with concentration. 'The office sends us out in the field sometimes. Spot checks, you know. Random Inspections – R.I.s – that's what

we call them. It's a very effective way of finding defaulters.'
His frown deepened. If he really had been a dog, he would
probably have been thinking about biting someone. 'It's
hush-hush, but you wouldn't believe some of the cases I
have to deal with. People trying to cheat the Revenue.
Barefaced fraud.'

'Disgusting,' Auntie Ag said. 'I hope you won't find
anyone like that around here.'

Her voice lifted towards the end, in the way people's
voices do when they want to ask a question but don't like
to put it into words.

'I can't talk about my work, of course,' Mr Lovesey said.
'It would contravene the Official Secrets Act.'

Next morning, Mr Lovesey went out again, with his briefcase in one hand, his umbrella in the other. An hour later,
after I'd done the beds and the dusting, Auntie Ag sent me
shopping. I wasn't keen to go – it was raining.

She wanted me to pay the newspaper bill and buy her
some cigarettes. And all of a sudden she decided that
she wanted sausages for lunch. That meant Lane's, the
butcher's. At this time of day, there was always a queue
at Lane's.

Auntie knew that as well as I did. So I guessed she wanted
to have another look at the first-floor front and didn't want
to be disturbed.

This was always Auntie's way with her gentleman lodgers.
She took her time. When she found Mr Plantin's special
magazines under the mattress, for example, she didn't say

anything about them for weeks. Not until she wanted to raise the rent, which happened to be when Mr Plantin had just applied for the Chief Librarian's job.

I saw Mr Lovesey when I came out of Lane's. He was standing outside, sheltering from the rain in the shop doorway and reading the adverts in the *Gazette*. I couldn't avoid him.

'Morning, sir,' I said.

'Good morning, Margaret Rose.' He glanced at my shopping bag. 'What's that you've got there?'

'Sausages, sir.'

'Will we be having them for supper?'

'No, sir. They're for lunch.'

'Pity,' Mr Lovesey said, looking sadder than ever. 'I like sausages. Goodbye, Margaret Rose.'

'I think we'll keep the sausages for supper,' Auntie said when I returned. 'Give the gentlemen a treat, eh?'

She was in a good mood, which made me think she'd found something when I was out. Or maybe she had just come up with a plan. She had been intending to give the gentlemen yesterday's cold tongue and a bit of salad for supper. She wouldn't waste sausages on them out of the kindness of her heart.

There were eleven sausages. At suppertime, Mr Lovesey, Mr Plantin and Auntie had three each and I had two. There was ice cream and jelly, Mr Plantin's favourite, for pudding. By the end of the meal, everyone was in a good mood.

'Mr Lovesey?' Auntie said as the three of them were leaving the room. 'A quick word, if I may take a minute or two of your valuable time. Come in the sitting room.'

'Of course.'

'I don't want to be disturbed, Margaret Rose,' Auntie said. 'You can listen to the wireless in the kitchen when you've washed up and laid the breakfast things. I'll come and find you when I want my Ovaltine.'

Later in the evening, I heard the clatter of typewriter keys from the first-floor front.

Mr Lovesey had spent a good twenty minutes with Auntie before going upstairs. He was still typing away when Auntie told me to make her Ovaltine.

He came down to the kitchen as I was washing up the milk saucepan. He had a brown envelope in his hand.

'When's the last collection?' he asked.

'Six-thirty from the box on the corner.'

'And the main Post Office?'

'That's ten-thirty, I think.'

He glanced at his watch. 'Good – I want this to go out tonight, you see. Could you run down and post it?'

'Yes, sir.' I put down the saucepan and dried my hands.

He held out the envelope. With his other hand, he jingled the change in his trouser pocket.

I took the envelope. It had OHMS at the top lefthand corner.

'Thank you, Margaret Rose,' Mr Lovesey said. 'That's very kind.'

I fetched my coat, which was hanging by the back door, and put it on.

Mr Lovesey was still there. He gave me a shilling. 'This for your trouble.'

'Thank you, sir.'

He went back upstairs. I told Auntie where I was going. She didn't ask any questions, but just nodded and sipped her Ovaltine.

In the porch, I held the envelope up to the light and read the typed address.

Private and Confidential
Mr M.Underhill
Underhill's Garage
Chepstow Road
Lydmouth

Mr Underhill's garage was about fifteen minutes' walk away. He was a big man with a bald head and a pale face that always seemed in need of a shave. He repaired all sorts of motor vehicles and bought and sold second-hand cars. He had a newly built showroom, a shop for spares, and a big workshop. Behind this was a walled yard packed with cars, lorries, tractors and even ambulances. Two Alsatians were chained up at the corner of the workshop during the day. At night, they roamed free.

Underhill's was a family business. Mrs Underhill did the accounts and helped out in the shop. They said she had the brains. Their two boys had left school and they worked for their dad as well. You often saw them washing cars or tinkering with engines.

Mr Underhill's younger brother was one of the mechanics. His name was Neil, and he was funny in the head. He probably wouldn't have got a job anywhere else – not just because he was funny in the head, but because he was sent to prison for six months after he broke someone's arms during a fight in the Bathurst Arms one Saturday night. Neil lived in a tumbledown bungalow attached to the shop.

Mr and Mrs Underhill had built a big house for themselves over the road. It was called Manderley, like Mr de Winter's house in the film, and in the book by Daphne du Maurier. (Mrs Underhill especially admired Laurence Olivier in the film.) The house had a balcony on the first floor and an attached double garage, as well as a tennis court and a swimming pool in the garden.

I knew all this because Mrs Underhill sometimes came to see Auntie Ag. They were both in the Women's Institute, and sometimes they worked together at Bring and Buy sales or doing the flower rota for St John's.

Mrs Underhill was not a lady who liked to hide her good fortune. That's how I knew about the swimming pool, the tennis court and much else, including the Underhills' summer holiday in Mallorca, which is an island that belongs to Spain, and which isn't pronounced how it is spelt.

Auntie Ag once called her 'that cow' when she thought I wasn't listening.

*

I tried to open the letter on my way to the Post Office, but it was too late – the gum had dried on the flap, and I could hardly steam open an envelope in the middle of the High Street at nine-thirty in the evening.

So I did as I was told and dropped it in the letterbox at the main Post Office.

The next morning, Auntie Ag gave Mr Lovesey an extra rasher of streaky bacon at breakfast. She was in the hall when he left for work, and handed him his hat and umbrella.

Almost like a wife. Now there was a thought.

When I did the rooms upstairs, I found a new maga-zine under Mr Plantin's mattress. I flicked through it – it's extraordinary what men like to look at, especially where ladies are concerned, but there's no harm in a girl knowing what she might be up against.

I struck lucky in Mr Lovesey's room too. Whoever he really was, he must have had proper Civil Service training at some point – he had made a carbon copy of his letter to Mr Underhill, and there it was in his suitcase.

The letter contained a lot of official phrases and ref-erences to various Codes and Orders. But what it said was simple enough. Mr Lovesey, HM Inspector of Taxes, intended to call on Mr Underhill at 9.30 a.m. this morning to make a Random Inspection of his books (as authorised by Tax Order B32, Section 8, paragraph 4), and to examine his accounts over the last three years.

If I learned one thing at the Lady Ruispidge Church of England Girls' Home, it's that you can't live without a dream. My dream was to go somewhere where you could make your dreams come true.

For me, I thought that was probably going to be London. After all, if my luggage tag was anything to go by, London might well have been where I came from in the first place. From what I had heard, my kind of dreams were more likely to come true in London than anywhere else.

Actually, I learned another thing at the Lady Ruispidge Church of England Girls' Home. The value of patience.

'Remember, Margaret Rose,' Miss Ingham said to me when she retired and went to live with her mother in Wigan. 'Good things come to her who waits.'

It took two days, all told, for Mr Lovesey to manage it. He must have had a lot of experience at doing his RIs.

At teatime on the first day, Mrs Underhill called unexpectedly at the house. When I opened the door, she barged into the hall without a by-your-leave.

'Where's your mistress?'

'In the sitting room.'

Auntie Ag wasn't my mistress. Miss Ingham had been very clear about that when I had come here five years ago. I was a home help, not a servant. Auntie Ag had often seemed rather less clear about the subject, but that wasn't the point.

Mrs Underhill's hair was a mess, and personally I wouldn't have been seen dead wearing a hat that colour with a maroon twinset.

She opened the sitting room door without knocking. 'Is that man really staying with you?'

'Who?' Auntie asked, all sweetness and light.

'Mr Lovesey, of course.'

'My Tax Inspector? Yes, of course. Such a nice gentleman.'

Mrs Underhill closed the door in my face. I tried to eavesdrop. But it was a close-fitting door, and they kept their voices down.

Auntie Ag gave the lodgers a glass of sherry before supper that evening. In all my years here that had never happened before, even when Mr Hargreaves had the first-floor front and Auntie Ag had had expectations.

After breakfast the following morning, she was lurking in the hall again when Mr Lovesey left the house. I was on the stairs, and I heard them having a whispered conversation.

The rest of the morning followed the same routine as any other morning. When I was doing the sitting room, however, I found a screwed-up ball of paper in the grate. It had fallen between the back of the grate and the rear wall of the hearth. The heat had charred one corner and turned the rest of the paper the colour of a strong cup of tea.

The paper was so brittle that it fell apart when I unwrapped the ball. But some of the pieces were large enough for me to make out that there was a pencilled list on it, and that the writing was Auntie Ag's. I could make sense of only four words, and they were all names, and all four belonged to people I knew.

Cooper-Lewis
Prout
Underhill
Lane

Mr Lane, as I've said, was our butcher. Miss Cooper-Lewis ran a private hotel on the Chepstow Road. (She and Auntie Ag had a long-running feud.) Mr Prout was the manager of the toy shop on the High Street.

'Underhill' was underlined.

Mr Lovesey came home unexpectedly as Auntie Ag and I were having lunch. I went to open the door when he rang the bell – only long-term lodgers were trusted with a key of their own.

So far, Mr Lovesey had been generally quite pleasant to deal with, despite his glum face. But now he ignored me completely and marched down the hall, calling Auntie's name.

She appeared in the dining-room doorway. They didn't say anything in front of me. She led him into the sitting room and closed the door.

Auntie's mince and mash was cooling on the plate. I carried the plate into the kitchen and put it in the oven, to keep warm. As I went through the hall on the way back, I tried my luck at the sitting-room door.

I couldn't hear a thing. So I took a chance and went up to Mr Lovesey's room. The first-floor front was immediately above Auntie's sitting room. I tiptoed across the floor to the fireplace, avoiding the two boards that creaked.

There was a capped gas pipe poking through a floor-board beside the hearth. It ran up from the room below. In the old days, it must have fed a light on the wall above. If you knelt down and put your ear to the side of the pipe, it was surprising the sounds that filtered up from below.

'... I can't go back there,' Mr Lovesey was saying, his voice distorted and muffled by the pipe.

'But you've got to.' Auntie Ag sounded agitated. 'You can't ask her to put it in the post, can you? And the longer you leave it ...'

'It's too dangerous. I'm sure the halfwit brother recognised my face. We were on the same wing for a couple of months, and he knows me as someone else. If I go again, even he might put two and two together. Couldn't she bring it to me here?'

I couldn't hear the next bit properly, though they were still talking. They had moved away from the fireplace or lowered their voices.

Then one thing very clearly. Auntie Ag said, 'In that case, it'll have to be Margaret Rose. There's nothing else for it.'

I strained to hear Mr Lovesey's reply.

But there was no reply, or not that I heard. Instead, the sitting-room door opened.

I was on the stairs in a flash. I was too late. They were already in the hall, their heads twisting up towards me.

'Where've you been?' Auntie Ag snapped.

'Powdering my nose,' I said. 'I put your lunch to keep warm in the oven. Shall I get it out now?'

*

For the rest of the day, everything went on as before. But something was different. I didn't get an inkling of what it was until I took Auntie Ag her Ovaltine.

She was sitting by the fire and smoking a cigarette, with a Denton Carbury detective novel open on her lap. She smiled up at me when I put the cup and saucer on the table with her lamp.

'Shut the door, Margaret Rose, would you? Come and sit down for a moment.'

That definitely wasn't normal. I sat in the armchair opposite hers.

'Don't look so worried, dear,' she said.

That was even less normal, if that's possible. Calling me 'dear', I mean.

'You know my friend Mrs Underhill?'

'Yes, Auntie.'

'Of course you do – she dropped in yesterday, didn't she, about the flowers for the week after Easter.'

I nodded, though I was pretty sure that church flowers had been the last thing on Mrs Underhill's mind.

'Well, I want you to pop over to her house tomorrow morning. You know? Opposite their garage? It's called Manderley.'

I nodded again.

'Go round to the back door. Mrs Underhill has been doing . . . has been helping with the W.I. accounts, and she wants me to check some figures for her and so on. It'll be a brown envelope with all the receipts and things in it. All right?'

'What time shall I go?'

'Let's say about ten-thirty.' Her voice hardened, returning to the tone she tended to use with me. 'And make sure you come straight home with it. They're confidential papers, and we'll all get in a lot of trouble if they're lost. You as much as anyone else. You wouldn't want that, I'm sure, would you?'

'No, Auntie,' I said.

Yes, you have to have dreams. But more than that, you have to take your chances when they come or else the dreams are just that. Dreams.

At Auntie's, I slept in the attic in a little room that had once been a box room. Auntie sometimes came up to snoop when I wasn't there. (I know that because I used that old trick of the hair between the door and its frame.)

Underneath my chest of drawers was a loose floorboard. It was there, in the dusty space between the joists, that I kept a biscuit tin that I'd found one day in Mr Forster's wastepaper basket.

My savings were inside. All the money I'd scraped together over the last five years. I had seven pound notes, eight ten-shilling notes, and a heap of silver and coppers. It came to seventeen pounds, six shillings and ninepence.

Money for dreams. Money for chances.

In the morning, I was up a little earlier than usual to make preparations. After breakfast, Mr Lovesey and Mr Plantin left the house as usual. Auntie Ag went into the sitting

room to smoke the first cigarette of the day and read the
paper.

While I was clearing away in the kitchen, I set aside some
bread and cheese for later. Dreams are all very well, but you
can't eat dreams.

A little after ten o'clock, Auntie Ag told me to get myself
ready.

'Remember,' she said. 'Come straight back from Mrs
Underhill's. You'd better tuck the envelope in your coat.
It'll be safer there.'

She let me out of the front door and watched me walking
down the path to the gate. I looked back and waved. Her
hand twitched in response, and she closed the door.

The front garden was separated from the pavement of
Victoria Road by a dusty laurel hedge above a low brick
wall. Once I was out of sight of the sitting room, I picked
up the bag, which I had hidden between the wall and hedge
before breakfast. It was a grey bag with a zip and plastic
handles. Miss Ingham had given it to me when I came to
live at Auntie's. It was big enough to contain everything
that mattered.

I walked down to the Chepstow Road and up to the
garage. Neil, Mr Underhill's younger brother, was fiddling
with the engine of a car parked on the oil-stained concrete
in front of his bungalow. He glanced up as I passed on the
other side of the road and watched me turning into the
drive of Manderley.

I went round to the back of the house. Mrs Underhill
opened the kitchen door before I had time to knock.

I hardly recognised her in her housecoat. She looked shorter, too, because she was wearing slippers, not heels. Her hair was in curlers and she hadn't done her make-up.

'It's Margaret Rose, isn't it?' She drew me inside and took a large manila envelope from the pocket of her pinafore. 'Don't lose that. Mind you take it home and give it to your mistress right away.'

'Yes, Mrs Underhill,' I said. I unzipped my bag and put the envelope on top.

'It's confidential,' she called after me, as I was leaving. 'That's why.'

I walked across the station yard to the ticket office. 'A second-class single to Birmingham, please.'

The next train was in fifteen minutes. Rather than hang about on the platform, I bought a copy of *Tit-Bits* and sat with it in the Ladies' Waiting Room. No one else was there. I tried to read but I couldn't concentrate. Auntie must be missing me by now.

It took an age for the train to come. When it did, it wheezed along the platform with painful slowness, trailing wisps of steam and smoke. The station wasn't crowded at this time of day, which made me feel I must stand out like a sore thumb. So I stayed in the Ladies' Waiting Room until the train had stopped moving. Then I ran outside.

A porter opened the door nearest me. I climbed aboard. Behind me, a spaniel towed a clergyman onto the train.

It was a corridor train and the sort that stops at every little station it can find. I walked down the train until I found a completely empty compartment near the luggage van. The whistle blew and the train pulled away from the station as painfully and as slowly as it had come.

I opened the magazine but I didn't even try to read it. I stared out of the window at the river, the spire of St John's and the town around it, enclosed by green hills. The train picked up a little speed, but not as much as I would have liked.

Leaving my coat and *Tit-Bits* on the seat, I carried my bag along the corridor to the toilet at the end. I sat down, unzipped the bag and took out the manila envelope. It was eight or nine inches long and about half that wide. The flap was held down with Sellotape.

I cut the end of the envelope with my nail scissors (thank you, Miss Ingham). Inside was a wad of banknotes more than half an inch thick and attached with an elastic band.

I spread them out like a hand of playing cards. Five-pound notes, mainly, and a few pounds. Two or three hundred pounds. Maybe more.

I didn't bother to count the money. I just sat there, looking at the banknotes, enjoying them, and feeling the happiness rise up inside me like a warm, pink cloud.

Auntie Ag and Mr Lovesey could hardly go to the police about the missing money. After all, Mr Lovesey wasn't Mr Lovesey. He was a fraud who had been to prison, and Auntie Ag was now his accessory before the fact or whatever they called it in detective stories.

Mr and Mrs Underhill couldn't complain, either. They had tried to bribe a Tax Inspector to avoid a Random

Inspection of their books. The fact he was a fake Inspector was neither here nor there.

I'd get off the train at Gloucester – the Birmingham ticket was just to throw Auntie Ag off my scent – and buy a ticket to London.

London, I thought, and with money in my pocket. The city where dreams come true.

I put the money away and pulled the chain. I went back to my compartment, placed the bag on the seat beside me and opened *Tit-Bits* again.

A moment later, the door slid open.

'Hello, Margaret Rose,' said Mr Lovesey or whoever he was. 'I thought I'd find you here.' He came into the compartment and closed the door. He set down his briefcase on the seat, placed his hat and umbrella on the luggage rack, and sat down on the facing seat, nearer the door than me.

I put down the magazine and stared at him.

'You've got something you shouldn't have,' he said. He didn't sound angry, just stating a fact. 'It belongs to the Government.'

'I don't know what you're talking about,' I said.

'It's as well I followed you. Just in case, I thought. How right I was.'

I said nothing.

'Where is it?' Mr Lovesey shuffled his bottom along the seat, bringing himself nearer to me. 'In that bag?'

'I don't know what you mean.'

I glanced away from him, up at the communication cord over the window.

'Don't touch that. Don't be a silly girl. Who are they going to believe, eh? You or me?'

There was a wood outside the window, the trees climbing up a ridge. The river was running parallel to us along the bottom of the valley. The train was very gradually slowing down.

'I'll say you tried to interfere with me,' I said.

Mr Lovesey sighed. 'Come on, Margaret Rose. No need for any unpleasantness, is there? I'm sure we can come to an arrangement.'

I stood up, which brought me in reach of the cord. But so did he.

The compartment door slid back.

Mr Lovesey swung round sharply. The ticket collector was in the doorway.

'Everything all right, Miss?'

'I . . . I . . .'

I broke off and cowered away from Mr Lovesey. The ticket collector wore a wedding ring and he looked like he might be a family man. I blinked, encouraging tears to fill my eyes. Another thing I'd learned at the Lady Ruispidge Church of England Girls' Home was how to make myself cry at will.

'What's up?' The ticket collector was frowning now. 'Is this man bothering you?'

The train was still slowing.

'I don't know,' I whimpered. 'He's . . . he's been acting funny.'

Mr Lovesey drew himself up. 'I assure you, I—'

'Let's see your ticket, sir.'

Mr Lovesey fumbled in his waistcoat pocket and produced a platform ticket.

'This ticket isn't valid for travel.'

'No, of course not,' Mr Lovesey said. 'The thing is, I decided to catch the train on impulse. I suddenly remembered something, an appointment, an important—'

'He was waiting outside the Ladies Waiting Room,' I said. 'He was staring at me through the window. Then he followed me on.'

The ticket inspector glanced from me to Mr Lovesey and back. 'But you say he hasn't actually *done* anything?'

'Not yet,' I said in a very small voice, and allowed two tears to brim over and trickle down my cheeks.

'This is nonsense,' Mr Lovesey said. 'Complete balderdash.'

The train was hardly moving now.

'I'll be the judge of that, sir,' the ticket collector said. 'One thing I know for sure, though, is you can't travel without a valid ticket.'

'Surely you can sell me—?'

'So you'll have to leave the train at the next station. You haven't come far, so I won't fine you – and you can thank your lucky stars for that.'

The train inched along the platform. We were coming into Mitchelbrook, a village that straggled along the main road. It was about five miles from Lydmouth. It wasn't even a proper station, just a halt where trains occasionally stopped.

'Come on. Out you go.'

Mr Lovesey looked at me. His shoulders moved in the ghost of a shrug. Then he left the compartment. The ticket collector followed him down the corridor.

I sat down and clutched my bag. I stared out of the window. The platform looked empty.

The guard blew his whistle. After an age, the train began to move again.

I saw Mr Lovesey one more time. He was standing close to the edge of the platform. For a moment, his melancholy, doglike eyes stared at me through the window, his head turning as the train slid past him.

Andrew Taylor is a crime and historical novelist who has been honoured with the Cartier Diamond Dagger of the Crime Writers' Association. He has also won the Historical Dagger three times. His books include the international bestseller, The American Boy *(a Richard and Judy selection); the Roth Trilogy (filmed for TV as Fallen Angel); the Lydmouth Series; the Dougal Series;* Bleeding Heart Square; The Anatomy of Ghosts; The Scent of Death; The Silent Boy; *and, most recently,* The Ashes of London.

Dreaming of Rain and Peter Lovesey

Ann Cleeves

I first met Peter at a CWA conference in Edinburgh. I hadn't met any published writers before and I was overawed to be in the same room as people I'd read and admired. Peter welcomed me to the group with his legendary charm and warmth. While I was embarrassed to admit that I'd been plucked from the slush pile he made it seem impressive and that I had every right to be there. I felt immediately that I was among friends and after more than twenty-five years that's still how I feel in the company of crime writers.

I met Peter Lovesey once at an event in a bookshop in Bath. It was a grey, drizzly day of the sort that you often get in the west country. Mild and the rain was soft, so if you tipped up your head it felt like tears on your face. It was before I was married and I did cry occasionally in those days, late at night in my room in the nurses' halls of residence. There were times when I felt lonely and that I didn't fit in; crime fiction was my escape and my solace. Peter Lovesey was won-derful, gentle and approachable like his novels. He signed

one of his books for me. I've still got it. It travelled with
me when we moved to the UAE, and I keep it in a drawer
besides my bed to reread at times of crisis.

I suppose Michael rescued me from loneliness. I met him
in the hospital. He was a professional rugby player and had
suffered an injury that he knew right from the beginning
would stop him playing again. I understand that he'd been
fearless as a player but the man I met in the ward was scared
and confused. As a young man, his future was mapped out:
he'd already played for his country when I first knew him,
and it was predicted that he'd go on to captain the team.
He didn't know anything except professional sport. Now,
it was as if he had no future at all. Perhaps he liked me
because I posed no threat. I've always been rather timid
and eager to please. He says that I helped him back onto his
feet and perhaps that's true, literally and metaphorically.
When he asked me to marry him I suspected even then that
it was out of gratitude, and I agreed because I was grateful
too that he'd noticed me.

I'm not quite sure why Michael went into teaching; he'd
always made it clear that he never liked children. There was
never any thought that *we* might have a family for example.
Perhaps he couldn't think of anything else that he was
suited for. More likely, I think he enjoys the power he has
over the children in his classes. He admits that he's a control freak and forcing the kids into physical activity means
that they're too tired to fight back. At least that's what he
says and he's only half-joking. He struggled a bit in his last
school – it must be hard when you've been famous and

celebrated to be a junior member of staff at the bottom of the heap – but he seems very happy where he is now, teaching physical education at an international school here in Dubai. The head's a rugby fan and was thrilled to employ him. Michael says he gets respect here from the kids and the other staff.

He likes the Emirate culture too, the positivity and the money. He even enjoys the weather. I've found it more difficult to fit in. Michael wouldn't think of me working and there's little for me to do. He'd even like to employ help in the house, but I wouldn't be comfortable with that. I have friends of course, other ex-pat women, but I suspect they find me a little boring for their taste. I'm not a confident driver, and I'm not very good at small talk, so I find it hard to get out and mix. They've stopped inviting me to coffee mornings and dinners. It's not that I'm completely unsociable: I joined a choir when we first arrived and more recently a book group. I've returned to the books of my youth, to the detective novels that kept me sane while I was training. I'm in need of escape and solace even more than I was then. Peter Lovesey's still my favourite.

Dubai is an intimidating city. It seems almost surreal with its jagged towers made of glass and metal, shining like gold and silver in the glare of the sun. It could be a monstrous science-fiction film set built in the desert. The metro has no drivers and the stations look just like flying saucers. Everything is hard and sharp and the heat sucks away all my energy. I'm haunted by dreams of rain, of mild westerly winds blowing over the Mendips, blurring the outlines of houses and churches. Sometimes I wake, drenched in sweat, imagining that I've been caught in a thunderstorm and I'm running down the streets of Bath in a downpour.

Peter Lovesey is coming to the Emirates Literature Festival. One of my friends brought a programme to the latest reading group. I've suggested that the group should read his novels, so we'd have intelligent questions for him before we attend his lecture. There will be a dinner too, each table hosted by one of the guest authors, and I imagine how wonderful it would be to be seated next to Peter. I might even pluck up courage to talk to him, to remind him that we met on a previous occasion.

I hope Michael will be happy for me to attend, despite the price of the ticket – he earns a very good tax-free wage, but he seems to begrudge me the small pleasures that would make life here a little more bearable. I don't think he would consider the Festival as an extravagance, however. Not because it attracts some of the most prestigious authors in the world, but because all the ex-pat wives will be there and he very much wants me to be a part of that social scene. It reflects well on him if I mix with the partners of senior bankers and executives.

The day before the Festival it rains. This isn't unheard of. Occasionally there are showers, brief and local. Usually they come to nothing. You can see where the individual raindrops have landed in the sand and then they disappear like magic as the heat dries them. But this morning there's a downpour; it only lasts for an hour but it brings the traffic to a standstill. The roads have no drainage because it was never considered necessary when they were being carved out of the desert, and there is standing water everywhere.

That evening Michael drops his bombshell. He comes in from work and I fetch a glass of juice out to the garden for him, so he can sit in the shade. This is his routine. He never thanks me for preparing the juice just as he likes it. If we employed a maid, I think he probably would thank her, because the ex-pat Brits are famous for treating their staff well and he understands how things should be done.

'We've been invited to Geoffrey's for dinner.' He's very excited. The head's dinners are legendary. Geoffrey has been in Dubai for years and he knows all the important people, Emirate and ex-pat. Geoffrey's wife used to be a diplomat here and has maintained all her contacts.

I'm not excited. I know it will be a dreadful evening to be endured not enjoyed, and afterwards Michael will criticise the way I looked, the people I spoke to and above all my lack of support for him.

'Lovely,' I murmur. 'When is it?' I hope I will have weeks to prepare.

'Tomorrow. I suppose he had a late cancellation and we're a kind of second best.' Michael frowns. He sees a slight in everything.

'But I can't go tomorrow! It's the night of the Festival dinner.' The words are out before I can stop them.

Michael's frown deepens. 'Of course you can go. It's not the bloody lecture is it? It's only a party.' And so, of course, the decision is made.

*

The next day it rains again. The schools are closed and the radio runs warnings about not leaving home. The Burj Khalifa, the tallest building in the world, is shrouded in cloud. I have done my best to prepare for this dinner and even Michael pays me a compliment of a kind: 'I wish you'd make this much effort when it's just you and me. It's not as if you have anything else to do.' We run to the car. Michael will drive there and I'll drive home because we know that wine and beer will be served. Usually the prospect of driving would make me anxious but tonight I'm shrouded in a depression that is as dense as the cloud and it seems a very small problem. The traffic is slow and Michael becomes impatient. He hates being late. He turns off the motorway into an underpass under the main carriageway; this will lead to a smaller road that will be a short cut to Geoffrey's house. 'All this bloody fuss about a bit of rain.'

It's dark by now. His headlights show that there's standing water in the underpass, but he ploughs on. He's an Englishman and rain won't deter him. As the car hits, it's clear that this is more than surface water; it's a flood many feet deep. The underpass is a well and it holds all the rain that has run off the hard, tarmacked roads. For a moment the car floats and then it starts to sink. I realize that if we stay where we are we will drown. Before the pressure becomes too powerful, I push open the passenger door, and climb out. The headlights short and everything is very dark. There's a faint rumble from the traffic above us. Outside the water is too deep for me to stand, but I know I can swim to safety. I hesitate for a moment. Michael can't swim and he's terrified of water – perhaps that was why he loved living in the desert. I still have time to drag open his door and help him to safety.

Then I think of Peter Lovesey and the cloud that blows in across the Mendips. I swim out of the underpass and climb up to the side of the motorway. I wait there for someone to stop and to rescue me. I won't get to the Festival dinner, but I'll make it back to Bath, with its rain that's gentle like tears.

Ann Cleeves is the bestselling author of the Vera and Shetland series; both have been adapted as successful television dramas. Her latest novel is The Moth Catcher. *The first of the Shetland novels,* Raven Black, *won the CWA Gold Dagger, and her earlier work includes a series with an ornithological background and another featuring Inspector Stephen Ramsay.*

The Walrus and the Spy

Catherine Aird

The first book of Peter's that I read was Wobble To Death, *and it made a great impression on me. Unfortunately my own connections with exotic sports are limited to editing two volumes of the standard (and only!) history of English Roller Hockey and having had a grandfather who captained England at water polo. I therefore cast my mind about in search of another connection and decided to set my (boyish) short story in the years in which he was born. I can remember them (just) although he won't be able to – but then, as they say in Yorkshire: he's 'nobbut a boy'.*

'Ah, there you are, Tyler.'

Henry Tyler had just stepped inside the entrance hall of the Mordaunt Club when he heard his name spoken behind him.

'The very man I was hoping to see,' said the voice.

'Morning, Carruthers,' sighed Tyler, who had been planning to have a quiet lunch away from his place of work – the Foreign Office in London.

'Are you lunching with anyone today, Tyler?'

'I had been heading for the Long Table,' admitted Henry Tyler. The Long Table was where those lunching either without guests or with other members of the Mordaunt Club customarily sat, automatically sitting next to whoever was already there. This usually guaranteed amiable but unspecific conversation which was exactly what Henry Tyler, escaping temporarily from the maelstrom of activity that was the Foreign Office in the late nineteen-thirties, had been hoping for.

'So you're not lunching with Herr von Ribbentrop or even Neville Chamberlain, then?'

'Neither,' said Henry Tyler acidly. 'And I've also actually reached Friday still sane and on my own two feet which I may say I consider quite a high achievement these days.'

'Nor Lord Halifax?' persisted Carruthers.

'You shouldn't joke about serious matters,' said Henry Tyler, who had been dealing with all three gentlemen lately and not liking it.

'Sorry, old chap. Look here, would you mind lunching with me?'

'Of course not,' said Henry untruthfully. Malcolm Carruthers worked for one of those nameless departments of State that people such as himself weren't even supposed to know existed, let alone what they got up to. Whatever it was they did, Henry was pretty sure it was well outside the Civil Service code. And that it was safer for a man in his position not to know.

'Alone,' added Carruthers pointedly.

'Naturally,' agreed Henry, who could see where this was leading.

'Truth is, Tyler, we've got a bit of a problem over at our place.' Malcolm Carruthers waved an arm vaguely in the general direction of Whitehall.

'Really?' said Henry politely. Something that was part of the Civil Service code was that you usually let each Ministry deal with its own problems. Treading on other departments' toes was not encouraged but then these were what the newspapers described as 'stirring times' and those in public office said privately were 'very worrying ones indeed'.

'You know Farnessnes Island, Tyler?'

'I do indeed. A valuable source of diatomous earth. Situated in the Baltic Sea and determined to stay neutral in the forthcoming conflict.' Henry thought he'd better rephrase this statement in the interests of public relations at the Foreign Office. 'Or, rather, in any international conflict that might soon occur.'

'Too right, old chap. I don't think they have a hope of keeping out of things myself but there you are.'

'But I take it that naturally you already have – er – some of your people established over there to be on the safe side.' Henry Tyler followed Carruthers to a table for two in a far corner of the Club's spacious dining-room.

'Sleepers?' Malcolm Carruthers looked pained. 'You bet we have.'

'And?'

'One of them has just sent us something that we can't

read. That is to say that we can read it in one sense because it's in English but not get the message.'

'En clair?'

'Oh, yes.' He looked a bit abashed. 'I'm sorry to say we haven't set up any other way just yet.'

'You'd better get on with doing so pretty smartly then,' advised Henry Tyler, adding hastily, 'but whatever you do don't say that I said so. In theory those people don't exist.'

'Understood. We're working on it, of course.'

'So?'

Carruthers made to get something out of his pocket but saw a waiter approaching and stayed his hand. 'I'll have the whitebait,' he said after a cursory glance at the menu.

'And I'll have the soup,' said Henry. It was the only matter on which so far he had had the opportunity of being decisive that day, his political masters being notably intransigent. He quoted lightly '"Beautiful, beautiful Soup".'

'Funny you should say that, Tyler.'

'Why?'

'There's something about the walrus and the carpenter – no, not only the carpenter – the walrus and the oysters in the message.'

'Ah, as I remember the oysters got eaten, didn't they?' said Henry thoughtfully. 'They were the victims.'

'Really?'

'I'll have you know, Carruthers, that the world of *Alice in Wonderland* describes my working life at the Foreign Office at the moment better than anything else.'

The other man was too concerned with his own problems

to respond to this. 'You see, Tyler, we know that this message must be highly important.'

'I'm sure it is,' agreed Henry warmly. 'People don't go to the trouble of putting things into code that aren't.'

'It's their Prime Minister, Beren, who's worrying us – he's a pretty wily fellow.'

'All prime ministers are wily,' said Henry feelingly. 'It's when they aren't that you need to worry.'

Carruthers ignored this nugget of political wisdom. 'We really need to know where Beren stands if – when – war comes.'

'The neutrality, I take it,' said Henry, breaking a roll in half, 'being purely nominal?'

'I'll say. But it will only stay that way on the surface. We're worried about which way it really will go, neutral or not, when the balloon goes up.'

'Quite unofficially, I take it?'

'Naturally. In theory it's none of our business,' said Carruthers, unfolding his napkin. 'We're just holding a watching brief over at our place. Ah, here comes my whitebait.'

'And,' continued Henry, gentle persistence being a prerequisite of his daily work, 'am I right in saying that if their Prime Minister is of another cast of mind from ours then a second very different but nameless power might be able to use his precious island as an unofficial base?'

'You've got it in one, old chap. It's got a name, hasn't it? That sort of thing?'

'Rendition,' said Henry, addressing himself to his soup. 'A weasel word if ever there was one.'

'That's it,' said Carruthers, tucking his napkin under his chin and starting to tackle his whitebait.

'And neutrality being what it is my own feeling is always that he who is not for us is against us.' Specious neutrality was something they had known quite a lot about in the Foreign Office over the years. They knew all about fence-sitting, too. Appeasement, on the other hand, was something they were only just beginning to learn about.

'You will help us, though, won't you?' said Carruthers persuasively. 'I may say our people have done all the usual things with the message and can't get anywhere with the text. It doesn't mean a thing as it reads and we really do need to know whether their head man's on our side or not. And the sooner, the better, of course. Time really is of the essence.'

'I've got our man in Berlin coming to see me this afternoon,' temporised Henry, 'but I'm hoping to go down to Calleshire to stay with my sister for the weekend which might give me a bit of time to take a look at it for you.'

'I hope our ambassador isn't going to be a good man sent to die abroad for his country,' muttered Carruthers morosely, twisting a more famous version of the sentiment to chime with the present national mood.

Obscurely pleased that Carruthers's Department had its feet on the ground, too, Henry said 'I'll take your message away with me if you like and see what I can do.'

Carruthers sat back and relaxed. When the waiter was safely out of earshot he fished a piece of paper out of his pocket and handed it over.

'I'm not making any promises, mind you,' warned Henry, pocketing a handwritten missive with the title E I S H T M O and turning his attention to the soup. 'But I'll do my best.'

Too well-trained a civil servant to look at anything confidential on a railway train, Henry reached Berebury Station early on the Friday evening with it still in his pocket. His sister, Wendy Witherington, met him on the platform.

'Good to see you, darling,' she said, giving him a kiss. 'Tim would have come to pick you up but he's collecting Edward and his friend Frobisher from their Scout meeting.'

Henry slung his Gladstone bag into the back of Wendy's car and climbed in beside her. 'In my young day we walked back from Scouts.'

'Tim's doing penance.'

'Whatever for?' Tim Witherington was the mildest of men in spite of having a limp and a medal, both collected in the March Push of 1918.

'He got Edward into trouble with his English master.'

'He should know better,' said Tim's brother-in-law unsympathetically.

'I know. Apparently the boys were being taught about not using double negatives.'

'Very important,' agreed Henry gravely.

'So Tim asked Edward if a noh play in a knot garden was one. He was just teasing him, of course.'

'But Edward didn't know that and asked his English master?' surmised Henry.

'That's right.'

'Who, like Queen Victoria, was not amused?'

'Exactly,' sighed Wendy. 'So now Tim is trying to earn some Brownie points.'

'You could always try Edward on "Yes, We have No Bananas",' suggested Henry.

'Don't you start,' said his sister, turning the car into their drive.

Henry received a rapturous welcome from his young niece, Jennifer, and minutes later from Edward, still in his Scout uniform.

'Supper in ten minutes, boys,' said their mother, 'but only after you've washed your hands.'

'Frobisher's staying, too, Uncle,' Edward explained. 'His people are away.' He stood in the hall and raised his right arm to a position very similar to that adopted by a questioner at a meeting. His left arm he kept tightly to his side.

'Acknowledge, correct,' chanted Frobisher immediately.

Edward Witherington dropped his right arm and raised his left one to an angle of forty-five degrees.

'Seven o'clock,' divined Frobisher promptly.

'We practised sending "you've been making errors" at our meeting tonight, too,' said Edward ingenuously, 'but we haven't made one yet.'

'I expect you will soon,' said Henry kindly, 'life being what it is. I take it you're learning semaphore?'

'That's right, Uncle,' beamed Edward, 'but it's quite difficult.'

'Much worse than Morse,' chimed in Frobisher. 'That was easy.'

Both boys suddenly started loudly chanting 'Every Indian should hold two major offices.'

'Many of them do,' said Henry moderately, his mind going straight to that distant part of the British Empire, trying to remember who it was there who went in for pluralism. Bureaucracy seemed more of an Indian forte.

'That will do,' said Wendy Witherington firmly, ushering the boys off in the direction of the bathroom.

It was not until the next morning that Henry took out the paper from Farnessnes. It was after Tim Witherington had gone off to play golf, plus-fours and all, and when the boys were in the garden sending signals in semaphore without flags. His sister waved him towards the kitchen table, promised coffee and asked how things were.

'Buzzing,' said Henry.

'It's the bad-tempered bees who produce the best honey,' said Wendy.

'Maybe,' he said. Bad temper was something that they tried to keep out of diplomacy although there was a school of thought, citing Napoleon Bonaparte, which considered charm to be just as dangerous. Now he came to think of it, Adolf Hitler was said to be personally charming, too. He put this interesting concept to the back of his mind should he ever have any spare time to think more about it and pulled the piece of paper out of his pocket. 'I've got a bit of delicate homework to do while everyone's out.'

'Secret?'

'I'd rate it as only being on a need-to-know basis,' he said, sophistry being raised to a high art in his world of diplomacy and double-dealing.

Wendy nodded her understanding of this. Before her marriage his sister had been the confidential secretary to a solicitor and thus knew the distinction. More importantly, she knew the true meaning of discretion, too.

'Take a look at this, then.' Henry couldn't think of any reason for not sharing the message with her on those terms. After all it had reached England through normal channels and the country was not at war with Farnessnes Island or indeed with any other country just at the moment. Moreover it was written in English: that its message was unintelligible was irrelevant. 'But don't tell anyone that you've seen it.'

'Of course not,' she said robustly, studying the message. 'What's the problem?'

'We're looking for a name or an office.'

'And it's not hidden in the text?'

'I'm afraid not.' Henry had already searched for any combination of letters that spelt Beren or even P.M. and found nothing. 'At least, not that anyone can see.'

She frowned and read the title of the message aloud. 'EISHTMO? Are you sure it shouldn't be Eskimo?'

'Farnessnes Island is a good bit north of here but it isn't quite as far north as that.'

Wendy pulled a chair up to the table and sat beside him. 'Even so, there's a walrus in the message and they don't come very far south.'

Henry smoothed out the crumpled message sheet as together they studied the words:

Greetings to you all – . . . I am writing to wish you well.
Including Rachel! What can I say about dear Rachel –
? As always she's great in her own sweet way. But oh
dear –!
   Do you remember her? And the walrus of course
   Never mind if you don't – but I do. And don't forget that
the walrus ate the oysters and that the carpenter didn't like
the butter too thick. The food here is very good – Even so I
shall be glad to get home – for the flowers – the sunshine. .
oh for all sorts of things: you know without my saying
   Peter

Henry scanned his sister's face. 'Anything in particular strike you, Wen?'

'Well,' she said slowly, 'one thing is the absence of commas. There should have been lots of them if the message was meant to be grammatical. And some more full stops, too.'

'Grammatical it certainly isn't,' he agreed. 'Edward's teacher wouldn't like it.'

Wendy Witherington gave a reminiscent smile. 'When I was working, Mr Benomley was the chief clerk at the office. He was ever so fierce and I remember one day he gave us a terrific lecture about the importance of getting the comma in the right place when we were taking down shorthand. Apparently the Last Will and Testament of a very rich man somewhere along the line had been challenged on the two possible meanings of a clause that had a comma which was in the wrong part of the sentence.'

'Quite right, too,' said Henry, who only wished that getting things right at the Foreign Office was as easy as putting commas in the correct place. 'Young typists can be deplorably careless, their minds usually still being on the night before.'

Ignoring this jibe, Wendy gave another smile. 'Tim used to wait for me outside the office every evening.'

'Then I bet you didn't have your mind on the job either.' Loyal member of the establishment that he was and a civil servant to boot, Henry Tyler didn't like to bring up the matter of the man in history of whom it was said 'was hanged for a comma'. It was the Court's decision in 1916 to put a comma in the unpunctuated original Norman text of the Treason Act of 1351, crucially altering its sense, which had enabled Sir Roger Casement to be hanged according to law. Instead of mentioning this, Henry said to his sister, 'Now, is there anything else that strikes you about this message?'

She knitted her eyebrows. 'It doesn't read exactly smoothly, does it?'

Since elegant prose went without saying in the Foreign Office, Henry readily agreed with her, adding 'There was someone, wasn't there, who spent the morning putting a comma in and the afternoon taking it out? I think it was Oscar Wilde.'

'So the message must have a hidden meaning,' she

reasoned aloud, demonstrating an admirable capacity for sticking to the point.

'Agreed,' he sighed, 'but what? Tell me that.'

Wendy looked up from the paper. 'And I take it that Rachel isn't the name you're looking for?'

'I'm afraid not, old thing.'

They were interrupted by an outburst of shouting from the garden, the boys' voices carrying clearly over the lawn. 'No, Frobisher,' bellowed Edward. 'You've got it wrong again. You should have both flags out halfway between your knees and your feet for the letter N.'

'Sorry,' called out Frobisher from the other end of the garden. 'I'll try again. Is that better?'

'And if you can't get the letter C right we'll never be rescued,' declared Edward Witherington in stentorian tones. 'We'd be drowned or something before the rescue people got the message.'

'I do wish they wouldn't shout,' sighed Wendy. 'The neighbours don't like it. What message is that anyway?' she asked Henry.

'I'm a bit rusty these days but if I remember rightly,' said Henry, frowning, 'in the semaphore system the letters N and C mean "I am in distress and require immediate assistance".'

'Give me the Morse code any day.' Wendy said, turning her attention again to the paper on the kitchen table. 'You know where you are with S.O.S.'

'Not if you're the boy who's standing on the burning deck,' said Henry lightly. 'Three dots, three dashes and three dots wouldn't get you very far at the bottom of a cliff either if you hadn't got a torch.'

'Henry,' said his sister suddenly in quite a different tone, 'now I come to think of it there are rather a lot of dots and dashes in this message.'

Henry Tyler pulled the paper back towards him and read it again. 'You're right,' he said slowly.

'Had you noticed, too?'

'There's a dash and then three dots to start with.' He stroked his chin. 'I wonder if that could stand for a letter?'

Wendy Witherington moved towards the kitchen window and called out to the boys to come in from the garden at once.

'Oh, Mum, why?' Edward called back. 'We're not doing anything wrong,'

'Now,' she said in the familiar maternal tone that brooked no nonsense.

The two boys presented themselves in the kitchen with celerity. 'What is it, Mum?' asked Edward. 'We're only playing.'

'Your uncle wants you,' said Wendy.

Both boys looked at Henry. 'What for?'

'I'm hunting the snark,' he said, 'and I need some help.'

'You said Morse was easy,' began Wendy, stepping in.

'Every Indian Should Hold Two Major Offices,' the two boys chanted again in unison.

'You said that yesterday,' began Henry. He should have paid more attention.

'But what does it mean?' asked Wendy.

Frobisher said earnestly, 'It's something to help you remember something, Mrs Witherington.'

'A mnemonic,' Henry said.

'But what does it mean?' persisted Wendy. 'What is it that you were trying to remember, boys?'

'The letters in Morse, Mum,' said Edward. 'E is one dot, I is two dots and S is three dots.'

'Everyone knows S is three dots,' said Frobisher, 'just like they know O is three dashes. It stands for "Save Our Souls".'

'Go on,' said Henry.

'H is four dots,' put in Edward, 'T is one dash, M is two dashes and ... '

'O is three dots,' said Frobisher, 'like I said.'

'EISHTMO,' exclaimed Henry, light dawning.

'That's what that mnenomic thing was all about, Uncle,' explained Edward. '"Every Indian Should Hold Two Major Offices". Eishtmo.'

'Geronimo!' Henry clapped his hands. 'We've got it!'

'No, Uncle,' said Edward patiently. 'Not Geronimo – it's Eishtmo.'

Wendy said, 'The boys haven't seen that film about the apaches with Geronimo in, Henry. Tim thought they were too young.'

'Nonsense,' said Henry roundly.

'What film?' asked Edward.

'Never you mind,' said his mother.

'What I want,' said Henry, turning back to the message, 'is to know what one dash and three dots stands for in Morse code.'

There was a long pause while Frobisher tried to extract something from a pocket. Eventually he withdrew an exceedingly grubby card and handed it to Henry after carefully detaching the remains of a toffee from it. Henry consulted it at once.

'The letter B,' he said. 'Now, you said E was one dot, didn't you?'

'There's a full stop at the end of the sentence,' said Wendy. 'That could be it, couldn't it?'

'If we're on the right track we need something that amounts to the letter R whatever that is.'

'Dot dash dot,' said Edward. 'I remember that one.'

Wendy looked at the message again. 'You'd have to use the dots from the exclamation and question marks with the dash between to make an R.'

'Nothing wrong with that,' said Henry. 'What comes next, Wen?'

'A full stop at the end of a sentence.'

'That'll do nicely for E. Then?'

'A dash and an exclamation mark.'

'A dash and a dot,' announced Edward eagerly, 'stands for N. Is that any good, Uncle?'

'You bet it is, my boy. Those letters spell the name of the man we're looking for. Beren.'

'Is he a goodie or a baddie, Mr Tyler?' asked Frobisher.

'I don't know yet,' said Henry grimly, 'but I hope to find out quite soon.'

'The next sentence is on a line of its own,' said Wendy, her head still bent over the text. 'I wonder what that means?'

'My guess is that it's a new word,' said Henry.

'It's all right, boys,' said Wendy. 'You can go back into the garden now.'

'And miss all the fun?' asked Edward. He turned to Henry. 'We can stay, Uncle, can't we? Besides, you might need us.'

'Only if your Mother says you may,' said Henry, well versed in disclaiming responsibility for actions over which he had had no control – such as The Treaty of Versailles: Alsace-Lorraine was a continual worry and Yugoslavia a great problem.

Wendy's head, however, was still bent over the message sheet. 'There's a question mark and a dash next.'

Both boys chanted 'The letter A.'

'Beren a – a what, I wonder,' murmured Henry.

'Go on, Uncle,' urged Edward. 'What comes next?'

'A dash and a dot,' said Henry, 'in a new sentence.'

'We've had that already, Mr Witherington,' pointed out Frobisher kindly. 'It's N.'

'Then there's a full stop and a dash,' said Wendy.

'An A,' chanted both boys in unison.

'Go on,' said Henry evenly, aware that the next letter was the one that mattered.

'Two dashes,' said Wendy.

Henry consulted Frobisher's card. 'That's M. What's next?'

'Two dots,' said Wendy.

'An I? That all? MI?'

'There's a colon next. Two dots.'

'Another I,' said Frobisher, retrieving the half-eaten toffee. He was about to put it in his mouth when he caught Wendy's eye and instead restored it to his pocket.

'That doesn't make sense, Uncle,' said Edward.

'No, said Henry. He knew, even if nobody else present did, that government departments called MI5 and MI6 existed. Perhaps there was one called MI1 but if there was, he didn't know anything about it. Certainly not whether Beren might be a member of it. It seemed highly unlikely. He pushed the paper away and sighed. 'Sorry, boys, I thought we might be getting somewhere.'

'Never mind, Uncle,' said Edward. 'It was worth a try.'

'You can go back out again now, boys,' said Wendy, slightly crestfallen too.

'No, you can't.' Henry sat up abruptly. 'Let me have another look at that card, Frobisher.'

Obediently the boy handed it across.

'I thought so,' said Henry. 'It wasn't MI at all. It was two dashes and two dots . . . '

'That's the letter Z, Uncle,' said Edward.

'That's right. Beren is a Nazi.'

'Beren is a Nazi,' chanted the boys.

'Just what we needed to know,' said Henry, starting to rise. 'I should have got there sooner. There's a big clue that I missed.'

'What was that?' asked Wendy.

'The walrus.'

His sister looked up at him. 'What's the walrus got to do with it?'

'Morse is an archaic word for the walrus,' said Henry, getting up on his feet. 'I think there's even a walrus Morse code. Your telephone's in the hall, isn't it?'

'Uncle ... ' began Edward.

'Yes?' Henry paused at the kitchen door.

'Is Little Bighorn a double negative or a single one?'

'Ask your father,' said Henry basely. 'I'm busy.'

Catherine Aird, winner of the Crime Writers' Association Diamond Dagger Award in 2015, is the author of some twenty-eight works of detective fiction, including three collections of short stories.

Unfinished Business

David Roberts

*No author relishes an enthusiast picking as his favourite book
an early title in his oeuvre and yet that's what I want to do. Peter
has published many fine books since* Swing, Swing Together *in
1976 but, perhaps for the simple reason it was the first of his books
I bought in hardback, it remains the book I most treasure. It has
two splendid detective heroes: Sergeant Cribb of Scotland Yard and
his colleague, Constable Thackeray.*

The book has a lightness of touch, a joie de vivre *reflected
in the jacket illustration by Joseph Wright. (I am well aware how
important the jacket illustration can be in attracting a potential
reader at twenty paces and this did it for me!) It shows three men
in a boat – not to forget the dog.*

*I touch my forelock to Peter by impertinently borrowing Cribb
and Thackeray though I have to report both resented it. And I
pay Jerome K. Jerome a brief tribute with a mention in passing
of Charles Dodgson – almost as mythical as Jerome K. Jerome. I
picture him in a boat rowing a little girl past Eton College.*

Peter gives his book a title drawn from the 'Eton Boating Song', not in fact Eton's official song which is 'Carmen Etonense', *but the Boating Song is sung on many school occasions including during the Procession of Boats on the Fourth of June.*

Most fictional detectives wrap up the mystery they are investigating in two or three hundred pages and that is just why we know they are fictional. In real life mysteries are not so quickly solved and many are never solved, sometimes because of the pressures brought upon the police by influential politicians or worse. I believe even Sergeant Cribb met his match at Eton and he naturally resents having his hands tied by the Commissioner not wishing to offend any important Old Etonian.

Tom will make him weep and wail;
   For with throwing thus my head
   King Lear

Sergeant Cribb looked at the young gentleman with disgust. A popinjay with his highly coloured waistcoat and his stick-up collar – he was, apparently, a member of Eton's select society, suitably known as Pop. Frederick Gore-Harefield indeed! What sort of a name was that? His insolence, his disregard for Cribb as a representative of Scotland Yard and his studied indifference to the death of an orphan boy was insufferable. But he did suffer it. He had no alternative.

'The dead boy, Tom, was a boot-boy, I understand? What is a boot-boy exactly?' Cribb inquired.

Mr Buckland, the housemaster, answered. 'He was more of an odd-job boy. He did any simple handyman work about the house and, of course, looked after the boys' boots. Tom looked after the gas lighting and just recently we have installed electric lights in the dining room. These need careful attention if they are not to fail and Tom was rather good at that.'

'And Tom was . . . ?'

'He was a charity boy from the workhouse – I mean the orphanage,' Buckland said. 'Eton charity.'

'I see.' Cribb turned back to the boy. 'So you have no idea how your wristwatch came to be attached to Tom's arm? It is your watch, is it not – something rare, unique even? It has your name engraved upon the back. You must have been very proud of it.' Cribb stroked his magnificent side-whiskers meditatively.

'It was my father's. He wore it in the Anglo-Burma war and it was a great honour that he should have entrusted it to me. He gave it to me when I was elected to Pop. Now it is ruined.'

'You did not wear it when you were rowing?'

'Certainly not. It is by no means waterproof. I put it with my clothes in the cupboard as I always do – for safekeeping.'

'Were you not frightened it might be stolen?'

'It never occurred to me. As you say, it had my name on it – or rather, my father's – and no one could have sold it. My father will be very upset when I tell him what has happened.'

'And you have no idea who might have . . . ?'

'I can only think that when we were rowing, Tom stole it. What other explanation can there be?'

'Why would he do that if as you say it had no value on the street?'

'I don't know – because he had seen me wear it? Perhaps he wanted to taunt me.'

'Taunt you? Why should he want to taunt you?'

The boy looked so forlorn Cribb was almost sorry for him. But then he said, and the savagery with which he spoke shocked the policeman: 'He deserved to die. I am only sorry I did not kill him myself.'

His thin lips curled in a travesty of a smile but his diamond-hard eyes were filled with rage or perhaps hate. Frederick Gore-Harefield might not have murdered the boot-boy himself but he knew more about it than he had yet chosen to admit.

They were in Mr Buckland's house – one of the old buildings off Judy's Passage. Cribb had learnt that the housemaster was referred to as 'M'Tutor' and he had also been informed that this boy was head of his house. Buckland seemed a nice enough fellow, but weak. He was naturally desperate that neither his house nor the school should be tainted by a police investigation into how Tom was killed and thrown into the river. Cribb watched the man wriggle nervously in his armchair.

'Please don't think, Sergeant, that we don't care how poor Tom came to this miserable end. He was not drowned, you say?'

'His neck was broken before he was thrown in the river and he had suffered a nasty blow to his head before death – probably the cause of death. If he had drowned there would have been water in his lungs. There was none.'

'And there are witnesses?'

'Not to his killing.' Cribb spoke as brutally as possible and was rewarded by seeing Buckland flinch, 'but the man we have interviewed saw the body being thrown in the river. We can assume he was done to death in the boathouse. Constable Thackeray is searching the place as we speak.'

'And the witness is reliable?'

'I believe so. He had nothing to gain from lying and he has no connection with the school. In fact he is a clergy-man. He happened to be rowing his daughter or perhaps his niece – a young girl anyway, past Rafts ... I have that name right, have I not?'

'Indeed, Sergeant,' Buckland smiled patronisingly. 'Where the boats – the whiffs and riggers and so on – are stored and launched. You will have to forgive me, Frederick,' Buckland said to the boy sitting beside him. 'As you know, I am no wet-bob – a cricketer in my youth, you see, Sergeant – so, on occasion, I do get these things wrong.'

'And has he got it wrong?' Sergeant Cribb inquired of the boy with exaggerated courtesy.

'No,' the young man said without elaboration. Clearly, the contempt with which he viewed Cribb extended to his housemaster.

'And this man claims to have seen someone tossing something into the river ... ?' Buckland prompted the policeman. 'Could he see who it was ... what he was doing?'

'Regrettably, he was too far away to be able to recognise any one person but he is certain he saw four men, or boys, throw something into the river. He had the feeling it was a body – like when the crew of an eight, after a victory, throw the cox in the water – or so I am told,' Cribb added, slightly embarrassed. 'There was quite a splash, you understand. He naturally thought he was witnessing horseplay or some prank but when the boys – if they were boys – had disappeared and he had seen no one swim back to shore, he rowed over to investigate.'

'A good citizen!' Buckland exclaimed. 'He is a clergyman, you say?'

'Indeed, a clergyman and a professor at Oxford.' Cribb referred to his notebook. 'The Rev Dodgson – a mathematician. One could hardly be more respectable,' Cribb added, looking up at the housemaster.

'Indeed, yes. "Forsooth, a great arithmetician, one Michael Cassio, a Florentine, a fellow almost damned in a fair wife" – I believe I have heard of him.'

Cribb looked bemused. 'Cassio?'

'I was quoting the Bard of Avon,' Buckland simpered. 'Dodgson, yes, I have definitely heard my wife mention him. He writes books for children.' Buckland saw that he was straying from the point. 'And he found poor Tom?'

'I do wish you would stop calling him "poor Tom", Sir,' the young man said with asperity, stung into speech it seemed by his tutor's limp response to what might have been a tragedy but was certainly not *King Lear* or even *Othello*. 'Tom was no defenceless child.'

'No,' agreed Mr Buckland. 'He was big for his age – fifteen or sixteen – not tall but muscular.'

'I happen to know he was a bareknuckle fighter,' the boy added, unprompted. 'He fought for money.'

'Not so much Poor Tom as Tom Sayers, eh?' Cribb said with an attempt at joviality.

Mr Buckland looked from the boy to the policeman, obviously unfamiliar with the name. 'Tom Sayers . . . ?'

Cribb explained: 'When I was a boy Sayers was a well-known figure. A heavyweight boxer, we would say today, but in the twenties the sport was unregulated – the London Prize Ring Rules were hardly regarded.'

'I see, I see!' Buckland broke in. 'But now Lord Queensbury has laid down a code—'

'The point is,' the young man interjected impatiently, 'Tom would have not been an easy man to surprise.'

'Surprise . . . ?' Mr Buckland echoed. 'Ah! I understand you, my boy. No, I agree. Tom always struck me as a strong young man. He would have been able to defend himself. But you say his neck was broken, Sergeant Cribb? Anyone can be knocked down from behind with a club . . . '

'Or an oar . . . ?' Cribb suggested.

'Or an oar, yes. Is that what you think happened, Sergeant Cribb?'

This was the first time the young man had used the policeman's name.

'It is possible. As I told you, at this very moment Constable Thackeray is examining the boathouse for evidence of the murder happening there, on the riverbank.'

'Murder!' Mr Buckland protested. 'Can we be sure it was murder?'

'I think we can,' Cribb replied.

Gore-Harefield looked pensive, and examined his well-polished shoes. Idly, Cribb wondered who had polished them. He remained silent for what seemed a long time watching the boy weigh up his options. As Cribb had hoped, he finally decided that an admission of sorts was safer than leaving this policeman to discover the oar with the bloodstains.

Frederick could not now remember why they had not tossed the oar into the water when they had disposed of Tom's body. Ah! Yes! He recalled that Charlie Power had pointed out that the oar would not sink but float around drawing attention to itself. None of them had bargained on Scotland Yard sending even a halfway competent detective to investigate the death of a common boot-boy. He wished now that they had got rid of the body some way down the river in a convenient clump of reeds or even at Boveney weir. But it is easy to be wise in retrospect.

The killing had been sudden, unexpected, unplanned, and they had panicked. Tom had ambushed them after they had returned from a practice row up river – part of their preparations for the Procession of Boats on the Fourth of June. He had demanded money – more money than last time. Money they simply had not got. Otherwise he would peach on them – or so he threatened. It had not occurred to the boys that he would hardly dare to do that.

The authorities would not look kindly on a ruffian like Tom Barker – that was his name even if the boys only knew him as Tom – blackmailing Eton boys. Rupert had swung an oar at him and quite by chance had hit him on the neck. Tom had fallen and struck his head on a stone block. When the boys gathered round him they discovered to their horror that he was dead. One good thing from their point of view was that there happened to be no one else in the boathouse at the time. In terror they had bundled the dead boy into the river, simply to be rid of the body.

'The truth is, Sergeant ... the truth is ...' the boy paused. What was the truth? Tom had tried to blackmail them and so Rupert had picked up an oar and swung it, hardly thinking he would do much damage, merely wishing to relieve his frustration. Frederick had no wish to get his friend into trouble but he could see that the truth would out. This policeman had something about him – something in his eyes – which told him that he could not be trifled with.

'The truth is what, Mr Gore-Harefield?' Cribb asked gently but insistently when the boy's hesitation had become a lengthy silence.

'The truth is, Sergeant, that Tom ... The truth is,' he repeated as though struggling to find the words, 'Tom was up to every sort of trick – anything to earn money, and who can blame him? At first he was almost one of us – our "master of revels". He was our sort of court jester. In fact we called him The Jester or sometimes Poacher. He would make us laugh. And then he would fix things for us. We would tell him what we felt like doing to relieve the boredom, don't you know ...'

Mr Buckland started to say something but Cribb stopped him with a commanding lift of his arm. The boy was confessing and he must be allowed to continue.

The words came now in a rush. 'He would take us hare coursing, poaching of course in winter, and in summer he would provide us with girls or take us to cockfights and once to a dogfight.'

'You and who else?' Cribb asked grimly.

'The four of us – the "Four Musketeers", he called us. Charlie Power, Rupert Penrose, Dan Frankland and myself.'

'Good heavens, Frederick!' Buckland seemed genuinely surprised. He must have been familiar with the peccadilloes of generations of boys – boys who had got up to all sorts of mischief to alleviate the boredom of learning Latin and Greek – but to go with girls of the town was a hanging offence. Well, obviously not literal hanging but any boy caught in a bordello would be immediately expelled, and beaten too.

'Yes. It was wrong of us, sir, but the temptation was too strong. There is a public house in Windsor – a low place where Tom took us to watch him fight, or bet on dog fights ... And we were stupid enough to bet more than we could afford. When we won – which was not often – the girls would come round us like wasps round a rotten apple to relieve us of our winnings ... Well, you can guess the rest.'

'He resorted to blackmail?'

'Yes, Sergeant. He said we owed him money and he would have it. He said we were rich and he was poor. He came down to the boathouse when we were about to go out on the river and jeered at us, demanded to be paid if we wanted to avoid being reported ... We sent him packing but when we returned ... well, he was waiting for us. But we did not set out to kill him. You must believe me. It was an accident.'

The insolent young man was now a blubbing boy crying for mercy but Cribb looked at him with disbelief and impatience. This was all an act to save his hide, he was sure of it. He should take the boy and the other three back to the police station for questioning and to be charged at least with manslaughter, if not murder.

But then Cribb remembered what the Commissioner had told him. The Commissioner had insisted that Cribb should be as gentle as possible in his questioning. Etonians were not normal schoolboys. That was why the local police had called in Scotland Yard the moment the body had been fished out of the Thames. This young fellow's uncle was the foreign secretary, no less. What a scandal it would be to have Mr Gore-Harefield arrested and charged with killing a servant. The yellow press – as the Americans called the sensationalist newspapers which thrived on scandal and murder – would delight in revealing the low company these Eton boys kept. It was unthinkable both for the boy's family and for the school. But perhaps he could do a bit of bargaining on his own account. He could say that if the boy hoped to avoid prison he must be sent to the Colonies.

Cribb sighed. He was not normally a prejudiced man but

he recognised that his instinctive dislike of all that Eton stood for – the dislike as instinctive as that of a dog for a cat – was robbing him of his native good sense. He would start again and, this time, try to be fair.

'It was an accident, was it? Your friend swinging at Tom with the oar?'

Buckland breathed more easily. Eagerly, he said, 'Yes, a terrible accident and perhaps the boys, if they *were* Eton boys – and that still has to be proved – panicked and instead of calling someone – me or the Dame – when they saw how badly he was hurt, threw the poor boy in the river ... to get rid of him,' he added unnecessarily.

'The Dame ... ? Cribb queried.

'You would say the Matron,' Buckland explained, sounding superior.

Cribb had noticed before, when investigating a murder in a Masonic Lodge, that a secret language added mystery and interest to activities and rituals which were quite banal stripped of abracadabra magic.

Frederick, looking glum, glanced at the policeman, seeming to regret already that he had admitted so much. A good lawyer would, Cribb knew, have the confession thrown out of court as being inadmissible as evidence. For the confession to be of use the boy would need to make a new statement with his lawyer and his parents beside him and that he was unlikely to do. There were the other three boys of course, but would they confess?

Gore-Harefield broke his silence, obviously thinking along the same lines. 'Sergeant, you understand I did not know what I was saying just now. I was just ... you know, making up a story. I mean, why are you so sure these were Eton boys who put the body in the river? Why pick on us? Surely it is more likely they were town ruffians or navvies. There are plenty of them camped up river near Queen's Eyot. Irish, I believe.'

'Don't try to be clever, boy,' Cribb said angrily. 'At least make your new story stand up to scrutiny. You don't deny the place where this all happened housed the school's boats? Not a place where a navvy would venture or, if he did, would go unchallenged. And why would ruffians seize upon a boy like Tom? One of themselves, you might say. Now, had the victim been someone like yourself – well worth robbing and from a different class – well then ... ' He hesitated and then added: 'I think you have said enough for the moment. Mr Buckland, I will leave Mr Gore-Harefield in your hands. I think the best thing would be if you could send for the parents of the four of them and explain the situation. We have to decide how to pursue this matter. Someone must be held to account for Tom's death. I am determined on that.'

Cribb, even to himself, sounded melodramatic but he felt that if he did not stick up for 'Poor Tom', no one else would. These Etonians were protected by a carapace of privilege, of powerful friends and relations. They would never suffer the consequences of their actions. Tom was an orphan and had no one on his side. He might have been a rogue but he did not deserve to die so casually, like a rat caught in a larder.

There was a knock on the door and Constable Thackeray appeared.

'Excuse me one moment,' Cribb said and went out of the room to talk to Thackeray in private.

'Have you found anything?'

'Yes, Sergeant. We found an oar with blood on it and Alf – the man in charge of the boathouse says – reluctantly – I might add – that he heard a splash but took no notice. I don't know why. You would have thought he would have investigated to make sure no one was drowning or what-have-you. Then five minutes later Mr Dodgson arrived in a bit of a flurry shouting for help. Together, using a boathook, they heaved the body onto the rafts. It was immediately clear that Tom – and Alf recognised him – was dead. Tom, apparently, used to hang about the boathouses looking to earn small sums of money heaving boats about. Alf then sent a messenger to summon the police and Mr Buckland.'

'Well, thank you, Thackeray. I have enough to make a preliminary report to the Commissioner. See what he suggests.' He sighed. 'How does it go?'

'How does what go?'

'The Eton Boating song. Something about "blade on the feather"?'

'Ah right! I get you, Sergeant Cribb.' Thackeray hummed to himself. '"Nothing in life shall sever the chain that is round us now". I heard it at the music hall. Very affecting. Patriotic.'

'Yes, indeed, Thackeray, but there's something about feathers.'

'Blade on the feather,' Thackeray sang in a deep base voice, 'shade off the trees. Swing, swing together, with your bodies between your knees.'

'Very good! You would be proud to be an Etonian, would you not?'

Thackeray just shrugged.

When they got to the boathouse Alf was helping a crew into a four. When he was finished, Thackeray introduced Cribb and asked to see the bloodied oar.

'Yes, here it is. I washed it in the river and put it to one side for you.'

'You *washed* it!' Thackeray exploded.

'Yes, was that wrong?'

As Thackeray went off to examine the oar, Cribb looked at Alf and understood without a word being spoken that the washing of the oar had been deliberate. Alf was doing what he must think of as his job: protecting the reputation of the school. A dejected Thackeray returned to confirm that the oar was no longer evidence of anything except Alf's presence of mind.

As Thackeray began to berate the boatman, Cribb told him not to bother. 'Nothing to do with spilt milk or spilt blood except mop it up, eh, Alf?'

Alf said nothing but tried to look innocent.

'All I can say, Alf, is that this is unfinished business. I will be back and you will cooperate with my investigation or otherwise ... '

Otherwise what? Cribb knew that Eton had defeated

him. Swing, swing together. That was Eton's philosophy. It had worked for hundreds of years and would work for hundreds more. Yes, unfinished business.

David Roberts was educated at Eton and McGill University, Montreal. He was a publisher for thirty years before turning his attention to crime. He has published a ten-book series set in the 1930s and featuring Lord Edward Corinth and Verity Browne.

The Adventure of the Marie Antoinette Necklace: A Case for Sherlock Holmes

David Stuart Davies

I first encountered Peter Lovesey through reading his Cribb novels and the resultant TV series, both of which were excellent. Then, when I was editor of Sherlock, *the crime fiction magazine, I met Peter for the first time to interview him and found him a most charming and helpful fellow. Later I had the cheek to ask him to write a Cribb story for* Sherlock. *With the kindness and courteous support that is typical of the man, he agreed and really helped to put a feather in the magazine's cap. Since then, I have encountered him often, especially at events involving the Crime Writers' Association, meetings that reinforce the first impression I had of Peter: a very clever, masterful crime writer who wears his brilliance with great modesty. Now, as a new boy in the Detection Club, I have the great honour to count myself one of his literary comrades. Just the thought of it makes me smile with delight.*

When the bright yellow summer sun blazes down on London from a clear blue sky, the Baker Street rooms that I share with my friend Sherlock Holmes turn into an oven. The ferocity of the heat concentrates in our sitting room, creating a kind of airless cell. Even an open window and wearing light clothing do not prevent a fine sheen of perspiration glossing my brow. I become restless and listless. All morning I had been turning from one periodical to another trying to take my mind off the stultifying temperature. Only a detailed account in *The Times* of the previous day's play in the Test Match at Lord's had held my attention for a short while. Holmes, on the other hand, seemed impervious to the heat and sat, as usual, in his dressing gown by the empty grate, cross-indexing his files.

I longed for some distraction and, remarkably, just before noon, I got it. We received a visitor: a tall, gaunt man of middle years, wearing a stern expression which was enhanced by a sharp, finely trimmed moustache. He stood before us, erect as a guardsman, clutching his bowler hat in both hands, addressing us as though we were a public meeting. He announced in the stiffest of manners that he was Algernon Courtney Brown, chief manservant to Lady Cora Bramingham, and required an audience with Mr Sherlock Holmes.

Holmes flashed a whimsical glance in my direction and I had some difficulty hiding my amusement at this comic performance. With a little effort I managed to turn my suppressed chuckle into a little cough.

'I am Sherlock Holmes,' said my friend. 'Pray take a seat, Mr Brown.'

'Courtney Brown,' the man corrected him.

Holmes responded with a nod and waved our strange visitor to a chair but the fellow did not move. 'I think it appropriate for me to remain standing, sir.'

'So be it,' said Holmes. 'What is the nature of your errand?'

'There has been a robbery – a theft. My mistress' diamond necklace has been stolen. She requires you to recover it for her.'

'Does she now?' replied my friend, a note of irritation in his voice.

'Indeed. It is the famous Marie Antoinette necklace. You will no doubt have heard of it.'

'I have heard of it,' said Holmes.

Indeed, the whole of London had heard of it: the necklace, a dazzling piece of jewellery consisting of 181 carats, was one of the few surviving treasures owned by the infamous Marie Antoinette. On the rare occasions when it was worn, at some state affair or high society event, necks craned to catch a glance of the shimmering bauble.

'My mistress held a small summer ball at her town house last evening. She wore the necklace and it was admired by all the guests. Later, before the ball was over, Lady Bramingham returned the precious item to the private safe in her bedroom, only to discover when she retired for the night that the item was missing.'

'Really,' said Holmes lightly.

'And so, my lady wishes to retain your services to recover the necklace.'

'Does she? And why then did she not come here herself in order to retain them?'

Courtney Brown seemed slightly amused by this suggestion. His hitherto immobile features softened and the hint of a smile touched his lips. 'It would not be appropriate for my mistress to involve herself in such a menial task as securing the services of a private enquiry agent,' he explained grandly.

Holmes' eyes flashed, but he retained his equanimity. 'What a pity, then, that I am too occupied at present to allot any time to solving your mistress' dilemma. I am engaged in a very complicated and demanding case at the moment involving the loss of a treasured pet monkey which is consuming all my energies and ingenuity.'

'But surely that cannot be of the same importance as the theft of the Marie Antoinette necklace and providing a service for Lady Bramingham.'

Holmes smiled sardonically. 'With me it is always the case and not the client that is of importance. However, if her ladyship deems it appropriate to visit me in person and lay before me all the details of the matter, I may well find a little time to assist her. It is so very difficult dealing with facts at second hand. With such a procedure, clues often fly out of the window. I suggest you pass on this information to her ladyship. And now, if you don't mind, I have some work to do ... '

Holmes rose and moved to his chemical bench and turned his back on our visitor. It was an act of dismissal.

Algernon Courtney Brown opened his mouth to protest

but thought better of it. I opened the door to enable him to make a swift exit. He was barely down the stairs before Holmes and I burst out laughing.

'What a gadfly. An Osric of the strongest hue,' my friend chortled, returning to his chair.

'Surely you are not going to sit down?' said I with mock approbation, in between chuckles. 'Don't you have an important case involving a lost monkey to attend to?'

This set us off laughing again.

'In truth, Watson, I can only feel sorry for the fellow, for after all he was only carrying out the orders of his mistress. It is she who is the arrogant one in this matter. A private enquiry agent, indeed!'

'Well, you certainly sent him off with a flea in his ear.'

Holmes reached over and picked up his violin from the table by his chair and stroked the mellow wood. 'Mmm, I suspect that we have not heard the last of this affair. But if the arrogant Lady Bramingham requires the services of Sherlock Holmes she must apply for them in person. Muhammed must come to the mountain.' So saying, he placed the violin under his chin and began to play a lively tune of his own composing.

It did not take long for Holmes' prediction to bear fruit. Some two hours later we heard the bell ring below, followed some moments later by an imperious knock on our door. Holmes bade the visitor enter and once more Mr Algernon Courtney Brown stepped over the threshold.

He gave a brief cough and then announced in stentorian

tones, 'Lady Cora Bramingham.' He stepped aside and the lady herself appeared in our doorway. She was a stout woman of middle years dressed in a full-skirted outfit fashioned from a luxurious material in a somewhat gaudy shade of peach which rustled noisily as she moved, rather like the crackling sheets of a newspaper that is being shaken vigorously. She peered at us through a lorgnette in a haughty and imperious manner.

'Which of you is Holmes?' she asked, her voice deep and commanding.

'I am he,' said my friend. 'Pray take a seat.'

She moved forward, examining the chair that Holmes had indicated before eventually sitting down. This operation appeared to be the signal for Courtney Brown to retreat. With practised discretion, he left the room silently.

'I gather that you refused to avail your services to my man and demanded that you dealt with the matter through me,' said Lady Bramingham tartly.

'An investigation cannot reach a successful conclusion if the essential details are relayed third hand. One has one's reputation to consider.' Holmes delivered this observation in his most charming manner with a gentle smile set on his features. It was a smile I was most familiar with: one that he used to flatter and disarm.

'Very well. What is it that you want to know?'

'Well, firstly, why have you come to me? I assume you have informed the police of the theft of your necklace.'

She nodded. 'Of course. But I have little faith in their abilities. I have had a number of constables blundering about my property and suffered a long interview with an Inspector Calloway. He seems to have the crudest ideas of how to tackle the crime.'

Holmes nodded sympathetically. 'I know the man and I am aware of his limitations.'

'That is why I wish to engage you to solve this dastardly misdemeanour and return my beloved necklace to me. I have been told you are the best in the business.'

My friend was obviously pleased to receive this accolade but he did not respond to it other than nodding his head gently. 'Tell me about last night and the relevant events which led up to your discovery that the necklace was missing.'

Lady Bramingham gave a sigh of irritation. No doubt she had already recited this information to Inspector Calloway and found it tedious to repeat the procedure. 'Very well,' she said after a brief pause. 'I am very proud of my necklace, a gift from my late husband on the occasion of our tenth wedding anniversary. Of course it is so precious, so valuable, that one has to take very great care of it and be scrupulous in choosing the occasions when one can wear it. Last night I held a small summer ball at my house in Chelsea. There were some sixty guests in attendance. The evening commenced with a drinks reception and I wore the necklace. As I circulated amongst the guests, it was most admired. One old gentleman, the Duke of Belcourt, stated that to observe it up close was the highlight of his year.' She gave a small affected laugh before continuing. 'Once the dancing commenced, I returned to my room and replaced the necklace in the safe in my boudoir, locked it and returned to the party.

'At the end of the evening when the guests had all gone, I returned to my boudoir to prepare myself for bed. I just couldn't resist one final look at my beloved necklace. Imagine my horror when I found the safe was unlocked and empty. The necklace was gone. I have to tell you, Mr Holmes, the shock of the matter overcame me and I fell in a swoon on the floor. It was in the early hours of the morning before I recovered my senses. I dressed quickly and roused the household and instructed Courtney Brown, my man, to send for the police.

'After the circus that resulted from their visit, it became quite clear to me that I needed a more expert hand in charge of this investigation than that lumbering Scotland Yard fellow.'

'Have you any thoughts who might have taken the necklace?'

Lady Bramingham shook her head decisively. 'None whatsoever.'

Holmes leaned back in his chair and steepled his fingers. 'Not an easy matter, then. The house full of people, waiters, guests and musicians . . .'

'A string quartet.'

'How was the safe opened?'

'I don't know. I locked it with a key which I kept in my evening bag. When I returned to my room the safe door was closed but was not locked.'

'Mmm, no doubt the lock had been picked, which suggests a professional thief rather than an opportunist. A planned robbery, then. You have list of those attending the ball last evening.'

Without a word, Lady Bramingham produced two folded sheets of blue notepaper from her capacious handbag.

Holmes scanned the lists and shook his head. 'I can see nothing of significance here,' he said, shaking his head, and then with a sudden movement my friend rose to his feet. 'Well, the first thing we must do is return with you and examine the scene of the crime.'

Lady Bramingham's mansion was sumptuous in the extreme, a gaudy advertisement to her wealth. On arrival she took us straight up to her boudoir, where Holmes began his investigations. At first he studied the small green safe which was concealed behind one of the long flowing drapes. He ran his magnifying glass over it in great detail, muttering softly to himself. 'Yes, yes,' he said at last, turning towards her ladyship. 'The scratches around the keyhole are quite fresh. There are infinitesimal particles of metal that have been scraped off around the aperture which bear witness of some burglary tool being applied to gain entry.'

Holmes pulled open the safe and peered inside. Apart from a small cushioned box – obviously the usual resting place of the necklace – it was empty. He then proceeded to examine the rest of the room, at one point lying down on the rich Persian rug which covered most of the floor, and studying it with his lens. His behaviour seemed to startle Lady Bramingham at first and then fascinate her.

At last, Holmes dusted himself down and joined us by

the door. 'Sadly,' he said, 'there is little to be learned from these quarters. The thief was a very careful fellow. However, I am interested in the ensemble of musicians that were playing here last night. Who were they?'

'The musicians? You don't really think—'

'I am curious, that is all.'

'They were called the Joseph Ambrose Quartet – and very good they were.'

'Did you engage them?'

Lady Bramingham gave a snort of irritation. 'Of course not, I leave all such arrangements to my man. I have no idea where he came up with these people.'

'Then perhaps we could have a word with him.'

We found Algernon Courtney Brown in his office attending to some papers on his desk. 'The musicians? I have their details here.' With dextrous efficiency he pulled out a sheet of cream foolscap from a file on the desk and handed it to my friend. 'There you are: the Joseph Ambrose Quartet. They were quite good. Two violins, a cello, with Mr Ambrose himself on piano.'

Holmes noted the name and address on his shirt cuff. 'Have they played here before?'

'On two previous occasions.'

'The same personnel? Surely there was a new face amongst them.'

'Ah, yes, I think you are correct . . . I do believe that one of the violinists was new to me.'

Holmes smiled. 'That is most interesting,' he observed in his practised enigmatic fashion.

We then visited the ballroom where the function of the previous evening had taken place. Various servants were tidying up, sweeping and polishing, returning the room to its pristine and ordered self. Lady Bramingham and I stood by the door while Holmes paraded the chamber. He seemed particularly interested in the rostrum holding several music stands. It was here, no doubt, where the musicians had performed. From behind the rostrum, he picked up a copy of a newspaper and examined it briefly before placing it back where he had found it.

At length Holmes joined us. 'I have seen all I need now, Lady Bramingham,' he said tersely.

'And . . . ? Do you hold out any hope, Mr Holmes?' Gone was the imperious and arrogant tone of earlier. The voice was tinged with emotion and desperation. For a fleeting moment I almost felt sorry for her.

'I shall need to investigate further before I respond to such a question. You must be patient, Lady Bramingham – and hope.'

Moments later we were in a cab heading for an address in Chiswick. 'I do believe you were taunting the lady, Holmes,' said I. 'I know you of old and I am certain from your demeanour that you have picked up some clue, some indication that will lead you to a solution, but you just didn't want to tell her ladyship in order to prolong her anxiety.'

Holmes laughed. 'You make me sound like a cruel ogre. However, there is some truth in what you say, but more importantly the threads of this mystery are so thin I do not want to grow too sanguine about the case until I am closer to a successful conclusion.'

'And where are we bound now?'

'To the home of Joseph Ambrose.'

The house was a pleasant villa situated a quiet leafy avenue away from the hustle and bustle of the main Chiswick High Road. A maid showed us into the sitting room of the musician, Joseph Ambrose, a handsome man in his fifties with grey hair, a neat Van Dyke beard and piercing blue eyes. He was sitting at the piano by the window making notations on a sheet of music.

'Mr Sherlock Holmes,' he said, gazing at the card my friend had sent through. 'The detective?'

'Yes, sir.'

'Good heavens. I don't know whether to be excited or apprehensive.' Ambrose smiled nervously. 'I trust you are not here to accuse me of some dastardly crime.'

Holmes ignored this comment. 'I come to ask you for some details regarding your quartet which performed at Lady Bramingham's summer ball last evening.'

'Really? What on earth for?'

'An item was taken – stolen – from her ladyship's private quarters and I am looking into the affair.'

'Dear me, I hope you are not suggesting that I or one of my fellow musicians was responsible for this misdemeanour.'

'That is what I am attempting to establish.'

'Why, this is infamous. We are a respectable, law abiding

set of individuals. How dare you come here accusing us of theft!'

'If you are, as you say, law-abiding individuals, there is nothing to fear. I just require the answers to a few questions. If you refuse, I suspect you will be visited by the authorities who will insist on your cooperation. By force if necessary.'

Ambrose's face paled and his shoulders slumped, his anger dissipating. 'Well, as an innocent man, I suppose as you say I have nothing to fear,' he said, at length.

'Quite.'

'What is it you want to know?'

'Your fellow musicians – you have known them for some time?'

'Indeed. The ensemble has been established for five years.'

'Has there not been a recent change in the personnel?'

'Well, yes. We had a new violinist last evening as a stop gap measure. For one night only. My usual man, Albert Fanshawe, suffered a fall while alighting from an omnibus last month and sprained his elbow and so was unable to perform.'

'Who was his replacement?'

'A fellow by the name of Arnold Jeffers. I must admit I shall not be using him again.'

'Why is that?'

'He proved to be a very poor performer. Quite amateurish, really. I am sorry I engaged him.'

'You must have known the quality of his playing before last night.'

Ambrose nodded. 'Yes, I must admit I was apprehensive. You see, when Mr Fanshawe had his accident, I advertised in the press for a violinist as a temporary replacement but to my surprise I received very few responses to my notice. But this Jeffers fellow was very keen and almost begged me to try him out at last night's soirée. So eager was he that he offered to play without receiving a fee.'

'Did he now?'

'I am afraid, Mr Holmes, this aspect rather than the quality of his playing affected my decision to engage him for this one occasion. Music is not always a lucrative profession. We save as many coins as we can.' Ambrose shook his head. 'It was a mistake; I realise that now. His skill with a bow was, I'm afraid, very limited. It became clear to me his real passion was cricket. He was forever keeping in touch with the test match through latest editions of the press rather than concentrating on his bowing. Well, we managed to get through the evening's performance at Lady Bramingham's without any real disasters but it certainly wasn't the ensemble's finest hour.'

'I assume you will not be using Mr Jeffers in future.'

Ambrose gave a bitter laugh. 'I will not. I just hope that he has not damaged our reputation. If he has, the blame must fall on me.'

'What did the fellow look like? Can you describe him to me?'

'He was a tall man of middle age. Grey hair and a walrus moustache and yet he had an athletic build. He was very active for a man of his years.'

'Did he possess any distinguishing features?'

Ambrose pursed his lips and thought for a moment. 'Not really ... Oh, wait a minute though. There was one rather odd thing about him. He possessed brown eyes, but there was a noticeable fleck of grey in one of them.'

'The right one?'

'Why, yes! How did you know?'

Holmes ignored the question. 'Do you have an address for this Mr Jeffers?'

'Yes. I have it somewhere.' He retrieved a little notebook from the inside pocket of his jacket and flicked through the pages. 'Ah, here we are: 277 Upper Street, Islington.'

In an instant Holmes was on his feet. 'Thank you, Mr Ambrose, you have been a great help. We will not detain you any longer. Come, Watson.'

My friend had reached the door before Ambrose or myself had time to react to his sudden departure.

Once out in the street, Holmes gave a gentle laugh. 'Well, friend Watson, I believe that everything is clear to me now and the matter is all but wrapped up.'

'You suspect this Jeffers fellow of the theft.'

'Yes, in a way,' came the guarded reply. Before I could press Holmes for an explanation he rattled on. 'I have an errand to perform and I am afraid I am going to send you on what I suspect is a wild goose chase, but it is simply a matter of crossing all the t's and dotting all the i's in this case. You will oblige me?'

I shrugged my shoulders. 'If I can be of assistance ... '

'Good man. I want you to take a cab and check out the address Ambrose gave us.'

'277 Upper Street, Islington.'

'Yes, the very one. Just ascertain if a fellow answering either the name or appearance of Arnold Jeffers as described by Ambrose resides there and then report back to me at Baker Street.'

'Why do you suspect this to be a wild goose chase?'

'I fear that may become obvious all too soon.'

'And what will you be doing in the meantime?'

He gave me a broad grin. 'I shall be renewing an old acquaintance.'

My trip to Upper Street in Islington was not so much a wild goose chase as a fool's errand. When I arrived there, I discovered that the premises housed the local police station, a fact I believe that Holmes already knew or at least suspected. Crossing t's and dotting i's indeed. I returned to Baker Street in a dark and petulant mood, ready to vent my anger on my fellow lodger. However, he had not returned and my ill temper had dissipated by early evening to be replaced by a growing curiosity as to where Holmes was. Evening shadows were beginning to form before he returned. I knew that he was in a good humour before he entered our chambers. I heard him rattle up the steps two at a time in a lively fashion indicating quite clearly to me that whatever was the nature of his mysterious errand, it had been a successful one.

'Ah, Watson,' he cried heartily, throwing himself down

in his chair opposite me. 'I am sorry to have kept you waiting for so long. I observe from the detritus on the table you
had the good sense to take an early dinner rather than wait
for my return. Very wise.'

'Your excursion was successful, I take it.'

'Indeed.'

'I wish I could say the same for mine. The address in
Islington turned out to be a police station.'

Holmes threw himself back in his chair in a paroxysm of
laughter. It was some moments before he brought his merriment under control. 'I am sorry, my dear fellow,' he said,
wiping a tear of laughter from his eye, 'I was fairly sure the
address was a false one – but I had to check. However that
it was . . . a police station. That was a touch, an undeniable
touch.' He laughed again and I could not help but join him
on this occasion, so infectious was his amusement.

'So,' I said at last, 'you say your trip was successful.'

'And rewarding.'

'Rewarding? In what way?'

In reply, he placed his hand to his inside pocket and
brought out a blue cloth bag. He tipped the contents onto
the hearth rug. There before me lay a brightly shimmering
necklace, its incandescence almost lighting up the room.

'The Marie Antoinette necklace,' I gasped.

'The very same.'

I scooped it up and held in gently in my hands. It was
indeed a magnificent piece of jewellery. Each stone was
expertly cut so that each facet radiated a vibrant luminosity.

'It is wonderful. How on earth . . . ?'

'Pour us both a brandy and soda and I will explain all,' said Holmes, beaming.

As the warm summer evening darkened, filling our Baker Street sitting room with soft cooling shadows, Holmes and I sat in the pleasant gloom nursing our glasses as he discussed the case.

'I was fairly convinced from the beginning that the theft of the necklace had been carried out by an audacious, experienced and very clever thief. There are very few of such fellows who fall into this category. One person came immediately to my mind. However, his name was not on the guest list and so I reasoned he must have adopted some kind of disguise – a talent of his – and got himself into the house in this assumed persona. At first I thought this might be a servant or other kind of menial. But then my investigations led me to believe it was a musician. It was an ideal role. In between the musical performances, he would be at liberty to walk around, mingle with the guests and when appropriate slip from view to carry out his nefarious operations.'

'But how did you deduce it was the musician – the new violinist in Ambrose's ensemble, I take it?'

'I will come to that later; suffice it to say that all the slender evidence I was able to muster pointed to one man: Arthur J. Raffles.'

'The cricketer?' I said, my eyebrows rising in surprise.

'The cricketer and amateur cracksman.'

'Surely not. He is a respectable gentleman.'

'Oh, yes, Watson. What better front for operating as a jewel thief. He and I have crossed swords before. He is an ingenious felon. He is the epitome of a refined gentleman crook – but a crook nonetheless. However, I must admit I have great respect for his talents.'

I shook my head in wonder. 'This is remarkable,' I said.

'After our visit to Joseph Ambrose, I went to the Albany where Raffles has his rooms and bearded our quick-witted collector of highly considered trifles in his den. He admitted me with a smile and a knowing glance that seemed to suggest that he had been expecting me.

'"How lovely to see you after all this time, Holmes," he said, waving me to a seat. "To what do I owe the pleasure of this visit?"

'"I have come for the necklace," I said.

'Raffles looked at me blankly. "Necklace? What necklace?"

'"Oh, don't let us play games, Raffles. You know as well as I do what necklace. The pretty little item that you rifled from Lady Bramingham's safe last evening in your persona as Arnold Jeffers."

'He laughed in a soft theatrical manner. "What an audacious claim. I think your detective faculties must be failing you. You have begun to talk nonsense, old fellow. Maybe it is time for you to retire."

'"That is the advice I had reserved for you." I rose from my chair and wandered to the back of the room where I snatched up a violin which was lying on a small side table. I had observed it as I entered the room. You know, Watson, of my ability to scan my surroundings in a matter of moments, to take in anything that may be of interest or use to me. The violin was brazenly on show. I plucked a few strings and gazed over at my host. "I would ask you to play me an old tune, Mr Jeffers, but I suspect after last night's dismal show you have admitted defeat and given up the instrument."

'Raffles gave me a knowing smile but said nothing.

'"Allow me to give you a piece of advice," I said. "If you do, in the future, resort to the fiddle again to aid you in some nefarious venture, do take care to clean your fingers most carefully. Last night at Lady Bramingham's you left distinct tell-tale traces of resin on the handle of the safe."

'The merriment in Raffles' eyes dimmed and his smile faded.

'"It certainly confirmed to me that a violinist was the culprit. A little clue that dear old Scotland Yard failed to notice."

'"So it was a violinist, but why pick on me?"

'"A violinist with limited ability with the instrument but a great facility at cracking safes and a love of sparkling things. The finger of suspicion was wavering in your direction. And then it was secured."

'"How so?"

'"Your love of cricket is well known and you could not resist bringing with you a copy of *The Times* to read their report on the Test Match. You left the paper folded over at this section behind the music podium. And of course, rather audaciously, you chose the name Arnold Jeffers, based on your own initials. Mr A. J. Raffles."

"'All this is interesting stuff, but in no way would it implicate me in the robbery to the satisfaction of the authorities."

"'Maybe not, but I am sure if we presented them with you wearing your disguise, the full moustache and grey wig and looked into your eyes, particularly the right one with the grey fleck so carefully described to me by Joseph Ambrose, I suspect even Scotland Yard would be ready to clap on the handcuffs."

'Although Raffles' demeanour did not alter at my revelations, I could see by the paling of his features and the tightening of the muscles around the jaw that my comments had hit home.

"'It may be that all the evidence would be too slender to secure a conviction," I admitted, "but the notoriety which the matter would create in the press would, I fear, damage your reputation both as a man of honour on and off the cricket field and lead you to be blacklisted from all the society functions that currently you so easily and readily attend. For whatever reason."

"'I always thought you were a clever fellow, Holmes, but I believe on this occasion you have excelled yourself. It seems I have been outwitted by the old fox. What do you intend to do?"

"'Return the necklace to its rightful owner, of course."

'Raffles sighed. "As with cricket, so it is with crime, one should never be a sore loser." He slipped his hand into the pocket of his smoking jacket and brought out the glittering prize. "It was a joyful venture. Great fun to bring off, despite those dull hours of violin practice to improve upon my basic skills." He fondled the necklace, stroking the gems gently as one might a favourite pet. "Of course, the real enjoyment in the game for me is in the pursuit; the spoils are just the pretty froth on the champagne. But, nevertheless, I am sad to let this beauty go."

'He handed it to me. "And what fate awaits me, I wonder. I shall need the cleverest of lawyers."

'"On this occasion, an umpire's warning will suffice. I shall take no further action in the matter, but be assured, Mr Raffles, should our paths cross again in a similar manner I shall do all I can to support the law in taking its full course."

'He paused, his eyebrows raised in surprise at what I had just said. After a while when the full import of my words had registered, he nodded his head graciously. "You are a gentleman, sir."'

'You let him go,' I cried.

'In this instance, yes, Watson. As I have intimated on several occasions in the past: I am not retained by the police to supply their deficiencies. The evidence against Raffles was slender and I have succeeded in the task given to me. The necklace has been retrieved and will be returned to its rightful owner. No real harm has been done and the incident provided a little brainwork to fend off that cursed ennui which is always lurking in some dark corner eager to engulf me.'

I opened my mouth to protest, but thought better of it. Holmes had made up his mind and he was not a man to be budged. With a sigh, he wandered over to the side table near the window and retrieved his violin. Within seconds a sweet sentimental melody was filling the warm air of our Baker Street sitting room, while an expression of beatific serenity settled on the face of Sherlock Holmes.

David Stuart Davies is a leading expert on Sherlock Holmes. The author of seven novels, two plays about the great detective and several books on the dramatised Holmes, he is an invested Baker Street Irregular. His Yorkshire Noir DI Paul Snow series is set in the 1980s, while private investigator Johnny Hawke inhabits 1940s London, and supernatural sleuth Luther Darke lurks in turn of the century London. David was editor of Sherlock *magazine, and edits* Red Herrings *for the Crime Writers Association.*

An End in Bath

Janet Laurence

In 1995 I'd had several books in my first series of crime novels published and the University of Vitoria in Spain invited me to address their Third Seminar on Crime Writing. It was a great honour but I hadn't done anything like that before and felt very nervous. Then, there at the airport, was Peter Lovesey, another invitee. I didn't have another worry. Peter was a wonderful guide and companion. The British Council had sponsored us both to address Spanish schoolchildren on creative writing and I loved hearing him tell them how he started his crime writing career by winning a competition organised by Macmillan. He was even able to show them the original flyer. For me, the whole trip was typical of Peter: a perfect gentleman, a wonderful writer, and someone who will always give another writer a helping hand, as he did for me again last year by providing a wonderful strapline for my latest book. Happy birthday, Peter, and may you have many more.

*

Irene was reading. When the doorbell rang she didn't answer. It couldn't be anybody she wanted to see. She turned a page of her book.

A long second ring pierced the calm and forced Irene to go to the door. On the step was a pleasant-looking young man with a thatch of bleached hair, sweatshirt, jeans and an immense rucksack.

'Yes?'

'Irene Wootton?'

'Can I help?' She did not make the offer sound promising.

'I'm Rod, your cousin from Oz.'

'My cousin?'

'My grandpa's your Uncle Malcolm.' Irene had a sudden memory of her father throwing a Christmas card from Australia on the fire. When her mother had objected that they were family, he'd said Malcolm was a disgrace and that he wanted nothing to do with his offspring.

'Good heavens! You must be ...' Irene thought rapidly, '... my first cousin once removed.'

'Removed! Don't like the sound of that! Thought I could spend some time with you. Being cousins and all. Tell you about Grandpa and the family.'

'Spend time with me?'

'Do you always repeat what people say to you, Cousin Irene?' The tone was playful and Irene was intrigued.

'I suppose you'd better come in.'

The young man promptly entered, glancing around the spacious hall. 'My, you live in some style. Put the backpack here, shall I?' He didn't wait for a response.

Irene eyed the battered piece of luggage leaning drunk-
enly against the wall. 'It's very big!'

'Flew into Heathrow from Sydney this morning. Quite a
trick finding my way to Bath.'

'You'd better take those trainers off, they don't look at
all clean. I suppose you could do with a cup of tea; kitchen's
along here.'

'Any chance of a cold stubby? My throat's as dry as a
dingo's backside.' He grinned cheerfully at her.

'I'm not going to ask what a stubby is; you'll have to make
do with tea.'

'Grandpa said your dad was a mean old sod but that you
might have a spot more human kindness.' He paused for a
moment, running a hand through the untidy haystack that
was his hair. 'Could 'ave been wrong of course,' he added,
twinkling at her.

His easy manner was refreshing. Irene made tea. After
an inspection of her neglected garden through the French
window, Rod joined her at the kitchen table.

'What are your plans for England?'

'Dad thinks I ought to get culture.'

'"Get culture"? How?'

'Well, Bath is pretty historical, yeah?'

'There's been a settlement here since before the Romans.'

'Right! And didn't the Romans take a lot of baths? I'm a
shower man meself, mind.'

Irene handed over a mug and offered a bowl of sugar
lumps. Rod popped several into his tea. 'Ripper,' he said,
drinking it straight down and accepting a refill.

'What did your grandfather say you should do?' Irene wished she knew more about her Australian relatives.

'Yeah, well, he believes in action. Was big in sheep farming, handed it on to my dad.'

'Did he help finance this trip?'

'Grandpa gave me the air fare but said I'd have to find the rest myself. Been doing this and that to earn the dollars. Can turn my hand to almost anything.'

'And your father?'

'Bit of past history there.' Rod's expression darkened. 'Said I'd have to pay my own way. In fact said he wouldn't mind if he never saw my face again. But Mum says I should enjoy myself.'

Irene studied Rod's face. He reminded her a little of herself at that age: determined and self-centred. 'Doesn't seem to trouble you being given the boot like that. How old are you?'

'Twenty-two.' With life before him; Irene felt all of her fifty-eight years.

'You been in work?'

'Sort of. Uni, odd jobs, you know. I can turn my hand to most things.'

'What degree did you take?'

'Biochemistry.'

'No job offers?' The lad was a mite too pleased with himself.

'Thought I'd continue my education over here before I settle for the old nine-to-five.'

'What are your plans?'

'Well, Cousin Irene, I sort of left that until my arrival, like.' He gave her an engaging grin.

'Hmm. Have you anywhere to stay?'

'Thought, well, sort of hoped, you'd be able to help me out there. While I imbibed – isn't that the word? – Bath and its history.'

'In other words, free board and lodging?'

'Wouldn't be for long and I could help you while I'm here. That nature reserve out there, for starters. I looked after a number of gardens back in Sydney.'

The last gardener had been sacked by her father a year ago, just before he died. Irene had thought the gradually increasing chaos a small price to pay for peace and quiet.

'Hmm,' she said.

'I know weeds from proper plants. It's March now, get a good start and it should look daisy-right by summer. Plus I can do DIY jobs.' He gave a cursory glance around the kitchen. 'Looks like you need a coat of paint on this place.'

The kitchen, like the rest of the house, hadn't been touched for the last thirty years.

By the end of the day, Rod was installed in a comfortable bedroom, Irene had cooked a cottage pie for supper, and he had made a start on the garden.

Over the next week Irene was surprised at how pleasant it was to have Rod living with her. He was cheerful, blunt and amusing. He explored Bath in the mornings, found a job in a local pub for the evenings and in the afternoons attacked the weeds, the rampant shrubs, and the hay meadow that was the lawn. 'I need a scythe,' he announced the second day. 'That mower ain't man enough for the job.'

Irene drove him to a garden centre. Arrangements were made for an industrial cutter to reduce the grass to a manageable level.

At the end of the second week, Rod and Irene stood on the ragged remains of the lawn. 'You're doing a great job,' Irene said.

Rod gave a self-satisfied look around the large garden. 'Beginning to look fair dinkum,' he drawled. 'This place all yours?'

'My father left it to me.'

'That would be my Great Uncle Alastair?'

Irene nodded.

'And he got it from his dad, right?'

Irene nodded again.

'And no doubt a handsome sum to go with it. Grandpa got nothing!'

She tried not to feel uncomfortable.

'Your dad being on the spot, no doubt he tied the whole thing up. That's what Grandpa thinks.' Fierce blue eyes looked into hers.

Irene went inside without saying anything.

Alastair Wootton, Irene's father, had been an overwhelming presence in her life; he'd made sure she knew what a disappointment his only child was. Female, hadn't gone in for law, never managed marriage. Nevertheless, when, twelve years ago, a widower on the brink of retirement, he suffered a stroke that robbed him of speech and condemned him to a wheelchair, Irene gave up her career as a librarian and moved into her old home to look after him. He'd immediately fired his housekeeper.

She hadn't found it easy. Her father indulged in fits of temper, throwing things with his one good hand, purple in the face, eyes bulging from his head. He grunted at her (Irene gradually learned what he meant) and wrote notes. Gratitude was foreign to him; criticism his default position. According to her father, Irene was extravagant. *I don't want to be bankrupt before I'm on my feet again,* he'd write. He'd had a brilliant career as a barrister and, latterly, a judge. No colleagues called. And his outrageous behaviour drove away her friends. Irene had to struggle to keep the temper she had inherited from him under control.

Finally she'd had enough. One day, with a furious grunt, he'd thrown a too-hot mug of tea at her and she'd screamed at him, thrusting her scorched face next to his. His good hand tried to push her away; she grabbed his shoulders and shook him, releasing hurt and anger built up over years.

He'd had another stroke, this one fatal. She was his sole legatee and had been left well provided for. Irene tried to feel guilty but instead was filled with relief.

Rod should have been an intrusion on her peace and quiet, instead he made her feel newly alive. She welcomed the odd Australian he brought back. One sunny afternoon, he and his mate, Bongo, were drinking coffee on the terrace.

'Hey,' said Bongo, studying the stucco façade of the Georgian building, 'this is one hell of a house. Must be worth a bob or two. Got any children, have you?'

Irene laughed. 'Unmarried and childless, that's me.'

'So what's going to happen to this lot when you go?'

She was taken aback. 'I ... don't know.'

'Who's your nearest relative?'

'I suppose that would be Rod's family.' Irene quickly gathered up the empty mugs and disappeared.

Next evening Rod asked her straight out, 'You made a will?'

Irene was lost for words.

'Only there's four of us back home, me and two brothers and a sister.'

'I see.'

Over the next few days, Irene did some thinking. Finally she made an appointment with the family solicitor.

Afterwards she told Rod, 'I've left it all to you. I'm not planning to leave this life soon, mind. We're a family with long-lived genes, witness your grandfather and my father. Don't look to inherit for another thirty or so years.'

'But it will all come to me?'

'Yes.' Then something made her add, 'Unless, of course, I change my mind.'

'Do you do that often?'

She laughed, a little nervously. 'Not often.'

They were sitting in the shabby kitchen over the remains of supper. Rod got up and hugged her for the first time. 'Thanks, Cousin Irene. I hope you live to a hundred.'

Irene told herself that she had made a good decision. Rod was a hard worker, the garden was beginning to look as though it would be a pleasure to sit in. And he'd only ever uttered one complaint, about a cat that haunted the place. 'Always under my feet, he is. I'll have to teach him better manners.' Rod would have to wait for his inheritance but perhaps she could do something for him in the meanwhile.

Three days later, she gave Rod an envelope.

She watched him study its contents.

'But this is for a trip to Paris!' He fingered the Euro notes she'd included.

She laughed, pleased with the effect of her surprise. 'It's a little gift from your aged first cousin once removed. The airline ticket is open-ended so you can return any time.'

'Beaut, mate! Grandpa'll have to eat his words about this side of the family.' Then his eyes narrowed. 'What's the catch? You don't want me back here?'

'Of course I do. Why ever not?'

He shrugged.

'So you like it here?'

'Yeah, it's right cool. Have you got a guide to Paris?'

A few weeks earlier she'd ordered a new kitchen. The men arrived to install it just after Rod left. Irene almost welcomed their noise and commotion; the house was proving curiously empty without him.

On a beautiful spring day, Irene went out into the garden, now emerging from its jungle state into bridal mode with virginal white and pink blossom. Under some trees, she found bluebells; perhaps it was time she learned about plants. She walked along a flagstoned path and relished the privacy – mature trees and shrubs guarded the garden from nosy neighbours.

At the end, newly revealed, was a wooden shed. She had forgotten all about it. When her mother had been alive, her father had treated it as his refuge, somewhere out of bounds to everyone else. The door was secured with an elaborate padlock. Irene walked round the back. Rod's efforts so far hadn't reached an impenetrable tangle of bushes, brambles and verdant weeds. Surely, though, in a corner, that was an elegant statue wreathed in ivy? Irene tried to push her way through, then stumbled on something just as the outside doorbell rang.

Expecting to deal with a delivery to do with the new kitchen, she was surprised to find a woman about her own age who looked at her hopefully. 'I've just moved to Bath and thought I must look you up.' Skilfully styled blonde hair and a chic scarlet jacket over a well-cut grey jersey dress prompted Irene's memory.

'Good heavens, it's Polly Jones! Come in.'

'My, this your home?'

'How about a cup of coffee? There are workmen in the kitchen but there's an electric kettle in the sitting room. It must be, what, fifteen years since we last met. Are you with Bath library now?'

They had both studied for a librarian's degree at the same university and afterwards found posts in Manchester.

They'd been very friendly. However, after Irene had moved back to Bath, contact had gradually dwindled to an annual exchange of Christmas cards.

As Irene dealt with the kettle, Polly wandered over to the window. 'My library closed. Isn't it terrible what's happening all over? No library positions unless you're a volunteer. But I've landed a job with that wonderful independent bookshop you've got here. So now I'm a bookseller.'

'Are you enjoying it?' Irene handed her a cup of coffee.

'I think I will, once I get used to the change. Today's my day off, in lieu of Saturdays! What a wonderful garden you've got. All due to you?'

Irene laughed. 'I know nothing about horticulture. The garden is all down to Rod.'

'And who is Rod, may I ask?'

Irene was not sure she liked Polly's touch of coyness; it reminded her how she'd always been curious about any man that was mentioned. 'He's a cousin from Australia. Early twenties. He's been staying with me but he's left for Paris.'

'You're a cougar!' Polly said.

'Revolting idea! I'm his aged Cousin Irene.'

'Who's providing him with a cushy billet!'

'Let's take our cups onto the terrace, it's lovely in the sun.'

Gradually they picked up the threads of their friendship. Then Polly asked for a tour of the garden. Still happily talking they walked right round, ending up behind the shed, where Polly stumbled just as Irene had. Beneath a pile of rotting leaves they found the body of a large cat.

'Ugh,' said Polly.

Irene looked at the attractively striped animal. 'I've often noticed it in the garden; it looks aged. Do you think it crawled here to die?'

Polly found a stick and gently turned the corpse over. 'Impossible to tell, but there's something odd about its neck. Perhaps a fox? Do you know its owner?'

Irene shook her head. 'I'd better ask around.' She looked at her watch. 'Lunchtime. I can't offer you anything here but there's quite a good trattoria within walking distance.' She felt relieved when Polly took a rain check.

Irene went round the neighbouring houses, discovered the dead cat's home and apologised to its very upset owner. Two days later an accusation of murder was made. According to a vet, the cat's neck had been broken. The owner, an elderly woman with coarse grey hair escaping from a bun, accused Irene's gardener. 'I heard him cursing one afternoon, then a most horrible cry. Garfield practically flew over the wall, his ears right back.'

'I'm sure Rod wouldn't have harmed him,' Irene said. 'It was probably a fox. I've seen them slinking through the garden.' Which was true.

Eventually the matter was settled with a cheque for the vet's fee and a new cat.

Irene put the incident behind her – not difficult as Polly had decided to take her in hand. 'You used to be a sharp dresser. Are you patronising the charity shops now? And those clips for your hair are ridiculous.'

Irene murmured something about ten years with no income.

'But you've money now, haven't you? You aren't spending it all on the new kitchen?'

'No, indeed,' Irene said.

It seemed Polly had been in Bath long enough to locate any number of really smart clothes shops plus an excellent hairdresser. Irene looked at the transformation of her mess of pepper-and-salt hair into a warm chestnut bob. What, she wondered, would Rod think?

The kitchen had been completed, Irene had a wardrobe of new clothes, and now she needed a new project.

She found it in the wooden shed. The padlock key was in her father's roll top desk, as was one to a cupboard inside the shed. It held piles of matching leather-bound diaries that went back nearly sixty years. The last stopped the day before his stroke, with the writing as black and bold as in the first. Irene took the three earliest back to the house and started to read with a pleasant sense of anticipation.

The first began with Alastair's arrival in a set of chambers at the Inns of Court. Little personality came through the writing. Mentions were made of the shortcomings of colleagues, brief comments on cases; with visits back home merely noted. Then came a mention of his younger brother, Malcolm, and for once the writing showed emotion. Rod's grandfather seemed to have been a ne'er-do-well. Ostensibly an undergraduate at London's Imperial College, it was soon plain he was a continuing problem:

arrests for drunk and disorderly; fraudulent cheques; landlords wanting recompense for damage; girls who were crying rape. Alastair dealt with it all, desperate not to be saddled with a criminal for a brother; it wouldn't, he confided to his diary, do his career any good. Finally, Malcolm was expelled and returned home to Bath.

Hungry for her supper, Irene closed the diary. As she enjoyed cooking in her new kitchen, she thought about Malcolm. Rod talked about his grandfather with admiration. What had happened to transform him? Or were Rod's standards different?

After supper she returned to the diaries. Soon after Malcolm arrived back in Bath, his parents disappeared on a round-the-world cruise to celebrate his father's retirement as a successful solicitor. Irene could just remember him, a man who spoke little and then usually to complain.

Alastair wrote that his father expected him to control his younger brother. *How I'm to do that, I have no idea. I'm due to go down to Bath next week. Dad says Malcolm's taken on the construction of a terrace outside the sitting room. I dread having to sort out the mess he'll make of it.*

Irene took the diary to bed with her.

It was after midnight before she turned out the light and lay in bed running the entries over and over in her head in a daze of disbelief.

For once her father's diary was far from concise and logical. Even his writing was jerky and difficult to read. Had Malcolm really brought a down-and-out back to the house, claiming he was going to turn the chap's life around by getting him to help build the terrace? Alastair had arrived from London to find the foundations dug and the necessary materials delivered, but little else had happened. Alastair had laid into his brother, calling him, according to the diary, a useless layabout. So now Malcolm had brought home a real 'useless layabout', so he could show how capable they could be. According to the diary, Alastair had given him a lecture then left to find some friends who 'spoke his language'. Irene translated 'lecture' into titanic rage.

Alastair recorded that he returned to find Malcolm in a drunken stupor beside the dead and badly battered body of the down-and-out. The account continued with a confused jumble of Alastair's reasons for not calling the police. Irene had no doubt that, whatever his attempts at justification, it wasn't Malcolm Alastair wanted to protect but his own career.

Sleep didn't come that night. In the morning Irene went downstairs in her dressing gown, and took a cup of coffee out to the terrace. A long shiver ran down her spine as she looked at the flagstones. Her mother had complained about their unevenness. 'They need relaying,' she'd said more than once. It never happened. Now she knew why.

Before her grandparents had returned from their cruise, Irene's father had given Malcolm two thousand pounds to emigrate to Australia. 'That's your lot,' he'd said. In those days it was a huge sum of money. *It has depleted my twenty-first birthday settlement from Dad*, Alastair wrote. *But if it gets rid of Malcolm, it'll be worth it.*

Apparently it had. Irene speed-read the following diaries. Little was noted about the emigrant. Alastair's parents complained over the lack of information, Alastair was relieved. *No idea,* he wrote some three years later, *what Malcolm's getting up to but no news is definitely good news.*

What was it Rod had said? That his grandfather had made a success of sheep farming? Somehow it didn't sound like Malcolm but what better career for a family's black sheep?

Irene wondered where Rod was now. He'd been away for eight weeks. Another postcard had come from Istanbul; Rod didn't 'do' emails. *Earning my keep,* he'd written. *Grandpa would be proud.* For some reason that did not reassure her.

Irene worked in the garden. She found she enjoyed choosing plants and designing schemes and looked forward to showing Rod her efforts. Bongo came round to see if she knew when he was returning.

'Don't you text each other?'

'Sent me an email from some cyber-café to say his mobile had been stolen.'

'What a shame. It was a really smart one.'

'Reckon he sold it,' said Bongo.

Walking in the garden with Polly one Sunday, Irene looked at the statue that was still wreathed in ivy. 'I really ought to rescue her,' she said with a laugh.

'And you should do something about all that jungle,' said Polly. 'What, exactly, is there?'

'The odd laurel, lots of brambles, some bamboo and isn't that cow parsley?'

'Whatever it is, you don't want it. Shall we start with the ivy?'

Instead, a heavy shower sent them indoors.

The following evening Polly came round for supper. Just as they started, the front door opened, there was the thud of a rucksack on the hall floor and there was Rod, looking tired and thin. 'Well!' he said, taking in the new kitchen.

'Hi!' Irene gave him a warm hug. 'Come and meet Polly.'

'I've heard such a lot about you.' Polly offered her hand.

'I've heard nothing about you,' he said.

'Polly's a face from my past,' said Irene. 'We've been catching up.'

'You've done wonders with the garden,' Polly told him.

'Yeah, well . . . you must have spent a mint of money and not only here.' He studied Irene. 'A new hairstyle, and that cardie looks like cashmere. Mum insisted Dad gave her one. This all your doing?' he asked Polly.

She smiled and said nothing.

Irene realised she wasn't going to get any compliments, opened the fridge and took out a Fosters. 'Your room's all ready. Hungry? We're about to eat, there's plenty for three.'

'Nah, want to see if my pub job's still open. Can you stand me some cash?'

'Of course.' Irene reached for her handbag and passed him a couple of twenty pound notes.

'Thanks.' He nodded to Polly. 'No doubt see you around, eh?'

'Oh, you will,' said Irene happily. As the front door closed behind him, Polly raised an eyebrow. 'Real charmer!'

'He's probably exhausted.' Irene opened a bottle of white wine. 'Come on, let's enjoy ourselves.'

Rod appeared in the morning with freshly washed hair and a bundle of dirty clothes. She showed him the washing machine in a brand new utility room. 'I'm planning on installing an ensuite shower for your room,' she said, adding powder to the loaded machine. No response from Rod. 'Polly's educating me in spending money. This house needs a total makeover. And I'm planning a trip abroad. It's time I discovered the outside world. Now, I'm longing to hear all about your travels. Have you got lots of pictures?'

'Nah, the mobile got snitched.' His glum expression deepened.

'What a shame.' She stopped herself saying she'd get him another one. 'I've really missed having you around, Rod.'

He flushed and looked a little shamefaced. 'I missed you, Cousin Irene. Coming back here it, well, it threw me a little. I mean, everything's changed.'

'Nothing's changed. I've just begun to realise how much I've got to be grateful for, including my cousin Rod.' She took a jar from a cupboard. 'Look what I've got for you.'

'Vegemite! Beauty! Where'd you get it?'

'Off the internet. I heard how you Aussies love the stuff.' She put a piece of bread in the toaster.

It seemed their relationship was back to where it had been before Rod left for Paris.

Gradually she heard about his travels. He'd managed to make the money she'd given him go amazingly far, augmented by odd jobs, exactly what he didn't explain.

'Now I want to go to South America.'

'Why not?' Irene said.

He started work in the garden again. She found him very attentive, making her cups of tea or coffee; sometimes scrambled eggs or fried egg on baked beans, both favourites of hers. If Polly was there, though, he'd disappear to her father's shed.

A few days after his return he brought her a mug of peppermint tea, saying he thought that would be better for her than English Breakfast.

One night out with Polly, she suffered terrible cramps and only just reached the ladies' loo before throwing up. Polly got Irene home and into bed. 'Call the doctor,' she said. But Irene felt better in the morning.

Soon she felt worse again. Her next evening with Polly was spent in the loo. Polly said if she refused to see a doctor, she must stay with her until she felt better. For several days Polly fed her thin slices of bare toast and mineral water.

When, much restored, Polly took her home, she suggested Irene was very careful over what she ate or drank. 'I've got to go back to Manchester for a few days. Why don't you come with me?'

Irene laughed. 'I'll be fine. Rod will look after me. Maybe his herbal tisanes are not quite the thing but I'll steer clear of them, promise. Ring me as soon as you get back.' She watched Polly drive away and went inside.

The Australian couple stood on the front step and listened while the bell rang in the depths of the house.

'I can tell no one's there,' said the woman. 'It sounds empty.'

Her husband shrugged. 'Beats me how you women think you can tell.'

'I just wish we'd had an answer to our letter, or our telephone calls. Pity we didn't have an email address.'

'Malcolm said it'd be fine.'

'Your dad thinks the world jumps to his bidding.' She rang the bell again. 'Why he gave that ticket to Rod, I'll never know.'

'Good on him, that's what I think.'

'He should have made him knuckle down to a proper job.'

'That was never going to work. Chucked out of Uni, avoiding arrest by the skin of his teeth, lord knows what else.' He peered anxiously at the door. 'Ned Kelly had nothing on Rod when he wants something. When I heard Dad had given him this address, I wanted to warn what's her name, Irene? But he said Rod deserved a chance to start with a clean sheet. How she's been coping with him, I can't imagine.' He grabbed the brass knocker and rapped loudly enough to wake the dead.

'Darren!' protested his wife.

'Someone's coming.'

The door was opened by a middle-aged woman. 'Can I help?'

'Are you Irene?'

The woman nodded.

'We're Rod's parents.'

The door was opened wide. 'So nice to meet you.'

Several cups of tea and slices of cake later Irene showed Hattie and Darren out. They'd told her how Rod seemed to have disappeared. No emails, no text messages, no Skype, just nothing. She'd tried to tell them that was the way Rod operated. He didn't want to be tied down. Or run the risk of anyone finding out where he was. Rather like his grandfather, Irene said. 'True,' said Darren. 'We were doing this trip anyway. Just hoped we'd catch up with him.'

'I'm afraid Rod went to South America several weeks ago. I bought him the ticket, a thanks for all his help with my garden. I'm hoping for a postcard.' She'd shown them the ones he'd sent from Europe.

They seemed a little happier. Said while they were in London, they'd see if the airline had any information. Though, as Rod's father said, the boy could never be relied on to do what was expected. He might even have cashed the ticket and gone off somewhere else entirely. Perhaps taken a tramp steamer to Vietnam!

After Rod's parents had left, Irene went and stood on the terrace. She looked at the statue at the end of the garden. Freed from its covering of ivy, it stood naked, at once virginal and available. Few, she thought, would notice the newly dug bank behind the shed, the new laurel bushes were taking nicely. Maybe, though, she should get rid of the long chef's knife. She'd been using it to cut away the statue's encroaching ivy while Rod dug out the bank's brambles and hemlock. If only he hadn't got so aggressive when she'd accused him of trying to poison her.

Afterwards, she'd had a choice, but a court case would have been drawn out and messy, its outcome uncertain. Instead, she'd gone for the alternative – and Irene was sure her father would have approved.

Janet Laurence is chiefly known for her crime novels. She has been cookery correspondent for the Daily Telegraph *and her first crime series featured a cordon bleu cook, Darina Lisle. She is currently writing the third in a historical mystery series set in Edwardian times. Other books include* Writing Crime Fiction, *and contemporary women's fiction under a pseudonym. She is an ex-Chairman of the Crime Writers' Association, and is currently Chairman of the CWA International Dagger judging panel. She lives in Somerset, runs crime writing courses and produces editorial assessments for aspiring novelists.*

The Marquis Wellington Jug

John Malcolm

The late nineteenth-century champion jockey, Fred Archer, who lost an 1876 Doncaster race by a short head, was responsible for the genesis of two crime novels over a hundred years later: Bertie and the Tinman *by Peter Lovesey, the first of three stories in which the Prince of Wales is put to detective use, and my novel* Mortal Ruin, *an account of the result of Moreton Frewen's disastrous bet on Archer at Doncaster. It was thus a great pleasure to meet Peter and talk to him about the jockey when* Bertie and the Tinman *was published in 1987.*

Peter was already famous as the author of The False Inspector Dew, *which had earned him the CWA's Gold Dagger. He and his wife Jax responded with enthusiasm to my approach and it has been a great pleasure to know them for a considerable time. It is a privilege to offer this short story as a tribute to Peter, with a glancing reference to his award-winning creation, just one title in his impressive list.*

*

It sits on my desk in cheerful contrast to the paperwork lying beside it. I keep its bright scarlet soldier turned to face me, with his yellow and silver touches highlighted against a sober white background. The beaky moulded face looking at me above its yellow lapels has cheeks tinged with red below the pointed slash of black hat skewered by a red cockade. The eyes reproach me for the upright fill of pencils and pens that the jug contains, as though to justify its presence next to the computer. Not that it needs justifying because, quite simply, I like to see it. Underneath one of the white hands protruding from a buttoned yellow cuff below the folded scarlet arms, you can discern the impressed lettering *Marquis Wellington* invaded by a tarnished silver line of decoration just above the moulded base. The military figure staring at me is somehow bulky and protruding, moulded into the side of the jug to produce an unmistakeable shape. The Peninsular War was in full spate when the jug was made. He wasn't a Marquis for long; within a year or so he was The Duke.

I was staring at it thoughtfully as the doorbell clanged and Lionel Yelland came striding in on his springy Italian leather shoes. I had heard the sound of his van pulling into my car park and knew that it would only be seconds before he came bustling past the stock in my shop, eyes alertly swivelling to take in what was new, preparing the presentation of some silver object or another from the depths of the smart leather case, an attaché growing towards a Gladstone, containing his current liquid assets.

That morning he was in country mode, wearing his

long hacking jacket and moleskin trousers, with twill shirt tucked neatly in at the waist. Clothes are important to Lionel. He used to be a roadie with a punk band and was known as Spikey due to the treatment of his hair and the needled penetration of his scraggy outfit. One day the scales fell from his eyes; he woke to realise that he and the band were obsolete anachronisms on a road rapidly losing its surface on the way to nowhere. He promptly left to take up another obsolete mobile occupation: that of runner to the antiques trade, competing with the internet like Canute waving angrily at a breaking Atlantic roller.

The hair was now short-cropped and the chin mostly smooth-shaven depending on the preferences of the lady of the moment. The impression he still cultivated was one of slightly menacing energy, useful when confronting boys trying to take illicit recordings or girls about to launch themselves at musicians, if musician is the right word to describe any of his disbanded ex-employers. Lionel was by instinct a minder; his violent care was very useful to me on occasion.

He held up the attaché-Gladstone and looked at me enquiringly. I got up and nodded in understanding.

'Come into the kitchen,' I said. 'We'll have a coffee.'

He put the bag down on the floor by the kitchen table after looking round again to satisfy himself that everything was still in the same place.

'How's Ellen?' The question was cautious. He was never sure about Ellen.

'She's down in Devon. Family matters. You're quite safe.'

He grinned. 'Did you hear the news about old Saunders?' He sat down next to his bag and started unbuckling the broad straps that were a feature of its design.

'No. What about him?'

Saunders was a picture restorer on the Haywards Heath road, down near Ardingly, conveniently halfway down to Brighton and Hove for the boys who were customers of Lionel's. His restoration had just the sort of touch the Brighton trade wanted: skies became a brighter blue, empty landscapes acquired a horse or a woman with a bundle of sticks, turbulent seascapes calmed down while sails filled. The domestic walls of southern England were cheered by the pleasant treatment Saunders gave to hundreds of dull but old canvases that were available at low cost to the furnishing trade.

'He's dead.'

'What?' I paused, kettle in hand.

'Dead. Killed. Knocked down on the main road not far from Wakehurst Place.'

'Good God.' I put the kettle down. 'That's terrible. He hardly ever went out. Dedicated to his studio, as he called it. Big shed in the back garden.'

'I know. But he went to the pub on Friday evenings and walked home. No pavement on the main road just there. I think he was a bit pissed. Hit and run, it was. Bastards.'

I put a mug of coffee in front of him and sat down with one for myself. It was a shock. I didn't use Saunders for restoration, but I had more than occasionally bought off him because he traded paintings on the side. If you got to them before he effected his improvements, they could be good business. Not that he didn't know what he was doing; he served a market. I liked him for his casually-worn expertise, his practical knowledge, and his contempt for those who thought of themselves as experts.

'Poor old Saunders. I suppose he walked so as to avoid the drink-drive laws. Or for exercise after being stuck in front of canvases all week. He was a good reliner too. Had his own table.'

'Tell me about it. I ran quite a few good pictures to him. And some bad ones. They came out much better.' Lionel sighed, took a sip of coffee, bent down to his bag and put a tissue paper bundle on the table. 'Wait for it,' he said. 'I think you'll like this.'

Lionel did a good line in small silver, decorative bits that were useful sidelines for me: mustard pots, pig and elephant pincushions, pepper pots shaped as watering cans, vinaigrettes, menu holders, decorative tableware that was always useful stock. I thought at first that he would build up to having his own shop, but things have gone against shops and he was too mobile for the cooperative constraints of an antiques centre. I had a feeling that he'd soon reach a logical conclusion: either give it up or become a catalogue business with a smart website for promotion and low cost storage like any commercial catalogue business. But then he'd miss the touring around, the chat, the coffee in countless kitchens like mine if not, like me, on the old A25 road between Westerham and Brasted, where I alighted not so long ago.

'Abracadabra,' he said, finishing the unwrapping to reveal a small medieval knight's helmet sitting squarely on its base, genuine silver, nicely made. What is known as a novelty item; a nineteenth century pepper pot disguised as head armour.

'Frederick Elkington,' he said, interrupting my first thoughts, 'Birmingham, 1874. Ordinary pepper or Cayenne. Comes through the perforated visor. How about that for four hundred quid?'

'Done.' I spoke without hesitation and he smiled knowingly.

'Thought you'd like it. What about an owl mustard pot, London 1845?'

'That'd be real money. Have you got it?'

'Not here. Punter wants four thousand for it. Thought I'd ask you first.'

'Is it kosher?'

He frowned. Lionel is touchy about his integrity. It was true that I'd never bought any goods of his that turned out to be dodgy. He was trustworthy, but other people are not always so; I couldn't help asking.

'Widow. Probate. Kosher for sure.'

'In that case it sounds good. Need to see it though.'

He nodded briskly and sipped some more coffee. 'Next time, then. Are you fit to view at Bradfield's?'

It was a viewing day at Bradfield's Auction Rooms, near East Grinstead. They had smartened up their premises considerably in the last year or so, attracting quite a bit of Brighton trade as well as some provincial and more central London boys. Their monthly Fine Art sales were quite good; usually worth a visit to see whether what looked right in the catalogue was really as attractive in the flesh. Although the telephone and internet make it easy to avoid travel, old habits die hard. There was a good coffee room to sit and exchange gossip in, quite apart from a nearby pub, so you could reassure the others you were still active, still alive and buying. I hadn't really been accepted by the Bradfield's bunch yet; it takes time for the local dealers to let you join their games. I was still an outsider, to them something of an impostor, feeling a bit like the False Inspector Dew: a guilty amateur masquerading as a cool professional.

'Oh, I'm fit all right,' I answered. 'I'm curious about the paintings this month. I never knew that old Mrs Penstone had such a collection of Modern British.'

One feature of the coming sale was, according to the catalogue I'd received online, the distinguished collection of the late Mrs Penstone, a wealthy old bird who lived in a Lutyens house in the Ashdown Forest and had been something of a terror to the local trade. She wanted everything at knockdown prices, demanded free delivery and delayed paying for as long as she could. A bit like old Queen Mary, the Hove dealer Danny Brooks used to say, the Teck lady that George V took on when his brother died. He claimed that one London porcelain retailer with a By Appointment sign used to pay a Buck House footman to tip him off when she set out shopping. That way he could hide the best stuff that was big money so she couldn't ask for it to be sent round and then forget to pay. But to be fair, Danny was a hot republican and might have made it up.

Mrs Penstone bought lots of things, from furniture and silver to textiles and paintings. Bradfield's were cock-a-hoop to get the contents out of her Lutyens house when it came to winding up her affairs. By order of the principal trustee, the blurb said, who was a nephew; she didn't have any children of her own. The domestic stuff was not as desirable as it used to be; the young market wants modern, clean lines and twentieth-century design. It isn't impressed by traditional taste, has no ambition to dine off mahogany. But there were plenty of senior citizens in Sussex and its neighbouring counties, enough to appreciate old Mrs Penstone's Chesterfields and Knole settees, quite apart from her Chippendale dining suite.

It was the paintings that were drawing in serious interest, though. What I think of as Modern British with a strong Slade School element in it has come to get some good money from collectors. It is insular painting of course, infused with a nostalgic melancholy that makes it irresistible to English emotion. This collection had some sought-after names. They were not top-notch examples of their work but there were some modest pictures by earlier painters, too: Wilson Steer, Gilman, Frances Hodgkins and, thinking of that jug on my desk, a William Nicholson. Mrs Penstone must have spent money.

'Pity they're selling it all up,' said Lionel, 'but the nephew who's inherited it says that inheritance tax is clobbering him rotten. He's a Penstone, too: Charles he's called, some sort of City gent. Lives in Essex. The Lutyens house is heavily mortgaged, according to reports; the old bird did an equity release and spent it all on her collection.'

'That should be allowable against inheritance tax. He can't be so badly off. I sold her a dresser by Gimson not so long ago and saw her house pretty thoroughly when I delivered it. Downstairs, anyway. There was some good kit in the place then but I didn't see all these paintings. Must have been upstairs. Owen Bradfield must be pleased to get this lot; some of it looks like big London auction rooms material.'

'Well, Charles is groaning about tax, apparently, as well as how she spent a lot on things that have dropped in value, like all that brown furniture. There's some Georgian silver left,' Lionel was putting the knight's helmet pepperpot to one side with a significant glance at me that had to do with money, 'but the London trade'll go for that. I'll be lucky to pick up a novelty item or two.'

'If you do,' I answered, 'I'll see you right on anything I fancy.'

We weren't going to bid against each other so technically we were forming an illegal two-man ring. But silver was Lionel's territory; I wouldn't intrude. As though following my train of thought he looked at me speculatively.

'The Penstone collection has got a Nicholson jug like yours in it,' he said.

Lionel knew the jug well. A year or so before, we had assembled the makings of a demo to mark the bicentenary of Waterloo, complete with a model of the battle. Among the Wellingtonia gathered in for sale was the jug, which he had brought to me. For old times' sake, I kept it, partly because there were a lot of similar Lord Wellington jugs made when he was in full gallop but not so many Marquis ones. I had a bit of a thing about Wellington; it amused and sometimes irritated my lady friend Ellen Stanton. She looked at the prints and cartoons, the shelf of books, the pottery and bust of the Great Duke by D'Orsay, with the superior female expression that implied that boys remained boys, still trailing the stamps, football records, cricket score boards, Scalextrics and Dinky toys that kept them happy while women got on with adult life.

Dream on, ladies; knowledge is power, including knowledge of big boys' toys.

I got up to look for some cash. 'Nicholson painted a Marquis jug on its own, sitting on a book, that was in the possession of Vivien Leigh when Lilian Browse produced her Catalogue Raisonné of his work in 1956. It was the one John Rothenstein said was so good.'

'This is titled *Zinnias in a Jug*,' said Lionel. 'And the jug is the one you've got. It says so in the catalogue; the write-up goes on about the jug being in Nicholson's other paintings. Is that right?'

'That's what is in the catalogue, yes. If it's right it's worth big money.'

'But?'

I finished my coffee whilst standing up. 'It is very rare for Nicholson to replicate items in his still life paintings. The Wellington jug is an exception. He used it singly in the

Vivien Leigh version and again in *The Nelson Jug.* So this
could be an important picture. We are going to see for our-
sclves. We can take my car. You can browse the silver while
I look at this item in the collection along with the other
canvases. Unless you'd rather go separately in your van?'

He shook his head as he stood up too. 'I like being
driven and I like saving petrol. On the way you can tell me
everything I need to know.' He put his mug down on the
draining board and went into the showroom to look at the
jug on my desk at the back while I counted out twenty notes
of twenty for him. You can't pay Lionel by cheque.

'He was Ben Nicholson's father, wasn't he?'

'Yes,' I said, 'that's how they thought of him for about
three or four decades. Not any longer, though. Ben's got
question marks about his work nowadays, but Sir William
hasn't. Let me give you the full Franklin lecture while
we tool down the lanes through Edenbridge into Sussex
bandit country.'

He grinned again and we motored along pleasantly
enough, me talking until we got to Bradfield's. The car
park was pretty full and I had to find a place at its edge
before we could get out. At the doorway Lionel split away
from me towards the silver, set out on a table at the far end
of the big auction rooms. I ambled through the viewers to
the staircase; paintings were always hung upstairs in the
smaller area near some offices.

There was a cluster of people moving slowly in front of
the paintings on display. Viewers could get right up to the
canvases but there were a couple of porters keeping a close

eye from short range. My eye caught the unmistakeable Nicholson still life of reddish flowers. Zinnias are a deep red described as 'showy' by the *Concise Oxford Dictionary* and he used them more than once. It was not such a big painting, about twelve inches by eighteen. An expensive still life of flowers in a vase that was sold in town a year or two back had included one of the silver lustre jugs or vases with which Nicholson liked to show off his technique; it went for a sum well into six figures. This one, as I got near it, had a jug like mine, set somewhat sideways, to hold the flowers in the same way that mine held my pens and pencils on my desk. The handle was slightly pointed towards you. Evidently it had aroused interest; Owen Bradfield was standing protectively near it with an expression of satisfied importance on his face. Next to him was a big middle-aged man in a pinstripe suit, hands in pockets. Bradfield nodded to me with a friendly expression before turning a little bit further towards the pinstripes to hear what the man was saying. This would presumably be the Penstone nephew, scanning the punters for potential big hitters prepared to stump up six figure sums for William Nicholson's work. Bradfield was probably telling him that I wasn't one. Moving a little bit closer to the painting, I heard the pinstripe say something about Rothenstein and then, with resentment in his tones:

'... minor master he called him, condescending beggar, the man was streets ahead of some of the artists Rothenstein wrote up and punted on the radio, supercilious bastard ...'

I smiled as I looked a little closer. Sir John Rothenstein, in his two-volume book *Modern English Painters*, described William Nicholson as a dandy who pioneered the spotted collar worn with the spotted shirt, a perfectionist whose anguished effort and technical brilliance were concerned with the surface of things. Rothenstein wrote that he was an unoriginal little master whose modest perfection produced the minor success that is today scorned in favour of heroic failure. It was harsh stuff. Penstone's resentment was understandable. As I took it in, I kept thinking about old Mrs Penstone and how this painting wasn't visible when I was there. So many paintings assembled here made me think, too, of poor dead old Saunders and his talents. A couple of people moved away while I was thinking, so that now I was on my own in front of the Nicholson. The estimate in the catalogue was forty to fifty thousand; a beckoning estimate, set at a level to lure in the big hitters.

It was like many of the 'minor master's' still-life paintings: he liked jugs, collected them, painted a view of one hundred of them in his remarkable *The Hundred Jugs*, now in Liverpool's Walker Art Gallery. Still life was one of his specialities. As I told Lionel, *The Marquis Wellington Jug* that Rothenstein praised – books often used the English word Marquess in the title, but the jug was impressed Marquis – was present in one other recorded work, *The Nelson Jug*, sold at Christie's in 1991. I stared hard at the zinnias, conscious of something wrong. A feeling of exposure started to creep over me. I was taking too long. Bradfield and Charles Penstone were now watching me intently. My presence in front of the painting began to feel like an accusation. Why was I worried about my expression? Was it revealing?

'Don't make it so bloody obvious, Franklin.'

The voice in my ear startled me. It was rasping in tone, roughened by smoking. Danny Brooks is a large man, coarsely built, liking to behave flamboyantly, trading in gilded and ormolu Regency furniture – flash gear – along with chandeliers and brazen mirrors down in Hove. His blotchy grey suit bulged and flapped around his abundant figure even though we were indoors. It was late morning and I caught a whiff of beer on his gusty breath as I found myself too near his florid features. Lionel called him the king of the ring; it was true that he liked to think of himself as one of the top dogs in these rooms. He and I had a short history of antagonism over mirrors at auction; for some reason he resented my presence, even though we were dealing in quite different fields. He cultivated the role of a hard-knock school of knowledge man, learnt in the practice of tough trade, and saw me as an educated twit, a false amateur taking business away from the professionals, an outsider trying to push in.

'What's obvious?' I looked straight at him, irritated by the strident, overdone interruption that was breaking all rules of decent etiquette.

'The way you look. You think it's dodgy, don't you?'

'Nothing of the sort. I haven't said a thing.'

He guffawed. 'You don't have to, Bill Franklin. Keeping schtumm?' He gestured towards Penstone and Bradfield. 'Acting the part of potential buyer and assessor on this one? Going to let them think you've got a hundred grand? You don't have to say anything; I can see you wouldn't spend it on this one even if you had it. Mind you, I wouldn't either.'

'You wouldn't what?' I was conscious that Bradfield and Penstone had moved a little nearer to us. They must have heard Danny Brooks loud and clear. Elsewhere, heads were turning. Their faces had congealed. I hate scenes; it was sheer bad luck that Brooks had turned up at exactly the wrong moment, full of beery aggro, raising hackles on my back.

'I wouldn't go for a dodgy Nicholson and I don't mind saying so. You're not going to say this was in the collection old Ma Penstone assembled. It wasn't. It's been put in the sale. But you're going to keep quiet like you usually do. Come on, Bill Franklin! Admit it.'

'Yes, come on.' Charles Penstone's voice, close to my ear, was low and hostile. His complexion was getting mottled. 'Let's have it out. I'm warning you, Brooks. And you, whoever you are. This is a fine original painting. It certainly was in my aunt's collection. I'll sue the arse off anyone who says that it wasn't.'

Unlike Danny, who smelt of beer, Penstone smelt of expensive aftershave. He and Owen Bradfield were very close to me now, in what I can only call confrontational mode. Bradfield was looking decidedly put out. Penstone's smooth-shaven face moved even closer to mine, setting in hostility as I stared straight back at him without yielding. Impulsively, muscles tense, he put a hand on my arm to grip it in what was not a friendly gesture. I braced myself stiffly as anger came in reaction to his grasp, but he took it off sharply, letting out a low cry of painful surprise.

'Let's keep it pleasant, shall we?' Lionel Yelland's voice from behind me was equally subdued but his face, emerging between Penstone and Bradfield, was set into what I knew to be rigidity before violence. 'No trouble please, gentlemen.'

He eased forward into the grouping in front of the painting. The vendors both moved back in alarm, Penstone rubbing his elbow.

'Brought your minder with you, then?' growled Danny, eyeing Lionel respectfully. 'Very wise.'

'I must ask you to leave.' Bradfield used his most pompous tones as he tried to gain control. 'All three of you. At once.'

He looked round as he spoke, to try and catch the eye of one or more of his porters, but they were studiously looking away from us. Lionel smiled one of his smiles that showed the small gaps between his teeth, like a crocodile yawning.

I was stung into revelation. This assembled scene was the last thing I wanted. There was no way I was going to buy the painting; it was true that I was there out of curiosity. I had been going to keep quiet. Lionel was looking at me without expression, almost relaxed. None of these other men would be any challenge to him, nor any of the porters.

I pointed at the jug holding the zinnias. 'I don't think that was a Wellington jug when Nicholson painted it. It's been overpainted, I'd say, reshaped into one. Cleverly done, the original jug altered just enough to bring the Duke's red coat into it and match the zinnias. Changes the value a lot. A coat of matt varnish put on so you'd have to have to have the right kit to detect the dabs of new paint. But it's not a Marquis jug as it says in the catalogue. It's one of the other ones, which were all impressed Lord Wellington, not Marquis, with General Hill on the other side. The Marquis jug has a yellow star on his red chest, signifying the Order of the Garter he was awarded early in 1813, after he was made Marquis and before he was made Duke. It's a very specific time frame. The way the jug is placed, you'd be bound to see it: a little yellow star. The flag beside him should be yellow and this one is green. William Nicholson didn't use a Lord Wellington jug. He had a Marquis one. Whoever altered the painting to make it more special must have used a Lord Wellington version for a model, to get the shape right. It looks the same, it's got the red coat, but without the star. That's a rarer jug to find.'

I paused to let it sink in.

'I wasn't going to say this. But old Saunders had one of those Lord Wellington jugs,' I said. 'Without the star. I saw it on a shelf in his shed. I often thought he'd like to use it.'

And I paused again.

There was a tense silence. Danny Brooks had a faint twisted smile on his lips.

'But he's dead,' he said. 'So he'll never tell us anything.'

Bradfield and Penstone stood silent, staring at me as though frozen by my exposition. Lionel touched my arm and gave me a slight jerk of the head. I moved back in response. Carefully we walked away from the paintings back down the staircase and through the crowded room.

No one got in the way.

'The silver wasn't up to much either,' Lionel said as we went through the outside door. 'The good stuff has all gone up to Town.'

'So would the paintings if they'd been better. Thanks for the backup, by the way.'

'My pleasure.'

We made our way carefully to the car. We were getting in when Danny Brooks came up, puffing a little.

'They've decided to withdraw it,' he wheezed. 'It won't be in the sale.'

'Good.'

'Bradfield is upset. You've made a real enemy out of Penstone. But Bradfield should thank you when he's had time to think about it. Wouldn't do his firm any good to sell a dud as pricey as that one.'

'Certainly not.'

'I supplied all the mirrors in that house. You can't tell me what was on the walls. I offered to buy my stuff back when she died but that greedy bugger wanted a big splash at Bradfield's.'

'Plus an added lot or so?'

He nodded at me. 'Old Saunders was good. I often had a beer with him. I hope they get the hit and run.'

'Me too.'

'I might give a copper I know a steer as to where to look.

There'll be a dented car with forensics locked away somewhere. Like a Lutyens stable block.'

'You do that,' I said. 'I liked old Saunders.'

'I will.'

He looked at Lionel for a moment and then back at me,
his blotchy suit flapping in the breeze like loose feathers
on a flustered rook.

He dug in his pockets for his mobile.

'Well,' he rasped, 'see you next time round, then? Or can
I buy you two a drink? After I've made this call?'

*John Malcolm was born in Chorlton-cum-Hardy, Manchester,
and spent a few boyhood years in Uruguay before returning to
school and university in England. He had a business career in
engineering, and is also the author of eighteen crime novels. He
was Chairman of the Crime Writers' Association in 1994-5 and
Chairman of Rye Art Gallery Trustees 1995-2005. He is also the
author (as John Andrews) of reference books on antique furniture
and is managing editor of* Antique Collecting *magazine. His
most recent crime novel,* A Damned Serious Business, *was
published in 2015, the bicentenary year of the battle of Waterloo,
for which Bill Franklin, narrator of this story, arranged a lethal
exhibition.*

A Question of Identity

Kate Charles

Peter Lovesey hooked me many years ago, when he introduced Sergeant Cribb to the world. Since then, and through many fine novels, he's remained one of my most admired writers. Though his series books are superb, my favourites have always been the quirky standalones: The False Inspector Dew, Rough Cider, On the Edge, The Reaper. *Thinking about why I enjoy these so much, I realised that these books, as well as many of his excellent short stories, often hinge on a question of identity – mistaken identity, assumed identity, hidden identity. That revelation was the inspiration for this short story. I've set it during the London Blitz, a landmark time during Peter's own life, when his childhood home was bombed out. I offer it to him with love and admiration.*

I got to know Vera quite well during those nights in the Anderson shelter. I suppose you would even say we became friends.

Mind you, we were very different sorts of girls. In peace-time it's unlikely that our paths would have ever crossed in a meaningful way. But war does make for strange bedfellows.

I'm a vicar's daughter from the country. That probably tells you all you need to know about me. Wartime gave me the opportunity to get away from the vicarage – from my life as an unpaid secretary to my father – and make a new life, of sorts, for myself in London.

Except that it didn't really turn out that way.

The only job my father would countenance for me was scarcely an improvement: working as a secretary and companion to his sister, my fearsome Aunt Iris.

Aunt Iris, a widow, lived in a tiny flat in Notting Hill, in what she liked to call 'reduced circumstances'. In practical terms that meant that there were no servants – that I was, in fact, her general dogsbody and slave, responsible for keeping her flat tidy, doing her washing and her shopping, preparing her meals, and anything else she felt was beneath her (which was virtually everything).

It also meant that there was no room for me to 'live in' – and hence why I found myself lodging in a shabby bedsit in Bayswater, sharing a bathroom and a kitchen with three other people. Including a girl called Vera.

Aunt Iris would have been horrified if she'd seen the house where I lodged. And she certainly would not have approved of my fellow residents.

Before the bombing started, I had scarcely exchanged more than a few words with any of them – with greasy-skinned Mr Robbins, who was a commercial traveller and seldom there; with Mrs Short, the fierce landlady, who terrified me. Or with Vera, so clearly not my kind of person. We all tended to avoid each other, timing our visits to the communal parts of the house quite carefully to that end.

And then Mr Hitler started dropping bombs above our heads. Poor old London – she bore the brunt of it, night after night, week after week, month after month.

Mrs Short had – begrudgingly, no doubt – paid one of the neighbours to install the Anderson shelter in the back garden, back at the beginning of the war. For months it had been unused. Then one night the sirens started their hair-raising racket, and off to the shelter we went.

On that first of many nights, Mrs Short had claimed one of the narrow benches, stretched out under a damp woollen blanket and gone promptly to sleep, snoring as peacefully as if she were in her own bed.

That left the bench on the other side for me and Vera. We sat together, cheek by jowl.

'Well,' said Vera, rolling her eyes. 'Here's a turn-up for the books!'

I couldn't help giggling, though I tried to muffle it. 'Don't wake her,' I cautioned in a whisper.

'Oh, that old baggage. She'll sleep through anything that bastard Hitler can chuck at us.'

So we started talking, and never really stopped.

The first thing I discovered about Vera, from that initial exchange, was that she was totally fearless. She wasn't afraid of Mrs Short, any more than she was afraid of Mr Hitler and his bombs. Nothing scared her, and that came as a total revelation to me. It had never occurred to me that you could live without fear – me, who was afraid of absolutely everything. One of the things – the most important thing – I learned from Vera was that fear only has power over you if you allow it to.

The second thing I found out was that Vera was alone in the world – even more than I was. I had Father and Aunt Iris; Vera had no one. Her parents had died a long time ago, and she had no siblings, no cousins. There had been boyfriends in her life before now – as attractive as she was, it would be very surprising if there had not been – but she was currently 'between men', as she told me with a laugh. Again, not a surprise: most of the men of our age were away in uniform, and the ones who were left didn't have much to offer a girl like Vera.

Vera worked in a shop in Oxford Street, she told me. It wasn't very exciting work, but it was respectable, and it paid the bills.

What she would have liked, if she'd had her choice of any career, was to be an actress. She would have been a good one, I always thought – she had a natural gift for mimicry, as was evidenced by the way she took off on our sleeping landlady so many times. To my delight, I must admit. I wouldn't have dared to mock Mrs Short myself, but loved hearing Vera do it. 'Short by name, short by nature,' she'd say. It always made me laugh.

We didn't really socialise a great deal outside of the Anderson shelter. Well, there wasn't much opportunity for that, was there? We both worked during the day – she at her shop, me at Aunt Iris' beck and call – and with the nightly bombing raids, any possible social life was pretty much on hold. Once or twice Vera tried to talk me into going to the pictures, but I was afraid to risk it.

Vera did start coming up to my room sometimes, on Sunday afternoons in particular. That was the one time of the week that neither one of us had to work: Aunt Iris, like my father, believed in keeping the Sabbath, so after church in the morning I had the afternoons to myself. Before Vera, I used to read a book or darn my stockings. But Vera had other ideas. She decided that I needed to wear some make-up, like she did – 'make a bit more of yourself', she always said. So she'd bring her powder and lipstick, and put it on me. It always made me feel silly, like some sort of painted doll, and I could only imagine what Aunt Iris would say if I ever showed up looking like that. Once I was 'made up', Vera would sit on my bed and chat, and then she'd start going through my wardrobe. Did I mention that we were pretty much the same size and shape? Vera's clothes, though, were nothing like mine. She wore fashionable frocks – the sort of thing Aunt Iris would have called flashy (with a disapproving sniff). But for some reason Vera was fascinated by my boring old clothes, and liked to try them on. This embarrassed me at first – my clothes were what you might call classic, the opposite of fashionable. Things that were made to last for the better part of a lifetime: tweed skirts, white blouses, hand-knit cardigans. With the pittance that Aunt Iris paid me, there wasn't much chance that any of my wardrobe would be replaced any time soon.

Anything left after I handed over my rent went on unglam-
orous necessities like vests and cotton stockings, once my
old ones had been darned almost to oblivion. Anyway, as I
said, I was embarrassed at first, but I soon realised that Vera
wasn't making fun of me – she was genuinely interested. I'd
never had a proper friend before, and had a lot to learn.

Vera may have been prettier and more self-assured than
me, but one area where I had an advantage over her was
in the kitchen. Father's frugality meant that, after Mother
died, from a young age I'd had to do all of the cooking at
home in the vicarage, and I'd developed my skills further
in Aunt Iris' kitchen, even under the limitations imposed
by rationing. I was good at stretching the rations in creative ways. Vera, on the other hand, could just about stretch
to popping a few sausages in a frying pan. As we got to
know each other better, we started eating together in the
evenings, between the time we each got home from work
and whenever the sirens would start up. She called it tea,
I called it supper, but whatever we called it, it was more
efficient that way: avoiding each other in the kitchen was a
luxury we couldn't afford, when we didn't know quite when
the sirens would begin. Mrs Short always had her main
meal at midday, and a snack later on, so she didn't intrude
on us during those early evenings in the kitchen.

Vera was happy to let me do the cooking, and even
though I'd usually had enough, after a day with Aunt Iris,
I didn't mind. I did take some pride in my abilities – which
Father probably would say was a sin. Well, maybe it was.

*

So now we come to the night I've been working up to – a night in early December, 1940.

It had been a bad week for bombing. Travelling round London, the city seemed a smouldering ruin. And I'd been doing a fair bit of travelling; Aunt Iris was more demanding, more crotchety than ever, sending me out on impossible errands and then giving me the sharp side of her tongue when I was unable to perform them to her standards, if at all. She'd fancied some fruit, and there was no fruit to be had, even after I'd queued for over an hour at the greengrocer. But Aunt Iris wasn't having it – I was a stupid, lazy girl who was probably out consorting with men instead of performing her duties. It was all I could do not to cry at the injustice of it all.

And then, to cap it all off, I got toothache.

If you've never had toothache, count yourself very fortunate indeed. If you have had it, you'll know what I mean when I say that there were moments when a bomb falling on my head would have been preferable to the agony I was experiencing. My face – my whole head – ached with an intensity it's impossible to describe.

So on my way back to my lodgings late that afternoon, I decided to call in at the dentist's office in the hope that he would still be in. But the dentist wasn't there, and neither was his office: where the building used to be, there was a hole in the ground. A giant cavity, you might say.

Now I did cry, standing on the pavement, looking into the hole and blubbing like a baby. I cried until my handkerchief was sodden, and realised that it wasn't doing my toothache any good.

There was nothing for it; I had to carry on. The sun was getting low in the sky, and soon the blackout would be in effect.

I let myself into the house, planning to creep upstairs to my room, bury my head under my pillow, and wait for a bomb to fall on it to put me out of my misery. But Vera must have heard my key in the lock, as she quickly emerged from the kitchen with a grin on her face.

'Come on through!' she commanded, beckoning me.

It was too early for Vera to be home, I realised through my pain. She had farther to come from her Oxford Street shop; she never got back before I did.

I followed her obediently into the kitchen. 'What are you doing here so early?'

'Sit down and I'll tell you.' She made a dramatic gesture in the direction of the kitchen table.

I sat. The way I was feeling, I couldn't do much else.

Vera's grin was splitting her face in two. 'I'm home early 'cause the shop was bombed out last night. It's gone.'

For the life of me, I couldn't understand why that would make her so happy. 'But that means you don't have a job.'

'Oh, but I do!' She flopped onto the chair opposite me. 'I didn't tell you about this sooner because I wasn't sure it was going to work out. But now it's all set, and the shop getting bombed just makes it easier. I'm going to get out of this bloody city! I'm leaving!'

I could hardly take in what she was saying. 'You're leaving?' I echoed stupidly.

'Tomorrow!' Vera gestured towards a battered suitcase

standing by the door, along with her gas mask. 'I'm packed, I'm ready to go.'

It all spilled out of her then: the plan she'd been hatching for weeks.

This had all come about, she told me, through one of her customers at the now-demolished shop. The customer had a friend in the West Country who was desperately looking for a girl to help her out as a cook at her boarding house. The woman had sent Vera a train ticket; she was leaving tomorrow.

I said the first thing that came into my head. 'But you can't cook! Did you tell her you could cook?'

Vera shrugged, then winked at me. 'I might have exaggerated just a bit. I'm sure I'll manage, and I'll learn on the job.' She reached for her handbag, which was sitting on the table, and extracted a wad of papers. 'Look. You can read the letters. She's desperate, like I said.'

She slapped them down in front of me and I flipped through them obediently, getting the general idea. Previous cook had joined the ATS, no one else suitable could be found, come as soon as possible. Light housekeeping duties, cooking for up to twelve people, room and board provided plus a modest salary. The last letter in the bundle contained instructions on finding the boarding house, and a train ticket to Bradford-on-Avon. A single, not a return.

I closed my eyes, feeling sicker than ever. I was going to lose my only friend. She was walking out of my life tomorrow.

Unworthily, I suppose, I was a bit hurt – hurt that she hadn't confided in me.

And even less worthily, I was envious. How wonderful it would be, I thought, to escape like that. Away from London and the bombs. Away from Aunt Iris. Away to the peaceful countryside. Light housekeeping duties and cooking – what bliss.

I put my head in my hands.

'Are you all right?' Vera asked belatedly, as she tucked the letters into her handbag and put it by her suitcase. 'You look all done in.'

'Toothache,' I said tersely, holding my jaw.

'Oh, poor you.' She jumped up. 'I'll tell you what. I'm going to cook us a slap-up tea tonight. I can use up all my rations – I can't really take them with me, can I? And it will give me some practice,' she added with a cheeky twinkle.

The last thing I felt like doing was eating anything, much less something cooked by Vera's inexpert hands. But I was too stunned to move.

Vera reached for the frying pan. 'Sausages and a bit of bacon. And eggs, of course.' She put the frying pan on the hob and disappeared into the larder.

When she emerged, a minute later, her arms laden with what seemed an unimaginable amount of food for one meal, I took in for the first time what she was wearing. It was my old housecoat, the one I wore in my room on Sunday afternoons when I didn't have to go anywhere. 'My housecoat,' I said, startled.

'I knew you wouldn't mind.' Vera deposited her load on

the table. 'I'd packed all of my clothes, except for my travelling costume, and I didn't want to wear that for cooking.'

She set about her task with more determination than skill, tossing the rashers of bacon and sausages into the frying pan, turning up the heat.

A few minutes later, she scooped out the charred meat and broke the eggs into the grease.

That was when the siren went off. Early – much earlier than usual.

'Oh, bugger it,' Vera said.

A few seconds later Mrs Short rushed through the kitchen, on her way to the back door and the Anderson shelter. 'Come along, girls,' she said as she skirted the table. 'You can have your tea later.' She yanked the light cord by the door just before she opened it, plunging the kitchen into darkness.

Our landlady was quickly followed by Mr Robbins, the other lodger. 'Hurry up,' he said over his shoulder. 'I think it's going to be a bad one tonight.'

It was the first time Mr Robbins had been here for over a week, which was fine with us; his occasional presence in the shelter was an irritant at the very least, with his bad breath and his dubious sense of humour.

'I suppose we'd better go now,' I said reluctantly, rubbing my jaw and starting to stand.

'Bugger it,' Vera repeated defiantly. 'Let's just stay here and eat our tea. It's my last night.' She went to the door, closed it with a shove, and pulled the cord to turn the overhead light back on.

On this occasion, I didn't take much convincing. The way I was feeling, I wasn't sure I would survive a long evening in the shelter in close proximity to Mrs Short's snores and Mr Robbins' noxious breath.

Vera dished up the greasy eggs and burnt meat, then put the plates on the table with a flourish, as if she were serving up a delectable banquet. 'Oh, bugger, I've forgot to brew the tea,' she exclaimed. She went back to the range and slammed the kettle on the hob. 'Go ahead and start, ducky. Don't wait for me,' she ordered.

I could hear the planes droning overhead. The bombs started, and they weren't that far away. Closer than I'd ever heard them before. Without enthusiasm, I forked a bit of egg into my mouth. Pain shot through my head.

Closer, and closer yet.

Then there was an almighty crash, so near it seemed to be just outside of the back door.

Without thinking, I jumped up and ran to the door.

'The blackout! Don't open the door!' Vera shouted.

And then there was an even more deafening crash, immediately overhead, and the ceiling came down.

I'm not sure how long I was unconscious. It might have been a matter of seconds, or perhaps a few minutes. Maybe even longer. I opened my eyes and looked at the search lights criss-crossing the sky above me, through a pall of smoke.

I remembered in that instant exactly what had happened. I was lying on the floor, but the back door frame had protected me from things falling from above. Gingerly I moved my arms, my legs. I seemed to be intact.

No worries now about violating the blackout: the kitchen, or whatever was left of it, was in darkness. Holding on to the door frame, I dragged myself to my feet and opened the back door.

There was a huge smoking crater in the back garden, where the Anderson shelter had been. A direct hit.

'Vera!' I cried. 'The Anderson's been hit! It's gone.' If we'd been in the shelter as usual, we would have been gone as well. I tried not to think about Mrs Short and Mr Robbins.

There was no answer from Vera.

I closed the door, carefully, and found the torch I kept in my skirt pocket. I switched it on and played it over what was left of the kitchen.

It took me a moment to find her, picking my way gingerly through the rubble.

She was on the floor, by the range. The range – ancient but sturdy – had evidently protected her legs. But her head, and much of the upper part of her body . . . were gone. Just gone.

Shocked to the core, sickened, I'm afraid that I vomited up whatever was in my stomach. I sank to the floor and clung to the table leg, shaking and crying.

Again, I'm not sure how long I was there. Dimly I heard the sound of sirens – not air-raid sirens, but the kind of sirens that meant emergency vehicles were on the way. Wardens, fire engines, paramedics, ambulances.

No paramedic in the world was going to be able to do anything for poor Vera. Nor for Mrs Short or Mr Robbins.

Me? I was, miraculously, all right. At least physically. At least, apart from my toothache. Which no longer seemed quite so important.

Without me here to tell them, I realised, the wardens wouldn't even know who Vera was.

It was then that I had the very first germ of my idea.

I got up and picked my way back to the door, with the help of my torch.

Vera's suitcase was there, just where she'd left it. Along with her gas mask and her handbag. Covered with a layer of dust and debris, but still there.

With a tiny stab of conscience, and a muttered prayer for forgiveness, I thumbed open the clasp of her handbag.

The letters from her new employer were there – I'd seen her put them there.

Her ration book was tucked into the back pocket. She must have retrieved it, I realised, from the spot behind the sugar canister where Mrs Short kept the household's ration books, her own and her lodgers' alike. I wondered whether Vera had told Mrs Short that she was going, or whether she had planned to do a flit. Not that it mattered any more.

And there was, of course, her identity card, as well as a thick wad of various other papers, including a duplicate birth certificate in the name of Vera V******. It was an unusual name, and I realised that I'd never before known what Vera's surname was. The subject had never come up.

I found her purse near the bottom of the handbag. It

held a few coins. Enough for a bus fare, or a cheese roll. Not enough to start a new life.

Beneath it, though, was a roll of banknotes. A large roll.

That was when I had a major attack of conscience.

I couldn't take Vera's money, I told myself sternly. I was a vicar's daughter. I'd never done a deliberately dishonest thing in my life.

But if I didn't take it, what would happen to it? Vera didn't need it any more, that was certain. And she had no family, no one to benefit from it.

The Crown would confiscate it, probably, if some crooked Warden didn't lift it first.

The sirens were getting nearer.

A new life. Was I brave enough to seize the chance?

If I went now, with Vera's case and her gas mask and her handbag, no one would know. No one would care.

They would find poor headless Vera, dressed in my old house-coat, and they would think it was me. Especially if I left my handbag nearby, with my identity card.

We were a similar size, a similar shape. No one would know.

Father would be sad, of course, I thought with a slight pang. And Aunt Iris would be furious, to be robbed of her slave. Ha!

But I would be . . . free. Free as a bird.

In the country, away from the cruel bombs. Light house-keeping duties and cooking.

I knew what Vera would have done, and somehow that made it easier. Vera would have seized the chance. She would have been brave enough – I had no doubt about that.

So I put my handbag on the remains of the kitchen table. I found Vera's coat on a peg by the door, and put it on. It fit like it belonged to me. I slung Vera's gas mask over my shoulder, slid the strap of her handbag over my arm, and picked up her suitcase.

I won't pretend that the journey itself was easy. Just getting to Paddington Station was difficult enough, let alone the train to the West Country. The train was crowded, smelly, slow; it seemed to take days. I was hungry and exhausted, still in shock, still suffering from toothache.

But I'll pass over all that, because when the train finally stopped at Bradford-on-Avon, I truly felt that the slate had been wiped clean and I was starting my life over. Reborn.

I was Vera V******. I was fearless; there was nothing I couldn't do.

My new employer was kind and suitably grateful. The duties were not in the least onerous. And Bradford was like paradise, after the hell-hole that London had become. After just a few days, my old life seemed like a bad dream from which I'd now awoken.

The thing that refused to leave me, though, was the toothache. Some days it was almost bearable; other days it drilled into my skull like a jackhammer. I couldn't go on ignoring it forever.

So one afternoon, when I'd finished clearing up after the midday meal, I sought out a dentist.

Directed by a helpful woman in the queue at the

butcher's shop, I found one in Bridge Street, near the town bridge and the tea rooms. Amazingly, I was told by the receptionist that Mr Timmons could see me that day, and the wait wouldn't be long. She gave me a card to fill out with my name and contact information. I'd scarcely finished it when I was called through to the consulting room.

Mr Timmons was a rather elderly gentleman, nicely spoken, with a reassuring air of competence. He introduced himself to me and shook my hand, then said, 'Now, my dear, if you'll just pop into the chair, and open your mouth for me, we'll soon get you sorted.'

I opened my mouth.

Mr Timmons tutted, then frowned. 'Nasty,' he said. 'It's cracked all the way through. It must be very painful.'

I nodded.

'You should have come sooner,' he chided gently. 'A week ago, I might have been able to save it. But now there's nothing for it. That tooth will have to come out.'

To say that the next half hour was unpleasant would be a vast understatement. The pain that tooth had given me over the past days was nothing to what I was in for in Mr Timmons' chair.

When it was all over, and I had a wad of cotton wool wedged in my bloody mouth, Mr Timmons patted me on the shoulder. 'Brave girl,' he said. 'Well done. You'll be fine now.'

I dragged myself out of the chair.

'Keep your mouth well rinsed out with salt water and take it easy for a day or two,' he said. 'If you can. Miss . . . ?'

'V******,' I responded as best I could through the cotton wool.

Mr Timmons frowned. 'V******? That's an unusual name.'

'Vera V******,' I repeated. 'Thank you, Mr Timmons.'

It was a few days later that the police came to the boarding house, looking for me. Fortunately I happened to be alone there that morning, in the kitchen, washing up after breakfast. I'd been humming to myself, one of the silly popular songs that Vera liked to sing. I answered the bell to find two men on the doorstep.

They introduced themselves to me as Detective Inspector Jennings and Detective Sergeant Boyd. 'We're looking for a Vera V******,' said the former, an older man with a seamed, hound-dog face.

'I'm Vera V******,' I confirmed. And I was – I was wearing one of Vera's pretty frocks under my pinny, and Vera's red lipstick.

'We'd like to ask you a few questions,' DS Boyd said, a West Country burr in his voice. He was the younger of the two, taller and not bad looking. 'May we come in?'

'Yes, of course.' I led them into the empty residents' lounge, my heart jumping uncomfortably in my chest. I'm Vera, I reminded myself. I'm not afraid of anything.

'May we see your identity card, please?' DI Jennings asked. His voice was polite, but he narrowed his eyes in a way that was not friendly.

I fetched my handbag and produced the card for them.

DI Jennings inspected it minutely, then handed it to his colleague, who followed suit, before giving it back to me.

He folded his arms across his chest and regarded me with that squinty look. 'You see, miss, we have reason to believe that you are not Vera V******.'

My heart twisted and plummeted, but I think that I kept my face perfectly still. 'But that's silly,' I said. 'I've showed you my identity card.'

'Do you have any other form of identification? Any other documents? A birth certificate, perhaps?'

I did. Vera's papers were no longer in my handbag; I'd put them in a safe place in my room, at the bottom of the chest of drawers. 'Just a moment,' I said.

A few minutes later I handed him the birth certificate. He scrutinised it, then shook his head. 'This is a duplicate, miss,' he pointed out. 'Not the original.'

'What difference does that make? It proves that I'm Vera V******.'

'It proves no such thing. Anyone can get a duplicate birth certificate, miss. You just have to go to Somerset House and ask for it.'

'But why—'

He cut across my words. 'Have you ever heard of identity theft, miss?'

I shook my head. Identity theft. I'd done it, of course, but I'd never heard it called that.

'It happens more than you'd think. If someone wants to disappear. They take the name of a real person who died, someone round their own age, and get a duplicate birth certificate issued in that name. And that's what we think you've done, miss.'

'No!' My indignation was real; I'd done no such thing. What I'd done had been ... instinctive. Spur-of-the-minute. They were talking about deliberate fraud. 'Why would you think that?'

'Sit down, miss.'

I sat, and the policeman with the hound-dog face explained.

They'd been alerted, he said, by a Mr Timmons, a local dentist. Mr Timmons had treated a young woman recently, and she had given her name as Vera V*****. But Mr Timmons, who had a good memory for his age, and also kept very thorough records, recalled that he had once had a patient by that name. And Vera V***** had died of meningitis at the age of twelve, half a dozen or so years ago. He still had her records, which he had checked, and they in no way matched the teeth of the young woman he had treated.

'There could be two people by that name,' I said defiantly. But my mind was racing. If Vera – my Vera – wasn't really Vera, then who was she? Why had she stolen the identity of a dead girl?

'There could be,' he agreed, his eyebrows signalling that he didn't believe that for a minute. 'We'll be going now, miss,' he said, leading his colleague to the door. 'But we'll be back.'

The younger, better-looking policeman turned for just a second at the door, and I swear that he winked at me. At *me*.

They might be back. But there was no way they could

prove anything, I told myself. And surely, in the middle of a war, they had better things to do than pursue a mere question of identity.

I squared my shoulders as I closed the front door firmly behind them.

I might not know who that girl was – my brave friend, who was now almost certainly buried under my former name. But I knew who I was. I was Vera. And I wasn't afraid of anything.

Kate Charles, a past Chairman of the Crime Writers' Association and the Barbara Pym Society, is American by birth but has lived in England for many years. A former parish administrator, she sets her books against the colourful backdrop of the Church of England. She has been co-organiser of the annual St. Hilda's Crime and Mystery Conference in Oxford since its beginnings in 1994 and was awarded the George N. Dove Award for her 'outstanding contribution to the serious study of mystery and crime fiction'. She lives on the English side of the Welsh borders with her husband and their Border Terrier.

The Mole Catcher's Daughter

Kate Ellis

As a young crime fiction fan – when writing crime novels of my own was just a distant dream – I have happy memories of settling down in front of the TV to watch the latest episode of Cribb. *With its intriguing mysteries and colourful portrayal of the life of a Victorian detective (dealing with many of the late nineteenth century's most topical issues)* Cribb *soon became essential viewing and gradually I became aware of its creator's name appearing in the credits. That name was Peter Lovesey.*

In addition to enjoying Alan Dobie's excellent TV portrayal of the eponymous detective, I became an avid reader of the Sergeant Cribb books. And from that time on, every time Peter Lovesey brought out another novel my heart has lifted as I've grabbed it eagerly off the shelves. Peter is one of the most talented and original crime writers at work today and I couldn't resist paying tribute to his first creation, Sergeant Cribb and his sidekick, Constable Thackeray, in The Mole Catcher's Daughter. *It only remains for me to wish Peter the happiest of special birthdays and many more excellent books to come.*

*

'Uncle Ted, when am I going to meet the sergeant?' We were on our way to St John's Wood when I asked my uncle the question that had been on my mind since we set out.

My uncle turned his head to look at me but it was hard to read his expression because his impressive beard has grown so bushy of late.

'You'll meet him presently. At this moment he's hot on the trail of the Paddington Strangler and, according to Chief Inspector Jowett, three unfortunate women take priority over one dead parlour maid. It's just you and me, my lad – two Thackerays together – but I'm sure we'll manage.' My uncle tapped the side of his nose. 'This'll be your chance to show those in charge what you're made of.'

I'd joined Scotland Yard with great hopes of being elevated to the new Criminal Investigation Department and I couldn't deny I was nervous. But Uncle Ted had a great deal of experience of plain clothes work so I knew I could rely on his guidance.

When we arrived at the house I was much impressed by its appearance. Although not of the grandest proportions, the white stucco villa stood in extensive lawned gardens and the surrounding trees lent it an air of isolation, even in that pleasant London suburb.

The perfection of the scene, however, was marred by small mounds of earth dotted over the fine lawn in front of the house, as if some eager treasure hunter had been digging for gold in random spots.

'Moles. Pesky little varmints,' Uncle Ted announced sagely as we approached the front door.

'Shouldn't we go round to the back, Uncle Ted?'

'The sergeant always prefers to use the front door when it's a murder,' he replied with a sniff.

'But we don't know if it is murder yet,' I pointed out. 'She might have poisoned herself by accident. Or taken her own life.'

Uncle Ted shook his head. 'According to the constable who attended the scene, no poison was found in her room. And she hadn't been out of doors all evening so she couldn't have taken it elsewhere. You'll learn, lad.'

'So she was poisoned by someone in the household?'

'Either that or she had a visitor. Shouldn't take us long to find out.'

'Some dastardly married sweetheart who wanted rid of her?' I said, my imagination conjuring all sorts of vile scenarios.

Uncle rolled his eyes and I could sense his frustration. I knew he'd rather be with Sergeant Cribb searching for the man the newspapers were calling the Paddington Strangler, but a woman had died and it was our duty to investigate. He operated the bell pull and I heard a harsh jangling within the house.

It was a full minute before the door was answered by a woman who was taller than the average. Thin with sharp features, she wore a black dress that hung off her gaunt frame and her dull brown hair, peppered with grey, gave her a severe look. She introduced herself as Mrs Keeler, Mr Guard's housekeeper, and I noted that her voice was deep and she pronounced her words carefully as though she was making a great effort to sound as refined as her social betters. As we were led into the drawing room, she told us her master was most upset about the recent tragedy.

Mr Guard stood as we entered the room. He was a diminutive, nervous man, half a head shorter than the housekeeper who'd returned to her duties as soon as she'd announced their arrival.

'What can I do for you, Sergeant?' The question came out in a squeak.

'Er ... it's Constable actually. Constable Thackeray at your service. And this is ... er, also Constable Thackeray.'

The man before us gave a nervous giggle. 'A job lot. I apologise, gentlemen, but recent events have disturbed me somewhat.'

'I quite understand, sir. Can you tell us what happened?' I said, earning myself a sideways glance from Uncle who, as the senior man, had assumed he'd be doing the talking.

Thankfully we were invited to sit before Mr Guard began his story – which turned out to be a long and convoluted one which I shall endeavour to simplify.

First thing that morning the parlour maid, a young woman called Eliza Crilley, failed to attend to her daily duties and when Mrs Keeler went down to her room in the basement to investigate, she found her dead, her body in a convulsed position on her bed, a dreadful grimace on her face. Mr Guard had been summoned immediately. It was most alarming, he said, and he hoped he'd never have to see the like of it again. The doctor was called and, having dismissed the possibility of lockjaw, he pronounced that she'd been poisoned. He suspected strychnine because he considered himself something of an expert on such matters.

'What time did the doctor say she died?' I asked because one glance at Uncle told me the account had rendered him speechless.

'He estimated it was shortly after she retired to bed and he suspects the noxious substance was administered in the cocoa she always drank last thing at night. Not that I'm familiar with her habits, of course, but that's what Mrs Keeler told me and an empty cup was found beside her bed. Eliza and Mrs Keeler are the only staff who live in and Mrs Keeler's room is on the upper floor so she was quite unaware of anything amiss. The doctor says poor Eliza must have suffered terrible convulsions, quite audible to those nearby, but in her isolation ...'

Guard took out a silk handkerchief and dabbed his eyes although I could see no sign of tears. Then he looked up, focusing his eyes on me rather than Uncle. 'I believe I know who is responsible,' he said in a whisper that sounded more like a hiss.

'Who might that be, sir?' my uncle asked, his notebook to the ready with pen poised over the page to write down the culprit's name.

'Early yesterday evening Mrs Keeler saw Eliza having words with the mole catcher. I asked Mrs Keeler to see to the matter but it seems Eliza was anxious to take on the task.'

'The mole catcher?'

'His name's Plum but, from the little I've seen of him, I wouldn't have thought him a violent man. However, Mrs Keeler tells me that strychnine is one of the tools of his trade.'

'Indeed,' my uncle said, as though he was familiar with the world of moles and their execution.

'Why did you ask Mrs Keeler to speak to Plum?'

'Because his treatment of the front lawn has failed. His poison has had no effect and I wished to complain,' said Mr Guard. 'As Eliza's room is in the basement anybody could have sneaked in there at the relevant time without alerting the rest of the household,' he added.

'And who is in your household, sir? Perhaps your wife . . . '

'I am unmarried, Constable. There is just myself and my lodger Mr Bennett who is out of the house at present. He works in a bank nearby. Mr Bennett is a mainstay of our local Amateur Dramatic Society, a pastime that occupies most of his spare time. And Mrs Keeler lives in, as I mentioned before.'

'How long has she worked for you?'

'Just three weeks. She came with the most excellent references. A woman of impeccable character by all accounts.'

'And the unfortunate Eliza?'

'A year. We also have a cook and a cleaner who come in daily and a woman who does the laundry each week. We are not a large household but,' his lips twitched upwards, 'I'd always hoped we were a happy one.'

'How were Eliza's relations with the rest of the household?'

'Very good, as far as I know. Mrs Keeler always spoke highly of her.'

'What is it you do for a living if you don't mind me asking, sir,' I asked, suddenly curious.

Guard's look told me he thought my question impertinent. 'I am the owner of four chemist's shops in the city.'

'You sell strychnine?' I asked, earning myself a stern look from Uncle Ted.

Guard looked flustered. 'Small quantities are used in some medicines, yes, but ... Is that relevant to your enquiries?'

Before I could reply my uncle spoke again. 'I think it's time we saw the body, sir, if that's convenient.'

I glanced out of the French window at the lawn ruined by the efforts of those industrious little creatures condemned to a hideous death by the man sitting before me, with Mr Plum assuming the role of the public executioner. And I suppressed a shudder.

It was Mrs Keeler who led us down the bare steps to the basement. Although it was a warm spring day, it seemed colder down there somehow. And darker. But this was where Eliza Crilley had lived and died.

Mrs Keeler marched gracelessly ahead of us down a narrow corridor and when I asked her how she got on with Eliza Crilley, she replied that she was a good and willing worker. Then she became more candid and revealed that Eliza had a taste for followers and she'd often had cause to chastise her for flirting with the tradesmen. It was clear that, with her employer out of earshot, she had no misgivings about speaking ill of the dead.

'Why did Eliza argue with the mole catcher?' I asked, taking advantage of her indiscreet mood. 'You say she flirted with tradesmen. Could she and the mole catcher have been sweethearts? Did you overhear a lovers' tiff?'

Mrs Keeler sniffed. 'He's old enough to be her father. But nothing would surprise me.'

'Mr Guard asked you to speak to him about his shoddy work, I believe?'

'That's right. But I had matters to attend to so Eliza offered to do it. Like I said, she was a willing worker. I can only assume that Plum didn't like the criticism.'

We had reached the door of Eliza's room and Mrs Keeler pushed it open before standing back and averting her eyes from what lay inside.

Somebody, the doctor perhaps, had covered Eliza's body with a sheet. Uncle Ted hesitated a moment before stepping forward and pulling it back to reveal the poor woman's face. I only glimpsed it a second before he flicked it back.

'Best not look, lad,' he whispered before marching from the room.

I hung back and when Uncle and Mrs Keeler were halfway down the corridor, I approached the bed and pulled the sheet back gently to reveal the corpse's face. What I saw made me catch my breath. Since joining the Force, I have come face to face with death many times but the look on the poor girl's contorted face brought to mind one who has seen the horrors of hell. I covered her up again and hurried from the room.

Half an hour later Uncle and I left the house. And as we walked towards the gate I saw a small heap of earth erupting like a miniature volcano on the manicured lawn beside the path.

George Plum's home was a small terraced cottage in the Lisson Grove area. A plaque next to his shabby front door told the passer-by that he was a Purveyor of Pest Control to the Gentry.

Uncle left it to me to raise the knocker and when the door opened he stepped forward.

Standing in the doorway was the most beautiful girl I have ever set eyes on. She was dainty of build with long fair locks held back with a blue ribbon the colour of her eyes and her red generous lips were slightly parted, as though Uncle's arrival had startled her. I felt it my duty to assure her that there was nothing to fear so I edged Uncle out of the way and held out my hand and introduced myself . . . which isn't how we are trained to do things at Scotland Yard. She took my hand, her eyes meeting mine, and I was aware of Uncle's disapproving glare.

'Now then, miss,' he said in a voice I can only describe as gruff. 'Is your father at home?'

Without a word she stood aside, watching me through lowered lashes. Then she instructed us to follow her and led us into the back yard where we found her father at work in a brick outhouse, pouring liquid into bottles with great care. When he became aware of our presence he barked at us to stay back, saying that the task he was performing was highly dangerous.

Once he had finished he washed his hands thoroughly under a rusty tap in the yard and I saw the girl pass him a towel before disappearing into the house.

Plum was a small man, bald with a pointed nose and the wizened look of one who spends a lot of time out of doors. My first thought was that he rather resembled the moles he sent to their eternal rest.

'What is it you want?' he said in an accent as thick as Uncle's own.

'You've been working at the house of a Mr Guard in Goldcrest Avenue, St John's Wood.'

Plum folded his arms. 'I wouldn't have thought he'd call you in for something so trifling. It's between me and him.'

'What is?' I asked.

'The moles. He said my poison hadn't worked and the blighters had taken on a new lease of life. I said I'd given the little bleeders enough strychnine to wipe out half the moles in London but he wasn't having any of it. Didn't even have the gumption to make his own complaint. Sent a slip of a girl to do his dirty work. Even the housekeeper never showed herself.'

'Was the girl's name Eliza?' I asked.

'She didn't introduce herself. But by her uniform, I'd say she's the parlour maid. Why don't you ask her?'

'That would be hard,' Uncle Ted said bluntly. 'She's dead and the doctor reckons she was poisoned with strychnine ... the stuff you use.'

Plum's mouth fell open and he shook his head. Despite my tender years I can recognise a liar when I see one and I reckoned his shock was genuine.

'According to a witness you argued with the girl,' Uncle said.

There was a long silence before he answered. 'My quarrel was with her master, not her. And I told her so.'

'The housekeeper heard raised voices.'

Plum sighed. 'I was angry and I'm sorry if I took it out on the girl. She was just the messenger and I had no reason to wish her dead. Why should I?'

'You'd never met Eliza Crilley before?' I asked, trying to see Plum in the role of Eliza's caddish lover and failing abysmally. I had seen her face and, even in its contorted state, I could tell that in life she'd been pretty enough to attract a more desirable kind of follower. Plum didn't even possess the attraction of riches which, I've heard, can make many a plain middle-aged man alluring to the opposite sex.

The mole catcher shook his head. 'Never in my life. My daughter, Jane, will tell you. Since my dear wife passed over she helps me with my work.'

'Did she accompany you to Mr Guard's residence yesterday?' I asked, suddenly eager to see her again.

'As a matter of fact, she did. And she witnessed my altercation with the unfortunate maid,' he added with a note of triumph. It seemed he had a witness. Although was a devoted daughter a reliable one?

He called Jane's name and she reappeared, wiping her hand on her clean white apron.

She was quick to back up her father's story, repeating his account unprompted, and I saw Uncle nod, as though he was satisfied we'd got to the truth.

I turned to Plum, who was looking pleased with himself. 'Did you at any time leave your poisons unattended while you were working at the house?'

'Of course. I never thought anything of it.'

'So anyone could have helped themselves?'

'I suppose ... ' Plum now wore a worried frown. 'But there's none missing. I would have noticed.'

I heard Jane's voice again. 'Father's right. There's no poison missing. I check the levels each night when we finish work.' She hesitated. 'I don't know whether this is important but after the maid had spoken to Father I saw a young man accost her at the back door. He was young, smartly dressed with dark hair and the most magnificent moustache,' she added with a pleasing flutter of her fine eyelashes. 'I noticed it particular.'

'You didn't catch his name, by any chance?' I asked, touching my own moustache which, although far from magnificent, I hoped would impress given time.

'No. But I'd seen him before. It is my belief that he lives there.'

I remembered Mr Guard mentioning a young lodger; a Mr Bennett who was employed in a nearby bank. It seemed that would be our next port of call.

As we departed I caught Miss Plum's eye and she gave me a coy smile.

'Will you be coming back?' she said as I passed her at the door.

Uncle gave my arm a hefty nudge. To my regret it was time to go.

The Manager of Pollard's bank clearly wasn't pleased when Uncle asked for a private word with Mr Bennett. I hoped that, should the young man prove entirely innocent of wrongdoing, his employer wouldn't make him suffer for our intrusion.

Mr Bennett, a lowly clerk, was permitted to use a poky unoccupied office behind the counter for our interview. He was indeed a good-looking young man and, although a few aitches were dropped here and there, he was well spoken and personable. Mind you, during my short time in the Force, I've learned not to judge too much by appearances.

'I'm shocked by what happened to Eliza,' Bennett began before Uncle could ask his first question. 'It was an appalling accident.'

'What makes you think it was an accident?' Uncle asked.

Bennett looked puzzled. 'I assumed ... Eliza had no reason to harm herself so what else could it be?'

'We're treating it as a case of murder,' Uncle said. 'You were seen talking to her yesterday soon after she had words with the mole catcher.'

'That's right, Constable. I told her it wasn't fair that Mr Guard should send her to do his dirty work. If he had a complaint he should have spoken to the man himself or at least sent Mrs Keeler.'

'According to Mrs Keeler, Eliza volunteered to speak to him.'

'That's just like Eliza. Mrs Keeler shouldn't have taken advantage of her good nature.'

As I watched his expression I recalled Mr Guard's revelation that Bennett had a taste for amateur dramatics. If his indignation on Eliza's behalf was feigned he would be an asset to any company of players.

'Did you notice anybody near Mr Plum's store of poisons in his absence?'

Bennett shook his head.

'What was your relationship with Eliza?'

Despite the man's famed acting abilities he couldn't suppress a blush. 'She was the parlour maid.'

'You were swift to leap to her defence when you thought she'd been given a task that was none of her concern.'

Bennett hesitated for a few moments. 'Very well, I confess I was fond of Eliza. But I assure you nothing improper took place.'

'Do you know anything that might throw any light on her tragic death?' I asked, glancing at Uncle who was listening attentively as though he approved of my question.

'There is one thing, but I'm not sure . . .'

'We need to know everything,' I said. 'However trivial it seems.'

'Very well.' He took a deep breath. 'Eliza and I used to meet in her room in the basement. Mrs Keeler's quarters are at the top of the house so Eliza was often on her own down there. She was a jolly sort of girl and I enjoyed her company. She had a taste for detective novels and there was nothing she liked better than a mystery. She followed notable cases in the newspapers and she was taking a particular interest in this Paddington Strangler. She liked to pick through every detail, even down to the police finding traces of red wool on the victims' necks.'

'Did she form any theories?' I couldn't resist asking the question.

'Oh, she always had some theory or other on the go. Then yesterday evening she told me she'd discovered something she intended to take to the police.'

Uncle caught my eye. 'Any idea what that something was?'

Bennett shook his head. 'When I asked her she said she'd tell me when she was certain.'

'Is that all?'

'She told me it was something surprising; said I'd be amazed.'

'Did she leave the house much?' I asked.

'Not often. Sometimes on a Sunday afternoon we'd go for a stroll in the park. She was from the country and I think I was her only friend in London.'

'Believe him?' Uncle Ted asked as we left the bank.

'I'm not sure,' I said. Because I wasn't. Bennett was plausible but he could easily have helped himself to Plum's poison if he'd been so minded.

'Perhaps Bennett himself was the source of her amazing

discovery,' I said. 'Perhaps he's trying to throw us off the scent.'

When we reached the station there was no sign of Sergeant Cribb and I could sense my uncle's disappointment. He'd hoped to share what we'd learned and take advantage of his superior's wisdom but the sergeant was still out pursuing the Paddington Strangler. Then, on his return, he would have to report his findings to Chief Inspector Jowett who was pacing his office like a caged lion, waiting for news.

And news came in the form of a plump constable who rushed into the station, stopping to catch his breath before addressing the sergeant behind the front desk.

'There's been another one, Sarg. Woman found in an alley. Doctor reckons she's been there since last night.'

'The Strangler?' I asked.

The constable confirmed that it was the same as the others. Then he continued. 'A man walking home from the Rose and Crown saw someone sneak out of the alley at eleven last night. He got a good look at him in the street light: around thirty; clean shaven; average height. Similar description to last time so I'd lay odds on it being our man. The sergeant's at the scene and he's not pleased, I can tell you. This monster's getting bolder by the minute.'

Before I could say anything the front door swung open and a young woman burst in. My heart performed a somersault when I recognised her as Jane Plum. And it was me she wished to speak to.

She took me to one side and I could see my uncle watching, straining to overhear what she had to say. But she lowered her voice. 'Something strange is going on,' she said.

When I asked her what she meant she began to explain, speaking in a whisper.

'Father had another complaint today. The moles of the district are thriving in spite of his best efforts. I think some-one's stolen some of his poison and swapped it for some harmless substance.'

I caught on fast. 'So somebody helped themselves to your Father's poison and used it to kill Eliza Crilley?'

'Yes. And I reckon this latest batch of poison smells very like the tonic Father takes as a pick me up. Looks almost the same too so ... '

'Your father substituted it by accident?'

'That's impossible. He takes the greatest care. Besides, none of his tonic is missing.'

'What tonic does he use?'

'Pulkinghorn's Perfect Pick Me Up. It's widely used by many men of a certain age, I believe.'

'When could the substitution have been made?'

'Mr Guard has two lawns, both plagued by moles of the most energetic kind. He treated one lawn two days before Eliza's death with the desired results. But the following day he treated the other and the moles carried on, bolder than ever. Father says the grass looks like a battlefield. It's the same with the garden he visited earlier today. I can only think that whoever killed Eliza changed the poison for the tonic on the day before her death when Father left his equipment unattended in Mr Guard's outhouse.'

As she spoke, ideas were forming in my head. Ideas so fantastic that I feared Uncle Ted would mock me if I voiced them. Then all of a sudden I was seized by an impulse to put my theories to the test and one look at Jane Plum's lovely face gave me fresh courage. 'Meet me this evening at Mr Guard's at a quarter past seven,' I said. 'Bring your father. Tell him Mr Guard wishes to discuss his moles.'

Jane only hesitated a moment before agreeing.

Uncle didn't seem too happy about the arrangements I'd made.

'I hope you know what you're doing, my lad,' he said gruffly but I didn't reply. My hopes echoed his own. If I failed and the sergeant found out about it, my ambition to enter the Criminal Investigation Department would come to nothing.

For the rest of the day I trudged the streets questioning all the mole catchers who operated in the district.

It was a risk I had to take.

Uncle and I arrived at Mr Guard's house at seven on the dot and when Mrs Keeler greeted us at the door she didn't look pleased about our arrival. Mr Guard, however, received us with wary curiosity and asked if there was any news. His question sounded like that of an innocent man but my mind was open to all possibilities.

Uncle Ted asked him to summon Mr Bennett and Mrs Keeler and when Bennett entered the room he fiddled with his shirt cuffs like a man with an uneasy conscience. As he took his seat I couldn't help remembering the witness's description of the Paddington Strangler. Although the man described had been clean shaven whereas Bennett possessed a moustache.

When Mrs Keeler was asked to sit on the sofa by the fire she looked most uncomfortable and perched on the edge of her seat as though preparing to flee. At seven fifteen the doorbell rang and she was about to stand when I told her I'd perform her customary duty and greet the visitor.

The reaction in the room when I returned with Plum and his daughter, Jane, was one of surprise, not least from Uncle Ted who gave me a questioning frown. The newcomers were invited to sit but Plum, awkward in his working clothes, said he preferred to stand if that was all the same with Mr Guard. Whereas Jane sat down awkwardly on a hard chair near the door.

Plum twisted his cap round and round in his soil-stained fingers. 'You wish to talk about the moles, sir. I can only apologise and offer to repeat the treatment free of charge. I really can't understand why—'

I interrupted, addressing the assembled company. 'Does anybody present take Pulkinghorn's Perfect Pick Me Up for their health?'

Plum raised his hand and so did Guard who appeared startled by the question. 'I do. What of it?'

Jane rose to her feet. 'I can assure you that none of Father's tonic is missing. He has only one bottle and that was in the cabinet this morning.'

'I don't doubt it, Miss Plum,' I said, giving her a

reassuring smile. 'Mr Guard, would you be good enough to check if any of yours is missing.'

Guard looked uneasy. 'No need, constable. I noticed this morning that a full bottle has gone from the bathroom cupboard. It's a complete mystery.'

'No mystery to the moles, I fear,' I said. 'Somebody swapped your tonic for Mr Plum's poison.'

'Well, I'll be . . . ' Plum exclaimed. 'Who would do such a thing?'

'Someone who couldn't risk you noticing the substitution, Mr Plum. The colour of the poison you use and the tonic is similar, is it not? The moles have been given a pick-me-up instead of a death sentence. No wonder they thrive.'

I glanced at Uncle Ted and put my hand to my stomach, steadying myself on a handy side table. 'Mr Guard. I feel a little unwell. May I use your . . . er . . . '

Guard stood up. 'Of course, my man. Mrs Keeler will show you . . . '

Mrs Keeler led me upstairs and showed me into a bathroom off the landing. As I stepped into the room with its green tiles, water closet and large cast iron bath I thanked the housekeeper and told her I could manage and that she should return to the drawing room.

I locked the door and ran the basin tap. Then, after a while, I let myself out quietly and ventured onto the landing, checking there was nobody about. I knew what I was looking for. And when I'd located the correct room I searched until I found it. My bizarre theory had been proved right and I couldn't wait to tell Sergeant Cribb.

I returned to the bathroom and turned off the tap before rushing downstairs and when I burst into the drawing room all eyes turned on me. This was my moment.

I stood in the centre of the room surveying the curious faces.

'I guessed that whoever swapped Mr Guard's tonic for Mr Plum's poison had some knowledge of the mole-catching business so earlier today I visited all the mole catchers of the district and asked some questions,' I began. 'I interviewed a catcher in Paddington who has two sons, the elder of whom followed his father into the business. The other, he told me, went into service and lost touch with his family, much to his widowed father's distress. This younger son, according to his father, has been strange and troubled throughout his life.'

I saw Plum gazing at the floor as if he'd rather be elsewhere. I had certain articles hidden behind my back and now I held them up for all to see.

'I found these hidden in a wardrobe upstairs.' I held up a man's shirt – I'd left the rest of the outfit where I'd found it – and a scarf, stretched out of shape. A red woollen scarf.

'Where on earth did you find them?' Mr Guard asked. I could hear the tremble of fear in his voice.

I looked around the assembled faces. 'I forgot to say, the name of the retired mole catcher was Keeler.' I swung round to face the housekeeper. 'Any relation, Mrs Keeler?'

She was standing near the door and she took a step back. 'Never heard of him.'

'Are you acquainted with the Keelers, Mr Plum?'

Plum was staring at Mrs Keeler, a puzzled look on his face. 'Not well, but I do recall old Keeler had two boys and the younger was a great trial to his poor parents.'

'No daughter?' I stared at Mrs Keeler and when our eyes met I knew the truth at last.

'Not that I've heard. But now you come to mention it, I can see a resemblance to . . . '

His words trailed off and I saw Jane whisper something in her father's ear as Mrs Keeler shifted in her seat.

'I don't expect you looked into Mrs Keeler's references too closely, did you, Mr Guard?'

I saw Guard's eyes widen, horrified. 'They were impeccable.'

'Eliza stumbled on your secret, didn't she, Mrs Keeler? Did she find something in your room? It was the perfect cover, wasn't it? Who would suspect a woman of being the Paddington Strangler?'

Before I could say another word the individual we'd known as Mrs Keeler tore across the room and burst through the French windows. I took off after him, closely followed by Uncle Ted. I could hear my uncle wheezing behind me as I chased the killer across the lawn and was delighted when I saw our quarry fall flat on his face.

When I saw that he'd stumbled on a mole hill and the brown wig he'd worn to accomplish his deception had fallen off and was lying some feet away, I couldn't help smiling.

*

'Sergeant Cribb, may I introduce you to my nephew, Jeremiah. A fine lad.'

'And the man responsible for catching the Paddington Strangler, if I'm not mistaken.'

I stood to attention. 'I had that privilege, Sergeant.'

'Tell me, lad, how did you know it was Keeler?'

'I realised someone from the house must have poisoned Eliza and at first I suspected Bennett. Then when I realised the killer had swapped Mr Guard's pick-me-up for the strychnine used by Plum, I knew it was someone with knowledge of the mole-catching trade, so I made a few enquiries. I realised the housekeeper had gone to great pains to avoid having any dealings with Mr Plum and that she'd sent Eliza out to deal with him when Mr Guard had asked her to see to the matter herself. I wondered whether this was significant and now I realise it was. Keeler was afraid Plum might recognise him or at least see a family resemblance. She – or should I say he – even tried to incriminate Plum who, of course, was entirely innocent.'

'When did you realised Keeler was the strangler?'

'Eliza Crilley seemed a blameless young woman and, hearing Mr Bennett's account of her interest in the Strangler case, I began to wonder if she'd stumbled on something, although I wasn't entirely sure until I searched Keeler's room in the attic. We'll never know for certain but I suspect Eliza suspected there was something strange about Mrs Keeler and couldn't contain her curiosity. Perhaps she even went so far as searching her room: she did tell Bennett she'd found evidence she intended to take to the police.'

'Becoming a woman and a housekeeper to a respectable man was the perfect cover for Keeler,' said Cribb.

'He'd been in service before and he'd altered his glowing references, adding an "s" to make Mr into Mrs. Housekeepers always assume the title of Mrs, even when they're single.'

'Well done, Constable.' A small smile appeared on the sergeant's face. 'We could do with men like you in the Criminal Investigation Department. I'll have a word with Chief Inspector Jowett.'

My heart soared. 'Thank you, Sergeant.'

I walked out into the foggy London street with Uncle Ted by my side. I was meeting Jane Plum that evening after work and all was right with my world.

'Looking forward to working with you again, Detective Constable,' Uncle Ted said with a chuckle placing his hand on my shoulder.

Kate Ellis was born and brought up in Liverpool and studied drama in Manchester. She is married with two grown-up sons and she first enjoyed literary success as winner of the 1990 North West Playwrights' Competition in Manchester. Her books reflect her keen interest in history and archaeology and, as well as many short stories, she has published five crime novels set in York and a standalone historical crime novel, The Devil's Priest. *However, she is best known for her Devon-based crime series featuring black archaeology graduate DI Wesley Peterson, the latest of which is* The House of Eyes. *Her standalone novel set in the aftermath of the First World War,* A High Mortality of Doves, *appeared in November 2016.*

The Trials of Margaret

L.C. Tyler

Peter and Jax Lovesey are close neighbours of ours, as these things go, in Sussex. We drive past the end of their road every time we go to Waitrose (though we would of course not presume to do so if we were merely on our way to the Co-Op). I therefore run into Peter quite often at events in and around Chichester. At the risk of embarrassing him I must say that Peter is much admired and greatly loved here both for his work and for his support of local writers and writing. I would therefore name as my favourite Lovesey book The Circle *— a tale of a murderous writers' circle based in Chichester. Peter says that, when he wrote it, he had no idea there was in fact a real Chichester Writers' Circle — but that they took it well.*

My story does not try to imitate Peter's splendid style (how could I?) or use his characters. It covers a shared interest in motive — in this case, how trivial and arbitrary the trigger for many, perhaps most, murders is. As one real murderer put it: 'If the carving knife hadn't been on the table when my husband came home, he would

*still be alive today.' Or, in this case, if something else hadn't been
in the drawer.*

*Happy birthday, Peter. I hope the story provides some amusement,
and that you will in due course reciprocate on my eightieth ...*

Margaret's first thought on waking was that she had had an
unusually good night's sleep. It was only as she rolled over
in bed and came face to face (as it were) with the back of
Lionel's head that she remembered she had murdered her
husband the evening before.

She rolled back again thoughtfully and then just stared
at the ceiling for a while. There was a crack in the plaster
that Lionel had been promising for months that he would
fix. He probably wouldn't be doing that now.

There were clearly things that she hadn't thought
through as well as she might, including what to do with
the body. Still, for the moment she could afford to lie there
and listen to the early morning birdsong and watch the
first rays of the sun flickering on the oak chest of drawers.
Such was the inward peace that she felt that she was only
slightly resentful that it was, strictly speaking, Lionel's turn
to make tea that morning. Somewhere in the house a clock
struck six, then another slightly further off, then another.
Lionel, in his pre-victim days, had always liked his clocks.
He spent half an hour every Sunday going round the
house winding them all; she thought she probably wouldn't
bother with that.

Margaret slowly slipped out of bed, trying not to disturb the duvet over her husband, and tiptoed out of the

room – it was unlikely she would wake Lionel, but it seemed more respectful somehow. It wasn't until she got to the kitchen that she allowed herself to start humming something from *South Pacific*.

Sitting at the table, tapping her foot to the tune and sipping her tea, she ran through the events of the night before. There had been the argument – what they had argued about wasn't so important as the fact that Lionel had flatly refused to see it as a problem of any sort. Men didn't see that sort of thing as a problem. Being a man had, frankly, been Lionel's fatal mistake. Afterwards, he had gone off to wind clocks or something and she had sat there regretting the fact that they did not keep cyanide handy under the kitchen sink. Then she had remembered that she did have a lot of sleeping pills that might be ground up very finely and put into something.

'Would you like an omelette for supper, Lionel?'

'That would be nice, dear,' he had replied, doubtless reflecting that she had got over whatever-it-was quite quickly this time. She opened a bottle of Chablis to go with the food. He had appreciated that and attributed his later drowsiness to the wine.

'I'd get an early night, dear, if I were you. I'll follow you up later.'

Oh yes, and when serving the two omelettes – the pill-laden one and her own – she had for a moment lost track of which was which, but then thought she could detect just a trace of white powder in the one in her left hand. It must have been the excitement of the moment, because she was always quite good at remembering, for example, which cup of tea had sugar in it and which did not. She had presumably got it right, because Lionel was dead and she wasn't.

She drained the last of her tea, then realisation finally hit her that she would have to Do Something fairly soon. The initial plan had not gone much beyond poisoning her husband. After that she had assumed there might be a certain amount of awkwardness. Now she thought it through, that awkwardness might include having to spend the rest of her life in prison – in pleasanter company than Lionel's of course, but still …

Lionel's body was too heavy for her to carry to the car unaided and, even then, it would be difficult dumping it in a river (or whatever you were supposed to do) without somebody noticing. She could bury it in the vegetable patch of course, but Lionel had always been the gardener in the family. And again, she was sure that her neighbour would find it odd that she was digging such a deep hole in the early hours of the morning.

The issue of the near-miss with the fatal omelette started an interesting second line of thought however. What if she were to claim that Lionel, not she, had cooked the omelettes (some husbands did such things apparently). What if he had done it with the intention of poisoning *her* and had then mixed up the plates, as she almost had, and eaten the deadlier supper of the two. In that case she would have woken up, gone down to make two cups of tea and then on her return to the marital bed discovered her husband already cold and stiff. She would initially have had no idea

what had caused his death, because (being *totally* innocent) how could she possibly guess that he would have ever
contemplated such a thing? So, she would have phoned
for an ambulance or something and then looked on with
innocent incredulity as events unfolded ...

It needed working on a bit, but that seemed the general
direction to go in.

'So, you had no idea,' said the policeman, 'what had caused
his death?'

Margaret wiped a tear from her eye and shook her head.
'He went to bed early,' she said. 'I didn't try to wake him
when I came to bed myself. It wasn't until I brought him a
nice cup of tea the following morning that I found I was
unable to ... unable to ...'

'Would you like a tissue?' asked the policeman.

'No, I'm fine. Really.'

'So you made tea and took it up. And then?' asked the
policeman.

'I dialled 999,' said Margaret. 'An ambulance came at
once, but it was too late. Too late! A heart attack, they
thought. At first, anyway. Until the autopsy report.'

'So you now know the cause of death?'

'Sleeping pills ...' Margaret fingered the top button of
her blouse and bit her lip.

'Do you know where he might have got them?'

'I checked the bedside table and mine were all gone.
Lionel must have found them and taken them.'

'He must have taken a large number of them. Is it

possible that he was trying to commit suicide? Had he ever expressed any suicidal thoughts?'

Margaret considered this. A simple 'yes' was tempting. On the other hand a brief discussion with any of Lionel's friends would contradict that. Lionel's joviality had been one of the more irritating of his characteristics. To lie quite so blatantly at this stage might attract suspicion. And the idea that he might have died trying to kill her was so much more appropriate.

'No. That's the odd thing. He didn't. I wondered, though ... You see, that last evening he made omelettes for the two of us. And I did notice sort of little white specks in one of them. I mean – what if he'd crumbled my pills into one of the omelettes intending to kill me, then mixed them up ...?'

The policeman looked at her oddly. 'Why would he do that?'

'Well, we had had a bit of an argument ...'

'What about?'

She told him. The policeman shook his head. 'Hardly enough to justify murder,' he said.

'On the contrary,' she said indignantly.

The policeman flicked through his notebook. 'Your neighbour reported overhearing an argument that evening,' he said. 'But we thought—'

'He was an irritating troublemaker?'

'That had occurred to us.'

'Well, yes, he is. But he can be trusted on that. There was an argument.'

'Your neighbour's evidence was that you had threatened to kill your husband.'

'Really? I doubt he heard that distinctly.'

'He says he did.'

'He's a bit deaf.'

'He told us he happened to have his ear pressed up against the wall, for some reason he can no longer remember. He heard every single word. It's just that it seemed a bit improbable, until now . . . '

'Look,' said Margaret, 'we had an argument, then Lionel tried to poison my omelette. Any idiot should be able to see that.'

'You're sure it wasn't the other way round?'

'Of course not,' said Margaret.

'Would you like to phone your lawyer now or later?' asked the policeman.

'It would,' said the barrister, 'be ridiculous to suppose that the argument that you had would cause you to poison your husband.'

'It wasn't exactly what we argued about that was so important,' said Margaret, 'so much as the fact that Lionel refused to see that it was actually a problem of any sort. Typical man.'

The barrister was pensive for a moment. 'Well,' he said, 'for my part, I can't imagine that any sensible jury would see it as a motive for murder.'

'But it may conversely have been enough to make *him* try to murder *me*,' said Margaret. 'You see, I have this theory . . . '

'I know you do,' said the barrister. He had a patronising manner not entirely unlike Lionel's. 'That's why we're where we are. Please leave this to me. I think we should stick to the facts, which are that there is no evidence that it wasn't suicide. That was what the police thought. That is what they would still think if you hadn't talked so much about omelettes.'

Fine. Suicide then, if that's what he reckoned.

'Which of course it *was*,' said Margaret.

'Precisely,' said the barrister.

The barrister was scarcely much older than her son, Margaret thought. 'Anyway,' she said, 'if any reasonable jury – I mean a jury of women – knew what Lionel had done and what he said, they would never convict me. Can we fix it so that I get a jury made up entirely of women?'

'No,' said the barrister.

'That seems very unreasonable.'

'The law sometimes is.'

'But I might just get an all-woman jury by pure chance?'

'The odds are two to the power of eleven against.'

'Sounds good enough to me,' said Margaret.

Margaret counted the jurors as they were sworn in. Nine women and three men. Hopefully the women would keep the three men under control.

The prosecution barrister outlined the case for the Crown. Margaret could see his heart wasn't really in it. Being a man too, he couldn't really see that what Lionel had done was worth killing anyone for. A lot of his questioning was perfunctory.

Margaret's neighbour gave evidence (after which he could forget any chance she'd ever take in a parcel for him again or warn him when the parking wardens were on the prowl). Yes, he'd heard the argument. They often argued. On this occasion she'd definitely threatened to kill him. It wasn't the first time he heard her say that. At this point, one or two of the female jurors glanced at Margaret sympathetically. She smiled back when she hoped the judge wasn't looking.

During the lunch break on the second day she got a text message from somebody claiming to be a member of the jury. *Hang in there, sister,* it read. She deleted it at once, but it gave her a comfortable glow all afternoon. When her turn came to be cross-examined she watched the jury carefully and noticed several women nodding in agreement with her answers. The male jurors looked less certain but, she was pleased to notice, they already had a beaten expression. They had been spoken to. Firmly.

'I think that went well,' said her barrister, removing his wig and easing his collar. 'Other than your raising that idea that he might have been trying to poison you. Could you *please* not do that?'

'It was worth a try.'

'No, it wasn't. You will kindly allow me to decide what is and isn't worth a try.'

'You are arguing the case very cogently.'

The barrister nodded. 'Yes,' he said. 'I am.'

That night she had another text message – goodness knows how they had found her phone number, but everything is out there on the internet if you look. It read: *Lionel was completely in the wrong. You have the full sympathy of nine out of twelve of the jury.*

Margaret deleted it. You couldn't be too careful. It would be a shame if they had to go for a retrial just because she had been chatting harmlessly to the jury.

On the third day she listened to the evidence of various expert witnesses with varying degrees of indifference. Let them pontificate on the effects of barbiturates. Let them quote statistics on suicides. Let them talk about the unlikelihood of blah, blah, blahdy, blah. This jury was never going to convict her. It would have been pleasant to show that professor of toxicology the texts she had received and to see his face when he realised how futile his words were.

She scanned the jury to see if she could guess who had sent her the messages. A young-ish woman in a batik dress, no make-up and hair tied in a bun looked both sympathetic and capable of locating her on the internet.

Margaret spent much of the afternoon working out what Lionel's clocks were worth and what she could do with the money once the trial was over. She'd always wanted to go to Bhutan.

That evening the text read: *Your barrister doesn't have a clue, does he? Still, we understand, though we did have to explain it to the men on the jury. We're with you all the way.*

*

On the fourth day both barristers summed up their cases to the jury. The barrister for the prosecution took the minimum time that he decently could to outline what he clearly saw as a very weak argument. He was undoubtedly expecting an acquittal. Her own barrister, however, proceeded slowly and methodically. The argument that had been overheard by the neighbour was, he said, utterly trivial. No reasonable man could believe it would be the motive for a murder. It could be true that somebody had put sleeping tablets into the omelette but, if so, could the jury really be certain who had done it? He rather thought not. People did commit suicide unexpectedly. And if the manner of this suicide was odd, surely the decision to end one's own life was in itself perverse? Logic – and at this point he looked at the male members of the jury – dictated that they could not possibly convict. He had strutted back to his seat, head held high.

Margaret watched her almost-all-women jury return to their room to deliberate.

'So how long until I get acquitted?' asked Margaret. 'I need to get to the travel agents. I want to book a flight to Bhutan.'

'We can't be certain ... ' said her barrister.

'Nine out of twelve of them are completely on my side,' said Margaret. 'I know that much.'

'You haven't had any contact with the jurors?' asked the barrister, frowning. 'That would mean that the jury would have to be dismissed, and you and they would be in contempt of court—'

'Chill,' said Margaret. It was what her children said to her. It sounded cool. 'Chill the beans, barrister.'

'Just so long as you haven't . . . '

Margaret looked at him with amused contempt.

'Of course not,' she said.

'Well,' said the barrister, 'if they reach a verdict in the first half hour or so it almost certainly means you have been found not guilty. The longer they take, the more doubters there must be and the less certain we are.'

It took the jury ten minutes.

'Guilty,' said the foreman of the jury.

The two barristers exchanged puzzled glances.

'But . . . ' said Margaret. She didn't quite hear what the judge said thereafter. She was expecting the foreman to suddenly smile and shake her head and say: 'Oh, sorry, did I say *guilty*? What *am* I like? I meant of course . . . ' But she didn't. One or two of the jurors smiled apologetically. The judge finished speaking. The jury filed out. Margaret was taken back to the cells.

As she walked along a dingy corridor a jolly ringtone announced a text message. She took out her phone and read it.

You have the sympathy of the whole jury, it said. *We'd have murdered the bastard for that too.*

L C Tyler was born in Essex and educated at Jesus College Oxford and City University. His comic crime series featuring author-and-agent duo Ethelred Tressider and Elsie Thirkettle has been twice nominated for Edgar awards in the US and won the Goldsboro Last Laugh Award (best comic crime novel of the year) twice with The Herring in the Library *and* Crooked Herring. *His new historical crime series, the latest of which is* A Masterpiece of Corruption, *features seventeenth-century lawyer, John Grey. He has lived all over the world but more recently has based in London and West Sussex. He is an Honorary Fellow of the Royal College of Paediatrics and Child Health and is currently Chair of the Crime Writers' Association.*

Ghost Station

Liza Cody

My friendship with Peter has been cemented over many years by several joint, sometimes bizarre, projects. It began in 1990 when Peter, Michael Z Lewin, Paula Gosling and I joined forces to write and rehearse a show we could take to the US – self-promotion without the loneliness. The idea worked: we even made a profit. Murder We Write *was followed by* Wanted For Murder *and some other peculiar notions, including a booklet called* The Ideas Experiment *and a CD I'd rather forget. During this time, with all the hard work, pratfalls and, sometimes, helpless laughter, Peter always refined and redefined the term 'perfect gentleman'. In fact almost five years passed before I realised he even knew any swear words. His wonderful Bath hero, Peter Diamond, works out of the now decommissioned Manvers Street Police Station. The cops themselves call a closing station a Ghost Station. My story is supposed to be sourly elegiac about the end of that particular era. Happy Birthday, Peter. With love and admiration for an unfailingly generous friend, and a great writer.*

*

Before that day I'd never been to Bath even as a tourist.
There was something gentrified and bookish about the city
which, I felt, excluded me.

Now, my supervising officer, McNabb, was driving the
unit the wrong way up a narrow one-way street. He was
swearing already, so I kept my mouth shut.

'Effing community policing, Shareen,' he snarled.
'Special Constables – they're crap. Why ain't Bath got a
proper force any more? Eh – tell me that?'

Someone rapped on my window. A round pink face
topped by a blue and white beanie grinned down at me.
He blew cider fumes in my face and said, 'Lost your way,
my lover?'

'How can you tell?' I asked, because it had been days
since anyone grinned at me, and months since anyone
called me his lover.

'They changed the sodding system,' McNabb said,
making a five-point turn, almost causing a pile-up, and
speeding back the way we'd come. 'This town's just a tourist
trap – they got nothing to do but foul up the roads.'

This tourist town where nothing happens was the site
of what we'd been told was a serious incident. We'd driven
over five miles through heavy traffic and mean mizzling
rain to attend: five miles on the A4, the most annoying
road in the West Country, while McNabb complained about
his regular partner who was on paternity leave. 'Why can't
they let the ladies have the babies? It's what they're good
at. What's wrong with the way things used to be? Eh – tell
me that?'

He was trying to provoke me into the sort of reply that he could repeat to his Neanderthal colleagues, which would've made me even less popular than I already was. I said nothing.

He solved the parking problem on Milsom Street by driving up on the pavement.

The serious incident was marked by a traffic cone, a faint smear on a bookshop window and a dripping wet Special Constable wearing a high-viz bib and a pissed-off expression.

He introduced himself as Ray Perkins. 'It's a knife crime.' He jerked his thumb at the rusty smear. 'It was a lot bigger half an hour ago,' he added pointedly. 'There's some more under the cone. Aren't they sending the Scientific Unit?'

'Why would they bother when we got Shareen? She's dynamite with bloodstains. Take some pictures, Shareen.'

All I had was the camera on my smartphone, and he knew it. He turned to Ray Perkins, and started to fire out questions.

My phone camera wasn't up to the job. The bloodstain didn't register at all, but I got a couple of great shots through the bookshop window of a display – a pile of hardback books, cunningly arranged in the shape of a diamond, that advertised an appearance by the author. The bloodstain never stood a chance.

'Useless,' McNabb crowed, confirming all his prejudices about me. 'This ain't no way to treat a scene of crime.'

'Tell me about it,' Perkins countered, sneezing. 'We don't even know the vic's name – the paramedics carted her off to the Royal United before we could ascertain her identity. It wasn't even a proper ambulance – my mate Suzie had to follow them there in a taxi. We're supposed to be a *foot* patrol.' He sniffed and wiped his nose on his sleeve.

McNabb gazed at him contemptuously. 'No proper cops, no proper scene of crime, no proper ambulance. This town's proper rubbish.'

'Get real.' Perkins fought back. '*I* didn't close the Manvers Street station. Don't you bitch to *me*, mate, *I* ain't the effing problem.'

'You ain't the fucking solution neither.' McNabb was as good at establishing an atmosphere of trust and co-operation as a scorpion. Two prickly guys scoring points off each other – my favourite on-the-job amusement.

Trying to prevent a disaster from becoming a catastrophe I held out my hand to Ray Perkins. 'Shareen Manasseh,' I said. 'This is Sergeant McNabb. Pleased to meet you.' Perkins looked as if he'd prefer to stay prickly, but he was forced to shake my hand. Reluctantly he said, 'Suzie will call from the hospital when she knows anything. But I'm as frustrated as you are. Everyone had scarpered by the time we got here so there's no witnesses except an old couple, the Ovendons, waiting in the café upstairs. I don't suppose they'll be much use.'

'I'll be the judge of that,' McNabb said. And then to me, 'We're finished out here unless you want to take forensic pictures of a wet traffic cone.'

I opened the bookshop door, and let Perkins lead the way upstairs.

'Is she dead?' the old woman, Mrs Ovendon, asked. 'I hope she didn't die. I thought he punched her.'

'All she said was, "Oh dear",' Mr Ovendon said. 'She leant against the window, and then she went down on her knees.'

'She just toppled over sideways.'

'We didn't see the knife.'

'So we didn't understand why she started bleeding,' Mrs Ovendon told us, bewildered. 'Does it always take so long for them to fall down and bleed?'

'Maybe it was because she was wearing a waterproof coat,' her husband said. 'She looked as surprised as we were.'

'Thanks for the description,' McNabb said when at last he could interrupt. 'But I asked you about the man with the knife.'

There's something horribly shaming to me about a woman bleeding in public. It's probably a remnant of the old religion. I've seen surprisingly little blood since joining the police force, but even so, although they try to hide it, my family seems nowadays to treat me as unclean. I don't go home much any more.

'We didn't see the knife,' Mrs O said. 'Just the blood.'

'He must've taken it with him,' her husband said. Both of them wore thick spectacles with brown plastic rims.

I was tired of looming over their teacups, cake crumbs and puzzled old eyes. I crouched down and said, 'Did you see the man who punched her?'

'Tall,' said Mrs O. She was very short – her feet dangled, like a child's, in mid-air.

'Young,' said the very old man.

'Scruffy.' She was neat in her brown coat, matching shoes and handbag. 'We weren't looking at him. We were looking at her.'

'Anything else?' I could almost hear McNabb's teeth grinding.

They looked even more confused and shook their heads. When my grandparents were as old as this they never went out unless one of their children or grandchildren drove with them.

I said, 'What made you notice *her*?'

'She gave the girl some money and then she petted the dog. That's right, isn't it, dear?'

'And I said, "It'll be her own fault if that big dog bites her hand." You don't touch a strange dog. You always warned the children, didn't you?'

'Of course I did,' Mrs O said with a fleck of pride. 'And neither one of them ever got bitten.'

'*What* girl?' McNabb almost shouted.

'She was selling the homeless magazine,' Mr O said.

'Another witness,' Perkins said. And then his phone rang.

I could see that McNabb wanted to tear it out of his hands. He restrained himself, and instead grabbed me by the arm and pulled me to my feet. He nodded to the old people and hissed, 'These two are a waste of skin. Go down and talk to the manager. Someone must've seen *something*. Then find that beggar. Do something useful for a change.' He was watching Perkins. He hated it when someone had more information than he did. It was not a trait that made him good at taking witness statements.

Leaving the Ovendons unprotected I went downstairs to find the manager. She was getting ready for the Meet The Author session, measuring peanuts into a bowl and placing wine glasses next to half a dozen bottles. An assistant was setting out chairs. They seemed to be expecting a big crowd. No one had time to talk.

Outside, the rain was heavier. A traffic warden was writing out a ticket for the unit. It was too late to stop him. I did not look forward to driving back to Keynsham with McNabb.

The blood on the window was gone. So was the red stain under the cone. The scarlet essence of a victim had slid, unresisting, into a gutter outside a bookshop in a tourist town where nothing happened.

I scanned the street looking for CCTV cameras. They are usually attached to street lamps, but weirdly it was only when I started looking for cameras that I noticed that there were no lamp-posts in Milsom Street. I was shocked – I am a trained observer but I hadn't noticed the absence of lamp-posts. How then could I blame anyone for not noticing a knife? I could hear McNabb's hectoring voice, No proper cops, no proper scene of crime, no proper witnesses, no proper lamp posts. So where *are* the sodding cameras? Eh – tell me that?

The streetlights, in fact, looked like large antique carriage lamps, and they were attached directly to the yellow stone walls. The cameras would be too. I just couldn't find any yet. But somewhere, in a bunker, would be a covert observer sitting in front of multiple monitors. This would be why the bean-counters somewhere could persuade the authorities it was safe and economic to close the Manvers Street station.

Of course, the covert observer would not be a police officer.

I settled my cap more firmly on my damp uncontrollable hair and took note of all the umbrellas, rain hats and hoods. Maybe even now a trained observer was manually tracking the man with the knife from camera to camera, plotting his route, noting into which rubbish bin he threw the weapon. A cop can dream, can't she?

Meanwhile, on the other side of the street a *Big Issue* seller was hawking his magazines from the shelter of the NatWest bank. 'All the news, views, blues, do's and don'ts you could possibly want – for less than the price of a cuppa cappuccino. I ain't begging, I'm working. Homeless but not hopeless . . . '

I crossed the road. He saw me coming, took in the uniform and the patter stopped abruptly. He was quite burly but sunken-cheeked.

'Don't go,' I said, and held out a few coins. He gave me his wettest magazine in return. 'The stabbing outside the bookshop? Were you here when it happened?'

'I'm always here,' he told me. 'I live here and when I die, I'll die here, and when I come back as a sodding ghost, I'll haunt here.' He had speedy, damaged eyes. 'I've never killed nobody except when I was serving my country, so don't you try to pin shit on me just cos I'm a rough sleeper.'

'Wasn't going to.' I smiled – a sad attempt to pacify those eyes. 'I just wanted to know if you saw what happened.'

'Someone pushed the lady down. It's her own fault – she shoulda been over here, buying from me. If she'd been in her proper place, over here, nothing woulda happened to her.'

'"Proper?"' I was becoming allergic to the word.

He stuck out his chest. 'See this here badge? I'm legit, on the up and up. I'm who she shoulda given her bunce to.'

'There was another seller—'

'That's where you're wrong, lady!' He thrust his head forward so aggressively that I nearly stepped back. 'What they do is pick up a mag from somewhere and *pretend* to be legit. That's stealing. You should stop them. What's that uniform for if it's not to stop thieves, eh?'

'Okay,' I said. 'But there *was* a girl selling, and the woman who got stabbed gave her money and patted her dog.'

'You don't know sod all, do you? Only time you show up is when a member of the posh class gets hit. The dog's bogus too. There's a bloke lives up the top of Broad Street got three dogs with blue eyes he hires out. You can make a load more dosh with a dog.'

The last time I saw my old nan was when I took her out to buy winter boots. There was a small black poodle tied up outside the shoe shop, and I couldn't persuade Nana to go inside until the owner came out to take it home. My nan had a very soft heart for small animals, but she didn't make it through the winter in spite of the boots.

'You look like you missed lunch,' said the man with the speedy eyes. 'I get like that meself – it's low blood sugar.'

'I had lunch,' I said, collecting myself and lying.

'Must be the weather, then. I bet you come from somewhere hot?'

'Yorkshire,' I said flatly.

His eyebrows shot up. 'I saw women looked like you in Iraq. You got war-zone all over your face.'

Suddenly I felt bone tired but I managed to ask, 'The girl across the road, has she got a name?'

He shrugged. 'I heard someone call her Dana. She's a meth-head.'

A big woman in a green hooded raincoat touched me on the arm and said, 'Did that poor lady die?'

'We don't know yet. Did you see what happened?'

'Oh no.' She blotted rain off blood-red lips. 'But my friend told me all about it. She was over there texting me when it happened.'

'What did *she* see?'

'Nothing – she was texting. I came as soon as I could because if the lady dies I want to buy some flowers to put on the spot.' She pointed to the flower stall just a few paces away, protected from the rain under an archway.

I said, 'We're hoping she'll be okay.'

'I won't bother then. You don't put flowers on the pavement unless they die, do you?'

The *Big Issue* seller said, 'Now that you've saved yourself a bundle on flowers, why don't you buy a magazine?'

'Oh, get a proper job,' she said, turning away.

'I got one,' he yelled after her. 'What do *you* do?'

He sighed. I sighed. Rain fell like a curtain between us.

He was almost right – a long time ago my people were desert people. They covered their dead with sand and placed rocks on top to stop animals digging them up and defiling their bodies. It meant too that they could find their relatives when they came that way again with extra stones to mark the place. That's how cairns are built – the first pyramids perhaps. Flowers, even if there were any, would have been useless.

'Eat something,' said the guy with damaged eyes. 'You're away with the fairies.' He wasn't concerned; just entertained.

'Dana?' I said to prove how sharp I could be. 'A dog with blue eyes? Anything else?'

'Nah,' he said. 'Now bugger off — you're keeping the punters away.'

I copied his name and badge number into my notebook – to punish him, I suppose. Cops need entertaining too.

The flower stall was very expensive. The arrangements were artistic and lavish – the sort that would look good on antique tables, pristine white tablecloths or brides.

The flower seller, more down to earth than her displays, said, 'I'm sorry, I didn't actually know anything had happened till the paramedics came. There was a big party of Chinese tourists, and the women wanted to take selfies in front of the flowers. It happens quite frequently. I couldn't see what was happening in the street.'

'But before that, did you notice a woman begging outside the bookshop?'

'There's *always* someone begging outside the bookshop –
they try to use the loo in there – it drives the manager
crazy. So, no. I didn't notice anyone in particular. They're
part of the furniture here. But I wish someone would tell
that chap outside the bank to shut up. He's got such a loud
voice I can't hear myself think.'

There was a proper lamp-post at the bottom of the street.
I spotted a camera mounted on it with a 180° view up
Milsom Street and around a higgledy-piggledy intersection.
Which way would it have been pointing when a 'posh class'
woman was pushed or punched?

A tourist came up and asked me the way to the Abbey. Of
course I didn't know, but rather than admit I didn't belong,
I pointed in the direction some other tourists were going.
In fact I needed to ask the way to Broad Street myself, so
reluctantly I made my way back to the bookshop.

'A beggar possibly called Dana, and a bloke up Broad
Street who hires out blue-eyed dogs? You're wasting your
time, *Officer* Manasseh. Worse, you're wasting *my* time.'
McNabb was staring in helpless rage at his parking ticket.
He wanted to blame me – I could see it in his little red eyes.
He didn't like me. There were many reasons but I couldn't
do a thing about any of them. I would just have to struggle
through this posting and then wait for the next. A homeless, refugee police officer – that was me.

Perkins, who was trying not to laugh about the parking
ticket, gave me directions to Broad Street. 'There's two

halfway houses on the corner of Broad and Bladud,' he said. 'And yeah, you do see some blue-eyed dogs that look like huskies round here.' He might have been helpful simply to spite McNabb, but I thanked him anyway.

'What was the news from the hospital?' I asked.

'Her name's Imogen Bron and she's in surgery now. She doesn't seem too badly hurt. Suzie wasn't allowed to interview her. She'll stay there till the lady can talk. We're going down to the council offices to see if we can look at the CCTV footage.'

'Fat chance,' McNabb snarled. 'It'll be all data-protection this, and data-protection that. Like data-protection trumps police work. Do they think we can do this job with both hands tied behind our backs? Eh – tell me that?'

'Shall I try to track down this Dana?' I asked.

'Shareen couldn't track down pepperoni on a pizza,' McNabb said to Perkins. 'No, my girl, you are going to drive me and *Mister* Perkins here to the council offices, and then you are going to park this effing unit somewhere legal.'

The council building was called One Stop Shop and it housed a police 'desk', all that remained of a complete police presence in the city. I had to agree with Perkins – it was a 'bit of a comedown'. According to him the ugly yellow stone block opposite One Stop Shop, that once housed Manvers Street Police Station, would soon be turned into science labs for Bath University.

'What this town needs is a few ram-raiders smashing windows and nicking all the merchandise,' lectured McNabb.

'That'd have all the sodding retailers clamouring to bring us back quick enough. That's all the councils listen to these days – pressure from poxy retailers ... ' He snorted. 'That's if the bleedin' villains could find their way through this stupid one-way system,' he added.

'It's the end of an era,' Perkins said wistfully.

For now Manvers Street was a ghost station with a No Parking sign in front of it. I had to go to the car park next door and pay.

With no orders except to 'stay put', I sat behind the wheel and watched a stream of people with wheelie-cases and backpacks flow to and from the train station at the end of the road. I stole one of McNabb's peppermints, and then I stole a toffee. The rain rolled drearily down the windscreen. I was hungry.

I was on a case: assault with a deadly weapon. I knew nothing about it. McNabb and Perkins were talking to the high-tech people who might or might not have watched the event, and who might or might not have recorded it, and who might or might not share the information. I had a low tech meth-head, Dana, pretending to be a *Big Issue* seller, drumming up sympathy with a blue-eyed dog, not her own. Imogen Bron gave her money, crouched to pat the dog and got herself knifed.

I was part of a half-hearted, overstretched police response, but would we pay even this much attention if it was Dana who took the knife instead of posh Imogen? If Dana had been knifed, would Posh Imogen have stayed around to give a witness statement? Maybe she would – she patted dogs and gave money to beggars, both attributes of a responsible, caring citizen who we have sworn to protect and serve. We've sworn to protect and serve Dana too, but sometimes it doesn't work out that way for meth-heads.

The windscreen was fogging up. I put my cap back on and left the unit in search of a sandwich. I found one, only a hundred yards from the ghost station, in a tiny, sticky floored caff in an alley between Manvers Street and what looked like a newly built retail citadel.

It's impossible for a police officer to eat on the job without breaking one ancient dietary law or another, and this place seemed to be the reason why – having not much more than ham, bacon, sausages and pork scratchings on the menu. I was about to get reacquainted with my old friends, cheese and pickle, when the woman serving me said, 'I wish you lot hadn't run out on us. Especially with all those homeless blokes at the shelter over the road. There's way more fighting than there used to be when you were next door to sort the buggers out. Now all you got is a couple of fat girls in the council office. I know, I seen 'em.'

Over the road, next door to the Ghost of Manvers Street, was a looming thundercloud of a church with its doors firmly closed. But leaning against them, trying to find shelter, were five ragged men. The one in front watched me cross the road. As I approached, he rolled up his sleeves and folded his arms. On one arm were tattoos of the name and insignia of a Welsh regiment; on the other was the hooded figure of Death gripping his scythe with skeletal hands.

'What?' he said belligerently, protected by tattoos, his long black hair rain-flattened against a cannonball skull.

'She brought us our tea,' said a scrawny, bearded bloke behind him. They were all staring at my cheese sandwich with the eyes of raptors.

I said, 'Do any of you know a young woman called Dana? She hasn't done anything, but she witnessed a stabbing while she was begging in front of a bookshop.' My voice, weaker than the sound of traffic, seemed to stop dead two inches from my mouth.

'Giss yer sarnie,' said someone else, 'or we won't say nothing.'

Five men; one woman's very overdue lunch. Another domination game. Hallelujah.

'Aw, starving?' I asked. 'Missed your lunch too? *All* of you?' I spoke to the bearded bloke because he had what looked like fresh ketchup on his moustache. A feeble way to fight oppression, I know, but then who was oppressing who, bearing in mind that I was wearing the uniform and had a bed of my own to sleep in at the end of the day. All the same, I was pissed off. I went on, 'Judging by the pub smell, you made your choice. Cheese and pickle's *my* choice. Get over it.' I turned round and marched away, tired of fighting the same battles over and over again. But I was tired of turning away and refusing to fight too. A win might give me encouragement, but I hardly ever won.

The sound of sniggering followed me halfway to the unit. Then the pounding of running feet stopped me. I spun round to face two of the younger men from the group coming to a halt in front of me. The shorter ginger one said, 'We decided to talk to you. Dana's gone and ain't no one gonna tell you where she went, so Taff said it was okay. See, she used to be a sweet kid, but the glass ruined her. Even her teeth's falling out and she ain't hardly over twenty yet. We drink, yeah, so *you* won't see the difference, but we hate synthetic drugs.' He himself wasn't much older, but already his skin was reddened and roughened by alcohol and weather. His teeth looked all right, though – scummy, but healthy.

His mate, shaven-headed and thin enough to be chronically ill, said, 'No names, right?' He wore a black hoodie and the deep dark eyes staring out at me were like a younger version of Taff's Death tattoo.

I said, 'What am I going to do? Run you all in?' I gestured over my shoulder to the ghost station behind me.

He laughed and his teeth were like a skull's teeth. Ginger said, 'You and who's army?'

'Yeah,' I agreed, because I didn't even know if there were any holding cells over the road at One Stop Shop and I couldn't arrest them and drive them all to Keynsham.

Death said, 'We heard what happened at the bookshop. We talked it over and we're pretty sure what musta went down – no one wanted to carve the *lady*. It's obvious – the knife was meant for Dana. That is why she's fucked off without saying bye-bye to anyone.'

Ginger said, 'It's the Countdown King. There – solved your crime for you.'

'Thanks,' I said. 'Who's the Countdown King?'

'Glass dealer.'

'He deals more than crystal meth,' Death told me. 'But what he does, like, when people owe him money, see, he puts a knife to their necks and says, "Gimme everything you got." And he goes, "Ten, nine, eight, seven ..." and that really freaks especially the girls. So they give him, like, even their rent money.'

'Has he ever actually cut someone?'

'Course he has,' Ginger said. 'They wouldn't be so shit-scared otherwise.'

'There's no one can make a bad time worse like a dealer,' Death said.

I thought: you should know. Because he reminded me so strongly of a heroin addict I knew up North when I was just a cadet. 'Who—?' I began.

'No names,' Death reminded me.

'And I've *got* to ask – sorry – where's Dana running to?'

'And I gotta *not* tell you,' said Death with his death's head grin.

'Well, thanks,' I said. 'Do you still want my lunch?'

'Nah,' Ginger said. 'We was just rattling your cage. We had fish fingers and chips at the shelter. And we'll be having chicken curry and rice tonight. All for free.' He fumbled in his pocket, brought out a pack of tobacco and retreated to the shelter of the church to roll his cigarette.

Death said, 'I'll take half.'

'Want to sit in the unit?' I asked, opening the wrapping.

'No. The others are watching.'

I handed him half my lunch. 'Anything you want to tell me?'

'No.' He took a big bite. 'Except I wasn't always like this.'

'What happened?' Because sometimes all you've got to give is five minutes.

'I was a nurse,' he said with his mouth full. 'I burned out. Something went wrong with my head. And then I got cancer.' He coughed. 'My mates call me Lucky.'

'I'm sorry,' I said, rather than stand silent like an idiot. 'Well, I certainly got you wrong. I thought you were a junkie.'

'That's one bullet I ducked. I meant what I said – I fucking hate dealers. Nothing you can do about the Countdown King, is there?'

'Not without a name.'

'You'll be gone by nightfall, I gotta live here.'

I waited while Death walked away before finishing my own half of lunch. It wasn't as soggy as I was.

'Where've you been?' McNabb said. 'Who's the junkie? You were supposed to wait in the car. Can't you do *anything* right?'

'Probably not,' I murmured sadly, wiping pickle off my upper lip. I noticed that McNabb had a dusting of fine white sugar on his tie. Conclusion: he'd been offered doughnuts at One Stop Shop. He never refused doughnuts.

'Well, you're driving me to the hospital,' he said. 'You'd better get that right. Mrs Bron's just come out of surgery. So maybe we'll get an answer or two from a reliable source. I don't want to leave it to Perkins' mate, Suzie – she'll be an even wetter shower than he is. I hate community cops. Did I say?'

'Might have, ' I said, turning the key. Two sodden cops sitting side by side in a confined space gave the unit the smell of mouldy bread. The windows steamed up immediately.

I found my way out of central Bath by following the Bristol signs. McNabb was right about the traffic system. Bath was a town designed for horses. Cars always seemed to be facing in the wrong direction.

He wasn't going to give me any information voluntarily. Information is power in his world, and power is to be kept tucked inside a clenched fist.

'What about the CCTV?' I asked in the end. 'Did you get to see anything?'

He grunted disgustedly. 'Didn't even get inside the bunker. Had to kick our heels till the supervisor deigned to come out and talk. Know what? I bet their famous system was down. I bet they fucked up royally and no one wants to admit it. No one wants to admit they should never have moved us out of Bath. They need us and they're too busy covering their arses to say so.'

Maybe I should leave the force and train to be a CCTV observer. Then I could deal with pictures, not personalities. Or blood. But I'd have to rely on unreliable technology and sit in a dark room watching TV all day. Which sounded quite restful compared to a car trip with McNabb. And at least I'd know when lunchtime was. But maybe I wouldn't know who I was working for. Because I suspected that the kind of penny-pinching city that cut its police force to the bone would farm out its surveillance to a penny-pinching private security firm.

McNabb said, 'So what did you do while I was getting nowhere at sodding One Stop Shop?'

Reluctantly I told him what Death and Ginger told me.

He said, 'I thought you people were supposed to have a reputation for brains. Instead you put the Ass into Manasseh.'

My brother's a history professor, my sister's an architect – while I am trying to find a hospital, trapped in a unit that smells of mouldy bread, with a man who gets off on making me crazy. Brains? Who needs 'em? Eh – tell me that?

They'll never forgive me in this area for the one time I put family before the force.

Bath's parking problems extended to the Royal United Hospital. McNabb ordered me to let him off at the main entrance, and then find somewhere legal to park. But before he could open his door a sleek silver grey Audi bristling with antennae pulled in beside us.

'Oh crap,' McNabb said. 'CI-fucking-D. All I needed to make today perfect. Stay here.'

I watched as he bustled over to the two CID men – two hard-arses I recognised from Keynsham – huddling with them under the overhang in front of the hospital's automatic doors. They didn't seem overjoyed to see him either. The doors slid open and a tubby woman wearing a Special's high-viz bib came out to join the group. She had greying blonde hair and no-nonsense body language which began to crumble after only two minutes in their company. I recognised the posture.

Five minutes later, having failed to make herself heard

over the roaring testosterone, she came over to me and let herself into the passenger side.

'Suzie,' she said, holding out her hand. I took it and introduced myself.

'Looks like we're surplus to requirements,' she said. 'Your boss says you're going off shift anyway. He said you're to give me a lift back to town.'

'Okay,' I said, starting the engine.

'I could catch the bus,' she offered without conviction.

'You're okay,' I said. As I drove off, out of the corner of my eye, I saw McNabb waving urgently at me. I pretended not to see him and accelerated away, saying, 'So, what's the story? Did you get to talk to Imogen Bron?'

'Lordy, what a mess!' She sighed. 'Know what? Some idiot rang in to say it was a mad Jihadist who stabbed Mrs Bron. That's why the big boys came over double-quick.'

'They'll love that,' I said.

'Oh, they did. Bath was on some terrorist hit list someone found. Paranoia reigns supreme. Which is why they didn't want to listen to me. I know Mrs Bron was out of it, but her sister turned up and said we should arrest Imogen's ex-husband. They're recently divorced and he went dipsy-doodle about her getting custody of the kids, and him paying too much maintenance. He'd been threatening her. Oh no, said the big boys, that's just a *woman's* story – always concentrating on small personal fears when there's big important man-stuff to be scared of.'

I said, 'Everyone's scared of something.' I was thinking about Death's hatred of drug dealers.

'Me, I'm scared of losing my job and not being able to feed my dogs,' Suzie said. 'You've no idea how insecure everyone in Bath is feeling right now.'

'I'm beginning to get a hint,' I said. 'Have you heard of a drug dealer called the Countdown King?'

'Heard of him; never actually come across him. It's shameful – Bath's such a rich city, and beggars cluster round wealth. Sometimes I think that all we do is enforce parking regs and stop beggars hassling tourists. But can we afford the time or manpower to stop predators hassling *them*?'

'Apparently not,' I said. And we drove along in companionable silence for a few minutes.

Then she said, 'Your boss is awfully rude, isn't he?'

'If you believe what's written on the wall of the ladies' bog in Keynsham he's a "massive twat".' We smiled sympathetically at each other.

'Well then,' she said, after a short pause, 'maybe I won't tell you that he ordered me to instruct you to turn round and go straight back to pick him up after dropping me off.'

I could hear his voice ranting about the CID shoving him off his case. *No proper information, no continuity. All I got is you. Why? Eh – tell me that?*

'You forgot,' I said, 'because . . . '

'Because I still have a report to write,' she said. 'Besides, I'm in a hurry. No, really. Can you drop me back at Milsom Street? I want to catch that Meet The Author event at the bookshop. He's my favourite writer – tells a cracking story. So, y'know, your boss's orders went clean out of my muddled little head.'

'What a shame,' I said.

So I drove back to Keynsham in peace, by myself.

Three weeks later I was transferred back to London. This was a great relief, but it meant that I never heard the end of the Bath story. Or stories. Because there's always more than one – it depends on your view point which one you accept.

At least, I thought, I'd never have to visit Bath again unless it was as a tourist.

Liza Cody was born in London. She has been employed as a furniture maker, graphic designer, and hair inserter at Madame Tussauds. She is the author of the Anna Lee series about a London private eye, and the Bucket Nut Trilogy which chronicles the adventures of a big bad ugly woman wrestler. There are several other mystery novels – most recently, Miss Terry *and* Lady Bag. *She is a huge Peter Lovesey fan and currently lives in Bath.*

The Suffragette's Tale

Marjorie Eccles

I first read the historical novels with which Peter Lovesey began his career, and was hooked right away. Humour is not always well placed in a crime novel, but the Sergeant Cribb books manage to be amusing and witty without ever descending to caricature, and the comic aspect never seems at odds with the clever plotting, the fast pace, the unexpected twists and the authentic background.

And who could forget Peter's other historical series with Bertie, Prince of Wales, that unlikely but extremely entertaining amateur sleuth? Three books only, but great fun. Told with a lightness of touch and an ironic glance at the questionable mores and customs of fashionable late Victorian/early Edwardian society, they are, needless to say, as devious and well plotted as any of his other series, and equally well researched. This particular story of mine relates to much the same period, in tribute to Peter.

In the late summer dusk, lights are appearing at the bedroom windows of the large country house as the guests staying there for the first partridge shoot of the season begin to dress for dinner. After a day out with the guns and a splendid bag to show for it, the men are ready to relax over a lavish meal and their host's excellent claret – and a game or two of cards afterwards, with one person at least hoping he might have more luck than the previous night. The women are powdered and scented, clasping on their jewellery and feeling more than ready to engage in sparkling and amusing conversation after a whole undiluted day in the company of the other women.

Outside in the shadowed garden, a nightingale sings. Stars prick the darkening sky. From the rose garden wafts the heavy scent of *Madame Alfred Carrière*, still blooming as she has all summer. The muntjac deer which lives out a solitary existence in the copse by the three-acre field gives out its eerie, hoarse bark, and Callie, the master's old retriever, raises her head and pauses, though briefly, in her evening amble. A rabbit chases across the lawn, making for the kitchen garden, but she ignores that, too. Her hunting days are over.

In the shadow of a majestic sequoia at the edge of the lawn, two women stand. They are wearing plain felt hats and dark clothes. Mrs Cope-Tredegar is a tall woman with an autocratic expression. The younger one, Miss Flora Daventry, has a sweet, round face framed by soft and waving brown hair. In her gloved hand is a heavy rock and attached to the rock is a folded piece of paper, securely tied on with a narrow ribbon. The paper holds a simple message, large and clear: VOTES FOR WOMEN!

Another light springs up in a darkened downstairs room and figures can be seen moving behind the French window. Miss Daventry clutches the rock tighter and her eyes sparkle. As the only girl in her family, with three brothers, she is no stranger to throwing a cricket ball, fast and accurately. They wait for some time longer. 'Now!' whispers Mrs Cope-Tredegar, and Flora swings back her arm and lets fly.

A satisfying crash of breaking glass, a shout. The dog gives one short, alarmed bark, then forgets she is old and makes enough noise to waken the dead. The two women release their held breath, look at each other and laugh, somewhat shakily. They pick up their skirts and run.

It is raining when the policeman arrives at the house in Belgravia. Not a heavy, drenching rain, but a miserable drizzle that slicks the London cobbles and leaves a dew of moisture on the raincoat and the moustache of the detective inspector from Scotland Yard, whose name is Potts.

Though only twenty years old, Flora Daventry has already come up against the law in her career as arsonist, shop window breaker and chainer-of-self-to-railings. She shows perfect composure when Potts is shown into the library, where she is working on a sketch for a handbill to be printed and distributed for the cause of women's suffrage. The composure is deceptive.

She has never encountered this particular inspector before and perhaps he is unaware of her past activities, though it will not take him long to find out if he cares to enquire. She has been arrested more than once, sometimes dragged by her hair into police vans, taken screaming into custody, and been brought before magistrates. Her name is on record, she has paid fines, been warned off with a caution. As yet, she has never been sent to prison. If that comes – and there is every likelihood it will – she is ready to face it, though smashing the window of a house in the country is hardly likely to warrant more than a charge of wilful damage to property, and is not the province of a detective inspector . . . surely?

He is a mournful-looking man, Detective Inspector Potts, who looks as though life does not come up to his expectations. He says he has bad news and suggests she might like someone else to be with her.

She shakes her head and says no, she doesn't think so, and stands gazing at him with limpid, innocent blue eyes, prepared for the reckoning, while underneath her crisp white poplin blouse her heart beats with slow, painful thuds. But it isn't the window-breaking he has come to see her about. He tells her it's his distressing duty to inform her that her fiancé, Mr Harry Carlyon, is dead.

Harry? *Harry*? She has to grasp the back of a chair for support. 'He's – he's had an accident?'

'Not an accident, no. Killed, I'm afraid, Miss Daventry,' says the detective sadly, and adds, in what is really a very kind voice, 'Are you sure you shouldn't ring for someone to be with you? You look very pale.'

'No, thank you, I'm quite all right. And there's no one else but the servants at home just now.'

Harry, dead! It can't be true. Harry, to whom she has

been engaged for more than two years. Although he is by
no means the brilliant match her mother had hoped for,
he is a young man of impeccable lineage, good-looking,
popular and charming, who laughs and says when she
marries him she will forget all that women's suffrage nonsense, and smiles again when she says she cannot and will
not. Her determination has not caused him to take fright
and back off from their engagement, however, understanding such resolve being totally foreign to his nature. He is
also, of course, only too aware that as the daughter of an
extremely rich and indulgent father, Flora will be more
than adequately provided for on her marriage. Which provides a future safeguard against Harry's greatest failing – a
tendency to overplay his hand at cards and gamble with
money he does not have.

'It can't be true,' she says through stiff lips. 'Are you
sure?'

'I'm afraid so. I'm extremely sorry.'

'But . . . how?'

The detective hesitates. 'Prepare yourself, Miss Daventry.
He was murdered, I very much regret to say. Or that's what
it amounts to. Manslaughter at the very least.' He sits on the
opposite side of the fireplace with his feet apart, planted
squarely on the Aubusson, a hand on each knee, while
Flora still clutches the chair-back. 'It had to happen, sooner
or later, the way these madwomen have been carrying on.
These pesky viragos, these suffragettes.'

And even in the terrible fear of what she knows she
is going to hear, Flora feels a hot tide of resentment.

Madwomen! Viragos! And worst of all – *suffragettes!* A silly, belittling term she hates, coined by journalists and taken up now by everyone. But it doesn't obscure what else she has heard. She feels a red flush of panic and disbelief rising under her pallor, a deep, searing scarlet that runs from her throat to her forehead. 'I – don't understand.'

DI Potts looks sadder than ever. 'I presume you are aware that Mr Carlyon was a guest of the MP, Sir Robert Spurling, this weekend? A shooting party at his residence in Hertfordshire?'

'No, I – yes, of course. I was invited too, but I had other arrangements.'

Protocol dictated that as Harry's fiancée, she had been invited to Conigsby, regardless of the fact that relations between herself and Robert Spurling have been cool, to say the least, ever since she refused his proposal of marriage – with more disdain and incredulity than tact, she has to admit. Her mother was distraught at Flora's throwing away her chance of becoming Lady Spurling, though her father, a self-made industrialist, had been philosophical. *Never liked the fella, anyway. Not too sound, either – financially.*

Flora herself has no regrets. For one thing, Spurling is nearly twenty years older than she is, a widower and a hardened gambler. For another, his reputation, especially with women, does not bear scrutiny. He is also a die-hard anti-suffragist.

When apprehended, admit responsibility for one's actions, and thereafter say nothing.

But this advice from the top has deserted Flora in the horror she now faces, and she asks to be told what has happened. Dreading to hear, yet needing desperately to know the truth.

Potts is watching her keenly now. 'Sir Robert's opposition to women having the vote is well known, is it not?'

She nods dumbly. Why else had she and Evadne Cope-Tredegar gone down to Hertfordshire?

He regards her sorrowfully and explains that just before dinner on the night before last, a large stone was thrown through a window at Conigsby House. Another act of violence by those who called themselves the WSPU, the Women's Social and Political Union. Doubtless as retaliation for Sir Robert's virulent anti-women's suffrage speech last week in Parliament. Unfortunately, the heavy stone had struck Mr Harry Carlyon on the head, killing him instantly.

Flora feels the blood drain from her face again and sits down abruptly as the world begins to spin around her.

Her clandestine activities with the WSPU have made Flora adept at getting out of the house unnoticed, reserving explanations for later. The next morning she manages to slip away early and takes a ticket at King's Cross for the nearest station to Conigsby. Outwardly conformist and respectable, wearing the same sober clothes as two days ago, she sits quietly in a Ladies Only compartment of the train, while inside her thoughts boil over, forcing her to relive once more the torments of a sleepless and guilt-ridden night.

She has fled the house, not sorry to escape the concerned tears of her mother, and Papa's gruff, embarrassed
sympathy, both of which conceal their opinions that nothing good could ever have come of this, meaning both her
engagement to Harry Carlyon and her involvement with
those women.

There is a touch of the martyr in Flora (as perhaps in
many of her fellow suffragists) and despite herself she is
feeling an overwhelming need to confess, to punish herself. But it will not help the Cause to add murder to the
list of what is already seen as their heinous list of crimes.
And most definitely, Flora does not want to hang, or even
to face imprisonment for the manslaughter of her fiancé.

Why Harry had been at Conigsby is really no mystery.
Flora is well aware of the gambling for high stakes that
goes on at these house parties: bridge, or more fashion-
ably baccarat, the favourite game of the Prince of Wales.
He had promised her he wouldn't accept Spurling's invitation, despising the man almost as much as she does, but
she knows Harry's promises. He had been convinced he
was currently on what he called his winning streak. And
when had Harry, with his ever-present, but rarely justified,
optimism that Lady Luck was currently on his side, ever
believed she would basely desert him? Oh, the waste! She
wishes she could cry and rid herself of the painfully hard
knot in her chest, but the tears won't come.

Flora was of that new breed of upper class young women
who are not content to live out their lives according to the
decrees of the society into which they have been born.

After leaving the schoolroom, despising the trivial, point-less social round of parties ahead, she had burned to do something useful and worthy with her life, but could not quite figure out what. After much pleading, her indulgent parents had allowed her to follow a course at a school of art. But after her bitter humiliation at being virtually written off as merely 'a very talented amateur' by those who taught her, she had left and resigned herself to the inevitable. Very soon she was dancing and being seen everywhere with Harry Carlyon, swept her off her feet by his gay insouci-ance. Had she met him after, rather than before she had been drawn into the women's rights cause, things might have been different; as it was she was already engaged to him when she agreed to attend a WSPU meeting with one of her former art school friends. A casual decision which opened up a whole new world for her.

Initially fired with the impassioned oratory of the principal speakers – their leader, Mrs Pankhurst, and her fiery daughter Christabel – she subsequently met other women for whom the pursuit of pleasure and the business of finding a well-to-do husband and having his children was not the be-all and end-all of existence. Many of them were women with money and time to spare. Some were well educated and making careers for themselves against all odds. None of them were afraid to speak their mind, regarding themselves as free spirits, pressing with increasing militancy for equality with men, demanding the unalienable right of women to have the vote. Daring to fight and flaunt both authority and custom, making a

statement by despising the currently elaborate, fashionable clothes and tight lacing in favour of practical, loose
and comfortable ones. Throwing off their inhibitions with
their corsets.

Flora was eagerly welcomed into the fold. At first she
was put to designing banners and leaflets, but that was not
nearly enough for her and very soon she was in the thick of
it, battling alongside the more militant section and enjoying every minute. Happy and fulfilled, with a purpose and
ideals to follow for the first time in her life.

Neither her father's thunderous disapproval nor the
tears and pleas of her mother had stopped her. They loved
her and had perhaps spoilt her, but they had always been
helpless at knowing what to do with her. In the end, they
had given up, thankful that Harry Carlyon, unsatisfactory
as he might be in many ways, was going to take her off their
hands. When she was a wife and mother she would have no
time for disruptive and unladylike activities.

And while Flora continued to wear Harry's ring, an
expensive, square-cut emerald he hadn't been able to
afford, she had come to see she could never marry him.
Apart from his airy dismissal of her suffrage activities, as
the first flush of attraction wore off, she had been forced to
admit that he was fundamentally weak, not always honest
and trustworthy, and not always as charming as he had first
seemed, either. He had a fine temper when roused. She
had been trying to find the right moment to break off their
engagement, but somehow it had never arrived.

*

Two days ago, she and Evadne had approached Conigsby House from the rear, a previously reconnoitred route across the fields, and after Flora had successfully accomplished her mission, counting on the element of surprise to give them time, they had fast retraced their steps to where a motorcar driven by a staunch, jolly girl called Ethel Turnbull had been waiting to drive them back to London. They had sung all the way home.

Today, after alighting at the branch-line station, Flora takes the conventional route to the big house and eventually turns down Conigsby's drive, but hesitates when she reaches the gravelled forecourt. It had rained heavily in the night and the garden looks fresh and green, but in the bright morning light the house itself appears less spruce and prosperous than it had when viewed in the scented, shadowy dusk. The white stucco is in need of a lick of paint and in the gravel a few weeds have sprung up where not one is usually permitted to raise its head. It has a shuttered look that is faintly menacing.

It's not too late yet to turn back. But Flora lifts her chin and marches to the front door. Her ring is answered, not by the butler or a parlour maid, but by a uniformed policeman. Momentarily taken aback, she doesn't know what to say when he asks what her business is.

'Sorry, miss, but I can't let anyone in.'

'Just a minute, Constable,' says a voice behind him. 'I'll take care of this.'

Detective Inspector Potts comes forward. He still looks melancholy, but his eyes are sharper and his glance is disapproving. 'What are you doing here, Miss Daventry? This is no place for you.'

She might almost have asked him the same question. She had not expected the police would still be here.

'Oh, these things take time,' he informs her, noting her surprise. 'People to see. Talking to everyone, you know. But we leave today. It's all over bar the shouting.' His glance rests on her. 'However, since you are here . . . '

A bolt of fear shoots through her. He knows, then. He knows she was involved, very likely he's always known. Why doesn't he arrest her immediately? 'I've come to see Sir Robert,' she tells him.

He considers her again, then beckons her to enter. Inside, she detects other signs that all perhaps is not well at Conigsby. Flowers stuck in vases by a servant who has no touch for arranging them, and doesn't care. Furniture not as well-polished as it ought to have been, the paintwork shabby. Tiny triangles of dust in the corners of unbrushed stair treads, the rods a little tarnished. It looks what it is: a house lacking a mistress, a wife-less house. A house needing money spent on it, moreover.

She follows Potts to a room at the back and catches her breath as they enter. *The* room. The room where Harry had died, which happens to be Sir Robert's business room, now put to rights. A central desk, a drinks cabinet, a gun cupboard and a small table by the French window covered by a plum-coloured chenille cloth. The broken glass has been cleared away and a new pane fitted into the window. You can still smell the putty. Outside, the garden stretches,

peacefully serene, *Madame Alfred Carrière* and the magnificent sequoia with the sweeping branches, beside which
she and Evadne had stood. Flora imagines the trajectory
of the rock she threw and works out that Harry must have
been standing just there by the table, with his back to the
window.

She doesn't think she can go through with this.

Sir Robert comes in. A handsome, fleshy man with soft
hands which repel her. He does not, thankfully, offer
a handshake. Nor condolences. 'Bad business,' is all he
says, while his cold eyes express contempt for her and the
Sisterhood she has embraced. He had once fixed his sights
on her as a future wife and hostess, mother to his potential
children, far more of a catch than that young pup, Carlyon,
who had usurped him. But Flora was one gamble he hadn't
won.

He goes to the drinks cabinet, pours himself a large
measure of Scotch and briefly holds up the decanter in
a token invitation. There are no takers. The door swings
silently inwards, and the old retriever ambles in, makes
immediately for Flora and offers her head to be stroked.

'Knows you, Miss Daventry, I see,' remarks Potts, as the
dog flops down and rests her head on Flora's feet.

'Oh yes, we're old friends, aren't we, Callie?'

'A good guard dog, I reckon, Sir Robert?'

Spurling laughs shortly. 'Too old for that now. But she
can still make a lot of noise when necessary. Should have
heard her after that window was smashed.'

'Though not before the stone was thrown?'

'No,' says Spurling, his eyes challenging Flora. 'She wouldn't bark at anyone she recognises.'

Flora waits, winding her fingers together. The moment has come, but Potts is taking his time. He extracts from his pocket a folded paper and spreads the creases out on the leather-topped desk. 'Do you recognise this, Miss Daventry?'

The three words stand out blackly, written in the curly, cursive calligraphy Flora learnt at art school, and which she's proud to use on her poster and handbill designs – a flamboyant gesture she hadn't been able to resist even for this. She might just as well have written her signature.

In a low voice she says, 'Yes, I wrote it.'

'Ha!' Spurling drains his whisky and puts the glass down with a thump.

The detective looks steadily at Flora, who wonders what he is thinking. Not easy to read, DI Potts, but evidently not averse to a little drama now and then, for he once more produces something from his pocket and with a conjurer's élan lays it alongside the note: the coloured ribbon Flora had used to tie the paper securely to the stone. *Gift-wrapped*, she'd said, laughing. How could she ever have imagined what the terrible result would be?

'Green, purple and white. The colours of the WSPU,' Potts states, and asks severely, 'Did you or did you not come here two days ago with the express intention of breaking that window, Miss Daventry?'

She does not avoid his eyes. 'That, or any other.'

Spurling is flushed with triumph. 'You see, Inspector!

Barefaced, incorrigible, the lot of them!' And to Flora, in a juvenile taunt that does not become a man of his standing, he declares, 'And now your fiancé is dead, through nobody's fault but your own.'

'So it would seem,' answers Flora quietly, her heart breaking with remorse. 'But that was entirely accidental.'

'A damned convenient accident, miss! It was no secret what Carlyon felt about your acting like a hooligan. Besides which, he'd grown to be something of a liability lately, hadn't he? Too many flutters? Too many debts for you to take care of?'

She is not going to lose her temper with this foolish man. 'On the contrary. Harry had been having a run of good luck recently. What he called a winning streak.'

'Pity it didn't last.'

Potts properly ignores this outrageous remark and Flora still keeps her control. 'Luck never does last, even Harry's. But any debts he incurred here ... I came today to settle them.'

At that, Spurling's head jerks up and he stares, as well he might. His eyes are like boiled gooseberries. Harry's straitened circumstances have always been common knowledge among his friends and acquaintances, though in the end he had somehow found money to repay what he owed. Most of them know, or suspect, that Flora is the source from whence it came. Still ...

Potts has taken out his notebook and is consulting it. 'I understand there was some card-playing here on the night in question, Sir Robert?'

Spurling is living proof of the fact that being an MP doesn't necessarily demand a high degree of intelligence, but even he knows there is no use in trying to sidestep this issue: Potts has been talking to the other guests, to those who had made up the card players, all of whom have been allowed to depart by now, and to the servants. He nods in surly agreement. 'Certainly, it's a sociable way of passing the time. We played baccarat for a while.'

'And the stakes were high?'

'No higher than usual.'

'We found very little money in Mr Carlyon's possession and from what I have gathered his "winning streak" gave out when you were playing?'

'If by that you mean he lost heavily, then yes, it did. To me mostly, as a matter of fact.'

Flora says evenly, 'Tell me the amount and you shall have it.'

But after a red-faced struggle between cupidity, his perhaps desperate need for money and his view of himself as a gentleman, he mutters gracelessly, 'Forget it. In the circumstances. Only a trifling sum.'

'Five hundred guineas!' Potts shakes his head like a sad bloodhound. 'That may be trifling to you, sir, but hardly so to most people – and from what I understand, certainly not to Mr Carlyon. I suggest that was what you were arguing about.'

'Arguing?'

'Raised voices were heard coming from here shortly before the window was smashed.'

Spurling takes refuge in bluster. 'We were having a few words, I admit. He wouldn't pay up. Offering me an IOU, if you please – with fat chance of that ever being redeemed! He turned damned offensive when I refused it and . . . well, you know how these arguments go . . . ' Spurling likes the sound of his own voice, and not only when giving an anti-suffrage speech, but it isn't serving him well now; it trails off and he changes tactics. 'Look here, aren't we rather losing sight of the main issue – what this young woman's senseless mischief has resulted in, not to say how convenient it was for her that her fiancé has died?'

That is monstrous, but Flora laughs scornfully. 'You are not actually suggesting, I hope, that I knew Harry was here at Conigsby – and in this room – and that I meant to kill him?'

Potts holds up a hand. 'You have a good aim, Miss Daventry, and good eyesight, I dare say, but not that good. Nevertheless, Mr Carlyon was killed.' He bends to a Gladstone bag on the floor, and this time brings out the fateful stone, which he places on the desk alongside his other exhibits. A knobbly, sizeable lump of Hertfordshire puddingstone, sharp flints embedded in a matrix of rock, which Evadne had picked up in the grounds here when they did their reconnoitre.

He becomes sternly official. 'Miss Daventry, you have admitted you threw this rock, and therefore I am obliged to charge you with trespass and wilful damage. And we have here unmistakable evidence, proof that it was undoubtedly the weapon that killed Mr Carlyon.' He turns the stone over. There is encrusted blood, and some of Harry's blond hairs sticking to it. Flora thinks she might be going to faint for the first time in her life and wishes she could, but she is made of stronger stuff.

'However ...' Potts gestures towards the coloured ribbon and the sheet of paper. 'Why, one must ask, are they not marked and bloodstained too, when they were wrapped around the rock?'

A pause, until Spurling laughs shortly and says, 'Well, not precisely wrapped around all of it. The note was folded quite small – you can see the creases – and tucked under the ribbon. Not obscuring the whole surface, by any means.' He looks rather pleased with his own explanation.

'Possible. But not highly probable.' Potts turns suddenly and whips the chenille cloth off the table by the window. There is a nasty, deep gouge in the polished mahogany. 'I'm told you asked for this cloth to be put on the table after the incident, Sir Robert. Damaged by the flying glass, you said.'

'That is so.' Another silence descends on the room.

At last Potts speaks, keeping his eyes on Spurling as he addresses him. 'I don't need to spell out to you exactly what happened, sir, do I? But for the benefit of Miss Daventry—'

Miss Daventry's wits, however, have been sharpened over the last eighteen months in her role as one of the hardened criminals many people believe she and her sisters have become. She looks from the table to Potts, then to Spurling, and knows immediately and for sure exactly what the detective is going to say. But first: 'What has happened to Harry's ring, Inspector?' she asks quietly.

Spurling looks thunderstruck, Potts less so. 'Ah yes, his ring, Miss Daventry,' he says. 'Well, Sir Robert?'

Spurling shrugs and finds sudden interest in a faded still life-hanging over the mantelpiece, slaughtered pheasants and a limp, bloodied hare.

'The ring was noticed during play that night. Lady Warmington in particular remembers Mr Carlyon wearing it, but we have not found it among the possessions he left behind. No doubt you can enlighten us further, Sir Robert.'

At last Spurling says stiffly, 'As a matter of fact, Carlyon offered it to me to pay off his debt.'

When they became engaged, Flora and Harry had exchanged rings and afterwards, Harry had delighted in wearing his constantly, swearing never to take it off: a heavy, antique rose-gold signet ring, worked with pavé-set diamonds. Flora herself had disliked it, regarding it as over-ornate, foppish and rather tasteless, but it was expensive, and what Harry himself had chosen.

'Be that as it may, Sir Robert, it seems to me that this rock, regrettably but undoubtedly thrown by Miss Daventry, crashed through the window. And that it hit – not Mr Carlyon, but this table. After the message had been read, Mr Carlyon turned his back to the room – possibly to open the French windows with intent to run out and catch whoever had thrown the stone. You, sir, then seized your chance and made use of the rock to kill him.'

An ugly flush rises to Spurling's face and he springs to his feet. 'That is pure supposition, not evidence! And entirely unjustified. I demand an apology! Carlyon and I were having an argument, I won't deny it, but why the devil should I kill him? It would hardly have brought me the money he owed me, even had he not already repaid me with that ring of his!'

'Very true, but reason rarely plays its part when anger is involved.'

Flora looks Spurling in the eye. 'For all his faults, Harry would not have given his engagement ring away. Even that one.'

Being an artist at heart and observing minute details is second nature to her, but Harry never suspected she knew he had exchanged the original ring at some point for a paste copy, and a rather inferior one at that. There had been little point in telling him she knew: the money he'd obtained by the exchange would have been long gone by then.

But she is not the only one with an eye for detail, and some of the people Harry gambled with are not exactly unaccustomed to selling off the family jewels for clever substitutes, and passing them off as real. The amusing idea that Harry had exchanged his engagement ring would not have gone unnoticed, especially by a woman as lynx-eyed as Lady Warmington in that department, nor kept from Potts in the course of his questioning.

She can almost find it in her to feel sorry for Spurling as he learns the truth. That he had killed Harry in a burst of temper, for the price of a flashy, worthless piece of jewellery.

'I'm sorry, Miss Daventry.'

And indeed, Potts is sorry. While Spurling has done the fatal deed, Flora Daventry cannot escape the fact that she has provided the means. By paying the penalty for the damage she has done, she will get the publicity which is the purpose of these women – brave, but wrong-headed – when they defy the law. But for what? For unrealistic ideals, a pie-in-the-sky dream, a dogged belief that one day, one way or another, women will succeed in winning the right to vote – and even, God help us – to take their share alongside men in governing the country.

Stranger things have happened, but he wouldn't put money on it.

Marjorie Eccles is the author of the contemporary series of Gil Mayo novels, and now writes crime novels set in the first half of the twentieth century. Her short stories have been broadcast, printed in magazines and included in anthologies. She is a past winner of the Malice Domestic Agatha short story award.

Murder and Its Motives

Martin Edwards

This story pays tribute to Peter Lovesey's abiding interest in true crime, which has provided much source material for his fiction. Two outstanding examples are The False Inspector Dew, *with its echoes of the Crippen case, and* Waxwork, *which drew on his reading about Victorian women poisoners, notably Florence Maybrick, Florence Bravo and Adelaide Bartlett.* Invitation to a Dynamite Party *was based on the real bombings that Irish nationalists carried out in London in the early 1880s, while there are references to the Jack the Ripper murders towards the end of* Swing, Swing Together *when a character was mistakenly named as a suspect.* Bertie and the Tinman *took as a starting point the strange suicide of the jockey Fred Archer and one of the characters, known as 'The Squire', was a genuine fraudster of the Victorian period. Peter Diamond's debut,* The Last Detective, *was inspired by two newspaper reports side by side in a Bath newspaper: one about an unsolved case of a missing girl and the other a description of a local beauty spot, Chew Valley Lake.*

A short story called 'Second Strings' was suggested by another newspaper piece, this time in the Evening Standard, *about a harp stolen from somebody's garden. But the principal influence on 'Murder and its Motives' is Peter's first published short mystery, 'The Bathroom'. A lovely anecdote about his efforts over a period of several years to persuade* Ellery Queen's Mystery Magazine *to accept 'The Bathroom' appears in an article he contributed to* The Tragedy of Errors *by Ellery Queen, a 'Lost Classic' published by Crippen & Landru in 1999. 'The Bathroom' appeared in Peter's first collection of short stories,* Butchers, *and it draws on the renowned case of George Joseph Smith. Peter's enduring fascination with Smith's crimes was reflected decades later in his highly enjoyable essay 'The Tale of Three Tubs', which appears in an anthology I edited for the Crime Writers' Association in 2015,* Truly Criminal.

When I discovered that Ursula was plotting Father's murder, my feelings were rather mixed. I burned with anger and outrage, naturally, but I was also conscious of a rare excitement bubbling inside me.

Until that moment, my life had been uneventful. I can scarcely remember the Norwich Blitz, when Hitler, for some strange reason, decided to devastate our quiet and ancient city. Even a bout of TB when I was seven years old proved mild and my gradual recovery was almost unfortunate, since I found being an invalid congenial, despite Mother's lack of sympathy and Father's barely concealed lack of interest. But Ursula's scheme gave me a rare opportunity. If I could only foil her plan, Father's everlasting gratitude was sure to be mine.

How vividly I remember Ursula's early days at work in our rambling bookshop. Her arrival was a breath of fresh air. Mother and Father quarrelled frequently – or to be precise, she was forever berating him, while he increased her fury by paying her no heed – and the rows were punctuated by periods of sulky silence. Ursula was vivacious, and happy to chatter with me when she wasn't busy serving customers or working on the accounts. At the age of ten, I thought her glamorous, although as I grew older and wiser, her voluptuous prettiness came to seem cheap and commonplace.

Mother loathed Ursula, but only had herself to blame. She'd nagged Father into employing someone who could make sense of the bookshop's chaotic finances, and Ursula was shrewd when it came to making ends meet.

'My parents were as poor as church mice,' she once told me, wincing at the memory. 'I learned the hard way about the value of money.'

In lieu of part of her wages, she occupied the top floor of the ramshackle building by the Yare which housed both our family and the shop. Father had previously resisted Mother's demand that we take in a lodger, to ease our perilous financial situation, but for Ursula, he was prepared to make an exception.

In his younger days, Father had worked as a solicitor's clerk, but for all his intelligence, he lacked the industry required to succeed in the legal profession. Because of his lifelong devotion to books, I presumed for a long time that he did at least possess expertise in pricing stock, but he often paid over the odds when bidding for auction lots. Ursula drew up a budget, and charmed him into keeping his purchases within the financial boundaries she laid down.

My parents' room was next to my cubbyhole at the rear of the ground floor, behind the shop and office. One night, long after I was supposed to have gone to sleep, Mother had raised her voice so high that I could hear her despite the thickness of the wall separating us.

'You'll have to choose. It's either her or me.'

Father is softly spoken, and I couldn't hear his answer. Whatever he said made her cry, a howl of anguish from a woman I'd never known shed a tear.

I'd never imagined the possibility of Ursula replacing Mother, but I found the prospect appealing. The following day, when Mother scolded me after reading my latest indifferent school report, I simply could not help myself.

'I wish Ursula was my mother, not you,' I blurted out.

Mother didn't slap me, for once. Instead, her pale features crumpled. For the first time in my life, I'd defeated her.

'Perhaps,' she muttered, 'before long, you'll get your chance. See how that turns out.'

I couldn't guess what she had in mind, but within twenty-four hours, she had walked out, and we never heard from her again. She took her suitcase, and didn't leave a note, far less bother to say goodbye. We were well rid of her, and I couldn't help saying so to Father. He simply shrugged, stroked my hair in an absent-minded way, and went back to reading his book.

Soon I became aware that Ursula was sharing Father's room, and within a few months of Mother's departure, she started referring to him as her husband. I didn't object, although I was beginning to tire of her. She'd persuaded Father to make her a partner in the business, and now she had the run of the place, she'd started putting on airs, and no longer had time to spare for me. When the two of us did talk, she'd offer advice about improving my appearance, which I had no intention of following. She used to say that if I didn't make an effort, I'd never attract a boy, but since I regarded boys in much the same way that I regarded acne, I took no notice. At least my continuing lack of scholastic progress didn't trouble her any more than it did Father. I loved reading almost as much as he did, but somehow that never translated into good marks in an English exam.

When I was old enough to leave school, it was agreed that I should take a temporary job in the shop until I decided what to do with my life. It wasn't suggested that I join the partnership, and I didn't much care. I've always lacked ambition, and there I take after Father. He's happiest with his nose in a book, and can never work up much enthusiasm for selling stock or trying to drum up custom. Mother used to say that his laziness drove her to distraction, and even Ursula began chiding him about his lack of interest in the state of the business. She reckoned that he'd only bought a bookshop because he'd read everything in the library.

A woman called Winnie, middle-aged and sharp-tongued, helped part-time in the shop, but she never got on with Ursula, and she flounced out after a particularly silly argument about whose turn it was to put the *Closed* sign on the door when we were shutting up for the day. Although we were seldom rushed off our feet, Ursula decided to employ someone else, and after I met the new recruit, I wondered if Ursula had contrived the final row with Winnie in order to create a vacancy for Richard.

She said she'd met him in the market one day, when a stallholder's barrow sent her flying, and he picked her up and helped her dust herself down. It may have been true, but I'm not sure I believed it. Whereas Ursula was sixteen years younger than Father, Richard was ten years her junior. I suppose he was good-looking, despite his weedy physique, weak chin, and prematurely thinning brown hair, although to my mind Father, with his unfashionably long hair and sleepy eyes, was much more handsome. Richard didn't have a job, because he'd come into money after the death of a wealthy aunt eighteen months earlier, enough for him to become a gentleman of leisure, and buy a cottage in Wroxham with grounds running down to the Broads. He was no sailor, however – asthmatic since childhood, he'd avoided war service, for which he was no doubt profoundly grateful – and he'd become bored. Since he claimed to love books – though I never saw him actually read one – Ursula's solution was to invite him to help out in the shop two or three days a week.

Right from the start, she treated him as one of the family. He had a taste for sherry, and would bring a bottle along when invited to dinner. I noticed that he usually consumed most of it himself, since neither Father nor I drank, and an over-fondness for alcohol wasn't among Ursula's vices. Richard was slightly closer to me in age than to Ursula, yet he and I had nothing in common, and seldom spoke to each other. Ursula, however, hung on his every word, and that he plainly regarded as his due.

Father's attitude towards him was vaguely affable. I understood why he relished an excuse for doing even less work in the shop, but I was taken aback when he agreed to Ursula's suggestion that Richard join the two of them in partnership, and contribute some cash to shore up the finances of the business. An even bigger surprise came when Father agreed that Richard could come and live in Ursula's old rooms at the top of our house. This was presented to me as a short-term expedient, while Richard's cottage was having its roof re-thatched, but since he could afford to live in luxury at the Maid's Head, or some other hotel, I began to wonder if there was more to it than met the eye.

One afternoon, I lugged a box of books down the steep flight of stone steps and through a door leading to the cellar beneath the shop. Father was having his usual after-lunch nap, and I was glad of something to do. Ursula and Richard were chatting away behind closed doors in the tiny office, and I found the sound of Ursula's muffled giggles as irritating as they were tedious. The cellar was dry, despite our proximity to the river, and Father called it the storage basement. There he kept paperbacks and cheap library editions for which there was no space upstairs. I'd never explored it, because I didn't like cobwebs or the mess of flaky plaster, and I'd once bumped my head on the low, boarded ceiling. Realising that I could hear voices from up above, I edged forward between tottering piles of books which formed an L-shape. A few paces later, I found another opening into a further area lying beneath the office and our private rooms at the back of the building.

I distinctly heard Richard whining through the floorboards. 'You know what they say, sweetheart. Two's company, three's a crowd.'

'It won't be long before it's just the pair of us,' Ursula said. 'Together forever.'

'This waiting is sheer torment.' Richard's petulance implied that this wasn't the first time she'd said so.

'We can't afford a mistake. Nobody must suspect. I've changed my mind about grinding up the light bulb. What if the doctor wasn't satisfied? Don't fret, I'll think of something soon.'

'Promise?'

'Cross my heart and hope to die.' She giggled. 'As you say, two's company ...'

The squelching noise that followed made me shudder with disgust. They were *kissing*.

For a moment I wondered if my mind was playing tricks on me. Father might be infuriatingly vague and wholly self-centred, but he was worth ten of Richard Latham. Richard was much younger, yes, but what could she see possibly see in him? And what on earth did she mean about grinding up a light bulb?

They were so preoccupied with each other that I was confident they didn't hear me retracing my steps. I hurried out of the cellar, and rather than returning to my work on the ground floor, where I might bump into them when they'd finished mauling each other, I scuttled up to the next floor, where most of the non-fiction books were displayed in two rooms. Staring me in the face was a set of shelves labelled *Criminology*. This was one of Father's favourite subjects, but the whys and wherefores of murder had never interested me. Yet as I thought about the conversation I'd overheard, it was all too clear that Ursula wasn't merely contemplating divorce or separation.

She had fallen head over heels for Richard, and meant to kill Father, so that she could have everything. The man she loved, two houses, and the business. *Two's company, three's a crowd.*

Several books facing me had evidently been put back carelessly. As I stretched out a hand to straighten them, the title on one spine caught my eye. *Murder and its Motives.* I found myself plucking it from the shelf, along with the fat volume next to it. Murder was a subject I knew little or nothing about. I hurried back to my room, ready to undertake some research.

Murder and its Motives was written by a woman with the unlikely name of F. Tennyson Jesse. She also happened to be responsible for the other book I'd removed from the shelf: this was *The Trial of Rattenbury and Stoner*, whoever they were. I flicked through the introduction to the book about motives, and within minutes I became engrossed in

Jesse's solemn discussion about the different reasons why one person might wish to kill another.

Gain. Revenge. Elimination. Jealousy. Lust of Killing. Conviction. Jesse had studied scores of famous murder cases, linking the culprits' motives to one or more of those headings. I found what she said strangely thrilling:

It has become a well-known commonplace that women, when they take to crime, are 'worse' – that is to say, more thorough – than men.

'Mary Ann!'

Ursula sounded in the mood to scold me for dereliction of duty, surely the ultimate example of the pot calling the kettle black. What did she have in mind for me once Father was dead and gone? Would I be exiled to work from dawn till dusk in a factory, or the mustard mill?

I trudged from my room, avoiding her eyes, and muttering that I had a headache. Father emerged yawning from their bedroom at the same moment, and the three of us almost collided in the passageway. I was seized by a sudden urge to announce to him that Ursula was contemplating his murder because she was in love with our lodger. One glance at his expression dissuaded me. He was contemplating Ursula with undisguised adoration. As far as he was concerned, she could do no wrong. If I told him what I had overheard, Ursula would invent some story to convince him I was lying out of spite, because she insisted on my earning my keep. I'd have infuriated him, and put her on her guard.

No. If I were to save him, I needed to be more subtle.

I would try to understand something about murder, and the psychology of people who committed it. I resolved to read the books by the Jesse woman, and anything else that might give me a clue to how murderers behaved, and how best to forestall their plans.

That evening, after picking at my food like a sparrow, I made an excuse about the return of my imaginary headache, and left the three of them at the dinner table. Richard had already polished off half the bottle of Harvey's Bristol Cream he had produced with his usual flourish before we sat down to eat.

Before I fell asleep I'd devoured both books, and that night I dreamed of Alma Rattenbury. Her lover, a chauffeur and handyman who lived in the family home, beat her elderly husband to death with a mallet, but it didn't do either of them any good. The boyfriend was convicted of murder and imprisoned; Alma was acquitted, but promptly committed suicide. In my dream, Alma had Ursula's face, while Richard was palely handsome in a chauffeur's livery. I was trying hopelessly to explain their conspiracy to a sceptical policeman when the alarm clock woke me up.

My headache persisted over the next few days, developing into a migraine once I had consulted an ancient medical dictionary about the appropriate symptoms. I managed to stay in my room most of the time, gulping down books about criminology as if they were on prescription. Nobody seemed to care much about what I was up to; since Richard was on the spot, there was always someone to look after the shop, and the lack of customers coming through the door meant it didn't need much looking after.

It was a strange time, almost surreal. Richard and Ursula seemed edgy and short-tempered, with poor Father blissfully unaware of any tension in the atmosphere. My mother had often accused him of being insensitive, and much as I loved him, I could see what she meant. Once or twice I'd even asked myself why I cared for him so much, when he seemed to find me less interesting than his books. The answer, I suppose, lay in his natural charm. When he paid me a compliment, however absent-mindedly, it never failed to thrill me. Perhaps in the past, my mother and Ursula had felt the same excitement.

Before long, I realised that Father and I were not the only students of famous crimes in the house. In the twenties, a married woman called Edith Thompson had taken a young lover, and written letters to him in which she contemplated shattering a light bulb and placing the shards in her husband's mashed potato. She had never gone through with it; instead, the lover battered her husband to death. Edith was also charged with murder, and the combination of her unwise correspondence and her shameful adultery was enough to condemn her to the gallows. Ursula had, presumably, taken the case as a dreadful warning.

Ursula's motive, I thought, was primarily Elimination. She wanted rid of Father so as to be with Richard. But there was also an element of Gain. She must want to keep the house and business, otherwise the two of them could simply decamp to Wroxham once the cottage's new thatched roof was in place. Presumably she was scouring for a foolproof method of murder. Unfortunately, it soon became apparent from my voracious reading of old murder cases that elaborate schemes were apt to unravel. Even William Palmer, the Rugeley Poisoner, who repeatedly got away with murders committed for reasons of Elimination and Gain, seemed to me to owe his success to an outrageous run of luck.

Was she planning to poison Father? When the coast was clear, I searched the kitchen, but failed to discover any bottles containing mysterious pills or sinister potions. Nor did I find clues in the room shared by Father and Ursula – or in Richard's domain on the top floor. There were no hidden pistols, no offensive weapons other than commonplace kitchen utensils. We did not have a garden, but a small backyard, so there was no reason to keep cyanide or any other weed or pest killer that could be put to homicidal use. Perhaps she had some other method in mind. Rickety wooden staircases connected three floors of books that were open to the public, and also the private part of the building. Might an accident be contrived, for instance by sawing through a banister? Surreptitious amateur detective work revealed no sign of any tampering.

As the days passed, I succumbed to an increasing desperation. Richard had developed a nervous tic, and was drinking more heavily than ever. Ursula began to chew at her crimson fingernails when she thought no one was watching. Father remained unruffled, but I noticed that his attitude towards her was more solicitous than ever, as if he recognised the symptoms of something amiss, without being able to diagnose the cause of her malaise.

I'd heard about the Phoney War, and the four of us seemed to be experiencing its domestic equivalent, huddled together, waiting for the storm to break. One evening after a silent meal of liver and bacon, while Richard concentrated on finishing the sherry, Ursula fiddled with her bracelet, and Father leafed through an auctioneer's catalogue, I felt I could bear it no longer, and burst into a wail.

'Something terrible is about to happen!'

'What on earth are you talking about, dear? You said you were better.' Ursula's eyes were wide with alarm. She gabbled. 'Is your head still hurting? Should I send for the doctor?'

'It's nothing to do with my head.'

Tears of frustration ran down my cheeks. Having grabbed everyone's attention, I had no idea what to do with it. The migraine might have been a fabrication, but my thoughts were muddled, and now my head really did hurt. I suppose I'd wanted the conspirators to realise that I knew they were up to, without making an explicit accusation that I could never substantiate. For Ursula to have addressed me as *dear* was uncharacteristic. She was plainly rattled, but Richard merely contemplated me through an alcoholic haze, his brain in a fuddle.

Father's expression suggested mild curiosity rather than concern. I longed to tell him what those two traitors were plotting against him under his own roof, but still I held back. If I'd managed to frighten Ursula, made her realise that I understood what she was up to, she might be deterred. Perhaps she and Richard would decamp to Wroxham, leaving us in peace. That would be a triumph of sorts. And yet … I raged inwardly at the thought that, far from suffering any punishment for her vile betrayal of Father, Ursula should be rewarded with a life of luxury. It was scant consolation that Richard was a drunkard and a weakling. She would relish taking charge.

'You'd be better off in bed,' An unaccustomed tenderness lit Father's dark brown eyes, almost as if he were seeing me for the very first time. Was it possible that he'd read my mind, and knew I was trying to protect him? 'Come on, Mary Ann. Take a book with you, and read yourself to sleep if you don't drop off at once. I'm going to turn in myself, and read a chapter or two before lights out. Tomorrow, I'm sure everything will seem different.'

'Goodnight,' Ursula said, while Richard volunteered an inarticulate grunt. I didn't bother to reply, but as I left the room, followed by Father, I saw Richard's eyes struggling to focus upon Ursula's ample bosom as she breathed out with relief.

'Try this,' Father said when we reached my bedroom door. He dropped a kiss on my cheek, and handed me a book he'd brought from the dining room. 'Unless it will disturb your sleep.'

Once I was snug under the covers, I peeked at the book. The author was William Roughead, and the title *Malice Domestic*. Roughead kept me so enthralled that I didn't spare a thought for what Ursula and Richard – in the unlikely event that he were still capable – might be getting up to once Father, too, was safely tucked up in bed with a book.

A scream woke me the following morning. I'd forgotten to set my alarm, and it was already ten past eight. Some sort of commotion was taking place upstairs. Ursula sounded hysterical. A wave of nausea overcame me. I was terrified that the conspirators had lost their nerve after my outburst, and killed Father in a state of panic. If they had murdered him, I vowed to myself, I would not rest until they too were dead. I struggled into my clothes, and stepped out of my room.

Father, fully dressed, was standing in the passageway, his arms around a shuddering Ursula. My knees almost buckled as relief overwhelmed me.

'What . . . what's wrong?' I stammered.

'Something very shocking has happened,' Father said. 'You'll have to be brave, Mary Ann. I'm afraid Richard is dead.'

'*Richard*?' I couldn't believe my ears.

'He's drowned,' Ursula sobbed. 'When he didn't get up, I went up to the top floor to see if he was all right. I found him in the bath . . . '

I spent the rest of the day in a daze, as Richard's body was taken away in an ambulance, and a police constable questioned us about what had happened. Apparently, my guesswork had been wide of the mark. Ursula had followed Father to their bedroom after only another five minutes, and she'd left Richard with what was left of the sherry. He was drunk, not for the first time, and she'd worried that he might break his neck by falling down the stairs when he tried to go up to bed, but he insisted he needed no help.

So the murder plot had been foiled, but I'd had nothing to do with it. Or had I? In my bewildered state, I couldn't tell if my outburst at the dinner table had played any part in what happened afterwards. It crossed my mind that Richard might have committed suicide. Had he panicked, believing that somehow I'd stumbled across his murderous secret? The evidence at the inquest seemed to rule that out. He'd simply filled the old, deep, copper bath with hot water – Ursula, resplendent in an expensive new black coat, said he made a point of taking a bath each evening – and having drunk himself into something close to a stupor, he'd dozed off, and drowned. The coroner, fat and pompous, probed the medical evidence, and suggested that Richard's asthma might have played a part in the tragedy, but it made no difference to the inevitable verdict of accidental death. With a few stern observations about the perils of alcohol calculated to earn a headline in the *Eastern Daily Press*, the coroner concluded the proceedings just in time for lunch.

I couldn't make up my mind what Richard's drowning meant to me. The conspiracy was dead, but Ursula was alive and kicking. Could I ever rest easy, knowing how she had behaved? What if a new young man appeared in her life – would Father ever be truly safe?

Forty-eight hours after the inquest, I had my answer. I'd carried another box of books down to the cellar when I heard Ursula's voice through the floorboards once again.

'I'm seeing the bank manager this afternoon. There should be no difficulty. The partnership deed was perfectly clear, and Richard didn't have any family to make a fuss. The charities which inherit the bulk of his estate should be duly thankful, rather than complaining that there's much less in the kitty than they hoped for.'

'You did well,' Father said.

'It wasn't easy, believe me.' A noisy sigh. 'Last night, I had a nightmare. Watching him gasp for breath as I pushed him underneath the water . . . '

'It's over now. I told you the plan was . . . watertight.'

Ursula brayed with laughter, but Father hushed her. 'Careful. We're still mourning our beloved partner, remember. Don't let Mary Ann hear you.'

'I'm still not sure about that girl, Jack. What was she playing at . . . that evening? If looks could kill, she'd have finished me on the spot before you had the chance to haul her off to bed. I even wonder . . . '

'What?'

'Those last few days, every time she looked at either Richard or me, her eyes were full of hate. It's as if she'd cottoned on to the story I was feeding him.'

'Don't worry about Mary Ann. Her evidence at the inquest was perfect, wasn't it? Trust me, she's a chip off the old block.'

'I can't help worrying, Jack. What's to become of her, anyway? How long do you expect me to put up with her moping about the place? Two's company, three's a crowd.'

Father murmured something inaudible, and once again

I heard the squelching nonsense of a long and passionate kiss. I crept back up the steps, and took refuge in my room.

I'd misunderstood everything. Yes, there had been a conspiracy, but between Father and that odious woman. Gain had been the motive for Richard Latham's death. Ursula had gained his confidence by pretending to fall for him, and to plan Father's murder – and then she had drowned him. Drunk and dozy, he'd been too feeble to defend himself. There hadn't even been any scratch marks or other signs of a struggle – or at least there were none by the time the emergency services arrived the next morning.

The template for the crime was obvious. Jesse and others had written about George Joseph Smith, notorious as the 'Brides in the Bath' killer. At first his *modus operandi* had proved successful; his mistake had been to keep repeating it until suspicion was aroused. Smith murdered for Gain, and so had Father and Ursula. Richard's money was what they wanted. He'd thought that the dividend from his investment in an ailing business would be Ursula's everlasting devotion. Father must have used his legal expertise to draft a partnership agreement that resulted in Richard – gullible, but naive enough to believe he held the upper hand – sinking funds into the partnership. No doubt they'd agreed the moneys would belong to the surviving partners after the death of one of them; Richard's mistake was to assume that he'd be one of the survivors. He made a perfect victim, with no nearest and dearest to ask awkward questions after his death.

Father, I was sure, had dreamed up the plan. His

knowledge of criminology– the story of the shattered light bulb, borrowed from Edith Thompson, for instance – gave Ursula's fake plot a veneer of plausibility, as well as supplying a means of murder. Smith had got away with his first murder, and so would they.

I had disliked Richard, and I couldn't bring myself to deplore what Father had done. On the contrary, I admired his cleverness. Even so, I felt consumed by despair. Father and Ursula were bound together more closely than I'd realised. They shared a deadly secret, and it would be impossible now to persuade him to give her up. I'd lost him to her forever.

Two's company, three's a crowd. Ursula would insist on ridding herself of me, of that I had no doubt. If only she had died as well as Richard …

For me, the next twenty-four hours were as nerve-racking as those which preceded Richard's death. I could not conceal my unease, and although Father seemed untroubled, Ursula was astute enough to recognise that my anxiety was not simply the result of an encounter with sudden death. As I nibbled at a sandwich over lunch, she tackled me head on.

'No wonder you're down in the dumps, Mary Ann. When I took a clean towel into your room, I saw you've been reading books about gory murders. It's not healthy, you know.'

Her tone was solicitous, the glint in her eyes menacing. Was she wondering how to stage a suicide? I imagined the proceedings at the inquest into my death, and Ursula, elegant in her black coat, telling the fat coroner how upset I'd been about Richard's death, making sure that there was no question of a verdict of Murder for Elimination.

I needed to turn the tables on Ursula, and exploit my recently acquired knowledge of murder cases so as to conjure up some way of removing her from our lives. Jealousy, Revenge, or Elimination? I certainly had no shortage of motives.

Eavesdropping on her private conversations with Father when I was supposed to be minding the shop might supply valuable information that would help in devising a plan. In mid-afternoon, when Father, fresh from his usual nap, popped into the office, I seized the opportunity to hurry down into the cellar again.

'She'll have to go,' Ursula was saying.

I could picture Father's familiar, perplexed expression. 'There's no rush, darling. Things will sort themselves out in time.'

'I'm sorry, Jack, but that's not good enough. At lunch, you could cut the atmosphere with a knife. I'm sure she suspects something.'

I couldn't catch his murmured reply, and as I moved forward to try to hear more of the conversation, my foot caught a piece of plaster sticking up out of the ground, and broke it off. Stifling a yelp of surprise, I saw that there was a small gap beneath the plaster. Taking care not to make a noise, I broke off some more plaster. Underneath the cellar was a dark hole. Something inside it smelled unpleasant. Taking a step backwards, I realised that a section of the floor – much of it covered with boxes and bric-a-brac – appeared to have been plastered more recently than the remainder of the cellar.

Having read *I Caught Crippen* by ex-Chief Inspector Walter Dew, I realised at once what lay beneath the cellar floor. Turning on my heel, I fled up the stairs, but before I could hide away in my room, I ran straight into Father.

'You've been sorting things out, down in the cellar,' he said pleasantly.

'Ye – es.'

'Shall we have a chin-wag about it?'

'I'm not sure . . . '

'Come on, nothing to be afraid of.' He smiled. 'I thought I heard you scrabbling about down below, and I sent Ursula out to the bank so that we wouldn't be disturbed.'

Obediently, I followed him into the office, and we sat on either side of the old roll-top desk. I felt nervous and uncertain, but I don't think I'd ever seen him looking so – so alive. He resembled a young boy who has gained a sudden insight into all the possibilities that life has to offer.

'I honestly thought I'd never say this, Mary Ann, but I do believe you're a chip off the old block.'

The same phrase he'd used when speaking to Ursula. But what exactly did he mean by it?

'You do?'

He treated me to one of his sleepy-eyed smiles, and I glowed inside. 'We share the same literary tastes, for one thing. Of all the thousands of books in the shop, it's the criminological titles, the *Notable British Trials* and all that, to which I always return. Utterly absorbing, don't you think?'

When I nodded vigorously, he took my hand. 'Funny,

isn't it? One can spend so long trying to find what life is about, and where our talents lie. It's a wonderful experience, to find one's true *métier* at last. And my guess is that you're on the brink of making that same wonderful discovery.'

'I'm ... still a little confused.'

'Of course. But let's not beat about the bush. It's a shame about your mother, but at the time it was the only solution. Truth to tell, I've never regretted it, not even when Ursula became more ... demanding.'

There was a conspiratorial look in his eye. 'I'm no businessman, as you well know, and if she hadn't persuaded Richard to take out a mortgage on his cottage, and put the money into the partnership, we'd all have been in Queer Street. You do understand, I had no choice?'

'Yes,' I said. 'It's just that Ursula ...'

'I know, I know. Don't worry about her.'

'But—'

'Honestly.' He squeezed my hand, and I saw his eyes were shining. 'As she would say, two's company, three's a crowd. I'll sort everything out, I promise. You do trust me, don't you?'

I hesitated for a split second, as Jesse's phrase skipped into my mind. Lust for Killing. Until this instant, I hadn't properly understood what it meant. Nor had I appreciated its addictive appeal.

And then I returned the pressure on his warm hand, and said, 'Of course I trust you, Father.'

Martin Edwards is the author of eighteen novels, the most recent of which is The Dungeon House. *His other publications include* The Golden Age of Murder, *a ground-breaking study of detective fiction which won the Edgar, Agatha and H.R.F. Keating awards in 2016; he has also won a CWA Dagger and the CWA Margery Allingham Prize. He is series consultant for the British Library's Crime Classics, and in 2015, he was elected eighth President of the Detection Club, an office previously held by G.K. Chesterton, Agatha Christie, and Dorothy L. Sayers.*

Alive or Dead

Michael Jecks

I've always loved Peter's work, especially his Bertie, Prince of Wales stories. He has been a successful and prolific writer, but he has also been a generous and amiable companion to many crime writers over the years. It's a real delight to be able to help honour him with this short story, which is a take on the idea of 'the perfect murder'. This is a subject that Peter himself has tackled with much ingenuity on a number of occasions; once, he even collaborated with four other gifted writers, Sarah Caudwell, Lawrence Block, Tony Hillerman, and Donald E. Westlake, on an entertaining book called The Perfect Murder.

19.20 *Wednesday*

On the day he decided she was going to die, he arrived home early. Closing the door quietly behind him, he stood in the narrow, darkened hallway, listening. The singing from the kitchen didn't falter, and he smiled as he hung his coat on a peg and eased his laptop's strap over his head, setting the bag by the chair.

It was the same most nights. Five years ago, when they'd started living together, she always came to greet him – but that was when they'd still been in lust. Now that was gone, and in its place there was an emptiness. It hurt.

The plan took time to form, of course. You don't decide to kill someone on the spur of the moment, not if you want to get away with it. It had to be perfect. Ideally, it should be clearly impossible for the murderer to have committed it. And figuring out the perfect, impossible crime wasn't easy.

At first he had thought he'd just divorce her. Get away, escape . . . but that was trouble from the start. It was messy, there was all that shit about splitting everything down the middle, records and CDs, the DVDs and books. He'd worked hard to get his collections built up, and he wasn't going to sell them. Or the house. He liked this place. She had bought it with her first husband and he couldn't afford to buy her out. Divorce would be ruinously expensive, and his income as an editor wasn't that great.

They'd kept up the illusion of a happy marriage. Julie never argued when they were out; no, both of them stored up the points scored and only when they got home did the vitriol start to get thrown. At least while they were out Malcolm could enjoy himself.

It was the job which had shown him how to go about this. Editors weren't generally thought to be prime candidates for murder, maybe, but Jesus! If the police only knew what strains and pressures they worked under, editors would be the first suspects in any murder.

Malcolm Field, a short, dark, dapper man, with lines of

anxiety at mouth and brow, smiled to himself. Yes. If they only knew.

Seven years ago he'd been responsible for the crime list at another publisher, and his efforts had paid off. He'd been headhunted when only twenty-nine. In those days he had thirty-two authors, and his list was top in the UK. Back then to be an editor was respected. Now all the power was held by accountants, and having once clutched it, they wouldn't let go. His best authors, the ones he liked and admired the most, were gone. Gradually his list had reduced until now he had only twelve. And he didn't *like* half of them. No point taking them to lunch – the ones who drank were boors, and the sober ones were dull, dull, dull.

He first met Julie at a party. He could remember seeing her for the first time so clearly. She was utterly beautiful: young, blonde, long-legged, full-hipped, with small, even teeth. Quite lovely. And a few days later he stumbled into her again.

That had been one hell of a day. He'd had a stand-up fight with the commissioning committee over a new writer, a *brilliant* new writer, whom he wanted to snap up. Rather than that, his colleagues voted half a million quid to buy a celeb's book. *Half a million.* Well, of course, the book only sold ten thousand copies, lost a fortune, and the celeb was delighted. He kept his cash. Meanwhile another publisher snapped up Malcolm's newbie. Who'd have thought a bloody story about a small-time crook in Plymouth would have sold so well? Malcolm bloody would, that's who! – but oh, no! The accountants wouldn't give him a measly fifteen thousand after paying so much to a celebrity 'name'. Too much to risk, they said. And that was that.

Meeting Julie again had felt like a dream. She'd been fresh, enlivening, exciting – and God, so hot! He'd wanted to rip her clothes off the first moment he saw her. She was a publicist, and wore these really sexy narrow-framed black glasses that went with the black dress she was wearing. He'd thought he'd gone to heaven when he woke up next to her in bed. He must have been pissed as a rat, but whatever he did with her that night must have struck a chord with her, because from that moment they were an item.

How times change.

She'd been honest right from the start. She had been married, she told him, and if they were to become serious, he had to understand she had never stopped loving her first husband. Her old man had been in the Twin Towers on 9/11, and although his body wasn't recovered, everyone knew he was dead. Luckily the Americans were understanding after that catastrophe, and they allowed death certificates to be issued even when the bodies weren't found. Julie was legally a widow.

Then it added to her strange allure – now it gave him the ideal murder. Because her husband had reappeared.

20.30 Thursday

Detective Sergeant Blake walked up the driveway with queasiness in his stomach. He didn't like homicide scenes. The sights and smells, the aura of violence and hatred. All too often the victim and perpetrator were married, killing from frustration, jealousy, or a split-second's rage.

Even in the dark he saw it was a large house, set back from the road behind a red-brick wall. Tiny lawn, paved parking area, garage. The house looked clean and fresh, almost new. Only the police milling about and the blue lights spoiled the image of middle-class aspiration.

Signing himself in with the officer at the door, Blake stepped inside to find a scene of forensic industry. Men and women in Tyvek jumpsuits, shoe-covers and gloves walked carefully, protecting the crime scene from contamination. Blake pulled on his own covering.

The bodies were in the conservatory. Blake swallowed, seeing the thick stream of blood that spread over the floor from the dining-room chair, out towards the wall where the bodies lay. The man's flies were undone, his trousers and pants halfway down his thighs.

Stanley Hughes, his Detective Constable, pointed to the blood with his biro. 'Sad one, sir. Looks like a robbery gone sour. The couple were in the dining room having sex, from the look of things. The intruder smashed the French windows there, probably unaware that they were inside, and found the couple. It made him panic, I guess, and he grabbed a knife from the table, stabbed the bloke, and beat up the woman. Probably a drug user desperate for his next fix.'

'Don't speculate. Follow the evidence. How is she?'

'In hospital, but not critical.'

Blake nodded and hunkered down. Malcolm Field lay

with his back to the wall, an expression of horror on his face, hands at the knife in his breast. The other man lay a short distance away. His hand was cut badly, and Blake wondered at someone smashing a French window with their bare hand. 'Any indication he was a drug taker?'

'No.'

'Because these clothes don't look like your typical lowlife's.'

'No.'

'And he would have had to come around the house, wouldn't he? He'd be able to see in. Even from the French windows, he'd see them rolling about on the carpet?'

Wednesday

Malcolm had first seen him last week.

That was how he thought of him now – *him*. Paul was his name: Paul Friedland, until 9/11 an international, superstar bond dealer. Older than Julie, he had been enormously rich, and they'd been happy together. When he died, she threw herself into her work, but never forgot him. Even when they'd moved in together, she'd been in love with the dead man. She kept his picture in a closed book on her desk.

It was his eyes that Malcolm noticed first. Dark, very dark, and haunted. In that pale face, it was hard to miss him, and the expression was so ... well, touching, like someone who'd seen a disaster. Which he had, of course. Malcolm's first reaction was to turn away, ashamed, like he'd met the glance of a beggar, but even as he did, his mind registered the features, wondering where he'd seen those eyes before. Later he saw the book in his bedroom, turned over the cover and saw the photo of Paul. It made the breath stop in his chest. It was *him*. Sure, he was thinner, but he looked good for someone who had been dead fifteen years.

The perfect plot. A chaos of husbands: one thought to be dead; a second to replace him, and then the first returns. Ideal for a novella as it stood: the confusion of the wife, her torment, forced to choose between her men; perhaps a little twist at the end when she can't pick, and decides to leave them both for ever . . . or she picks both, and they share? It could be a comedy like that. Not many laughs just now, though, Malcolm told himself.

He watched his wife through the open door. She hadn't even heard him. Perhaps that was why she was happy. His arrival home nowadays didn't usually give her much joy.

Her first husband and she had lived here in Amersham in the early nineties. When they moved to America, they'd kept the house and rented it out, keeping it as an investment. With Paul's bonuses they bought a small apartment with a view. 'If you leaned out the window and squinted *very* hard,' Julie chuckled throatily, 'you could just see Central Park.'

She hadn't wanted to stay in New York when Paul died. Too many memories. She sold the apartment and came back here to Hundred Acres Lane. When they met, Malcolm sold his old cottage and moved in with her. He adored the large rooms, the big windows, and in particular the bright conservatory. In the summer he sat there with the French windows wide and read his manuscripts sipping wine. Losing that comfort was unthinkable. He *couldn't* lose this house.

He passed from the hallway into the long dining room at the rear of the house, and out into the conservatory. In his mind he had the murder scene already prepared. The French doors were closed. He would open them later and smash the glass. First . . . well, first he needed a wine bottle. The brick was already here, their doorstop for when the weather was hot.

It was a simple plan. A perfect plan. No one could possibly accuse Malcolm of guilt – his innocence was obvious. He was going to be the innocent witness to his wife's murder, the unwilling victim of an attempted murder.

Thursday

Blake stood outside the French windows with Hughes and stared at the house. 'So this intruder knocked her down, then grabbed a knife and killed the householder, or stiffed the householder first and then knocked her down? Why'd he stab the man and let go the knife?'

'Like I said, Sarge. He came in, saw the couple and panicked. He'd looked through the windows and couldn't see them.'

'Because they were on the floor, you said,' Blake said. He peered in through the window. 'Except I can see them on the floor there perfectly clearly. So would he. So why did he smash the glass and go inside?'

*

Wednesday

Malcolm saw him again when he got off the train after work two days ago. Paul looked scruffy and confused, his face grey-complexioned like a life-long smoker's. He was scarred with more wrinkles, but he was definitely the man in her photo: her first husband. Malcolm followed him to a pub, and entered after him.

Jim had been landlord there all the time Malcolm had lived in Amersham, and Malcolm occasionally dropped in with Julie. The place had rooms upstairs, and over a beer or two Malcolm asked the landlord if anyone was using them.

'One guy, yes.'

'I just saw someone. Looked a bit – um – tatty?' Malcolm said, taking a sip of beer as Jim dropped his change onto the counter.

'Yeah. He looks like he's not had an easy time of it,' Jim agreed.

Malcolm was spurred by a devil to say, 'He looks just like Julie's first husband.'

While polishing the counter, Jim threw him a look. 'She's divorced?'

'No. He was in the Twin Towers. They never found the body.'

His ruminative tone was enough to make Jim stop and frown. 'You don't think he survived it?'

'Jim, did you see the film of the plane hitting the second tower? No one would have survived that, it'd be impossible. No, I think it's just a coincidence, that's all.'

'Suppose so,' Jim said. 'Wouldn't want Julie to have a shock, though. Do you think it *could* be him? Perhaps he was knocked on the head and has only just regained his memory, or something? It happens, you know.'

Malcolm silently blessed the editors of Jim's tabloid newspaper. They always preferred coincidences to facts and pandered to the daftest superstitions. Like many who devoted their spare moments to gaping at the latest shock revelations of Lady Diana's death (which reappeared every Monday) or who read with absorption news of alien visitations (which Jim didn't *believe*, of course, but you never could tell, not when you thought about how many planets there were up there), Jim was always prepared to take the most extreme and unlikely possibility as being Gospel truth. There was not a conspiracy theory on the internet which Jim couldn't accommodate in his gullible mind. Accepting that a long-dead husband had returned to life was child's play to him.

Malcolm thought about Paul as he walked home. Why was he here? Did he want his wife back, his life back? And *how* had he survived the blast and collapse?

That prompted a new line of thought: if he had been traumatised, what had happened to him? The Americans were keen on checking a man's identity at every turn. Someone without a credit card might as well be invisible – he wouldn't survive five seconds in the banking system – but this man had survived years without using his own name and cards. If he had, the Americans would never have given Julie his death certificate.

He must have deliberately fled and hidden himself. A fugitive. So why come back here?

Thursday

Later that morning, Blake sat at his desk and stared at the photograph. 'You're sure?'

'Yes, sir. The landlord was quite certain that the man had been staying with him for a few days. The dead house-holder, Field, saw him and mentioned he looked like her first husband. He died in the Twin Towers.'

'And this photograph was kept by her on her dressing table. So now we can forget the idea of a robbery, can't we, Hughes?' Blake said. He stood and stared out of the window with his hands in his pockets. 'This man appeared, saw them together, broke the window, ran in, killed the man and tried to kill the woman.'

'Perhaps he was just furious to see his wife with this man?'

'But there was a death certificate issued. The Americans thought he was dead. Did he pretend to die?'

'Maybe he wanted to claim on his life insurance and run off? But she would have had to make the claim, wouldn't she?' Hughes guessed. 'She'd have known he was alive. Perhaps he thought she was still loyal to him, found her with her new husband, and got so jealous he ran in and—'

'But a few days ago he was sitting in a bar and chatting with this bloke. Why?'

*

Wednesday

The more Malcolm had considered the conundrum, the more certain he was that Paul had been the victim of a terrible loss of memory as a result of the trauma. He'd lost his mind, forgotten his name, quite likely. Something triggered the recovery of memories: the name of his town, a mental picture of the house, or perhaps the vague recollection of a woman he had loved.

It was perfect, Malcolm told himself again as he locked the French windows. She mustn't escape. 'Darling?'

He walked through the dining room and into the kitchen. 'How are you?' he asked, holding out his hands.

The singing stopped. She turned and faced him with an expression of sharp enquiry – or was it hatred? He merited a swift peck on the cheek, but that was all, and then she was back at the hob, stirring, a large glass of red in the other hand. 'Lay the table. It's curry.'

'Good! My favourite,' he enthused, collecting mats and cutlery and setting them out.

He had studied the best crime stories, and he knew that in almost all inevitably the criminal must lose. In the last pages, he or she would be caught and exposed, or die. There had to be a spurious justice in crime fiction. The baddie couldn't possibly win.

In the real world, murderers did get away with it. And Malcolm had been very careful. He hadn't taken out a new insurance policy. There had been no point; they'd both taken large life policies when they married so that if either died there would be a buffer for the survivor, and her death would bring in an entirely unsuspicious quarter of a million. No policeman would think he'd planned this so long ago, so whatever happened, he would be safe.

Julie came out with the food on a tray. With the plates there were two wine glasses. Hers was refilled, his was empty. Dangling from her left hand was a winebox..

Eating, Malcolm felt an overwhelming sense that the world was all right. Soon his plan would be executed – the pun made him smile – and although he'd have a necessary headache, he'd be richer and free. With the money, he could take a holiday. Compassionate leave after this hideous and traumatic event. He'd always fancied a safari in Kenya. See the animals in their natural habitat. And there was Mombasa, with all that sand and sunshine.

'Are you all right?' she demanded as his eyes fixed on the view in the middle distance: the veldt, a waterhole, majestic elephants trumpeting, warthogs splashing, an impala or two shaking their heads . . .

'Eh? Sorry. Just thinking about a typescript I read today.'

'Must have been funny to make you grin like that.'

He smiled again, this time patiently, and she snorted with disgust and tossed her splendid fair hair.

Malcolm's mind returned to the visit he'd paid to the pub last night. He'd ordered, and cast about the room as if with disinterest, but then registered shock on seeing Paul sitting alone in the corner. Paul had flinched like a man expecting to be punched.

Malcolm mugged appallingly, like the worse ham actor,

but there were only a couple of people to notice. 'Aren't you Paul? Paul Friedland?'

The man was pale, and his haunted eyes looked red-rimmed from lack of sleep. 'No, no! I'm Henry. Henry Doe.'

That, Malcolm thought, was proof. John Doe was the standard name for any unidentified body in America. Any reader of modern crime fiction knew that. Clearly when he'd been found, the institution had given him that moniker, but since 'John Doe' was always a dead man, someone with a sense of humour had given him 'Henry' as a Christian name. It gave Malcolm a feeling of power and security. This man was plasticene waiting to be moulded to his will.

'Paul,' he insisted, and tried to fit a wry expression to his face. 'I should know. Your picture's still on Julie's bedside table. From your marriage to her.'

'Is this some sort of joke?'

'No joke. My God!'

Malcolm had finished his drink and ordered another. By the end of three pints, Paul was more relaxed and garrulous. Yes, he had been found wandering the streets of Manhattan after 9/11, and taken to an asylum. He wouldn't talk about his time there, but admitted that he started having flashbacks of Amersham and a woman a year ago, and only recently had he started to remember bits and pieces of his past. Just over a month ago, his memory began to return. He recalled a house, an apartment, a woman – all with startling clarity – and had to come back to England to learn who he was. It was a struggle to persuade the doctors, but in the end he managed it, and ... well, here he was.

Perfect, Malcolm considered. And now, all he need do was bludgeon Julie. He had intended to use a wine bottle – the cardboard winebox was useless for that. Still, he could persuade her to drink another bottle. She never turned down a drink. And then, when she was down, he would wipe every surface in the room to add verisimilitude to his story, before opening the door that led into the garden. Smashing the glass would be easy. The brick was already there. Throw it through the glass panels and the story was begun.

A burglar had broken in. Preparing to ransack the place, he saw Julie, struck her with a deadly blow and then knocked her gallant husband down as he tried to protect her, before making off empty-handed.

That was the story. There were details, of course. He must strike quickly – he couldn't have too many bludgeon-marks, and then, when he'd knocked in the glass of the door, he would lift her to scatter some fragments beneath her to make it appear that the glass was broken before she fell. Yes. Easy. Then back into the house, unlocking the French windows, to trash the sitting room briefly – you see, it's all in the story. That's what matters. The police would initially think that the burglar had come in on a quick smash-and-grab, had been accosted by the owners, struck them both down, killing her, sadly, and then fled. And if they were on the ball, they'd make the natural assumption, that her husband had killed her. Everyone knew that when there was a murder, it was the spouse who 'dunit'.

Only later would they gather from Malcolm's broken tale that her first husband had not died in America as everyone had thought, but instead had made it here to take back the woman he adored, and when Paul realised he couldn't have her back, he killed her, knocking Malcolm down when he tried to stop the murder. In the dark, Malcolm didn't recognise him. That was the detail, of course, that would make the cops believe him: the fact that Malcolm wouldn't point the finger. There'd be no need. They'd soon learn all they needed when they started asking around.

Malcolm could play his part perfectly. The only tricky element was where he had to knock himself out, but he'd planned for that, too. After he'd knocked her out with the bottle, he'd use the brick to actually kill her. Striking her with a corner would be lethal. He'd checked it in the pathologist's text book that was published by a sister imprint in his company: the point would concentrate the mass of the brick, and would smash her skull. He glanced at her, chewing steadily opposite him, and yawned. The brick would kill Julie, and then he'd rub the bloody weapon on his own scalp to mix her blood on his hair, and finally, he would throw the thing up into the air a short way and head-butt it. He felt a twinge of concern at that, but it was the only way to add veracity to his story. It was going to hurt like hell, but there was nothing he could do to prevent it.

So, he would collapse at the side of his wife, the brick smothered in her blood and probably some quantity of his as well, and a short while later, Paul would appear in the garden as Malcolm had suggested. So that he could peer through the French windows and see the woman he thought might be his wife. Malcolm had suggested that, 'so she won't be too distressed'. It was his master-stroke.

'If she sees you in the street, Paul, what'll she do? She'd be convinced she was seeing a ghost, wouldn't she? God, you could give her a heart attack. Look, I'll tell you what. I'll make sure we eat in the conservatory tomorrow night. You come round to the back – there's a gate at the side – and peer in through the windows. Right? That way, you can see if you recognise her or not. Then we can meet up the day after and talk about it, eh?'

He had played it perfectly. The concerned husband who didn't want to see another man robbed. No one could have been more considerate. Paul would see the bodies, raise the alarm, and who would believe him when he said he'd not hurt either Julie or Malcolm. Malcolm would reluctantly admit that he had met Paul, that Paul had broken into their house, and Julie refused to leave with him, so he attacked her with a bottle, and then hit Malcolm with their doorstop.

'Not his fault, officer. You can see it from his point of view, I suppose,' he rehearsed and smiled.

The wine was getting to him. He'd best take it easy. The excitement, the adrenalin, they could make him miss his mark and screw up. No chance he could do that today. This must be absolutely perfect.

Nonchalantly he glanced at his watch and tried to control the shock. It was much later than he'd planned. He had to move quickly. 'Darling, d'you think you'd like some more wine?'

'Don't you think you've had enough already?'

'Don't be like that,' he said with a smile. It was hard to be cross with the woman when her life was to be cut short so soon. 'I'd like another. Shall I get a bottle?'

'There's plenty left in the box if you want it.'

Bloody woman! 'I find it a little sweet.'

He stood, and felt some surprise at how his legs wanted to fold.

'Are you all right?' Her voice was suddenly concerned. 'You've gone quite pale ... you're not going to be sick, are you?'

Six Weeks Later

The investigation into the deaths was detailed, but took little time. As the Super said, there really wasn't much to do. Everyone knew about the tragedy, and all three were victims, really.

Hughes had managed to track down the home where Paul Friedland had been living and discovered his medical records. There was no mystery, no fraud. It was a simple, tragic story. Friedland had been injured in the Twin Towers attack, and somehow got heavily sedated. He was discovered that evening, wandering the streets, soaked and traumatised to the extent that he could not even remember his name. There were so many injured and mentally scarred that this surprised no one. He was soon admitted to a sanatorium, and there he remained.

It was clear what had happened; why he had turned to murder. The couple had been indulging in postprandial intercourse when Paul Friedland saw them: a man with *his* wife. Checks showed that he had been released from a mental institution only five weeks before as flashbacks of memory came to him. Apparently he remembered being entombed, he remembered tumbling into the Hudson, and the horror of it had never left him. More memories returned and he followed them to Amersham.

Detective Sergeant Blake read the report a third time, sighed, closed the file, opened it again, shook his head, and pushed it closed with the palm of his hand, leaving his hand on it as though it might reopen of its own accord if left to its own devices. In his mind, he saw the photos of the three bodies again, the blood, and the knife. The two men, and her, wife to both, lying half naked between them.

The phone rang and he took it up in his other hand. 'Yes? Oh. Yes, I'm ready.'

He stood as she entered. The pretty woman with the red, tearful eyes and mourning black that suited her blonde hair so well.

'I am glad you are recovered from your ordeal,' he said sympathetically, and Julie nodded gratefully as she sank into her chair.

'It was so horrible. Just when I was over Paul's death, and then he turns up . . .'

'I cannot imagine,' he said sympathetically.

'I never would have thought . . . I thought it was a ghost

at first. There I was with poor Malcolm, and suddenly Paul was with us.'

'There is no need to go through it again, Mrs Friedland.' Using her first married name still sounded odd, but as she had pointed out, since her first husband was still alive when she remarried, she felt she owed him that small sign of respect. How she could cope, he didn't understand. She had seen Friedland stab her husband, and then her husband struck him with a brick before he died. Friedland attacked her, punching her, but Field's blow had disorientated him. She grasped the brick and managed to bludgeon him in terror.

'It just felt so weird, you know? I thought such a thing would be impossible after the Twin Towers. I lost him once then, and now I have again, as well as poor Malcolm ... He didn't deserve that!'

He made some compassionate noises, but really, there was nothing he could add to help her. 'It's a terrible case, of course, but no blame can attach to you. You were quite right to act as you did. It was self-defence.'

Wednesday

Malcolm didn't feel sick, no, but very sort of 'floaty', as if he could dissipate like a wisp of smoke in a puff of wind. Sluggishly, he tried to stand, but his legs felt like lead. He had to grab the table for support. 'I can't ...'

'No. I wanted you quiet, darling.'

He looked at her in surprise. 'What?'

'The drug, dear, the Rohypnol in your dinner.'

'What? What are you talking about?' he demanded. His tongue felt too large for his mouth, and he tried to shake his head.

'I didn't want you to escape,' she said with a chuckle, standing, and walked to him. She took up the bread knife and stabbed him. He felt the blade deep in the chest like a sliver of ice. 'Dear God, Malcolm, you didn't think I could bear to live with you for ever, did you?' she asked as he sank to the floor, staring up at her. He shuffled backwards, away from her, trying to escape as she stalked after him.

'No, darling. I never wanted to live with you. But I couldn't get rid of you too quickly. That would have been obvious after I made you take out the life policy. Anyway, losing another husband so fast would have been a problem, wouldn't it? Anyone would think I was careless.'

'You've killed me!' he croaked. He could feel the blood bubbling in his chest.

'Yes, well, sorry about that,' she said with apparent sympathy. 'But you really have been a pain in the arse for the last year or so. No fun at all. So, sorry, but it had to happen.'

'I feel so weak!'

'Ah, that will be the Rohypnol. They call it a date-rape drug, you know. I gave it to you the first night we met – it was the only way to get you into my bed without being bored stupid by your wittering on about that author.'

'He was—'

'Whatever,' she said, cutting him off with a bored shake of her head. 'So I gave you more to slow you down tonight. It worked, didn't it? Almost tasteless. Rather like you.'

'You won't get away with it,' he whispered.

'Last time I had to be lucky. The two towers being hit on the morning when Paul had overslept. That was a real stroke of luck, that was. I drugged him with a coffee laced with R, and when everyone was plugged into their TVs or out in the streets, I helped him downstairs and put him in the trunk of the car. Later, when the roads were still clear, I took him to a bridge over the East River, and just let him slide into the water. Simple. Even better, apparently R means you lose your memory while under it, so he lost his memory. Mind you, I gave him enough to tranquilise a herd of wild elephants. I'm surprised he didn't die. I only gave you a little to slow you down.'

'Didn't work!' Malcolm muttered, but he wasn't sure she could hear him over his chattering teeth.

'It took me a while to track him down. Then I send him a letter. He flew over here to see me, although he wasn't sure I was really his wife. Now he's going to see something that the police will think must drive him mad. She smiled and began to undo his flies. 'Just one more little detail, petal,' she cooed as she massaged.

As he slumped sideways, he saw between her thighs the pale, anxious face appear at the windows, and felt a slight satisfaction that she wouldn't get away with it – but then he realised what she had said, what she had planned.

Six Weeks Later
Walking her to the door of his office, Blake watched as she slowly passed down the hall to the lifts, and turned to

glance at him. She lifted a hand and waved it to him before holding the tissue up to her eyes again and leaving as the doors opened.

And that was the last time he saw her. Many times Blake would wonder about that beautiful young woman, and then one day he caught sight of her in his wife's magazine.

NEW HAPPINESS OF THIRD-TIME WIDOW the headline read, and he took it up to read. Julie had married again: a casino-owner in Nevada, who had seen her at a gaming table and taken a fancy to her. Sadly, he'd died in a helicopter crash when trying to show a section of the Grand Canyon. A successful pilot, he had succumbed to an engine failure.

No policeman likes coincidence. Once, perhaps; twice in a lifetime, possibly; but three accidental or incidental deaths widowing her? Suddenly Blake felt a cold certainty in his belly, and he looked at the picture of her new fiancé. He looked very old, and Blake wondered how much he was worth.

Alive or dead.

Michael Jecks has published forty titles, five more collaborative novels, and many contributions to anthologies. The Death Ship of Dartmouth was shortlisted for the Theakston's Old Peculier Crime Novel of the Year Award, and his work has been celebrated by the fountain pen manufacturers Conway Stewart and Visconti. The founder of Medieval Murderers, he has served on the committee of the Historical Writers' Association and as Chair of the Crime Writers' Association. He became Secretary of the Detection Club in 2016, and lives on Dartmoor with his wife and two children.

The Right Thing

Michael Z Lewin

I met Peter thirty years ago in Bath where later we each set many stories. And, since that time, we have shared many an adventure. Most dramatic of these was a series of public appearances when, usually with Liza Cody and early on with Paula Gosling, we presented 'shows' to illustrate aspects of the arts and crafts of mystery writing. And there were many high points: Peter juggling behind his back, singing his 'Autopsy Scene', choking on a peanut in Leeds, finding our audience volunteer already had a prosthetic hand when we had an imminent gag involving our own prosthetic hand . . . Even once getting the giggles. Yes, Peter. The giggles. *And we visited many a high spot, including Oklahoma City, Melksham, a St. Louis library with a statue donated by Mussolini, and Seattle. Seattle* was *a high spot: we got a standing ovation. Ah, happy memories. But apart from Peter's unfailingly charming, tolerant, gentlemanly nature, one aspect of getting to know him has been the slow adding, over* years, *to the information about his personal history. Yes, early on we knew he taught English to a future Olympic champion and world record holder, but it was ages before we heard that his house as a child was bombed in the Blitz, and that he'd piloted airplanes in his National Service and that he'd shovelled elephant shit at a circus. A man of many parts, Peter. And an all-round good bloke.*

'Are you all right?' Marie asked her friend Cassie. 'Because you haven't said a thing about my new necklace and we've been sitting here for *five minutes*.' Marie lifted the intricately carved black disc that dangled from a white silk cord round her neck. 'It's *jet*. That's a rare stone, if you didn't know, and it comes from the sea. And it's *very* expensive.'

'Yeah, sorry,' Cassie said. 'It's nice.'

'Nice?' Marie echoed. 'Nice? You are so impervious to art, Cas. This is *ancient*. A magical love token with runes no one's ever translated. And bordered by roses, which have always been *the* symbol of love.' In fact she had no idea what the carvings meant, but that's what they *could* mean.

'Very nice. And pretty. Very pretty.'

'Sorry. I know your Kenny doesn't give you beautiful, expensive presents for no reason at all and just because he loves you. I should be more considerate.'

Marie sipped from her cappuccino and looked out the window. She continued to play with the disc. To be honest, Wayne was a bit rough for her taste and not very attuned to things cultural. It would have been so cool if he was, say, an actor or a singer while still looking tough and gorgeous like he did. But it was crystal clear – jet clear – that he really liked her. Loved her probably, even though he hadn't said it yet. She tossed her hair.

And gifts like this ... Well! No other girl in Marie's friendship group got gifts like this from a boyfriend.

Cassie moved from her chair to study the black disc in the light from the window. 'Oh, that's beautiful. And all the carving looks modern despite being that old. So you don't know what the symbols mean?'

'I just said they've never been translated.' Marie gave up. If Cassie wasn't able to concentrate on a gift from a boyfriend, she was clearly distracted by something important. More important than the homework they'd met to talk about. A play for drama class that had to be at least ten minutes long, though preferably twenty. It hadn't been going well. Miss Nackenhorst, their drama teacher, had urged everyone to write about what they knew. But what did she and Cassie know? It was all proving too hard.

'What's wrong?' Marie asked.

'It's Kenny.'

'Is he pushing you again?'

'No, it's not that. Not anything like that. It's his sister's tablet.'

'*What?*'

'Her tablet.' Cassie sighed heavily, deeply. Sighed again. 'O-K. His sister's gone on holiday, to Lanzarote, with her boyfriend.'

'The rugby player?'

Nodding, 'Which is a massive secret, right, which you already know. So, Kenny's parents were away for the weekend and Saturday night he wanted me to come to his but I convinced him to have a party instead and his parents were cool with that. A lot cooler than they would have been if I'd been there alone with him. Anyway, word got around and like twenty people came – you were at the movies with Wayne. And somebody stole his sister's tablet.'

'*What?*'

'His sister's new tablet. Someone stole it.'

'Who?'

'He doesn't know. And it's just horrible to think that someone at his *party* would do something like that.'

'Has he told his parents? Or the police?'

'God, no. They'd never let him have friends over again. And his sister's going to kill him, because she left it and her phone behind on purpose so that their parents couldn't contact her because she's supposedly in a cottage in Wales on a hen week, you know? But that's not all.'

'What?'

'Kenny's seen it. The tablet. He's seen it for sale on eBay.'

'Who's selling it?'

'It's a code name – MrTech99. He has no idea who it is. But it's the same tablet all right. His sister has a Brooklyn Beckham sticker on hers, and the picture of the tablet for sale on eBay actually shows the sticker. It's totally his sister's tablet.'

'Oooh, Cas, you do mix in the second division, don't you.' Marie fondled the jet roses.

'Well, Wayne's not exactly everything a heart could desire,' Cassie said. 'Although, I'm surprised he has such good taste in jewellery, because he always struck me as likely to be *third* division where choosing pretty presents was concerned.'

'Wayne has hidden depths. And he chose me, didn't he, which shows he completely knows what's beautiful.' But Marie was a bit cross with Cassie because part of her agreed with her friend. Wayne was less than perfect.

Tuesday night was one of the regular family dinnertimes at the Lunghis. All eight were in attendance. Papa and Mama, Gina and Angelo – Marie's parents – Rosetta and Salvatore, Angelo's siblings – and David, Marie's brother.

At such dinners they always talked about the family business, a detective agency started by Papa decades ago. This night Angelo went first and updated everyone about a case of mistaken identity that he was testifying about in court. 'I forget sometimes,' he said, 'just how tedious court proceedings can be.'

'But they pay,' the Old Man – Papa – said. It sounded like a statement, but it was really an attempt to have the fact affirmed. He didn't entirely remember the details of Angelo's case but sometimes his progeny had a disconcerting inclination to work for free. Perhaps they were too comfortable. Perhaps he should threaten disinheritance. That would buck up their inclinations. Huh.

'They pay, Papa,' Gina said. Gina worked mostly from the office and she knew all the business's details.

'Good,' the Old Man said. Gina he trusted. 'Good. My client also pays.'

Although the Old Man no longer worked on the agency's

bread-and-butter cases – for lawyers and other professionals – he had developed a niche market of his own, doing
detective work for older people. Sometimes older clients
preferred to work with an older detective. One who could
see things from their perspective. And who maybe wasn't so
busy. And a detective who didn't mind if a case was 'small'.

The Old Man's current client was a posh lady who lived
on one of the hills that overlooked the ancient centre of
Bath. Mrs Angstrom had lots of money, which was why
she'd come to the Lunghis. The Old Man was investigating
her niece's three children. She didn't want to leave money
to gold-diggers and all three of these children were suddenly being attentive. Had they heard about her illness?
How could that be?

Someone of Papa's age could understand her concern.
Of course he could. And there was no need to spell out to
her that when it came to the computer side of his investigations he got some younger help. Perhaps he didn't spell
out that the help was from a teenager, his grandson. But
help was help.

Although there was nothing substantively new to report,
the Old Man did offer for consideration a new theory about
what was happening. That it was Mrs Angstrom's niece
herself digging for the gold. If one of the children came
into money, the child would support its mother. 'That's
what a child would do,' he said. 'A good child.' He turned
to Mama for support. Mama smiled. The new angle on the
case had actually been hers, though she was happy not to
be credited.

The other adults were entirely content for the Old Man to continue his line of enquiries. 'Just as long as she pays,' Salvatore said waggishly.

'Of *course* she pays,' the Old Man said. 'Huh!'

Salvatore was a painter and only worked on cases which called for extra manpower, or when he was in need of more money than he managed as a painter and, more recently, an art teacher.

His sister, Rosetta, did work in the business, but almost exclusively by handling the family's finances and its technical equipment. On this evening, however, neither sibling had anything to say about cases. Each was currently more interested in personal romantic 'cases' with developments that weren't yet ready to be reported to the family. Reported to Mama, to be specific.

The family matriarch wanted nothing more before she died than to see her remaining two children married. Or partnered. She would settle for partnered. She was that modern and flexible.

But after years of urgings, hints and subtle subterfuges, Mama felt her time was running out. An idea sparked by her husband's current case had led her to think about her own will. Could she make it a condition that neither Rosetta nor Salvatore would inherit without being married? Or partnered?

And could she do such a thing without her husband knowing until it was done? He surely would disapprove – for him inheritance was straightforward: everything to her, and then the children equally. He had talked of such things in the course of ruminations on behalf of Mrs Angstrom.

So Mama's plans too were not ready for sharing. Because her real goal was to make things happen while she was still alive.

'I have a new case, actually,' Marie said as the final plates of linguini with scallops were being cleared. 'And before you ask, yes, my client is paying.' She had taken a pound off Cassie in order to be able to make this statement truthfully.

All the adults looked at Marie. She was a dramatic girl – even for a teenager in her first A-level year. But a case? She had never once brought the agency a case.

'A case of what?' Marie's younger brother, David asked. 'Nail polish?' David, a geek, aspired to be the family wit. But although he was also preoccupied by his own loves – computers and, currently, a girl in the Fourth Year who looked up to him as an older man – he was also serious about the business. He loved being his grandfather's silent partner.

'My client,' Marie said, 'who wishes to remain anonymous, is trying to recover a stolen tablet. The tablet in question was stolen Saturday night by person or persons unknown, but it is now being offered for sale on eBay. The identification of the tablet is absolute. I bring the case to the family because my client wants us to get the tablet back without involving the police – who would undoubtedly keep it as evidence for months. My plan, with my client's approval, is to challenge the thief face-to-face with proof that the tablet he is trying to sell is stolen. I will *threaten* to go to the police if he doesn't turn the tablet over to me. But awesome as I am, I think I might not be intimidating enough on my own, so I would like one or more of the family's adult males to accompany me and back me up with a video and audio record of what's said and done. If the thief doubts my intentions, showing him that we have him on video will convince him. Is somebody willing to help me, or should I go on my own? Either way, I'm confident we'll have a satisfied customer.' Satisfying customers was another of the Old Man's mantras.

Marie liked that her presentation had gone much as she'd rehearsed it and without interruption, even from David. Was there some way this situation could be used in the play with Cassie? She'd already written and learned the speech.

'Marie has brought us a case,' the Old Man said.

'Wonderful,' Mama said. She knew that such an initiative from their granddaughter would please her husband, put him in a good mood. Maybe make it a good time to talk about conditions in her will.

'But such a fuss about a tablet?' the Old Man said. 'For a pill? Can it be legal?'

'Tablet is what they call a kind of computer nowadays,' Marie said.

'So why not call it a computer?' The Old Man looked around the table for support. When none was forthcoming he said, 'Huh!' Then, 'Gelato. I'll have gelato, I think. For energy, for this confrontation with a master criminal.'

Gina and Angelo were cautious and they were certainly reluctant to encourage the Old Man, or Marie, to confront anybody who was selling stolen goods. 'I don't know—' Angelo began.

But Gina cut him off. 'How much money is the thief asking for the stolen tablet?'

'A hundred and thirty pounds,' Marie said.

'For a second-hand tablet?' David said. 'Is it made of *gold* nail polish?' David hated to give up on jokes he felt had been underappreciated. But this reference to nail polish was also met with silence. Ah well. He said, 'Sellers on eBay usually post items to purchasers. How are you going to meet this thief face-to-face?'

'I've thought of that,' Marie said. 'I'll say I want to collect it in person to avoid postage and the risk of damage. And the eBay listing says the seller lives in Bath. I think my plan is a lock.'

'Marie,' her father said, beginning again, 'we don't take anonymous clients. And if you think I'm going to let you go to the premises of someone who is selling stolen goods, you're . . . '

'Crazy?' David offered.

'Mistaken,' Gina said.

'I've said I don't want to go alone,' Marie said.

But it was David again who raised another pertinent problem. 'If this perp is from Bath, mightn't he recognise our family's name when we agree to buy the tablet?'

Marie hadn't thought of that, and since the thief had been at Kenny's party, he was very likely to be a fellow student. Her name was legend at the school. Even wimpy David was known in some circles.

Further discussion established that although the second and third generation Lunghis all had eBay accounts, only Salvatore's did not include the family name: he was 'painter42'.

'You are ashamed of our name?' the Old Man complained loudly.

'Why 42?' Gina asked.

'Because 42 is the answer to everything,' Salvatore said.

Only David laughed, having read *Hitchhiker's Guide to the Galaxy* three times.

Cassie's identity as Marie's client was also revealed. But reluctance to get involved was overcome when the Old Man said, 'We must help this girl, who is a friend of Marie's.' And anyway it really was a novelty to have Marie so involved in anything related to the business.

'Does your Cassie get pocket money? Or have a job?' the Old Man asked. It was a question that also accepted that the agency was not going to make proper money from this case. Mama looked at her husband with interest. Was he becoming flexible in his old age?

A postprandial meeting of the adults produced a plan. Salvatore would contact the seller and express a wish to buy the tablet, so long as he could see it working first. He also wished to avoid postage costs by collecting it in person. Salvatore made the approach to MrTech99 on his phone while the adults shared some wine in the living room.

Except for the Old Man and Mama who had retreated to their flat at the top of the family property. The Old Man was tired and he still had work to do on his case. 'David,' he'd said, 'do you have a few minutes?'

Marie had gone to her room, no doubt to report events to Cassie. Marie wore her moods close to the surface. Marie was happy.

'I don't know about all this,' Angelo said. He drank some wine. He savoured it. 'Ah.'

'Do you think Marie's not telling the real story?' Rosetta said.

'What do you think?' Angelo asked Gina.

'The tablet is there on eBay,' Salvatore said. 'The picture shows the Brooklyn Beckham sticker. And the item location is listed as Bath.'

'Could she just be trying to get us to buy her this computer?' Angelo asked.

'Her own tablet is streets better than this one,' Rosetta said, looking at the specs on Salvatore's phone. She'd been responsible for buying it for Marie's birthday. An all-singing-all-dancing machine, it could easily last her through university, if she went. And Rosetta'd got a very good deal.

'I think we suck it and see,' Gina said. 'But with more people rather than fewer, depending on what kind of meeting Sally can set up for the transfer.'

'What if the perp won't just hand the tablet over?' Angelo said.

'Give him the money and use our video record to get the police to arrest him?' Gina suggested. 'The video probably wouldn't be accepted in court but our testimony would.'

'*Another* court case? Oh wonderful.' Angelo drank again from his wine.

They did not consider their plan to be 'a lock', but it was the best they could devise with the information they had. And before the second bottle of wine was finished, Salvatore had exchanged several emails with 'MrTech99' through eBay's contact system.

I want to buy the tablet you're offering, subject to confirmation that it works, Salvatore had written.

It works.

I can come to Bath to pick it up. You can demonstrate that it works then.

OK, but if you're not paying by PayPal, I'll need cash.

Discount for cash? Say £100?

£120. That's my best offer.

OK. Does it have an instruction manual?

You can get one online.

What about a warranty?

You'll see it working. It's got its charger. I'm a private seller, not a business, and it's always worked perfectly for me.

I'll need an address and a time and your mobile number in case I'm delayed. Parking in Bath is awful.

I'll meet you in the Pig and Fiddle. Nine o'clock tomorrow night. That's on the corner of Broad Street and Saracen Street. There's a car park around the corner.

A pub? That makes this sound dodgy.

I'm going out with mates. If you want me to post it to you, pay the full price and P&P and you'll have it in a couple of days.

OK, the Pig and Fiddle at nine tomorrow then. But I will need to see it working.

I'll make sure it's charged. And you're paying cash, right. No cheques.

Cash. One-twenty. How will I know you?

I'll be the guy with the tablet next to his pint.

And the phone number?
MrTech99 provided a mobile number.

In fact the Pig and Fiddle was only a couple of minutes' walk from the Lunghis' home and workplace. But it could have been miles away as far as Marie was concerned: she was adamant that she would be at the pub for the transfer. Salvatore could locate the thief and let him show the tablet. But Marie would be there too, saying the tablet was being bought for her. And it was she who would challenge the thief with identification of the tablet as stolen. Salvatore would already be recording the conversation with a concealed audio recorder.

Angelo and Rosetta, in another location, would be recording the transaction on video. Their new video recorder looked like a phone. It would *seem* that Rosetta was taking pictures of her boyfriend, while she was actually focusing over her brother's shoulder with high-quality close-ups and directional audio. They would leave their table and move around, if necessary.

They would set out for the pub at eight-fifteen. Even Marie. Even though it was a school night.

Marie wanted to invite Cassie's Kenny, but the adults said no because the thief would recognize Kenny. They were already worried he would recognise Marie, but she reassured them on *that* score. She was a drama student: she would disguise herself. She had wigs. No one would recognize her as a blonde with heart-shaped sunglasses.

Picturing the showdown, she saw herself standing before the perp, whipping off the wig and glasses. 'Busted!' she would declare. She rehearsed her tone of voice with Cassie during lunch at school. Cassie was impressed by Marie's bravery.

And Kenny was grateful to have a chance of getting out of his fix, no matter how indebted he would end up being to Cassie's melodramatic friend. He still had no idea who'd stolen the tablet. His imagination was not his main appeal to Cassie.

'Now, what to wear ... ?' Marie said to Cassie on the phone after school. 'Nothing that's really *me*, but I will, after all, be on video.'

By eight-thirty the Lunghis were in position. The Pig and Fiddle had two entrances with its bar in the middle. Angelo and Rosetta took a table opposite the bar from which they had good views of both doorways and most of the pub. If the thief led Salvatore somewhere else – outside to tables under awnings, for instance – they'd do their best to follow inconspicuously.

Salvatore and Marie shared a small table against a wall near the main entrance but they were making no pretence of conversation. Salvatore was immersed in a book called *The Tooth Tattoo*. His blonde 'friend' was texting Cassie: *30 minutes and counting*.

Then Wayne walked in.

For a moment Marie thought it was coincidence, a happy accident. He would be *so* impressed that she was working on a family case. But then she saw that he had something under his arm, wrapped in a carrier bag.

The penny dropped. Or, being Melodramatic Marie, what dropped was a two-pound coin. Surely not. Then *surely* ...

'I'm going to the loo, Uncle Sal,' she told Salvatore.

'OK,' he said, without looking up.

There was no time to take account of her father and aunt. Marie presented herself in front of her boyfriend.

'Hel*lo* there,' Wayne said with the crinkled-mouthed smile that had so charmed her when they first met outside the drama studio at school. He'd said he was lost. Then later confessed that he'd been waiting for a chance to speak to her.

They stood silent for a moment. Shocked, Marie realised that he had not recognised her. The *idiot*.

'Wayne ... ' she said in an urgent whisper, whipping off the sunglasses.

'Marie?' He stood there, jaw hanging.

'Of course it's Marie, you dolt. And you are about to get busted.'

'*What*?'

'There are three plain-clothes policemen just waiting for you to "sell" the tablet under your arm to painter42.'

Mouth still open, Wayne looked dimly around the room.

Marie said, 'As soon as you take the hundred and twenty quid they'll arrest you for selling stolen goods and thieving it in the first place. They'll have you on audio and on video. They'll march you out in handcuffs. They'll lock you up forever.'

'I ... I didn't thieve it.' But Wayne showed signs of panic. 'Wha ... ? How do *you* know?'

'My family's business is a *detective* agency. We *know* these things.'

Wayne turned toward the door.

'*No*, idiot,' Marie said. 'They'll get you before you can

take two steps. You're in possession of stolen property.
Come with me. *Now.*' She took his arm and conducted him
past the bar, past Angelo and Rosetta, and up the stairs past
a sequence of cartoons: Julius Caesar Pig, Admiral Nelson
Pig . . . They marched into the Ladies.

Wayne was too numbed to object.

Once inside, Marie spun him to face her. 'Give it to me.
Give it to me.'

Wayne handed over the carrier bag.

She could feel what it was but she had to look. Brooklyn
Beckham looked back at her. 'I am *so* disappointed in you,
Wayne Mount. I cannot begin to tell you.'

'But I didn't thieve it. You know that. You could be my
alibi.'

That's what he thought of her? As an *alibi*? Pigs might fly.

'Please, Marie.'

'Get out, Wayne. While you still can. Go back through
the pub the way you came in. Look around as if you were
expecting to meet someone. Act like the person isn't
there – can you do *that* much acting? Then shake your head
like the person's let you down and leave slowly. *Slowly.* It's
your only chance.'

'But . . . ' Wayne stretched a hand toward the carrier bag.
'When do I get it back?'

'You *don't*, you idiot. It's not *yours*.'

'But Freddie will kill me.'

'Freddie who?' But then she knew. He was in the Upper
Sixth and going out with Kim. 'Tell him this is what happens when he steals from friends of mine. Tell him if he

doesn't like it, he can come down to the police station with me after school and see if *they* tell me to give it back to him. Now move, Wayne. *Move!*'

A toilet flushed in one of the two stalls. Wayne looked. Marie made a wide-eyed face. 'You're in the ladies' loos, *idiot*. What are you? A pervert?'

Wayne turned and left.

A hippy-dressed woman in her thirties emerged from the stall, straightened her clothes and went to one of the two basins. Marie slipped into the other stall. As she turned to close the door she saw the woman looking at her in the mirror. '*What?*' Marie shouted, and slammed the door. It bounced open. She closed it and bolted it, muttering, 'Perv.'

Safely alone, she wanted to sit but there was no lid. All she could do was stand where she was, breathing hard. Then lean against the door hugging the tablet. Things fell into place. Like how Wayne could have so much money to spend on her without having a job. How could she have been so *stupid*?

The problem was that she had *really* liked him. How he looked. How he carried himself. That he appreciated her clever quips without needing to try to match them.

How could he have *done* this to her?

She began to cry. Even though Marie Lunghi never cried.

The detectives were home again well before ten. 'So?' Gina asked.

'A no-show,' Angelo said.

'I rang him at five past nine,' Salvatore said, 'to ask if he was somewhere in the pub. But he didn't answer. I tried again fifteen minutes later and the phone was turned off. Again, around nine-thirty, it was still off.'

'So we called it,' Angelo said. 'But Rosetta has some lovely tapes of me mugging for the camera.'

'Not tapes,' Rosetta said. 'It's all digital. We could upload it straight to YouTube – if it were more interesting. I wonder, does anything on YouTube ever get no views at all?'

'Oh dear,' Gina said. 'Marie, you look upset.'

'I'm just unhappy that Cassie's Kenny won't get his tablet back.'

Gina considered. 'We *could* report it to the police.'

'Isn't Kenny the one who should do that?' Angelo asked. 'Which isn't to say they're likely to do much for him.'

'It's not exactly finding a severed foot in a public park,' Rosetta said, referring to a recent city event.

'But,' Gina said, '*we* can try to make contact with MrTech99 again to see what his story is. Salvatore?'

'Yeah, I can do that.' But he was clearly without enthusiasm. He was more interested in what would happen next in his book than in events with MrTech.

David appeared in the living room from his bedroom, wreathed in smiles. 'MrTech99 has deleted the eBay listing. Do I *deduce* that things went as planned?'

'He's taken down the listing?' Angelo said. 'That's surprising.'

'Why?' David said.

'Because we never met him. We didn't get the tablet.'

'But what's that Marie has in the carrier bag?'

No one had noticed the carrier bag.

Marie said, 'Homework, *idiot*. I took homework. It *is* a school night.'

'Wow,' Kenny said in the lunchroom next day. He stared at the tablet as if he could hardly believe it. 'Wow. Thank you soo much, Marie. You really saved my bacon.'

'He loves his bacon,' Cassie said. She and Marie giggled.

Kenny looked from one to the other. 'Really,' he said. 'I don't know what I would have done.'

'Just keep Freddie out of your house from now on,' Marie said.

'Freddie? That's who it was?' Kenny looked around the lunchroom. Apparently not seeing Freddie he turned back to the girls. 'Wayne's over there, Marie.'

'Wayne who?' She looked sternly at Cassie, who responded only by drawing a finger across her throat.

Kenny saw the gesture. 'Oh yeah? Well, his loss,' he said, trying to chime in, although he knew perfectly well what all the girls saw in Wayne.

But Cassie said, 'We *are* going to work on the play tonight, aren't we?'

'Oh yes,' Marie said. 'I have just the story. It has drama, tension and redemption.'

'Wow,' Cassie said.

'I've spent far too much of my school career trying to live

my family down. I'm going to embrace my inner detective. It's all about how a teenager comes to have money without *working* for it, and the nasty consequences.'

'Wow,' Kenny said.

'But are you going to tell Kim?' Cassie said. 'We could meet her after school.'

'*You* meet her after school,' Marie said. 'Haven't I done enough?' She tossed her hair. 'Besides, I've got something else I have to do. Something really, really hard.'

Bath used to have a police station on Manvers Street but the building had been sold to the city's expanding university. The area's police HQ was now miles away, in the cheaper town of Keynsham. The only remaining fixed police presence in the city was a cubbyhole in Bath's local government 'One Stop Shop'.

Complain about uncollected rubbish, pay a parking ticket, apply for benefits, report a murder: all under the one roof.

Marie had never been in the One Stop Shop before. She was directed to a counter well off to the side where two young police officers sat.

'May I help you?' A female officer in her twenties who looked weary.

Marie breathed heavily. What she'd resolved to do here was not a natural thing for her.

A bloke cop looked on, but said nothing. Perhaps the woman took all the female enquiries.

The young woman saw Marie's uncertainty. 'If you'd like

to speak confidentially, there's a room where we can talk in private.'

'Please,' Marie said.

'I'm Constable Phillips,' the woman said as she got up. 'Haley.' She left the cubbyhole by a side door and then led Marie across a narrow corridor to a small room fronted with opaque glass. The room had a few chairs, a small table and some electrical equipment by a wall. The glass in an outside window was also opaque.

'Have a seat,' Haley Phillips said.

Marie sat.

'Now what can I do for you ... ?'

'Marie.'

'Is it about some kind of crime, Marie?'

Marie was *so* out of her element. At school among friends, or just with her family, she was brash and boisterous. She always had something to say and was ready to say it. But here ... She was not just with a stranger, but with the *police*. This was the law. This was the real world.

This was hard.

But it had to be done. From her bag she took an envelope and passed it to Constable Phillips. Who studied it for a moment and then looked inside.

She pulled out the jet necklace. She looked into the envelope. Finding nothing more, she examined the necklace more closely. 'Unusual,' she said, looking to Marie to explain.

'It's jet. A rare and expensive stone that's found in the sea. Those are roses.'

'Interesting.'

'I found it. In the street.'

'And . . . ?'

'I'm turning it in. I thought it might be stolen or something. But it's not mine. And it's so beautiful, someone will be missing it,' Marie said sadly. She was missing it already – its warm weight against her neck, the strange runes that were probably symbols of love, the roses. What *could* they all mean but love?

It wasn't that she loved Wayne exactly. But with a gift like this – for no special *reason* – she'd thought he must love her. But Wayne had not turned out to be the real thing, any more than the disc was a real gift. Wayne was bogus. Strictly second division. Or third. Or Fourth! And she'd never settle for less than the best again. Even if it meant she lived her whole life without love! Even if she never had another boyfriend until she went to university!

'Marie?' It was Officer Phillips.

'Yes?'

'We have a procedure for lost items.'

'Good. Thank you.'

'But if no one claims it then in six weeks you can have it back. If you want it.'

'Have it back? I can?'

'That's what the law says, unless, say, there's reason to believe it's connected to a crime. But if you just found it in the street . . . ? I'll need your contact details. If you'd want it.'

'No,' Marie said. 'I think not.'

*

Michael Z Lewin has been writing mystery novels, short stories, plays and other things for more than forty years. He hails from Indianapolis, Indiana, but has lived in the West Country since 1971 and Bath since 2000. The story in this collection features the Lunghis, who have operated their Bath family detective agency in three novels and several stories.

The Super Recogniser of Vík

Michael Ridpath

It is hard to believe Peter is now eighty. I have just finished Down Among the Dead Men, *published when he was still only seventy-nine. The book features a number of A-level art students. My own daughters have recently emerged from studying art at sixth form, and I am amazed at how well Peter has managed to capture the thought processes and speech patterns of the teenage female artist. The result of six decades of observing, listening and transferring real life to paper, no doubt. Perhaps when I am eighty I will be that good? Dream on.*

'How was London, Árni?'

Magnus looked up as he heard his younger partner's suitcase trundle into the Violent Crimes Unit.

Árni grinned. 'Great. A very useful four days.'

'Did you see the Hotspurs play?'

'Spurs, Magnus. Spurs. And yes we won, one-nil. Against Manchester City. A great result.'

Magnus grunted. One of the several bits of Icelandic

culture he hadn't yet got to grips with was their love of English soccer teams. He had played football himself, real football, a running back for his high school team back in Massachusetts. He dimly remembered kicking a ball around as a child on his grandparent's farm on Snaefellsnes, but he had only really got into sport when he had moved to America at the age of twelve. What with one thing and another he had become a cop and joined the Homicide Unit of the Boston Police Department. So, when the National Police Commissioner of Iceland had gone to the States in search of big-city modern police experience to help out with big-city modern police problems in Reykjavík, he had alighted on Magnus as about the only Icelandic-speaking homicide detective in the US.

It was the same spirit of keeping up with modern police methods that had prompted the Commissioner to send someone to London on an anti-terrorism course. That person had been Árni.

'Did you learn anything useful?' Magnus asked.

'Sure. I think I can guarantee the safety of our international rail terminal and our entire subway system.'

Magnus rolled his eyes. There were no trains in Iceland. And no subway system. But were there any terrorists? Probably not, but you could never be too careful. The Commissioner was right to be wary of complacency in Niceland. Serious crime wasn't common, but when it happened it could be nasty, as Magnus had already discovered.

Why send Árni, though? He was a nice guy, but hardly Iceland's smartest detective. Yet he was brave and he was loyal: he had once taken a bullet for Magnus, literally. And his uncle was head of CID in the Reykjavík Metropolitan Police.

Árni sat himself in the chair on the other side of Magnus' desk. His eyes were shining. Uh-oh. It looked suspiciously as if Árni had had an idea.

'I've had an idea,' Árni said.

'Yes?'

'I was sitting next to this British woman on the course. A sergeant. Ingeborg Smith.'

'Ingiborg? Is her mother Icelandic?'

'No, it's spelled with an "e", the Swedish way, but she says she's completely English. Very nice. She looks Nordic – blonde, you know. She's from Bath in the west of England. We had a drink in a pub.'

'Árni, are you in love?' Magnus was troubled. A lovesick Árni could be a real problem.

'No! No. There were a group of us from the course. But she told me about this special unit in the Metropolitan Police in London. "Super Recognisers".'

'Super recognisers?'

'Apparently a very small proportion of the general population have excellent recall of faces. They can remember thousands and so they can match and cross-reference images of suspects better than any normal human, or for that matter any computer. The Met has a team of seven of them, police officers recruited from all over the country, and they've had some great success.'

'Doing what?'

'Looking at CCTV. Identifying suspects. Making arrests.'

'And?'

'I thought we could use one for the Raffles Case.'

'You mean the Thingholt jewellery burglaries. You know how Baldur hates you calling it the Raffles Case.'

'Have you got anywhere with it yet?' Árni asked.

'No. Nothing.' It was frustrating. There had been three burglaries of very expensive jewellery from houses in the wealthy section of Thingholt, the hill in the centre of Reykjavík. Despite trying for two months, CID had been unable to break open the case. Detectives from the Violent Crimes Unit had been drafted in to help their colleagues. Iceland was an island, you would have thought it would be difficult to dispose of such distinctive pieces without someone somewhere in Iceland's criminal community hearing something, but there had been not a whisper. No forensic evidence to speak of. An indistinct CCTV image of a figure in a balaclava inside one of the houses, and some more from a neighbouring property of a succession of people walking down the street that evening. The burglar could be any one of them, or possibly someone else entirely. Without a name, the press had dubbed him 'Raffles of Reykjavík'.

They had had no luck with the CCTV images either. There were about thirty possibles, which had been divided up among a team of detectives who had laboriously checked the photographs against known criminals. One match, but the man had just been released from the prison at Litla Hraun, and so could not have performed two of the three burglaries.

The real problem was that the neighbours were worried that all their beautiful jewellery would be stolen. And the neighbours in that particular area of Reykjavík were either politicians, or the people who funded the politicians.

Baldur, the head of the unit, wanted the case solved. Árni's uncle, the head of CID, wanted the case solved. The National Police Commissioner wanted the case solved. The press wanted Raffles to strike again, so they could really lay into Reykjavík's incompetent police force.

'Then let's bring in a super recogniser,' Árni said.

'Isn't that too late? It would have been useful last week, but we've already checked the CCTV images and found nothing.'

'No. We get the super recogniser to check them against ordinary people in the city. Lots of them.'

'What, he wanders around the streets of Reykjavík staring at strangers?'

'Not quite. The shopping malls. He monitors the security cameras in the Kringlan mall. And Smáralind.'

Those were the two biggest malls in Reykjavík. In the country.

'OK, I see that quite a few people go to those places. But not everyone in the whole country.'

'Of course not,' said Árni. 'But if Raffles is a jewel thief he's going to like buying stuff, isn't he? And we know he spends time in the centre of Reykjavík, if only turning over rich people's houses.'

It was a dumb idea. But it might work. Maybe.

'Where do we get the super recogniser from? Did you bring one back from London?'

'We get one from Iceland.'

'How exactly do we find one of these super recognisers here?'

'I've done it already,' said Árni. 'My cousin, Gulli.'

'He's a super recogniser?'

'At the age of twelve he could identify every sheep in his valley. And then they tested him in the next valley over and he could do those as well. That's thousands of sheep! It was miraculous. You should have seen it, Magnus.'

Magnus closed his eyes and for a moment yearned for the old days of processing homicide victims in Roxbury. Policing in Iceland was . . . well . . . different.

'OK. So your cousin Gulli is an expert at identifying sheep. How do we know he can recall human faces?'

'There's an online test. We give it to him. If he passes, we get him to monitor the CCTV feeds for a week and we pick up anyone he identifies.'

'Where does he live?'

'Near Vík.'

'But that's two hundred kilometres away!'

'Got a better idea?'

Vík was a settlement of three hundred souls, clinging to the far southernmost edge of Iceland. Gulli's farm was a few kilometres out of town, in the crumpled belt of green between the majestic Mýrdal glacier to the north and the sea to the south. To the west brooded Eyjafjallajökull, the volcano which had belched ash and meltwater over this part of Iceland a few years before.

The farm was one of several reached by a straight track running off the main ring road around the island. Magnus parked his Range Rover, bought dirt cheap off a bankrupt bankster right after the crash, and climbed out of the car to inhale the fresh air blown in from the North Atlantic. It was always good to get out of Reykjavík. The cries of seabirds rent the air: terns, puffins and guillemots. He looked over the deep grey stretch of sea, and spotted the famous Reynisdrangar rocks, three basalt columns rearing out of the waves a few metres beyond the cliffs. Local legend had it that they were a three-masted ship and two female trolls that had been frozen to stone when the trolls were caught by the rising sun while dragging the ship out of the sea.

The farm seemed prosperous and well maintained: the classic Icelandic set-up of white concrete walls, red corrugated metal roof, lush green home meadow, a barn big enough to hold several hundred sheep and large plastic-coated bales of hay. There were few sheep in sight – they were up on the hills for the summer.

A tall, thin boy, dressed in the farmer's uniform of blue overalls, emerged from the barn to greet them.

'This is my cousin, Gulli,' said Árni, proudly.

Gulli held out his hand and Magnus shook it as the boy looked away and blushed. On closer inspection, Magnus could see that he was not a boy at all, but a man in his mid-twenties: tall like Árni, a protruding Adam's apple like

Árni, and weedy like Árni. No, weedier. Not a great asset around the farm, Magnus suspected.

'Come inside and have some coffee,' Gulli said, still not catching Magnus's eye.

Árni introduced Magnus to Gulli's mother, Bogga, a thin woman in her fifties with delicate features and long blonde hair tied in a plait. Despite her slight frame, she exuded that toughness and competence typical of Icelandic farming women. She gave Árni a hug and swiftly produced coffee and cakes – *vínarbraud,* the Icelandic version of Danish pastries. Nice.

Árni explained his idea to Gulli, who seemed intrigued. Árni then whipped out his laptop and put Gulli through his paces with the online test devised by a British psychology professor. It involved studying more and more obscure images of faces and matching them. Magnus and Árni had tried it earlier. Magnus had scored 58 out of a possible 80, Árni scored 39. Gulli scored 80. With no difficulty. It was amazing. Árni was right: the man's ability to recall faces was extraordinary.

Árni glanced at Magnus. Magnus nodded.

'So will you help us?' Árni asked him. 'Will you come to Reykjavík and help us find this Raffles?'

Gulli's enthusiasm left him. 'I'd like to, Árni, I really would. But there's no chance Dad would let me – is there, Mum?'

'Probably not. But you can ask him. Here he is.'

Out of the kitchen window, Magnus could see a broad-shouldered slab of a man striding towards the house purposefully, a red and white Icelandic sheepdog at his heels. He crashed into the house, kicked off his boots, and greeted Árni gruffly. For a moment, but only for a moment, Árni's enthusiastic friendliness was dampened, but then he introduced the farmer to Magnus as his Uncle Thór.

Árni explained what they wanted Gulli to do, and then he asked his uncle whether Gulli could come to Reykjavík to help them for a week or two.

Thór frowned. Six decades of wind and rain had etched his strong square face with a thousand tiny wrinkles. 'No,' he said. 'That's out of the question. We need Gulli here, we can't spare him.'

There was something about the man's stubbornness that riled Magnus, the idea that nothing could possibly be more important than his son's labour on the farm.

'Your son is an extraordinary individual,' Magnus said. 'No one else can do this in Iceland. And it's an important case. You must have read about it.'

'A lot of rich people losing jewellery they don't need,' said Thór. 'You wouldn't send someone all the way here from Reykjavík if my tractor had been stolen, would you? And what did you do when my dog was run over by some townie a couple of years ago? Nothing.'

Magnus didn't answer. Árni had explained that this uncle was from the other side of the family from his police-chief uncle. So, no, Thór couldn't expect much help from the Reykjavík Metropolitan Police.

'Well, would you?'

'Probably not,' Magnus admitted. There was no chance

of persuading the old bastard, he could see that now. A four-hundred-kilometre round trip wasted. Árni should have seen this coming.

The farmer reached down and grabbed a *vínarbraud*. As he munched his frown deepened. He glanced at his son. Then he bent down to scratch his dog behind the ears. The dog's tongue slipped out of its mouth and a curled tail beat from side to side on the floor.

'What do you think, Frakkur?'

Everyone else was quiet, letting Thór, or the dog, decide.

The farmer stood up. 'You know what?' He turned to Magnus. 'Why not? One week. That's all. Take him for a week.'

It was late by the time Magnus got home, after nine o'clock, but it was still light. Gulli was installed in a cheap hotel, a very cheap hotel, and looking forward to starting work in the Kringlan Mall the next morning. Perhaps infected with Árni's enthusiasm, Magnus was beginning to think that the idea might actually work.

Magnus lived on the top floor of a tiny house with a lime green corrugated metal roof on Njálsgata, in the centre of Reykjavík. His landlady was Katrín, Árni's sister, and Magnus passed her in her Gothic finery on her way out. She was an occasional backing singer in a not-very-good band.

'I saw your cousin Gulli, today,' Magnus said. 'In Vík.'

'What on earth were you doing there?'

'He's helping us with our enquiries. We think he might be able to identify the jewel thief we're after.'

Katrín raised a spiked eyebrow. 'Was that my brother's idea?'

Magnus nodded.

Katrín shook her head. 'That figures,' she said, as she walked off.

The Kringlan was Iceland's first shopping mall, not far from Reykjavík city centre. Magnus and Árni showed Gulli the pictures of the thirty passers-by, and set him up in a small, airless room in the management offices of the mall, with the photographs easily at hand. He joined a security officer in front of a bank of TV monitors as the first customers of the day rolled up. Magnus was pleased to see Gulli was taking his task seriously; whether he could keep his concentration going for the whole week was another question. Three policeman, two uniforms and one in plain clothes, stood by ready to arrest the suspect when Gulli spotted him.

The security guard, Siggi, eyed Gulli suspiciously. He was a small man of about forty with buck teeth and a newspaper, which he seemed quite keen to read.

No luck the first day. On the second, Gulli spotted two suspects from the Thingholt CCTV images. When they were questioned, one turned out to be a thirty-year-old flight attendant with Icelandair who was in Toronto on the night of the third burglary, and the other was a businessman, the next-door neighbour of the victim, on his way home. Nothing suspicious about that. The speed and accuracy of Gulli's ability to spot the suspects was impressive:

Magnus was sure he wouldn't have been able to do it. Siggi was impressed.

That afternoon, on his way out after checking up on Gulli, Magnus was surprised to see Gulli's mother Bogga drinking coffee at a café on the ground floor of the mall. He caught her eye and smiled, but she pretended not to see him. He wondered what she was doing there. Fussing over her son in the big city, no doubt, and embarrassed at being caught out.

On the third day, three more suspects and two shoplifters. Two of the suspects were neighbours and the third, a middle-aged divorced woman living alone, had no alibi, but it was hard to believe she was a real jewel thief. A detective was tasked with checking into her background, just in case.

Árni's idea was working to some extent, although it was looking unlikely that Gulli would spot even half of the thirty people on the Thingholt CCTV feed by the end of the week. But, as Árni had said, it was better than nothing. Following the results so far, a couple of detectives went around the houses in the immediate neighbourhood to eliminate the images of neighbours, which turned out to be eleven in number.

Nothing on the fourth day. Two unlikely leads on the fifth, and then on the fifth evening, a Monday, Magnus was called out to a serious assault in Vesturbaer, a smart section of town just up from the Old Harbour. A young lawyer, Jósef Kjartansson, had been badly beaten up by an intruder in his ground-floor apartment. Magnus went first to the scene, and then to the hospital, where Jósef was in bed with a leg broken in two places. He was due to be operated on in the morning.

'I hope you are going to get the bastard who did this,' he said. His chubby face was flushed, and covered with a film of sweat. He had that air of entitlement that young successful Icelanders occasionally brandished, which always rubbed Magnus up the wrong way. Magnus took an instant dislike to the man, but he tried to control it.

'We will get him,' Magnus said. And he would. He pulled out his notebook. 'Tell me what happened.'

'I came back from work about seven o'clock. I dumped my briefcase, took off my jacket and went through to my bedroom. I noticed the flat was cold, and in the bedroom the back window was open. It had been broken.'

'I saw that,' said Magnus. The back window was accessed through a tiny garden that was out of sight from neighbours.

'Yeah. So I assumed that I had been burgled. Maybe this Raffles I've read about? So I went through to the living room to see what had been nicked and there was this guy waiting for me, wearing a balaclava.'

Magnus listened – he would get a description later in the interview.

'I was shocked. The guy stood up. I asked him what the hell he was doing there.

'Then, out of nowhere, he produced this metal crowbar and swung it at my legs. He was fast, and I went down. Then he hit me again in the thigh, really hard. I could hear it crack.

'I screamed. "What was that for?" I said.

'"Bassi," he said. And then he was gone. He left through the bedroom. Must have climbed back out the window.'

'Bassi? Who is Bassi?'

'How the hell would I know?' The chubby face was red now. 'That's for you to find out.'

'All right, but I could use some help from you, Jósef. Do you have any idea at all who it might be?'

'I don't know anyone of that name.'

'Are you sure? A friend's nickname?'

'Of course I'm bloody sure!'

Jósef, indignant and in pain, was of very little help. His description of the intruder was nothing better than 'medium height or maybe a bit tall'. Magnus showed him the image from inside one of the burgled houses of the jewel thief in his balaclava, but Jósef couldn't tell whether it was the same man or, for that matter, whether it was the same balaclava. As for the voice – he was a native Icelander. Could have been young, but maybe he was older. No idea what he was wearing.

Useless.

After twenty minutes Magnus found his sympathy veering away from Jósef and towards whoever had broken his legs.

Jósef was convinced he had no enemies, no jilted girlfriends or jealous lovers. He worked for a law firm that was still unravelling the mess at the Icelandic banks during the crash. He hadn't testified or acted against any of the bankers who had been sent to jail.

But somebody didn't like him. And, despite the fact Jósef was a jerk, Magnus would find out who.

Back at police headquarters, Magnus looked up the name 'Bassi'. Iceland had a list of official names by which babies could be registered, and Bassi had only been added in 2010. It was more likely to be a nickname – it meant either bass, as in bass guitar, or a little bear. He checked the criminal database. Then the phone directory, which was listed by first name, not last name as in most other countries. Nothing.

It was a serious assault and so the forensic team had gone to work with little result. No fingerprints, some fibres, indistinct footprints in the garden. Once he had heard that the jewel thief had worn a balaclava, Jósef was convinced that he had been attacked by 'Raffles'. Magnus thought it unlikely. It looked as if nothing had been taken, and a bachelor, even a yuppie lawyer, would not own the kind of jewellery that had tempted the burglar before. It seemed to Magnus that the intruder had been waiting for Jósef with the intention of doing him serious harm.

Time to do some legwork. Interview Jósef's neighbours, his friends, his work colleagues. Someone would hate him enough to beat him up. Someone would know someone who was called Bassi. Someone big, bearded and bearlike perhaps, or someone with a deep voice.

But the following morning, Raffles of Reykjavík was on the front page again. A journalist had got to Jósef in hospital, who had advanced his theory that he had been attacked by the burglar. This was not a good development. If the richest inhabitants of Reykjavík could not go to sleep at night without the fear of being beaten up by a violent burglar, they would not be happy. Results would be demanded, quick results.

Which was fair enough, Magnus had to admit. But he was damn sure that the man in the balaclava who had assaulted the young lawyer was not the man in a balaclava who had stolen the jewels.

He did the legwork. Spoke to Jósef's colleagues, spoke to neighbours, looked over his flat again, studied the forensics reports. It was a residential street, so plenty people had walked up and down it that evening. There were no CCTV images this time, but two local kids of about fourteen had been spotted hanging round smoking, and someone had noticed a woman in a red coat walking back and forth along the road. No description. Nothing to go on.

And after a promising start, Gulli wasn't coming up with anything either.

It was Gulli's last day, and Magnus and Árni went to the Smáralind mall, where they had moved him in hope of better luck or at least a different set of customers, to take him out to dinner. Thór had been insistent that he couldn't spare his son any longer, and Gulli, of course, had been unwilling to stand up to him.

They went to a restaurant on Laugavegur, the main shopping street in the centre of town, near Thingholt where the jewel thief had struck. Gulli seemed to have enjoyed his week in Reykjavík, despite spending most of it in a

windowless room staring at screens. And he was excited
about catching the shoplifters.

When they had finished, they walked him back to the
hotel, which was close to the police station.

'Did your mother stay at the same place as you?' Magnus
asked.

'What?' Gulli said.

'Your mother. I saw her on Thursday, just outside the mall.
I assumed she was visiting you.' Or checking up on you.

'My mother didn't come to Reykjavík.'

'But I saw her, I'm sure,' said Magnus.

'No,' said Gulli. But he was staring down at his feet and
blushing.

He's lying. Magnus thought. He considered pushing Gulli
on it – Magnus's instinct when someone was lying to him
was to try to find out the truth – but it seemed mean. The
poor kid had done a lot for the police already that week.

Why would he lie about seeing his mother?

Embarrassment, probably. He was ashamed to admit
that his Mum was checking up on him. It was a long way to
travel from Vík to do that.

Gulli raised his eyes towards the Hallgrímskirkja, the
smooth concrete church on the crest of Reykjavík's high-
est hill, which was glimmering in the dusk, illuminated by
subtle lighting.

Then he stiffened and turned.

'That's him!' he said. He was staring at the back of a man
who had just strolled past them on the pavement, heading
back towards the centre of town.

Magnus didn't need to ask who it was that Gulli had seen. He strode briskly after the man, who turned when he heard Magnus coming.

'Stop!' Magnus commanded. 'I'm a policeman.'

The man, who was in his twenties, hesitated, and then ran. Magnus sprinted after him, chased him up a side street, and brought him to the ground with a crunching American-football-style tackle, knocking all the breath out of him.

Within seconds the suspect was cuffed, face down on the pavement. From what Magnus could see of the man's face pressed against the pavement, he was indeed one of the younger men from the Thingholt CCTV images. In theory innocent men do sometimes run from the police. In theory this young, agile suspect might turn out to be yet another false lead. But Magnus was pretty sure he had caught Raffles of Reykjavík.

'On your feet!' Magnus commanded, dragging the man upright. 'Now, what's your name?'

'Hey, cool it,' the man said, in English. 'I don't speak Icelandic. What's the problem?'

'Your problem, buddy, is that you have stolen a whole lot of jewellery, and you have been caught. You're coming with us to the police station to tell us all about it.'

'I don't know what you're talking about!' said the man.

But he did. His name was Ruud van der Linden, he was Dutch, and he was the boyfriend of a girl who worked with an upmarket florist in Thingholt. When they searched her apartment, the police found a pair of diamond and sapphire earrings in a plastic bag stuffed into a jar of flour. Van der Linden was smart; he had a degree in electric engineering and had worked for a burglar alarm company in Rotterdam. He had returned to his home country on a regular basis, smuggling the jewels to sell in Holland. Case closed.

Magnus wasn't the lead detective on the case, so he wasn't involved in the interview, but he hung around at his desk, waiting to hear the result.

A word was written on the notepad by his computer. *Bassi.*

Van der Linden clearly wasn't the guy who had beaten up Jósef; he didn't speak Icelandic.

So, who was Bassi?

The word meant 'bear', or rather 'little bear'. Magnus's little brother Óli had had a teddy bear named Bassi. Magnus thought there might be some saga warrior with that name. He had read all the sagas, many of them several times, but he couldn't recall which one had a Bassi. Was Handar-Bassi the full name? Maybe he was imagining it.

There was also something else from his childhood. Not just Óli's bear. Someone at the neighbouring farm. The farmer? His wife? His kids?

Or an animal?

An animal.

Magnus knew who Bassi was. He grabbed his jacket and rushed out of the police station. It was a quick drive to the hospital, but it was late and the nurses tried to stop Magnus disturbing their patient.

'I only have one quick question,' he said. 'I'll be two minutes, that's all.'

Jósef was awake, and he said he was happy to speak to Magnus and answer his question.

Which he did.

As Magnus left the hospital, he took out his phone and called Árni.

'You're driving Gulli back to Vík tomorrow?'

'Yes,' said Árni.

'Do you mind if I take him instead?'

'Um . . . Sure, Magnus. If you want.' He sounded pleased at the reprieve from the long drive there and back.

The weather was foul the next morning; grey clouds bursting with moisture enveloped Magnus's car for most of the journey across the southern plain of Iceland, until they passed the waterfall of Skógafoss, the clouds lifted, and the soft white topping of the Mýrdal glacier gleamed in the newly escaped sun.

Gulli was excited by Raffles's arrest the previous evening and proud of his role in it. He would have stayed on in Reykjavík to bask in the glory for another couple of days if he could, but his father had ordered him back. And Magnus had said it was probably for the best.

They approached the farm along the straight track, Magnus driving slowly. There were animals about.

He pulled up outside the farm next to a pick-up truck.

'Do you want to come in for a cup of coffee?' said Gulli.

'I will, thank you,' said Magnus. 'I can't resist your mother's *vínarbraud.*'

Magnus took off his shoes at the front door, and noticed the red coat on the coat hook.

Both Gulli's parents were in the kitchen, already drinking coffee, the paper open in front of his father. They greeted Gulli, and Magnus who congratulated them on their son's success.

'Sit down and have some coffee,' said Bogga, with a welcome smile. Even the previously suspicious Thór was smiling. Proud of his son, no doubt.

The sheepdog hauled itself to its feet and ambled over to say hello. Magnus bent down to scratch him behind the ears. 'Lovely dog,' he said. 'Is he the same colour as Bassi?'

The family froze. Silence. Magnus let his question hang there.

'Who is Bassi?' said Thór.

'Your dog,' said Magnus. 'The one you told me about that got run over by the townie from Reykjavík. The townie who is in hospital with a leg broken in two places. The dog was called Bassi, wasn't he? You must have been very fond of him.'

Gulli was staring at the ceiling. Bogga's mouth was open and she was looking at her husband for a reaction. Thór was staring at Magnus. He didn't answer.

'I wondered what Bogga was doing outside the Kringlan Mall, especially when Gulli denied she had even been in

Reykjavík. Thór, you realized that there was a chance that Gulli might recognise the man who ran over your dog when he was driving too fast along the track. I asked Jósef last night, and he admitted it was true, and that he had driven off without stopping. He said that a farm hand had seen him. Which was you, wasn't it, Gulli?'

Gulli swallowed and nodded. Thór's stare switched from Magnus to Gulli, his anger rising by the minute.

'So, you stationed Bogga near the entrance to the mall. If and when Gulli spotted the man who had run over Bassi, he would let his mother know, and she would follow him. Which she did, to Vesturbaer. Then the next day, you, Thór, would wait for him in his apartment to break his legs.'

'He deserved it,' said the farmer. 'All these tourists come driving out to the cliffs. And they drive too fast – the Icelanders are worse than the foreigners. I loved Bassi, but he was a stupid dog; he used to rush out and chase the cars. The guy was driving too fast, but even so he could have braked in time if he had been paying attention. But he didn't. And after he ran poor Bassi over, he just drove off, without stopping. Gulli saw him, though.'

The farmer glanced at his son. 'He needed to be taught a lesson, if we could only find him.'

'Maybe,' said Magnus. 'But you can't go around breaking people's legs, even if they deserve it. You are all under arrest. I'll take you to the station in Vík.'

Magnus had brought along three sets of handcuffs for the job. For a moment he thought Thór might try to resist. The farmer got to his feet and stared at Magnus. Magnus stared back. The man was strong, but Magnus was younger and fitter.

'Resisting arrest will make this so much worse,' Magnus said.

Thór nodded. He bent down and patted his dog. 'We can't leave Frakkur here alone.'

'I'll make sure nothing happens to the dog.'

Magnus spent the rest of the morning and the afternoon taking statements, filling in paperwork, and arranging for the family to be transferred to police headquarters in Reykjavík the next day. An enterprising journalist had driven over to Vík from Reykjavík to interview the man who had caught Raffles, and had got himself a fine scoop. Although Magnus hadn't said anything, and hadn't allowed the journalist to speak to Gulli or his parents, it was impossible to conceal that they had been arrested, and the neighbours were capable of putting two and two together.

But the neighbours would look after the farm. And Frakkur, the dog.

As Magnus was driving back towards Reykjavík, with the setting sun ahead of him, the Westman Islands rising out of the glittering sea to his left, and Eyjafjallajökull slumbering to his right, his phone rang.

'Hi, Magnus, it's Árni.'

'Oh, hi Árni.'

'I've just heard about Uncle Thór. And Gulli. Who would have thought it?'

A suspicion reared up in Magnus's mind. Why had Árni

been so keen to get his cousin down to Reykjavík looking at faces?

'You, Árni. You would have thought it.'

'What? What do you mean, Magnus? You don't think I had anything to do with it, do you?'

Was Árni that smart? Possibly. Possibly not.

Magnus hesitated and grinned. He chose to decide that Árni wasn't.

'No, Árni, of course not. Turned out your idea was not so dumb after all. As soon as I get back to Reykjavík, I'll buy you a beer.'

Author's Note. There are actually two people with the name Bassi in Iceland's phone directory, but it seemed unfair to drag real people into my fictional crime. And thanks to Lilja for her help.

Before becoming a writer, Michael Ridpath used to work as a bond trader in the City of London. After writing eight financial thrillers, he began the 'Fire and Ice' series, featuring the Icelandic detective Magnus Jonson. He has also written two spy novels set at the beginning of World War II.

Digging Deep

Ruth Dudley Edwards

I read Wobble to Death *when it came out in 1970 and loved it and other Sergeant Cribb books, so – as a diffident rookie crime writer – when I joined the CWA in the 1980s, I was nervous about meeting such a luminary as Peter. He proved to be kind, unassuming and consistently supportive. He was funny too. I was at Magna Cum Murder in Muncie, Indiana, in 1996, when Peter's response to the frequent honking of freight trains through the night was to go to reception and ask politely when the hotel was due to arrive in St Louis.*

I present this very short story by way of affectionate tribute; I'm not sure if Peter has ventured into 'flash fiction' himself, but his short stories display his versatility splendidly, and include wonderful experiments with style and structure such as 'Youdunnit', in which the reader becomes the killer, and the epistolary 'Arabella's Answer'.

She hated everything about his bloody allotment.

He never talked about anything any more except

potting, propagating, digging, weeding, slug-trapping and all the other mind-numbingly boring things he did there.

Except when he was sitting in his armchair in the evenings drooling over his blasted catalogues and droning on about mattocks and dibbles.

And demanding praise for the unexciting vegetables he brought her that must have cost about ten quid a pound to produce.

She cracked the evening he asked her to view his big surprise, which turned out to be a second allotment, with a section newly dug and ready for turnip plants.

After she had fatally stabbed him with his new telescopic tree lopper, she buried him deep, planted the turnips over him and worked out what to say when she reported him missing.

The police seemed only mildly interested in the disappearance of an elderly man with a drink problem who had developed a habit of walking at night on the cliffs when he'd had several over the eight.

It would be tidier if his body was washed up, said the solicitor, but since they owned the house jointly and shared a bank account, she'd be OK.

She wasn't, though, once she realised that she couldn't take the risk of letting anyone else have the allotment in case they dug too deep.

And since the first allotment was clearly the superior in location, to avoid suspicion she had to hold on to both.

The rules specified that neglect would lead to reallocation.

She knew almost nothing about gardening, but she did grasp that among her challenges would be figuring out a way of preventing his corpse from suspiciously enriching the soil.

A pragmatic woman, she told everyone she needed to mourn her husband by embracing his hobby, and prepared herself for a life of horticultural atonement.

It was what he would have wanted.

Ruth Dudley Edwards is an historian and journalist. The targets of her satirical crime novels include academia, the civil service, the House of Lords, literary prizes, the art market and political correctness. She won the CrimeFest Last Laugh Award for Murdering Americans *(2008), the CWA Non-Fiction Gold Dagger for* Aftermath: the Omagh bombings and the families' pursuit of justice *(2010) and the Goldsboro Last Laugh Award for* Killing the Emperors *(2013).*

A Sonnet for Peter Lovesey, on reaching the age of eighty

Simon Brett

I knew the name Peter Lovesey long before I met its owner. In 1969 I read news of a competition for a first crime novel, which offered the very juicy prize of £1,000. This encouraged me to complete a book I'd been thinking about for some time. Based on my experience of being a department store Father Christmas, it was entitled – inevitably – Death in Toys and started with the murder of Santa in his own grotto. I submitted my manuscript and waited. I heard nothing. Finally I read in the press that the £1,000 had been won by someone called Peter Lovesey with a novel entitled Wobble to Death. *That was the first time I heard of someone whom I have got to know well over the years and of whom I never think without admiration and affection.*

P raise? Praise for Peter Lovesey's always due.
E numerating all your works would fill
T ime we don't have. Let's mention just a few.
E ach series never fails to please and thrill.

R ight, first there's Sergeant Cribb who never fails,
L uring Victorian villains down the path
O n to the gallows. Then the Prince of Wales –
V ictorian too – and Diamond in Bath.
E xcellent are the standalones you've done,
S hort stories great – and books by Peter Lear.
E very kind of Dagger you have won –
Y ou've even got a Diamond souvenir!
8 0? You can't be! Let's raise a glass of fizz (and
O bserve the attic picture's rather wizened).

Simon Brett has published over ninety books. Many are crime novels featuring Charles Paris, Mrs Pargeter, Carole and Jude from Fethering, or Blotto and Twinks. For television and radio he wrote After Henry and No Commitments. He was President of the Detection Club from 2001 to 2015, and was awarded an OBE in the 2016 New Year's Honours for 'Services to Literature'.

A Village Affair

Susan Moody

For all I'm aware, Peter Lovesey is a domestic tyrant, a mugger of old ladies, and cheats at cards. Somehow I doubt it. His genial smile, his kind features and his absolute focus on any question asked of him, no matter how trivial, speak quite clearly of the man we know him to be. Always kind, always courteous, always encouraging to lesser writers than himself, and always ready for a laugh. Long may he reign.

Everyone loved Peter Jacques, with his shock of white hair, his bright blue eyes and embracing smile. He lived in a small, elaborately pargetted house at the end of Florey Lane, close to the railway cutting, and you could often see him out digging in his vegetable garden, waving as the London train trundled past. I always waved back, as I had been doing since I was a child, though I don't suppose he could see me. My parents had known him from university days and he'd stood as godfather when I was christened at St Barnabas. The three of us often turned out to watch

Peter lead the local rugby side to victory as their formidable centre forward.

Like my father, he'd been a solicitor with Lewes Cribb & Diamond, based in Belminster – the same firm I work for now – and with or without his wife, Peter was often round at our house. He'd been married to Bethany for years, though over time, she had become something of a hermit. Once an active member of the community (church flowers, lollipop lady, President of the Gardening Club and so on), we saw less and less of her as the years went by. There were no children, which Peter told us was one of the reasons for Bethany's increasingly reclusive behaviour.

'She feels a failure, you see, can't persuade her other-wise,' Peter told my parents, a glass of wine in his hand, legs stretched comfortably in front of the log fire. His mouth twisted. 'She feels she's let me down.'

'It's not necessarily her fault, old boy,' my father said. 'In fact, it's more likely to be yours.'

'I keep telling her that, but she still thinks it's down to her. She finds it embarrassing,' continued Peter. 'Coffee-mornings, supper parties and the like, everyone else seems to be talking about their kids' achievements, or their grandchildrens', and she can't join in. She feels she can't compete, d'you see?'

'She's never struck me as the competitive sort,' my mother said.

'Perhaps "compete" is the wrong word. It's more that she can't take part in the conversation, feels left out.' Peter shrugged his big shoulders. 'Nowadays she finds it easier not to go out at all.'

'Sounds as though she might be agoraphobic,' said my father. 'Has she seen anyone about it? Talked to a professional?'

'No. Can't get her out of the house, to be honest.'

'Tell her I'll pop round for a coffee,' my mother said. 'It might be less of an ordeal for her.'

'That's kind of you, Sarah.' Peter gave her his warm smile. 'I know she'd appreciate that.'

'How long exactly is it?' my mother said, when he'd gone. 'Since we last saw her, I mean?'

'Years,' I said, after a pause. 'Literally years.'

I realised for the first time how gradually, over time, we'd become used to seeing Peter on his own.

As luck would have it, my mother told me later, she'd never been able to contact Bethany when she called.

'So not agoraphobia, then,' commented my father.

'It doesn't look like it.'

'Unless she just doesn't want to answer the door,' I put in.

'It's not that. Especially as Lillian Lear told me she'd spotted her at the market in Belminster last month. In fact, I'm not sure Lillian didn't mention seeing Bethany getting onto the London train, too.'

My father laughed. 'Maybe it's just village-phobia, then.'

It seemed slightly odd to me, that Lillian should see her in Belminster, while Peter said he couldn't get her out of the house. But the older I get, the stranger I realize that humankind is.

Lillian Lear was a relative newcomer, one of those women no self-respecting village can afford to be without.

An energetic big-boned widow of long-standing, able to turn her hand to anything, from pouring concrete to fixing a leaking roof. She galvanised and bullied us all to the point of irritation, setting up committees to help indigenous famers in Peru or teaching deprived children to read or organising Bring And Buy sales in aid of St Barnabas. She was very friendly with Peter and Bethany, always inviting them round to her place or getting Peter involved with local affairs. They shared a keen interest in opera and I know that more than once the three of them had set off for Covent Garden or the Coliseum to take in some production there.

I won't say Peter was the life and soul of the village, because there were plenty of others who were more sociable, more involved in local events. But he did have a finger in a lot of pies. Sang in the local choir. Played masterful bridge at the Bridge Club, refereed local rugby matches, running up and down the pitch in shorts, with a whistle at his lips. Acted as Scoutmaster to the local troop. Entered the Men Only chutney competition at the summer fête – and if anyone suspected that it was Bethany who'd produced the winning chutney, none of us said so.

So when Peter retired, it was decided to throw him a party in the Village Hall.

'It'll be a way to bring us all together,' Lillian said. 'Not just a party for Peter, but a way to add to our community spirit.' She had said the exact same thing when she organised the village's Jubilee Party for the Queen's fiftieth year on the throne, and ten years later, for the Diamond Jubilee.

After those two national events, the celebration of Peter Jacques's retirement seemed a bit of an anticlimax, but never mind. As Lillian said gaily, and often, 'Any excuse for a party!' Or, in Lillian's case, any excuse to cosy up to Peter Jacques, which is what I suspected she was doing.

'Shall we see Bethany at your party?' I asked Peter, bumping into him at the weekly Farmers' Market.

He pushed his lips back and forth in that way people do, to convey doubt. To my surprise and horror, his blue eyes filled with tears.

'Peter!' I said. 'What on earth is the matter?'

He looked up and down the street and then leaned towards me, like someone afraid of being overheard. 'The truth is,' he said, and there was a heartbreaking tremor in his voice. 'The truth is, Bethany . . . has left me.'

'*What?*'

He nodded miserably.

'But this is terrible news, Peter.' I put a sympathetic hand on his arm. 'Do you know where she went?'

'No. But it's obvious she couldn't stand it a moment longer.'

'Stand what?'

'Me. Us. Our life together.' He seemed to crumple right in front of my eyes.

I was flabbergasted. 'Have you heard from her since?'

'Not a word.'

'When was this?'

He looked away from me, then back. 'You're not going to believe this, but about four years ago.'

'Four *years* – but that's impossible, surely.' I did a quick mental calculation and realized that we were all so used to Bethany's absence that it could indeed have been four years or even longer since our last news of her. We never realize how insidiously time slides past. 'Why didn't you *say* anything?'

'Didn't want people knocking at the door, trying to be sympathetic, even though most of them scarcely knew my poor Beth. Didn't want women turning up with *food* – tuna casseroles and macaroni cheese and so on. You know what they're like. Wanting to mother me. Wanting to manage me. Besides, I always hoped that Bethany would see that I wasn't as bad as all that, and come back.'

I steered him towards one of the benches set around the village green. 'But Peter,' I said. 'Don't you think you should have informed the police? Or at the very least, *us*?'

'Why?'

'Because . . .' I cast around for reasons. ' . . . because maybe she didn't leave of her own accord. Or maybe she took off without identification on her, had an accident and was killed. Or had her identification stolen and was murdered by the thief. Or . . .' Wilder and wilder possibilities jumped into my head. ' . . . maybe she lost her memory and is waiting for you somewhere, not knowing who she is or where she comes from, wondering why you don't come and rescue her.'

'That's . . . that's *horrible*.' He shut out my words by covering his ears with his big gardener's hands.

'Sorry. But you really need to think about it.'

'She's not a missing person,' he said. 'She *chose* to leave.'

'But I've just given you several reasons why maybe she didn't have any option. That maybe she was abducted or ... or *some*thing.'

'She's dead,' he said. 'I just know it.'

'Does Lillian Lear know?'

He nodded miserably. 'She's the only one, besides you. I think that's why she wants to throw this party. To cheer me up.'

Around us was the bustle of the Market: baskets of onions, homemade cakes and misshapen carrots, homemade jams and jellies, boxes of potatoes. Women stood behind glass counters dispensing cups of tea from the big urns and selling slightly distorted cheese scones or slices of rich chocolate cake. I wondered where Bethany could have gone. And why. There must have been much more to it than a feeling of not belonging because she had no children. Besides, it was a long time ago.

When I told my mother, she said, 'You know what? I wouldn't be surprised if Peter's done away with her. Poor Bethany must have been pretty dreary to live with.'

'But he seemed so upset when he told me,' I said.

'He could have been putting it on.'

'If he'd really done away with her, wouldn't he have told people she'd gone?'

'Maybe. Maybe not.'

I laughed disbelievingly. 'Why would you think one of your closest friends might be a murderer, for goodness sake?'

My mother wasn't the sort to tap the side of her nose in a knowing fashion, but she came pretty close. Raised her eyebrows. Pursed her lips. Shook her head slightly from side to side.

'Anyway, where would Peter have hidden the body?' I asked.

'All that digging! Need I say more?'

'Mother, *honestly.*'

But later, I thought about the gardening. It would have been easy enough to dig a grave in that soft, much-worked-over soil. And easy enough to dispose of enough clothes, passports, and so on in the bonfire. And easy enough for a well-built rugby player to carry the slight body of his wife out to the garden.

I considered the mounds of prize-winning vegetables he produced each year, the succulent green beans, the delicious new potatoes that he so often gave me. And the beautiful roses which bloomed more profusely for him than for the rest of us. I felt slightly nauseous. Had they been fertilized by poor Bethany's remains?

The more I thought about it, the more I wondered if my mother could possibly be right.

In the end, feeling like a Judas, I called in at the police station in Belminster, explained my niggling worries to my friend Inspector Bertie Prince. 'The thing is, Bertie,' I said, in conclusion, 'his story may well be true, and I doubt if you've got reasonable cause to apply for a search warrant. Nonetheless . . .'

'Peter Jacques,' he said thoughtfully. 'Actually, I wouldn't be all that surprised. Tell you what: we both used to turn out for the Belminster Battlers, in the old days. I can easily dream up some excuse to call on him. Might not get anywhere, but at least I can test the air, see if I sense anything not quite kosher. Why don't you come with me?'

We duly turned on Peter's doorstep. He seemed delighted to see us and we were invited in for a cuppa. The two of them recalled stupendous games of the past, triumphs on the pitch, terrible referees who robbed the Battlers of matches they should rightfully have won.

'It's lovely to see you again, Bertie,' Peter said eventually. His blue eyes sparkled. 'I've missed rugby, I must say.'

Bertie glanced round. 'Bethany not here?' he said casually.

'She's gone,' Peter said.

'Gone?' Bertie raised his eyebrows. 'On holiday, is she?'

'She's left.'

'Left?'

In a sudden violent movement, Peter stood up and went over to the little desk which stood against a wall. He came back with an envelope from which he extracted a piece of paper. 'Since you've brought it up, this is all I've heard from my wife in over four years.'

'But good God, man, why didn't you report it?'

'Just what I asked,' I said.

'Read it.' Peter passed the paper over. 'Better still, read it aloud.'

Bertie cleared his throat. '*Peter,*' he read. '*I can't stand living here in the village for another day. I want something more from life than petty gossip and jam-making. So I'm sorry but I'm leaving you. Don't waste your time looking for me. I'm not coming back.'*

'I felt humiliated. Didn't want anyone to realise my wife had left me.' He shrugged. 'I've got used to being on my own. And there are . . . compensations.'

He meant Lillian Lear, I was sure of it.

Time passed. I stayed on in the village. Married. Had one child, then a second. Found my first grey hairs. Was promoted at work. And *always* refused any gifts of vegetables from Peter.

In other words, I got on with my life. Peter and Lillian had gradually become recognised as a couple, spending all their time together, in and out of each other's houses, often staying overnight in one place or the other. Peter seemed as genial as always, yet niggles occasionally surfaced at the back of my brain. Was Bethany Jacques lying there in the well-dug-over earth of Peter's vegetable garden? Decomposing? Providing fertilizer?

And then one day ambulances appeared in Florey Lane, followed by police cars. It turned out that Peter Jacques had suffered a massive stroke. He was taken to the hospital in Belminster, where Lillian Lear sat assiduously by his bed, day after day, for the five weeks it took him to die. She organized his funeral service and the wake which followed. It was the end of an era.

Despite the fact that he was my godfather and, as far as we knew, had no kin, I was still astounded to discover that Peter had left me his house. We moved in to the pretty cottage. The children were as happy as could be to have so much garden to run around in. They always waved as the London train went lumbering by, though we couldn't see if anyone waved back.

All my old doubts returned. Were they playing above the final resting place of a murder victim? It took me over a year to ascertain that in all likelihood, they were not. We called in a contractor to excavate the vegetable patch, and another to build a small swimming pool at the other end of the garden. We had the lawn dug up and professionally laid, and had the foundations installed for a small summer house, and in another area, a pretty little pergola. No trace of human remains was found. If there were bones, they were elsewhere. Maybe my mother – and I – had been entirely wrong, and Peter was blameless. Maybe Bethany was living the life in London or Edinburgh, in California or Australia. I stopped worrying about it.

Shortly after that, Lillian Lear was diagnosed with terminal cancer. It looked as though Peter Jacques' company was what had kept her active and lively. 'With Peter gone, the poor woman's got nothing left to live for,' my mother said. 'It's very sad.'

The village rallied round, as it always did. Lillian's last months were as happy as we could make them. 'Any excuse for a party,' someone said, echoing Lillian's mantra, and indeed we seemed to spend nearly every weekend finding some excuse or other for a sociable gathering, until Lillian could no longer make it out of bed. In her very final days, she would lie there with a look of apprehension, even terror on her face. She'd moved on, turned inward, was beyond us now.

I held her hand sometimes. I wanted to say that it would be all right . . . but how did I know that it would? Of course I did not.

The Barnetts, the couple who bought her house, had ambitious plans. They built a big conservatory. Turned two of the attics into charming guest bedrooms. Enlarged the kitchen. Started on converting the barn where Lillian used to keep her dogs. The husband was a portrait-painter, the wife a renowned ceramicist, so the idea was to install two large studios, one each.

And then once again police cars wailed down the High Street and pulled into the small gravelled courtyard in front of Lillian's house. No ambulances this time, but police tape, white coveralls, a stretcher. I stopped in to see Bertie Prince at the station. Like the rest of the village, I was agog to know what was going on.

'Looks like you were half-right,' he said, leaning back in his chair.

'How?'

'Bethany Jacques was definitely done away with, poor woman,' he said. 'But not by Peter.'

'Lillian?' I said. 'Lillian *Lear*?'

He nodded. 'The Barnetts wanted to convert the barn and found there was dry-rot or death-watch-beetle or some such in the roof beams, so they brought someone in to pull out all the tongue-and-groove which lined the ceiling. And guess what . . . '

I didn't need to guess. 'Bethany.'

'That's right. She must have been bonked on the head, fracturing her skull, must have died almost immediately. Then she was stuffed between two intersecting beams before Lillian put up the boarding and boxed her in.'

'Not difficult, when you consider big strong Lillian and tiny Bethany,' I said. 'But why would she do such a thing?'

'To clear the decks, as far as Peter was concerned, I should imagine.'

'But we both saw the farewell note she wrote to him. And it was definitely her writing

. . . I'd recognize it anywhere.'

'My guess is that Lillian stood over her and forced her to write it. Then took her time to spread rumours about having seen Bethany in Belminster or at the railway station.'

'Poor Peter,' I said. 'What a blessing that he never knew.'

Bertie stared up at the ceiling. 'Isn't it, though?'

Susan Moody has published thirty-five suspense novels, including two series and many standalone novels. Quick and the Dead, *a new series featuring Alexandra Quick, has just been published with a second in the series,* Quick off the Mark, *due out later this year. Her popular Penny Wanawake novels have just been republished.*

Susan is the organiser of Deal Noir, a new crime convention. She has been Chair of the Crime Writers' Association, a Writer-in-Residence at the universities of Tasmania and Copenhagen, and President of the International Association of Crime Writers.

She is a huge fan of Peter Lovesey's books.

Spies, Superheroes and Stolen Goods

Peter Lovesey's memories
of the Detection Club in the 1970s

Martin Edwards asked me for some memories of my years as a member of the Detection Club. First I wish to thank everyone who contributed stories to this collection. I'm more than a little surprised to find myself in this position, as the bishop said to the actress, but it gives me great pleasure. In particular I thank Martin for thinking of it and doing the editing. Putting together an anthology is never as simple as you hope, and this was undertaken in his first year as our President.

Most of the names I will mention should now be prefaced with the words 'the late', but how depressing that would be. Instead I shall try to find words that capture them in the years I was lucky enough to know them.

Agatha Christie was the president when I was invited to join, but the letter in July 1974 came from Michael Underwood, explaining that he was chairman. In a follow-up letter the club secretary, Mary Kelly, delicately phrased it, 'in view of occasional disappointments in recent years we can't build too firmly on her being there.' Mary also suggested I thought for a week or two about something I held sacred, to swear by during the initiation ceremony. 'Past examples include cows, the river Alph, royalty statements, the last chapter of *Persuasion* and writing in bed,' she added. 'As several members will be initiated we'd be grateful if you could keep your sacred object brief; to one word if possible.' One word! This club is a tight ship, I thought.

In its heyday the club had its own premises, first in Gerrard Street, Soho, and later Kingly Street, off Regent Street. The rent, which must have been considerable, was derived from radio productions and books, but by the time I joined there were no club rooms and the main activity was using knives and forks. The subscription was still officially a guinea and I was told a pound would be preferred by the treasurer to keep the accounting simple. I have seen a receipt showing that in 1932 Dorothy L. Sayers purchased her life membership for a pound.

The 'several members' joining in 1974 were Gwendoline Butler, John le Carré, Ngaio Marsh and me. To be in such company was in itself daunting, regardless of the prospect of an initiation ceremony. I didn't know at the time that Ngaio Marsh was unwell and wouldn't attend and that le Carré rarely ventured out of Cornwall.

So on that first evening Gwen Butler and I were the two initiates. The wording of the ceremony was, I believe, pretty close to the original version written by Dorothy L.

Sayers soon after the club was founded in 1930. Sometimes described as a secret ritual, it had been disclosed to the world as early as 1933 in an article in the *Strand* magazine by G.K. Chesterton, the first President. Indeed, in 1935 when Anthony Gilbert, E.R. Punshon and Gladys Mitchell were initiated, the ceremony was broadcast on radio. Margery Allingham wrote in a letter in 1958: 'Last week I went to the annual dinner of the Detection Club ... and I had the honour of carrying the Skull on a cushion. We are all a bit white-headed for such nonsense not to be in rather alarming taste.'

By 1974 the principle that only writers of detective stories should be admitted had long since been abandoned. In our candlelit procession were spy and thriller specialists such as Eric Ambler, William Haggard and Dick Francis who must have kept their fingers crossed when they had promised that their detectives would 'well and truly detect the crimes presented to them'. Shocking to admit, I can't recall what I claimed to hold sacred when I placed my hand on Eric the Skull with his torch-bulb eyes. It was more than one word, for sure.

The guest speaker that evening was Roy Fuller, the recently retired Professor of Poetry at Oxford and also author of three well regarded crime stories written between 1948 and 1954. Listening to him speak with authority about those father figures of the detective story, Poe, Collins and Dickens, and their influence on his writing, I found myself wondering why he wasn't about to be initiated into the club instead of me, a newcomer to the genre.

I soon discovered that certain other members were as apprehensive as I about the company we were keeping. One slight figure was positively furtive, and she was Mary Kelly. 'You're tall,' she said. 'Do you mind shielding me from someone I'm trying to avoid?' 'Who's that?' I asked. 'Tell you later,' she said. It emerged, much later, that we had a *publisher* in our ranks and Mary, a writer of undoubted talent, winner of the CWA Gold Dagger in 1961, was overdue in delivering a book. George Hardinge – Lord Hardinge of Penshurst – was a brilliant crime editor who had steered many an author away from pitfalls in plotting, first at Collins and latterly at Macmillan. In the guise of George Milner he had also written several crime novels of his own. As one of George's many 'discoveries' I had always found him agreeable company, but Mary had a conscience and wasn't writing at all, and she continued to seek ways of escape from George. She never did produce that book.

I learned in time that part of the game was a gentle jockeying for position at dinner – at least at the Garrick Club, where there was no table plan. You looked for someone compatible and that could be a challenge. We all had common ground in writing crime novels, but socially and politically some of us were at opposite poles. There were four peers of the realm. There were also a few would-be peers who assumed everyone around them spent their spare time shooting at pheasants and small mammals. At the opposite extreme were several former members of the Communist party. To spice the mix, a significant number had served long careers in the secret service.

Among the latter, John Bingham (Lord Clanmorris), was said by John le Carré to have been a main inspiration for George Smiley; there was Sir John Masterman, who had devised the wartime double-cross system of turning Nazi spies into double agents; and a third ex-spook (there were almost certainly more in our midst) was Kenneth Benton who in a thirty-year career in MI6 had worked in Vienna, Riga, Madrid and Rome. In Madrid he headed a team that identified nineteen Nazi agents, including the renowned double agent code-named Garbo. Kenneth's boss at one stage was Kim Philby, of whom he said after the defection, 'He had no loyalties, either to HMG or friends or to the women he married. We had liked and admired him and were left feeling unclean.'

The ex-spies were disarming dinner companions and put everyone totally at ease, as I suppose a spy should. I did wonder how Cecil Day Lewis (Nicholas Blake), also known as Red Cecil and under observation by MI5 for years ('He seldom wears a hat and is not altogether smart in dress,' allegedly stated one report that smacked of desperation), must have coped surrounded by them, but he had died shortly before I joined.

Innocent that I was, I learned of Kenneth Benton's secret past only when I attended his memorial service on the club's behalf in 1999. It was in Chichester Cathedral and well attended. Someone remarked to me, 'Headquarters must be empty this afternoon.' 'Which headquarters is that?' I asked. He gave me a look. The eulogy enlightened me.

Despite the potential for discord, Detection Club

evenings were friendly to a fault, even at the more formal dinners when we couldn't choose who we sat with. The seating plan was devised by the secretary and must have been an art form in itself. In 1975 Mary Kelly handed over the reins to Douglas Rutherford, a former housemaster at Eton who had served in British intelligence (what else?) during the war and understood better than most the wheels within wheels. He was also our treasurer for many years and steered us through three changes of president. His wife Meg took over both roles after his death in 1988.

All differences aside, there were those like Christianna Brand who were known to enjoy a little baiting of the unwary. I was relieved that Christianna made a point of befriending some of the newer members such as Robert Barnard and me. Bob and I both looked forward to the letters she regularly sent after the dinners, always headed 'Darling' and so libellous that it would be uncharitable to quote any part of them, even at this distance in time.

The greatest pleasure was sharing a table with the wits of the club. Listening to Peter Dickinson, Michael Kenyon, Robert Barnard or Christianna in full flow was a privilege and a joy. I treasure a memory of a slightly inebriated Edmund Crispin talking dismissively about the incidental music he wrote for the cinema, including *Doctor in the House* and the first half-dozen of the *Carry On* series ('Years and years of Charles Hawtrey falling over his own feet. In the end I had to give up. It almost gave me a breakdown.'). After insights like that some of our guest speakers paled in comparison.

These were the extroverts. But I also valued the friendships made in one-to-one conversations. In particular there
were the women writers with careers going back in some
cases to the golden age years. Elizabeth Ferrars travelled
from Edinburgh for the meetings and rarely missed one.
I don't know how she was able to spare the time, for she
wrote more than sixty novels in fifty years. Celia Fremlin
was not so prolific, but always thought-provoking. She was
proud of having been admitted to the Detection Club in
spite of writing novels that had 'no policemen, no detectives and quite often no murder'. She told fascinating
stories of her experiences working with Tom Harrisson
on Mass Observation and she once surprised me by saying
her Hampstead house was left unlocked day and night.
Another favourite of mine was Dr Josephine Bell, who was,
I believe, the most senior member and usually carried Eric
the Skull into the initiation ceremony. She invited my wife
Jax and me for a meal in her idyllic Jasmine Cottage, a
listed eighteenth-century building in Puttenham, a Surrey
village, and it seemed the perfect setting for a golden age
writer. Then there was a lady with a twinkle in her eye who
introduced herself as Guy Cullingford and said I could call
her Constance. She was the writer of *Post Mortem*, one of
the most original and amusing crime novels I have read.

Meeting certain members evoked memories from my
teenage years. Macdonald Hastings had been the 'special
investigator' of the *Eagle* comic that was a weekly highlight
of my schooldays. After reading the front page about Dan
Dare I would eagerly turn the pages to read about Mac's

latest challenge: the Cresta run; deep-sea diving; castaway on a desert island; at the sharp end of a knife-throwing act; piloting a Tiger Moth plane; riding a camel across the Sahara. Yet here was my superhero bespectacled in a brown suit sitting beside me at the AGM. He told me the best assignment he ever had was editing the *Strand* magazine because it kept him in Savile Row suits and handmade shoes for five years, but unfortunately under his editorship it folded, so he was pleased when the *Eagle* job came along. At twenty-six, he'd married an ex-chorus girl twice his age. They were together only a few months but he ended up paying her maintenance for the rest of her life. His detective novels were about an insurance investigator called Cork. 'Keeps me afloat,' he said.

Another name familiar from my youth was Val Gielgud, so often mentioned on radio. I remembered vividly a dramatisation of Sherlock Holmes from the mid-1950s with a cast to die for: John Gielgud as Holmes; Ralph Richardson as Watson; Orson Welles as Moriarty; and Val Gielgud in one episode as Mycroft. I wasn't bold enough to speak to Val about the impression the series made on me. *The Speckled Band* had given me a nightmare. He was remarkably prolific as an author considering that he was Head of Drama at the BBC. And his personal life was busy, too. He tied the knot five times.

At one meeting, Margaret Yorke invited Jax and me to join 'a few of us from Oxford' at her cottage in Long Crendon to greet a coachload of Texans. Margaret was a dynamo, great fun, a tireless campaigner for Public

Lending Right and libraries, deeply interested in all that
was going on and with firm views on many topics. When
Michael Gilbert once revealed in an interview that he did
all his writing on his commuter train, the 8.37 to Victoria
('If you can write a page and a half in fifty minutes, as I
do, you can finish a novel in just thirty weeks, which makes
me extremely interested to know how full-time writers
fill their time.') Margaret took it personally and wrote to
the Crime Writers' Association deploring such behaviour
('Michael Gilbert's profession as a lawyer has provided
him with expert knowledge and material for his successful
novels. Others spend a lot of time in research. It seems that
his prose needs no revision or sharpening before delivery
to the publisher. Others are lesser mortals.'). 'Really a bit
shocking, I thought,' Christianna Brand wrote to me on
a postcard. I doubt whether Michael and Margaret were
seated beside each other at the next dinner. But the party
at the cottage was the first of several and the 'few' were
Colin Dexter, Anthony Price and James McClure. The stars
and stripes were hoisted in welcome and we all basked in
Texan superlatives.

After Dame Agatha's death in 1976 we elected Julian
Symons as President. In 1972 Julian had published a history
of the crime novel called *Bloody Murder* unsparing in its
treatment of several fellow members. On the whole it may
have been better to have been omitted altogether from
Julian's book than to have it written that you were 'once
highly regarded' (Josephine Bell and Gladys Mitchell);
'engaging, but rather too hectic' (Christianna Brand); 'very

variable' (John Bingham); 'more interested in pure adventure stories than in any kind of mystery' (Dick Francis and Gavin Lyall); checked by some restraint from 'writing in a way that fully expresses his personality' (Michael Gilbert); and 'interestingly odd' (H.R.F. Keating). Perhaps it was my imagination, but I always felt a certain tension descend when Julian presided at the AGM, even though we had little of controversy to debate except the price of the dinners and the suitability of candidates for election. Believe it or not, in 1978 we had fifteen nominations and only four were chosen. Yet six years later it was decided nobody was worthy of election. A big plus of Julian's presidency was his influence in the literary world. He persuaded notable friends to address us. Besides Roy Fuller, I particularly remember A.J. (Freddie) Ayer, Pamela Hansford Johnson, who came with her husband C.P. Snow, John Mortimer, Ludovic Kennedy and Sir Huw Wheldon.

I got to know Julian better on a trip Jax and I made with him in 1991 to the Semana Negra in Spain when he was the age I am now and was to receive a Grand Master award. He embarked on it with gusto – too much of it, perhaps, for while climbing a steep hill he aggravated an Achilles tendon injury and was limping for the rest of the trip. The ceremony took place in a funfair against the noise of merry-go-rounds and the distractions of flashing lights and crowd movement. Unfazed, Julian hobbled to the dais and delivered his acceptance speech with grace and wit. Yet the fates had worse in store. While tidying his room that evening he accidentally threw away his airline ticket.

The hotel couldn't find it, and this was in the days before you could print your boarding pass on any computer. Next day Jax and I managed to organise a replacement ticket at a travel agent's. Much relieved, Julian limped with us to a seedy café that had the single merit of being a few steps from the hotel. Over iced tea, he began to reminisce on the theme of what life can throw at you, and it was funny and enchanting. I had long been in awe of this man, regarding him as essentially serious-minded. I'm sure he was about the things that mattered, but this was another, self-deprecating side. He talked of his problems as a young man editing *Twentieth Century Verse* on a shoestring, trying to cope with the vagaries of poets, in particular, Dylan Thomas; of sitting at long intervals for a portrait by Wyndham Lewis that took ten years to complete; and of being chased by George Orwell's dog. 'I can't think why. It behaved like a lamb with every other visitor.' It was a privileged time.

H.R.F. Keating, known to us all as Harry, took over as President in 1985 and his style was more laid-back than Julian's. My memories of Harry went back some years. I was one of the few who could recall him before he grew the magnificent beard. Like Julian, he was an expert on the history of crime writing and produced a number of books about the genre that I treasure, unfailingly positive, entertaining and authoritative. Also like Julian he had a vulnerable side not always evident, but echoed in Inspector Ghote, coping admirably even when beset by problems. When Harry got to eighty (astute readers will see a theme emerging here) I edited for the club a collection of short stories in his honour entitled *The Verdict of Us All*.

Harry's copy was presented to him at the annual dinner at the Ritz in 2006. The guest speaker that year was Douglas Greene, the owner of Crippen & Landru, the American publishers of the book – and this one. While researching his definitive biography, *John Dickson Carr: The Man Who Explained Miracles*, Doug had learned more about the early history of the club than any of us knew. Carr had been admitted to the club in 1936 and became its honorary secretary. Doug Greene was able to clarify a matter so steeped in obscurity that it had begun to worry us. When exactly was the Detection Club founded? Some of our literature suggested 1932, and Julian Symons had confidently quoted this date in an introduction he wrote for a 1978 club anthology called *Verdict of Thirteen*. When challenged by someone, Julian wrote to the *Sunday Times* offering a magnum of champagne to any reader who could prove him wrong. Would you believe it? – some anorak unearthed a letter to the *Times Literary Supplement* from members of the club dated 1930. I don't know whether Julian parted with the champagne.

Doug was able to reveal that Anthony Berkeley wrote to G.K. Chesterton on 27 December, 1929, proposing the formation of a club and inviting him to be its first Honorary President. On 4 January, 1930, he made a list of 'members to date'. It is safe to say we were founded in 1930.

Inspired by all this, I did some digging of my own into the origins of Eric the Skull. The Dorothy L. Sayers Society invited me to give their annual lecture in 2011. I know my limitations. My scant knowledge of DLS and her books wouldn't pass muster among experts, but I could ambush them with a talk about the secret life of Eric (who, it has long been whispered, ought to be renamed Erica). I enjoyed myself ferreting out the memoirs of some of the original members of the club. It was revealed in an essay by Gladys Mitchell that Eric was *stolen* from one of the London teaching hospitals by a young Australian doctor called Denis Browne, the husband of Helen Simpson, who was admitted to the club as an associate member in 1931. Denis Browne, like almost everyone else I have mentioned, is dead, and I don't think this disclosure will harm his reputation. As Sir Denis Browne, KCVO, he is remembered as the Father of Paediatric Surgery. It is comforting to know that Eric was stolen by a great man, but it doesn't altogether absolve us of the crime. When you think about it, the Detection Club has welcomed to its ranks 180 of the great and the good, but every one of us over the years has handled stolen property.

Peter Lovesey, 2016

Peter Lovesey

Bibliography

Sergeant Cribb series
Wobble to Death (1970)
The Detective Wore Silk Drawers (1971)
Abracadaver (1972)
Mad Hatter's Holiday (1973)
Invitation to a Dynamite Party (1974) (US: The Tick of Death)
A Case of Spirits (1975)
Swing, Swing Together (1976)
Waxwork (1978)

Albert Edward, Prince of Wales series
Bertie and the Tinman (1987)
Bertie and the Seven Bodies (1990)
Bertie and the Crime of Passion (1993)

Peter Diamond series
The Last Detective (1991)
Diamond Solitaire (1992)

The Summons (1995)
Bloodhounds (1996)
Upon a Dark Night (1997)
The Vault (1999)
Diamond Dust (2002)
The House Sitter (2003)
The Secret Hangman (2007)
Skeleton Hill (2009)
Stagestruck (2011)
Cop to Corpse (2012)
The Tooth Tattoo (2013)
The Stone Wife (2014)
Down Among the Dead Men (2015)
Another One Goes Tonight (2016)

Hen Mallin series
The Circle (2005)
The Headhunters (2008)

Other fiction
Goldengirl (as Peter Lear) (1977)
Spider Girl (as Peter Lear) (aka In Suspense) (1980)
The False Inspector Dew (1982)
Keystone (1983)
Rough Cider (1986)
The Secret of Spandau (as Peter Lear) (1986)
On the Edge (1989) (aka Dead Gorgeous)
The Reaper (2000)
Remaindered (2014)

Short stories
Butchers and other Stories of Crime (1985)
The Crime Of Miss Oyster Brown and Other Stories (1994)
Do Not Exceed The Stated Dose (1998)
The Sedgemoor Strangler and Other Stories of Crime (2002)
Murder on the Short List (2008)

Edited Anthologies
The Black Cabinet (1989)
Third Culprit (with Liza Cody and Michael Z Lewin) (1994)
The Verdict of Us All (2006)

Non Fiction
The Kings of Distance (1968)
The Guide to UK Track & Field Literature 1175-1968 (with Tom McNab)
The Official Centenary History of the Amateur Athletic Association (1979)
An Athletics Compendium (with Andrew Huxtable and Tom McNab)

Awards

Wobble to Death – Macmillan/Panther First Crime Novel 1970 (winner)

Mad Hatter's Holiday – CWA Gold/Silver Dagger 1973 (shortlist)

A Case of Spirits – Prix du Roman d'Aventures 1987 (winner)

Swing, Swing Together – Grand Prix de Littérature Policière 1985 (winner)

Waxwork – CWA Silver Dagger 1978 (winner)

The False Inspector Dew – CWA Gold Dagger 1982 (winner); Dagger of Daggers 2006 (shortlist)

Rough Cider – MWA Edgar Award 1987 (winner)

The Last Detective – Anthony Award 1991 (winner)

The Summons – CWA Silver Dagger 1995 (winner); MWA Edgar Award 1995 (shortlist)

Bloodhounds – CWA Silver Dagger 1996 (winner); Barry Award 1996 (winner); Macavity Award 1996 (winner)

The Reaper – Barry Award 2000 (shortlist); Prix du Roman d'Aventures 2004 (Jury selection)

Diamond Dust – Barry Award 2002 (shortlist)
The House Sitter – Macavity Award 2003 (winner); Los Angeles Times Book Prize 2003 (shortlist); Barry Award 2003 (shortlist)
CWA Cartier Diamond Dagger 2000

© Kate Shemilt

Peter Lovesey